PRAISE FOR HILARY DARTT

Jasmine's Pact

"Hilary Dartt has done it again. Her wit and poignant writing style brings the characters of three very different sisters to life in this first book of her new trilogy. Jasmine's Pact explores the very real nature of relationships that most of us can relate to."

RACHELLE SPARKS

"…Full of romance, tension, sarcasm and humor. I didn't want it to end. Hilary Dartt is a real talent."

EMILY WHITE

The Dating Intervention

"It was very hilarious, had loads of funny accidents and still had a way of being sincere and romantic … I also liked how much it was based around friendship, which added a nice, fresh take on a romance story. This is easily a five-star read."

NATURAL BRI BLOG

ALSO BY HILARY DARTT

The Intervention Series

The Dating Intervention

The Marriage Intervention

The Motherhood Intervention

The Garden Club Series

Studying Sequoia

Just Holly

The Seedling Homestead Series

The Order of Composition

The Architecture of Vision

The Structure of Perfection

JASMINE'S PACT

BOOK ONE IN THE GARDEN CLUB SERIES

HILARY DARTT

DEDICATION

For Rachelle, my first newsroom buddy,
and my forever friend.

CHAPTER ONE

Jasmine Carr recognized Parker Abbott's voice before he finished saying her name. The *Daily Trumpet's* newsroom buzzed with activity, but when Parker spoke, the hive of ringing phones, fingers flying over keyboards, and reporters coming and going came to a stop so abrupt Jasmine could practically see desks sliding across the floor.

"Jasmine," Parker said when she answered her phone. "Happy birthday."

Her body recognized his voice, too, surprising her by going all tingly at the memory of his hands on her skin. She stood up, unable to contain the energy that image conjured up.

"Happy birthday, Parker," she said. "It's been a while."

He laughed, and a hot blue flame flared up in her belly at the sound. He said, "It's been fourteen years. You know what today is, right?"

She nodded, then licked her lips, cleared her throat, and said, "It's my thirtieth birthday."

"Right," he said. "And my thirty-first. Which means we have business to discuss. I believe you have a promise to make good on."

It's not that she'd forgotten their agreement. In fact, she'd realized recently that she'd unconsciously put her Real Life on hold, thinking she'd decide what she really wanted to do when she turned thirty. But with everything that had happened during the past decade, the pact she'd made with Parker had slipped to the back of her mind. A swarm of bees took up residence in her stomach. Again, she nodded, and again, she had to remind herself that he couldn't see her nodding.

"I guess I do," she said.

"I just booked my plane ticket. I'll be out there in a week."

So many questions ran through her mind. Where did he live? What had he been up to? Did he have a job? Was he still unreasonably sexy? When the two of them were together, would their chemistry still create entirely new elements?

An impatient voice cut into her thoughts, destroying the images of Parker's mouth devouring hers.

Jasmine's editor, Mikey Stockman, stood next to her desk, tapping his fat fingers on his thigh. "Jasmine."

She jumped and brought her imagination's film reel to a stop. "Look, Parker, I've got to go. I'll see you in a week."

"Hey, Mikey," she said. "What do you need?"

"What I need is for my features reporter to stop getting all twitterpated on the phone."

Could he tell?

"I'm not twitterpated," Jasmine said, barely managing not to stutter on the lie.

"Yeah, you are. See? There's a pen out of place." Jasmine hurried to put the rogue pen back in her banana slug coffee mug. Mikey went on, "Next time you're going to have phone sex, do it on your lunch break. Look, I've gotta talk to you. I know you've got that Cookies for Heroes thing to go to, but make some time for me when you get back, okay? And bring me a cookie."

"You're not a—"

"I know I'm not a hero, Jasmine. Just bring me a damn cookie."

Her face still radiating an embarrassed heat related to Mikey's phone sex comment, Jasmine picked up her purse and turned around to leave. As she got to the door, Mikey said, "And Jasmine?"

One hand on the door handle, she turned to look at him.

"Go relieve some of that ... tension before you come back."

Jasmine pushed open the door to the parking lot and squinted into the bright late-morning fog. *Okay, so I am a little weak in the knees,* she thought.

"What's wrong with *you*?"

Liza Carmack, reminiscent of smoky clubs and expensive brandy with her long fingernails and scratchy voice, stood in a swirling cloud of cigarette smoke on the patio.

"Why does everyone think something's wrong with me?" Jasmine said. She put up a hand to shade her eyes, but it didn't help. "It's just bright out here. Is it still summer? I am so ready for fall. This fog is killing me."

Liza, her long red hair tumbling down her back, lifted a shoulder (and her cigarette hand, faux pink diamond sparkling) in a lazy shrug. Of course, she ignored Jasmine's weather talk and said, "You just look a little—well, a little twitterpated."

When Jasmine flinched, Liza was quick to add, "It's not a bad thing, honey. I'm just so used to seeing you calm." She laughed, the sound raspy. "Imperturbable. I've seen a lot in my years, dear. You're twitterpated."

Jasmine pressed her lips together and shook her head. "I'll see you in a bit."

"Bring me a cookie," Liza called after her. Jasmine, who was now digging through her purse, looking for her sunglasses, gave her a dismissive wave. She heard Liza's laugh, rough and loud like it belonged at one end of a long wooden bar, and she couldn't help but smile. She realized her sunglasses were still perched on her head and she huffed out another sigh as she got into the car.

As Jasmine drove through Seabreeze, she thought about what Liza had said. "Imperturbable."

It wasn't that Jasmine was imperturbable, not really. The truth: she was shy. When she was a child, her parents had always said —"Only teasing, of course, honey"—that she should have been born a gopher so she could pop underground whenever she felt too exposed. Which was pretty much all the time. Needless to say, her sisters had called her a gopher for years, which only exacerbated things. Not only would she become paralyzed by shyness, but she also constantly worried they'd call out, "Gopher!" at the most inopportune times, like when she was walking across the cafeteria with a tray of food.

Mikey Stockman calling her twitterpated and using the term phone sex in the same breath was akin to being called a gopher. It made her long for some deep and twisting, very private, possibly endless underground tunnel. After buckling her purse into the passenger seat, setting up her phone for easy viewing and call access in the front cup holder, and then triple-checking behind the car, Jasmine backed out of her parking spot.

As she drove, she ran through the details of the Fourth Annual Cookies for Heroes event. Every year, elementary students brought baked goods to school and served them with milk to local police officers and firefighters. Without warning, Jasmine's train of thought jumped onto a different track. She drummed her fingers on the steering wheel.

Parker Abbott. He sounded exactly the same, so much so that her memories of him were starting to wake from a deep sleep, stretching and yawning and about ready to dance. Out of reflex, Jasmine checked her phone to see if he'd called again. She looked at her call log. Denver area code. What was in Denver? A zoo. A whiskey tour. Would Parker be into those kinds of things? She didn't even know him now.

She'd last seen him when he was seventeen, a strapping, muscular surfer with black hair and amber eyes and a smile as wide as the horizon. She shivered at the memory of Parker with the top half of his wet suit stripped down, ocean water glistening on his torso, his cold hands on her hot skin.

She wasn't sure she could concentrate on Cookies for Heroes. At the first stop light she came to, she scrubbed her hands over her face. It was the same story every year, really. She'd get some nice quotes from heroes and some cute quotes from kids. She'd head back to the newsroom and whip the story out.

Then, she could think about Parker Abbott and his sexy voice.

She could think about Parker Abbott and the promise she'd made him fourteen years ago.

"I MADE these cookies with my mom," said Alex MacIlvoy, a first grader with thick glasses and a bit of an underbite. "I put too much salt in, but that's okay. Mom said we can just wing it. Just don't tell the heroes. Want to taste one?"

"I never turn down a cookie," Jasmine told him. She took a bite. "This is good," she said. "Really good. Chocolate chips with butterscotch?"

"Yeah," Alex said. "And I was just kidding about too much salt. Wanted to see if you'd taste it."

Charmed, Jasmine laughed. "You know, I'm glad I decided to stop and talk to you before I left. I saved the best for last."

She leaned in to whisper to him: "Do you think you could sneak me a couple of those cookies? My boss asked me to bring one back. And one of the other reporters, too."

Alex smiled. "I'll hook you up. Newspaper people are heroes, too."

Jasmine shrugged. "That's nice of you to say. But I think we're talking about people who put their lives on the line, here. Police, fire-fighters, soldiers."

Alex handed her three cookies. "One for you, too," he said.

Usually, Jasmine's mind turned over the parts and pieces of her story on the way back to the newsroom, formulating the lead, inserting the strongest quotes and compiling all the bits and pieces of information so that when she sat at her desk, her fingers beat out a quick, steady rhythm on the keyboard, the story writing itself.

Today, though, she couldn't concentrate on cookies or heroes or even Alex MacIlvoy's adorable smiling face. Even though Mikey Stockman had asked her to meet with him when she got back, she took the longest route possible, following the winding coast like a tour of her past with Parker.

There was the pizza place where they shared their first kiss over pepperoni and sodas. Just a ways further down was the spot where they sat on the cliffs one New Year's Day and watched the waves while writing out their goals for the year. How funny, Jasmine thought, to remember what they'd hoped for back then. She wanted to run her first half marathon, and he wanted to surf in the Lighthouse Point surf competition. What would her goals be, now? She wasn't sure. She'd run a handful of marathons in the past few years, and she'd won a couple of awards at work. She'd have to think about that. And what about Parker's goals?

She turned left to head back into the heart of town, and passed the coffee shop where she always stopped to pick up tea and coffee Friday mornings during their junior year of high school. And the burrito shop with the greasy, salty corn chips they so loved. They'd gorge on those chips, with salsa and guacamole, until they were so stuffed they had to take their burritos to go.

She'd been devastated when Parker's family moved halfway around the world. At first, every landmark produced a fresh round of tears. Over time, the tears turned to fond memories. The truth was, though, she couldn't even remember the last time she'd thought of Parker, until he called today.

By the time she got back to the *Daily Trumpet*, she felt scattered and, she hated to admit, quite a bit twitterpated at the thought of seeing him again.

Well, not just seeing him, said her inner voice. *But also feeling his body against yours.*

"You brought us cookies," Liza said when Jasmine walked into the newsroom. Jasmine, hoping to avoid any further conversations about her lack of imperturbability, tossed the bag onto Liza's desk.

"Share with Mikey," she said.

"I will, later," Liza said. "If I haven't eaten them by the time his visitor leaves."

"Who's his visitor?"

"No idea," Liza said. "Some puppy, still wet behind the ears. New photog. Good looking, too."

Just then, Mikey's voice reverberated throughout the newsroom. "Jasmine Carr. So glad you made it. Take the long way back?" She felt a blush creeping up her neck but didn't have time to stop it before Mikey boomed, "Come on in, there's someone I want you to meet."

Jasmine shrugged at Liza, who arched a seagull-shaped eyebrow in response. As Jasmine walked across the newsroom, she glanced around to see if anyone was watching her. She knew it was unreasonable.

The only other reporters in the newsroom at the moment—Perry Marks, city reporter and Jessie Pinkerton, education reporter—were laser-focused on their own work. Perry yelled into his phone, hitting his desktop repeatedly with his pointer finger, and Jessie alternately leaned over a stack of papers on her desk and typed maniacally. Still, Jasmine straightened her shirt as she passed them, all the while wondering why she'd worn a button-down shirt today. She hated button-down shirts. The buttons always went sideways and the hem never stayed tucked in evenly. On one side of the desk, Mikey leaned back in his chair, hands clasped behind his head and one leg crossed over the other. On the other side of the desk …

Whoa.

Jasmine might be shy, but she was still human. The visitor was young, as Liza had said, but he probably had a few years on Jasmine. His close cropped, curly hair was the color of sand when the sun hit it first thing in the morning. And his eyes—a green like the ice plant that covered the hillside going down to the beach. He wore an expensive-looking pair of jeans, scuffed cowboy boots, and a white collared shirt. His face looked like some master sculptor had created it as a tribute to masculine perfection. And the way he looked at her, like he was at once searching for clues and coming to a conclusion, made Jasmine want to pull her sweater more tightly around her body, for privacy. Only, she wasn't wearing a sweater.

She felt her throat working as her brain tried to reconnect and come up with something appropriate to say.

Mikey cleared his throat, and Jasmine jumped. She wondered if he'd call her out on being twitterpated again. "Jasmine Carr, meet Hudson Stover, photojournalist," he said.

Jasmine extended a hand, and Mikey added, "Your new partner."

"My partner?" Jasmine said, in a squeak. She chastised herself then, because repeating someone's statement as a question was one of her biggest pet peeves.

"Yes," Mikey said.

It wasn't until this Hudson character sat back in his chair and crossed his arms as if to say, "Let the show begin," that Jasmine realized she'd really liked the feel of his hand in hers. Something about it had given her a little jolt. Now her stomach was fluttering.

Jasmine shifted her weight from one foot to the other and put a hand on her hip to quell the nervous energy, but found herself making a closer and unabashed inspection of Hudson Stover, photo-journalist. Although his clothes screamed city mouse, his hands were calloused, and (*my, my*) he had big muscles. Although his legs stretched from here to Texas, his shoulders were broad and sinewy. He was no stranger to hard work, then. Jasmine licked her lips. She swallowed and jumped when Mikey spoke again.

"We're going to be switching things up a little," he said.

Doom took hold as a tiny flicker in Jasmine's stomach, and began to expand, to morph into a full-sized flame. She hated change. The only thing she hated worse than change was the feeling that she had no control. And at this moment, Mikey was feeding her a change-and-no-control sandwich.

"As you know," Mikey said, "Liza's taking a few weeks off to visit her daughter and the new baby. And we need to cover her beat while she's gone. Since you have kind of a non-essential beat, I thought we'd bring you in on Liza's."

Jasmine gritted her teeth. Features were essential. Without features, you'd have a newspaper full of gloom and doom. Surely he didn't expect Jasmine to cover Liza's entire job. The woman was a pro, with more than thirty years on the police beat and a contacts list to match. As for Jasmine's own beat—features and health—and the constant pressure from Mikey and his bosses to produce a front-page-worthy feature story every day, it would be impossible to cover crime and courts at the same time. She would fail at both. Readers would notice, Mikey would fire her, and she'd have to face all her sources whenever she ran into them in Seabreeze.

When Jasmine opened her mouth to interrupt, Mikey stopped her by raising a hand. "Now, I know I can't expect you to cover your own entire beat and hers, too, which is why we're breaking things up. Together, you and Hudson will cover crime. And I'm thinking of putting the new reporter on courts."

"The new reporter?" Jasmine almost kicked herself for her second infraction. What was going on here? The world was spinning out of control.

Mikey put his hands together as if he were praying. "Yes, Jasmine. A new reporter. She's coming in next week. I have a feeling the two of you will get along just fine. Anyway, I want you and Hudson to work together so you can show him the ropes, the best watering holes, all that good stuff. That is, if you think you can do it without getting twitterpated."

Without meaning to, Jasmine glanced at Hudson to gauge his reaction. Something flashed in his eyes, but she couldn't quite define it.

She could, however, define the urge that rose up in her own body. She tried to push it back down, but the visual of her straddling Hudson in that chair took over. Jasmine closed her eyes, just briefly, to clear the vision. She'd been neglecting that urge for years and there was no reason to give in to it now.

Then she opened her eyes and Hudson smiled at her, a megawatt grin that showed all of his perfectly straight, blazing white teeth. His eyes sparkled and she couldn't help but smile back. The urge returned.

With a loud grunt, Mikey heaved himself out of his chair and stood up. He gestured to the door. "That's all I've got for you today, Jasmine. I'm going to take Hudson down to human resources to get his paperwork done. You guys can connect tomorrow."

As Mikey and Hudson walked through the newsroom on their way out, she heard Mikey say to Hudson, "You'll like that Jasmine, I just know it. Look, she brought me a cookie because she thinks I'm a hero. Want to split it?"

CHAPTER TWO

Jasmine Carr met Parker Abbott by accident. Parker called it Fate, but Jasmine didn't believe in Fate. People chose their paths, and Life resulted from the complicated intertwining of these choices. Sure, coincidence existed, but it held no particular meaning or importance.

It was sophomore year. A late spring rainstorm moved in one Saturday and sat right over Seabreeze. It saturated the grass and filled the streets. It caused mudslides and road closures. School was closed that Monday and Jasmine and her sisters celebrated with pedicures and popcorn, "Sixteen Candles" and "The Breakfast Club" in the background.

That Tuesday morning, Parker missed the bus. He would later swear the bus came early that day, pulling away from the curb with a splash just as he exited his front door. Although he came out one minute later than usual, that should have put him at the bus stop in time for the bus's arrival. Fate made the bus early.

"But school buses never come early," Jasmine would say, every time the conversation arose.

Over the course of the next couple of months, Parker told everyone the story of how he and Jasmine met. Parker's parents were already at work, and it was Parker's responsibility to make sure his little brother, Ryder, was dressed and ready each morning. Ryder, a top student in the freshman class, was supposed to turn in his science fair project that morning. When he brought it out to the bus stop, the rain caused the ink on his display board to run, creating a rainbow of words that melted together. He'd printed everything out on the ink jet, and insisted on going back inside to print it all again. Today was the deadline to turn in the project, and he couldn't take it in looking like this. It would only take a few minutes, Ryder said, and his chances of winning any kind of prize would be nil if he didn't fix the poster.

Besides, they had seven minutes until the bus was due to arrive. Plenty of time, Ryder said.

In an effort to hurry the repair project along, Parker went inside with Ryder, and began gluing the freshly printed graphs and bullet-point lists and hypotheses to the display board as Ryder printed them out.

This time, they got smart and wrapped a plastic garbage bag around the display board to protect Ryder's masterpiece. When they walked out their front door to catch the bus, the bus was pulling away from the curb.

The rain was still pouring down, or as Parker's parents would say, "It's raining so hard the animals are starting to pair up." And now they had to walk to school.

The Abbott boys trudged along the sidewalk, their shoes making *squelch* sounds and the hems of their pants becoming soggy. They used Ryder's display board as an umbrella, but the wind blew the rain hard onto their backs. Parker muttered to himself about Ryder making them late, and Ryder muttered to himself about Parker not having a work ethic. In fact, he said to himself loudly enough for Parker to hear, Parker hadn't even completed a science fair project.

No, Parker hadn't completed a science fair project, he muttered in response, but at least he'd be on time for school, if it wasn't for Ryder. Parker despised being late. Loathed it. Although their father, a sergeant in the Army, hammered punctuality into his sons' heads, Ryder never seemed to pick up on it and they'd spent countless hours of their lives being lectured on timeliness.

At that moment, during this muttered argument, a car pulled up next to them at the curb. Parker gritted his teeth and rolled his eyes. Could it get any worse? Were they now going to be trailed by some senior bullies who would splash them repeatedly as they walked along? He'd heard of it happening.

Then the car stopped. Parker hunched his shoulders and walked faster. Ryder did the same.

Of course, the situation looked quite a bit different from Jasmine's point of view. Warm and dry and toasty in her mother's van, she turned down the Dave Matthews Band when she noticed two boys walking in the pouring rain, using a huge piece of plastic-covered cardboard as an umbrella.

"I feel so bad for those boys," she said aloud to her mom and her two sisters, Sequoia and Holly. Her mom slowed down.

"Why don't they have an umbrella?" Sequoia, the oldest and master of all things practical, said. "That was really stupid. It's been raining for like, three days. It's not like they didn't have any warning."

Jasmine, always willing to hear the entire story before making judgments, said, "Maybe something happened. Maybe they lost their umbrella. Maybe it broke. Should we offer them a ride, Mom?"

"Jasmine, they could be, like, serial killers or something," Holly, the youngest sister, said. "I can't believe you'd offer two strangers a ride."

Jasmine exchanged a look with her mom, and Sequoia laughed. "Ridiculous, Holly. They're kids. Look at their shoes. Those are expensive. And that one kid is wearing a leather jacket. I'm sure he's not a serial killer. Serial killers wear trench coats."

It seemed like sound reasoning, Jasmine thought. Mom must have thought so too, because she pulled up to the curb and stopped next to the boys.

The boys walked faster, and Mom let the van roll forward to keep up with them.

"Well, go on, Jasmine," Mom said. "This was your idea. Offer them a ride."

Jasmine's first thought was that her mom was probably trying to get her to practice talking to strangers. She always joked that while all the other parents were giving their kids the "Don't Talk to Strangers" lessons, she was begging Jasmine to talk to someone, *anyone!*

Jasmine took a deep breath and rolled down her window. She found that she couldn't speak. Sequoia nudged her and she cleared her throat. The older boy, taller by about six inches, scowled as he turned toward the van.

"Well, he doesn't look very friendly," Holly said.

Jasmine, put off by the scowl, began to roll up the window, but Sequoia reached across her and pressed the button down. "Want a ride?"

The younger boy grinned and nodded. The older one continued to scowl.

Sequoia laughed, and Jasmine, not to be deterred from completing her own act of kindness for the day, opened the door and stepped into the rain.

Initially, Parker would tell Jasmine later, he experienced profound relief. The van wasn't full of older kids planning a splash fest as they drove to school. He felt his shoulders relaxing, but his apprehension didn't dissipate completely until Jasmine got out of the car and smiled at him.

"I'm Jasmine," she said, extending a hand.

She's an angel, said a voice inside Parker's head.

He tried to speak, but had to clear the scratchiness from his throat. "I'm Parker."

His uneasiness made Jasmine feel much more relaxed.

"And I'm Ryder." His little brother, all enthusiasm, greeted Jasmine and shook her hand with far too little abandon.

"We saw you walking," Jasmine said, "And it's so wet and cold, and so, we, um, wanted to offer you a ride to school. Seabreeze High, right?"

Parker grunted and Ryder said, "Yep! Freshman, of course."

"Oh, my sister's a freshman," Jasmine said, pointing to the van. "Holly."

The three of them stood there for a moment, the rain catching in

Jasmine's eyelashes and dripping off the piece of cardboard the boys still held over their heads. Jasmine looked from Ryder's face to Parker's, and then, when thunder rumbled, she remembered the reason they were there.

"Oh! I'm so sorry. So, do you want a ride?"

Ryder nodded and immediately headed toward the van. Parker remained where he stood, looking at Jasmine with something in his expression that caught her off guard. It was a hint of a smile, but something else, too.

"We're gonna be late," Sequoia called through the rain.

Jasmine quirked an eyebrow at Parker and he followed her to the van.

That day at lunch, Parker approached Jasmine. She sat with her friends on the concrete steps in front of the gym, and was stunned into silence as he walked towards her, his gaze locked on hers.

There was something so … intense about him.

"Jasmine," he said.

Not for the first time in her life, Jasmine was at a loss for words. The way he said her name made it sound like it was some kind of dessert melting in his mouth. She felt her own mouth drop open before Hannah Kirk elbowed her and she snapped it shut again.

"Parker," she said.

Without waiting for an invitation, he sat down next to her. Hannah left the scene with a less-than-casual, "I'll see you later, Jas."

"Look," he said. "I just wanted to thank you for stopping for Ryder and me this morning. I was kind of—well, I didn't get a chance to thank you."

"You're welcome," she said. "You did bolt when we got here. I thought it's just because you didn't want to be seen with the Carr girls, getting out of a minivan."

He chuckled, his expression still serious, then stood up and kicked at the concrete stair with the toe of his Converse. "Believe me, it's a step up."

After that, he walked away, and Jasmine spent the next two periods—geometry and photography—thinking about him, wondering what he looked like when he smiled.

The school year lasted only a few more weeks, during which they passed each other in the halls several times. Parker would usually studiously ignore Jasmine, but one day he made eye contact and gave her the smallest possible nod. It was an acknowledgement, at least, and it left her loopy for the rest of the day. She couldn't even finish her math test, and Mrs. Piper had to call on her three times just for Jasmine to stumble through her answer to the bell question in photography. Something about f-stops.

Then, on the first day of the new school year, which dawned cool and sunny, Jasmine walked into her biology class and found that Mr. Z. (short for Zillman) had assigned seats. She sat down at hers, and took out the textbook from her Spanish class. If she could finish the homework assignment—conjugating -ar verbs—before she got home, she'd have more time to watch "Law and Order" with Holly and Sequoia. Although Holly never finished her assignments early, and Jasmine and Sequoia always ended up waiting for her, anyway.

Some sixth sense put Jasmine's body on alert, and its accuracy was confirmed when she heard someone say, "I think this is the beginning of a beautiful friendship."

Parker.

He slid onto the stool next to hers. And finally, she saw his smile.

"Are you my lab partner?" Jasmine said. Hope rose in her chest.

"I am," he said. "Congratulations."

The tingling she'd felt in her fingertips turned into a foreign warm feeling that spread through her torso and down into her stomach, and she felt a goofy smile spreading across her face. These new sensations made her a tiny bit bolder than usual.

"I'd congratulate you, too, if I weren't a total freak about guts and stuff," she said. "I might let you down when we dissect earthworms."

The bell rang and Jasmine shut her Spanish book. She dropped it into her backpack, not even a little disappointed that she hadn't finished her homework. In fact, she wasn't disappointed that she hadn't even started her homework.

"I'm pretty sure earthworms don't have any guts," Parker said.

"And besides, you couldn't let me down. You've rescued me once and I'm sure you'll do it again."

Jasmine giggled, then clapped a hand over her mouth, embarrassed. Mr. Z. rapped on his desk with a ruler to signal the start of class. Jasmine faced forward and Mr. Z. Began droning on about "policies and procedures," and "classroom safety."

Parker slid a sheet of paper across the table, wedging it under Jasmine's elbow. She lifted her elbow and slid it over to her side. When she read what it said, a new flurry of energy made its way through her body.

Would you like to have dinner with me?

Parker had drawn three little check boxes underneath, labeled, *Yes, this weekend, No, never,* and *Hmm. I don't know. Maybe next weekend.*

Jasmine, her face almost unbearably hot with pleasure or embarrassment or both, pressed her lips together to keep from laughing, and used the lab pencil to check the first box.

Friday night, Parker knocked on Jasmine's front door at precisely six o'clock. Jasmine, dressed and primped with the help of her two sisters—Sequoia made sure her outfit was practical, yet sexy, and Holly applied her makeup "so you don't look like a deranged clown"—answered it and yelped with surprise.

Parker stood on the doorstep, looking bashful. His dad stood behind him.

"You must be Jasmine," his dad said. "I'm David Abbott, Parker's dad."

Parker's dad walked Jasmine and Parker out to the car, where he insisted Parker drive them to dinner.

"I have my learner's permit," Parker said, looking at Jasmine in the rearview mirror.

"Eyes on the road, Son," Mr. Abbott said.

"I turn sixteen a week from Monday, and I'm taking my driver's test then. So Dad's making me practice today, I guess." He shrugged a shoulder.

"Hold still, Son," Mr. Abbott said. "Nice and steady."

Jasmine smiled when Parker winked at her in the rearview mirror.

"Concentrate, Parker," Mr. Abbott said. "Drive now, chat later."

They made the rest of the drive in relative silence, with only occasional interruptions from Mr. Abbott: "Look over your shoulder before you signal, Son. And never drive behind a Volvo or in front of a Honda."

Finally, they arrived at the restaurant, Linda's. Parker's dad took the car to run errands.

The restaurant's bright colors and cheerful decorations amplified Jasmine's festive mood, and the almost-too-loud mariachi music made her want to get up and dance. The server brought them a bowl of corn chips, and Parker grabbed one and popped it into his mouth before she'd even finished setting it down.

"I love the chips," he said.

"Me, too," Jasmine said. "They're perfect."

Parker considered it a sign that they both loved the chips and guacamole—with a dash of salt and a sprinkle of lime juice—and Jasmine laughed him off.

"Fate is overrated," she told him. "You make your own luck. You choose your own way."

"Sage advice coming from a fifteen-year-old," he said.

"Fourteen. I'll be fifteen a week from Monday," she said.

"Wait. So we, like, share a birthday?" he said.

She nodded. "I didn't say anything in the car because I didn't want to make a big deal of it. Since you were talking about your license and everything. And concentrating."

"And because you're shy," he said.

"I am not."

"You're so shy. And it's totally cool. Anyway, the two of us sharing a birthday is another sign," he said, nodding as though this single fact proved his hypothesis. "We were meant to meet."

Parker asked Jasmine what she planned to order, and when it was the same as what he always ordered (chicken and cheese enchiladas), he gave her a meaningful look. She found it so endearing when he ordered for her that she walked him through her usual orders at the hot spots she frequented: orange chicken at the Chinese place, a bacon ranch chicken sandwich with curly fries at the Burger Stop. They spent the next hour discussing favorite movies and favorite books, least favorite actors and most-watched cartoons.

"I seriously cannot believe I've met someone else who loves 'Home Alone' as much as I do!" Parker said at one point, and Jasmine said, "Same with 'Ice, Ice, Baby.'"

The similarities were so plentiful that the two of them were in stitches by the time the server brought their bill.

"How have we never met before this?" Jasmine said as they sat outside on the patio, waiting for Mr. Abbott to pick them up.

It was a rhetorical question, and Parker didn't answer it then, because he knew the answer would seal their relationship's fate as a tragedy.

CHAPTER THREE

To Jasmine, the length of time between her first date with Parker and their first kiss stretched into an eternity. Only a few weeks passed, but it felt like longer, since the two of them spent every spare moment together. After school, they studied at the public library. At night when they were each at home, they talked on the phone until well past bedtime. Once he got his driver's license, Parker drove Jasmine to school each morning.

Every weekend, Parker came up with new adventures for them to experience together. He took Jasmine biking along West Cliff Drive, hiking in the redwoods, crab hunting at the harbor. Each of them became an instant member of the other's family, staying for dinner or a movie or both at every opportunity. But still no kissing.

Because the Carr residence was home to three teenage girls, issues of "Teen" and "Seventeen" stacked up in corners and under pillows, each one containing something kissing-related.

"What kind of kisser are you?" one quiz aimed to find out. "What his kissing says about him," another article promised to reveal. Sequoia and Holly pressed her to complete the quizzes, and she did. She couldn't bring herself to admit they hadn't actually consummated their relationship with a kiss. Jasmine spent countless hours wondering how Parker's lips would feel, imagining how his tongue would explore her mouth … and taking quizzes based solely on her fantasies.

Whenever they saw each other, he did nothing more than wrap her in a hug. She suspected she was at fault. After all, she'd admitted to being shy, and she liked the way he took control of things, from ordering her meals to choosing their dates and planning their activities. Maybe he was just waiting for the right moment. He didn't want to rush her.

Finally, one cold day just before winter break, Mr. Z. sent Parker and Jasmine to the library to check out a few reference books. The school's classrooms opened to outdoor corridors, and Jasmine shivered as the winter breeze picked up. She could sense something different in Parker's stride, something determined. She noticed but wrote it off as purpose, the feeling of importance that he'd been assigned a special task. She told herself he was avoiding eye contact because he didn't want to become distracted.

Inside the library, they stood side by side in front of the bookshelf, running their fingers along the spines to find the books Mr. Z. wanted.

Parker linked his fingers with Jasmine's, and she felt her stomach tighten. Then he ran his hand up her arm. She turned her head to smile at him, and he leaned toward her and kissed her. His lips were warm and firm, and her mouth opened slightly in response to the kiss. In that one instant, she felt so many things she'd never experienced before. Her "lady parts" (so named by Sequoia) reacted in a very serious manner, and she had an overwhelming need for him to touch her there and everywhere else.

She'd kissed other boys before. Jeremy Dawson, her first high school crush, behind the snack shack at the homecoming game and Aaron Gomez, her cross country running partner, behind a redwood tree on a long trail run. But she'd never kissed anyone like this.

Then, just as quickly as the kiss had started, it was over.

Jasmine's heart was beating a million miles an hour, and she tried to slow it down by breathing deeply, without letting Parker see how much it had affected her. He grinned at her and pulled out the book he was looking for.

A minute later, she found the book she needed, and they headed back to class. The air between them crackled with voltage for the rest of the period, every beating pulse pulling her body towards his.

SOMEHOW, during the fifteen months Jasmine and Parker dated, the issue of Parker's dad being in the military never fazed Jasmine. She later thought it should have, but her feelings for Parker blinded her to the practical matter of a military family's constant moves. One night, when Jasmine was at Parker's house for dinner, Mr. Abbott began talking, casually, about the family's upcoming transfer to an Army base in Spain.

It was news to Jasmine. Parker never mentioned he was moving, much less moving halfway around the world. Having suddenly lost her appetite, she dropped her fork onto her plate. It clattered, and everyone around the table went silent.

"Uh, Jas, did you even know we're moving?" Ryder asked.

She noticed Parker had taken a sudden interest in his food, and felt a powerful rush of anger. Why hadn't he told her? Why had he let her fall for him if he knew he was going to *Spain*?

"Um, he didn't mention that, no," Jasmine said.

Parker's mom, Cindy, sucked in a breath so loudly Jasmine would have laughed under other circumstances. But she gathered her wits and found her voice and said, "Parker, why don't you and Jasmine go for a nice walk and we'll clear the table?"

She stood up and motioned (not discreetly) for Ryder and Mr. Abbott to do the same. Parker pushed back his chair, the scraping sounds it made against the tile floor deafening in the sudden silence. Jasmine followed him out the front door, her legs barely bending enough to lift her feet off the floor. When he went right, she went left.

Hot, furious tears filled her eyes, and she used her fists to wipe them away.

"Jasmine!" Parker had jogged to catch up with her, and he grabbed her wrist and spun her around. When he saw that she was crying, he pulled her close.

"I'm so sorry," he whispered. "I just didn't want to ruin the time we had left."

He explained that he'd kept the move a secret to protect both of them. He'd done it for her as much as he'd done it for himself, to shield them from the pain of suffering through a long, drawn-out good-bye. And Jasmine understood. She was grateful he'd tried to look after her feelings.

But that didn't make her feelings any less strong. At sixteen, the mere idea of Parker moving away was the worst pain she'd ever known, and even as she calmed down enough to let him take her hand and walk her to the coast so they could watch the sunset paint the sky, she sobbed and sobbed at the thought of doing it alone in just a few weeks. She cried until her eyes were dry, and then she cried some more, her body convulsing until her stomach muscles were sore. Parker stood next to her at the railing along East Cliff, and rubbed her back. He'd run out of apologies, and she didn't want to hear them, anyway.

"Will you walk me in?" Jasmine said later that night when Parker drove her home. It was late and the house was dark. Everyone was asleep.

Without speaking, Jasmine led Parker upstairs to her bedroom. She shut the door and locked it, then turned around to face him. She kissed him, gently at first, and then a little harder. In that moment, she felt that if only she could convey the enormity of her feelings for him, she could leave a permanent imprint on his soul.

Parker brought his hands up to cup her face, and she inhaled the smell of the linen-scented soap he used. She put her arms around his waist and pulled his body against hers. He moaned and his hands made their way to her breasts. She could feel her nipples pressing against his palms, and that awareness sent a quivery feeling right down to her lady parts.

She shivered, and Parker smiled against her mouth.

"You like that?" he asked, and she wondered why they'd never done this before.

Yes, they'd kissed, but it was always so chaste, in an upright position on the couch or at school or the front door. They'd never been locked away anywhere intimate. She nodded and kissed him again, and he continued massaging her breasts until she thought she might explode. She took one of his hands and moved it down to her lady parts. He made a guttural sound that turned her on even more.

He began rubbing her through her skirt, and the quivery feeling intensified so she felt like she had to arch against him. He lifted her skirt and pulled her panties down, and when his hand touched her, she cried out.

"I want to make love to you," he said, even while he moved his fingers back and forth against her.

She led him towards the bed, and as they walked, he pulled her shirt up and over her head, then ran his hands up her torso again. Just as the backs of her legs touched the mattress, he knelt down and kissed her just below the belly button.

Why had she waited so long for this?

Because she hadn't even known she was waiting.

Parker took off his own shirt, but when he went to unbuckle his belt, she stopped him.

"Let me," she said, and she unbuckled it and unbuttoned his jeans carefully, forcing herself to move slowly so she wouldn't seem clumsy.

She gasped when she pulled down his underwear; she'd never seen an erection before and it was bigger than she expected.

He laughed. "I'll go slow. It's my first time, too."

THE NIGHT before the Abbotts were scheduled to leave, Parker and Jasmine sat on the end of Jasmine's bed, both of them in tears.

"This isn't good-bye," Parker said. "We can still be together."

"Will we be, like, pen pals, or something?" Jasmine said. In her mind, she ran through the conversation she'd rehearsed with Sequoia and Holly. She knew she was making the right decision, but the words were still so hard to say. "In case you forgot, you're moving halfway around the world, not just down the block."

She felt powerless to stop the sarcasm from coming out of her mouth like death rays, and didn't even try. Still, guilt crept in when she saw Parker's downcast eyes.

"Sorry," she said. She blotted her own eyes with a tissue and made an effort to soften her tone. "It's just that this feels impossible. I don't want us to spend our lives missing each other, when our time apart is indefinite."

Sequoia had come up with that sentence, and Jasmine had to admit, it made sense.

"Who knows when we'll see each other again? Besides, you deserve to date people when you're in Spain, or wherever you end up. And I deserve to date people here. I don't want to spend the rest of my high school career feeling like I can't go on a date or sit next to someone on the homecoming float, you know? And I don't want you to feel that way, either."

"We could go to the same college," Parker said, but they both knew they couldn't. Mr. Abbott was insisting on an Ivy League school, and Jasmine would have to work her way through community college for at least a couple of years.

Jasmine shook her head.

"I have an idea," Parker said. "What if we make a pact?"

"Oh, I've heard of these pacts," Jasmine said. She couldn't help but laugh, just a little. "These pacts happen when one person doesn't want to be with the other. Like, 'I'm too good for you right now, but I'll date you in ten years if I'm still single and desperate.' That's not what's happening here, is it?"

"Not at all," he said. "But you're right. You should be free to enjoy the rest of your high school career and your college years, and it would be impractical for us to stay together. But what if we meet up when we're, say, forty, and give it a try?"

"Forty? That's way too old. We could both be married and divorced by then. If we're both still single, there's a reason why. It's because we're both jerks, and I guarantee you neither of us is going to like the other."

"Fine. How about thirty?" Parker said.

"Wait. Is that too old?

"Fate put us together once," Parker said, "and I have a feeling she's going to bring us together again. Guys mature more slowly, anyway. I know you're going to want the best of me."

Jasmine laughed. Then, nervous again, she ran her hand over the bedspread. "But what if we, like, hate each other? People change."

"Jas. We both know there's something here." Parker lifted her chin with his finger, forcing her to look at him. "Right?"

She felt her eyes tearing up for the billionth time in two weeks. "Right," she said.

"So, if it's meant to be, it will still be there when we're thirty."

She leaned into him, and he wrapped his arms around her.

"Still," she said. "I think we should add some kind of structure. Like a minimum requirement. What if we say we give it a serious try for a month? One month."

"That sounds fine," he said. "But I don't think it's going to take a month for us to remember what this feels like."

They made love one last time, and Parker was gone the next day.

CHAPTER FOUR

"I CALL THIS MEETING OF THE GARDEN CLUB TO ORDER," JASMINE SAID. "It's my thirtieth birthday and I have an announcement to make."

The Carr girls had called themselves The Garden Club since Sequoia was eight, Jasmine was six, and Holly was four. They'd just gained enough awareness to realize their parents had named them all after flora, and the idea of creating a secret club around that theme was just too much to pass up.

The three of them now stood in the kitchen of Jasmine's apartment, Holly and Sequoia on one side of the island and Jasmine on the other. Jasmine had made them pre-dinner cocktails—Moscow Mules—and they sipped them and ate salted almonds to pass the time before their dinner reservation.

"You're finally going to settle down?" Sequoia said, and Holly chimed in, "You've finally lost your virginity?"

"You know I lost my virginity a long time ago," Jasmine said. "But actually, this news falls into both of those categories."

Holly did a fake gasp, and Sequoia raised her eyebrows, waiting.

"I got a phone call today," Jasmine said.

She waited for some flicker of recognition on her sisters' faces, but nothing. Completely blank.

"It's my thirtieth birthday?" she tried. Still nothing. To give them a little more time to guess, she began opening windows to let in the almost-crisp, almost-fall air. Still, nothing. Even though she had her back to them, Jasmine could picture Sequoia and Holly gesturing at each other, maybe even whispering together, trying to figure out what she was trying to tell them. Finally, she gave up on them. She turned around to face them.

"Do you remember—"

"Ohmigod!" Holly said, flapping one hand at Jasmine. The realization had struck, and awareness brought her eyes to a sharp focus on Jasmine's. "Parker! Parker Abbott! He called you! You're thirty, he's thirty-one, the pact! How could we have forgotten?"

She set down her glass and gripped Jasmine by the elbows. "So what happened?"

"Yeah," Sequoia said. "Dish. What did he say?"

Holly interrupted before Jasmine could even begin. "He was really good-looking, wasn't he? I still remember thinking he was really handsome. Even though I was kind of young for that sort of thing. Oh, wow. I can't believe he called you. I mean, have you even stayed in touch with him? I wonder what he looks like now."

"Let her talk," Sequoia said. "Geez."

Holly giggled and Jasmine, suddenly and inexplicably shy, said, "No, I haven't really talked to him since high school. I mean, at first we'd talk on the phone every once in a while, but with the time zones and everything it was hard. And then we both just got so busy. I've tried looking him up on social media sites a few times, but he's just not on there. And then today, out of the blue, he calls me. I'm at work and I'm about to head out for that Cookies for Heroes thing, you know? And my phone rings. So of course I answer it. Didn't even look at the number."

She could tell she was rambling and was relieved when Holly cut her off: "So what did he say?"

"I'm about to tell you," Jasmine said. "He said he's coming here in a week."

"Here?!" Holly said. "He's coming here?"

"Let her talk," Sequoia said again.

"Yes, he's coming here," Jasmine said.

"Wait, when? When is he coming? We have to go lingerie shopping. You need to get your eyebrows waxed. And your lady parts."

"He's coming in a week, he said," Jasmine said.

"She just said that," Sequoia said.

"Oh," Holly said. "Right. Anyway. Cancel our dinner reservation. We need to hit the mall. Or the sex shop."

"I'm scandalized," Jasmine said. "We are doing no such thing. I want to have a nice birthday dinner with my sisters. I don't think I'm going to do any lingerie shopping just yet. And I'm definitely not hitting the sex shop."

For lunch, Jasmine had chosen Pâtisserie, her longtime favorite spot, not only because it was her favorite, but also because she knew it would drive her sisters crazy. She loved the pastel-colored lanterns and bouquets. She loved the cushioned chairs and the festive candles.

"I don't know why you always pick these places, Jas," Sequoia said. She pointed to the entrees section of the menu. "Look. It's not practical at all."

"I know," Holly said. "It's like three pieces of lettuce with a sprinkle of Feta cheese and they charge you fifteen bucks. No protein. Not a single gram."

Jasmine's smile was evil laced with sugar. "Wish me a happy birthday and eat your salad."

"I could go for a big burger," Sequoia said, and Holly said, "Nah, a fat tofu burrito."

"Anyway," Holly said. "I'm so happy you're here with me."

"Cheers, Jas," Holly said. "To a year that's sure to be filled with adventure."

"As long as said adventure doesn't involve dyeing your hair leopard print, like Holly's," Sequoia said.

"Hey," Holly said, putting a hand to her newly-colored hair. "It's on trend."

Jasmine raised her glass, her sisters clinked theirs against it, and before Holly even finished swallowing her sip of lemonade, she was talking again: "So, are you gonna, like, meet up with Parker when he comes?"

"Holly, would you just let it go?" Sequoia said. "Let her decide on her own, without your romantic heart influencing her. I mean, wasn't it your idea that she just wait and wait for him to come back? And where would that have gotten her? I mean, actually, I think she kind of did that, subconsciously. And that's why she's still alone and lonely after all this time."

"I'm not lonely. And I didn't do that," Jasmine said.

"You don't think you did, but you did," Sequoia said.

"Only because it's Fate that the two of them be together," Holly said.

They were out of control.

Jasmine held up a hand. "First of all, I can't really stop him from coming, can I? And yes, I'll admit, I'm totally curious. I've thought about him over the years. Less frequently, you know, as I've gotten older, but certain things just trigger those memories." She slapped her hand on the table. "Bam! Just rushing back."

A few weeks ago, she'd been at the high school for a story about the debate team. She'd met the kids and their advisor in the library, and couldn't help but walk through the reference section where she and Parker had shared their first kiss. She experienced the feeling of his fingers entangled with hers, her heart beating fast and hard.

And a few weeks before that, she'd walked along East Cliff drive, as she'd done thousands of times since Parker left—thousands of times without thinking of him—and had the strong urge to go sit on the pilings where they spent so many Friday evenings. A spray of ocean water rose up against the pilings and rained down on her, bringing a vivid memory of one evening when she and Parker had sat in the very same spot to watch the sunset. They'd been discussing something so serious. She couldn't even remember now what it was. Out of nowhere (it wasn't really out of nowhere, but it seemed like it in the moment), a wave hit the pilings and sprayed upward, showering them with cold, salty water. They jumped up, yelling and laughing and running towards drier land. Every time they talked about it later, they broke into raucous laughter, doubled over.

Now, a decade and a half later, Jasmine smiled at that memory, and had to fight the urge to giggle like her teenage self would. The other Pâtisserie patrons would probably not appreciate giggling.

With some effort, Jasmine pulled herself out of the past. "We really had some good times," she said to her sisters.

"But you've changed, Jas," Sequoia said. "I mean, you've evolved since then."

"Don't you think Parker has, too?" Holly said. "She should at least give him a chance. At least meet up with him."

The server brought out the next course: a French Onion soup Jasmine often daydreamed about when she was driving to an interview or rushing to meet a deadline.

"But there's the pact," Sequoia reminded Holly. "If she meets up with him, it's a nonverbal agreement to move forward with the terms of the pact and she has to date him for what, Jas, a month?"

Jasmine nodded. "Yeah. But do you really think—"

"Yes, I really think you meeting up with him is the beginning of moving forward with the pact. You're sucked in for a month."

"Surely he won't hold me to that," Jasmine said. "I mean, if there's no connection."

"Oh, there's gonna be a connection," Holly said. She wiggled her eyebrows. "Considering you haven't had sex with anyone since."

Jasmine sipped her soup. It was true. She hadn't had sex with anyone since. The fact was kind of humiliating.

Sensing Jasmine's embarrassment, Sequoia changed the subject: "What else is new?"

Jasmine filled them in on her new assignment at work, and while Holly clapped her hands in excitement, Sequoia folded her hands together and tipped her head just slightly forward so she was looking at Jasmine from under her eyebrows.

"Uh oh, I recognize that look," Holly said, pointing at Sequoia. "That's your bossy look."

"It totally is," Jasmine said. "Dish, sister."

"I don't know," Sequoia said. She blew on a spoonful of soup. "Don't you think it's a conflict of interest?"

"What do you mean?" Jasmine said.

"I mean, I'm a cop," Sequoia said. "I work for Seabreeze PD. You're going to be covering some of my cases, probably."

Jasmine shrugged a shoulder. "I can be fair and unbiased, even where you're involved." Sequoia sucked on her lips but didn't say anything else, which made Jasmine speak compulsively: "Plus, I'll be training this new guy, Hudson. He's a photojournalist, but I guess we'll be matched up. Partners."

"Your ears are turning red," Holly said. "Is he hot?"

"Are they?" Jasmine said.

"They are," Sequoia said.

"Is he?" Holly said.

"He's hot," Jasmine said. "But not regular hot. City slicker hot. You know that's not my type. Although he wears cowboy boots. Real ones."

"Well, it could be your type," Holly said. She put an ice cube in her soup and stirred as it melted.

"Not with Parker reemerging on the scene," Sequoia said. "Let's be practical." The waiter set their entrées on the table. "Unlike this food."

"What's new with you?" Holly asked, nudging Sequoia. "You've been quiet."

Sequoia poked at her chicken breast medallion with her fork. She sighed. "I don't know. I got this new supervisor, and you know I usually get along with people, but this woman's a crazy, psychotic creeper."

"Wow, that's a great insult," Jasmine said.

"You're the wordsmith, not me," Sequoia said. "And anyway, she is."

"Why is she a creeper?" Holly said.

"I don't know," Sequoia said. Her mouth twisted into a scowl. "I can't really put my finger on it. My sixth sense is going off, big time. She's definitely unfriendly, but it isn't that. I mean, I'm unfriendly."

Holly snorted, and Sequoia flashed her a grin before continuing. "I know she's been here only a short time, but it doesn't seem like her decisions are coming from the right place. I'd certainly make different choices."

"Weren't you going to test for that promotion?" Jasmine said. "When's that?"

"It's a month from today, actually," Sequoia said. "But even if I come out first on the list of candidates for sergeant, it could be a while before a position opens up. I think there's one guy retiring soon, which is why they're offering the test, but if I'm second on the list and a second position doesn't open up, I'm stuck with Ms. Creeper for the rest of my career."

"Maybe she's just nervous, because she's new," Holly said. "I'm sure she'll come around."

"And I'm sure unicorns fly," Sequoia said. "And sprinkle glitter."

Jasmine reached across the table and squeezed Holly's hand. "Sequoia didn't mean it," she said. "It's that time of the month for her."

When a ghost of a smile crossed Holly's face, Jasmine said, "What's new with you, anyway? We haven't talked about what you're doing."

In a voice that sounded more like a mumble than her typical, enthusiastic timbre, she said, "Nothing really."

"Didn't you say earlier that you had something to tell us at dinner?" Sequoia said.

"That was before you said unicorns fly," Holly said.

"Stop pouting," Sequoia said, and Jasmine said, "Tell us."

"Fine," Holly said, and some of the usual light came back into her eyes. "I'm getting certified as a personal trainer. You know, I spend so much time at the gym and everything, and working as a temp just isn't really my style. Skirt suits and collared shirts are so not me."

"So," Sequoia said, drawing out the word, "you're making your career choices based on wardrobe now."

Jasmine stomped on Sequoia's foot under the table. Of course, Sequoia didn't even flinch.

Jasmine said, "That's great, Holly. You'll be a business owner now. You can teach classes and do personal training and all that stuff. You're going to be great at it."

Sequoia nodded. "That really is great. I didn't mean what I said about your wardrobe. Fitness really is the perfect field for you, for that neon-sign buzzing you've got going on. I think you'll like it a lot."

It was true. Personal training would fit Holly, with her naturally toned muscles and constant high energy.

The server brought over a tray of fake dessert items, and although Jasmine would have preferred the chocolate fudge cake, she selected the raspberry lemon cake because she knew they'd all like it. Holly would have chosen the raspberry cheesecake ("work hard, eat well!" she'd say) and Sequoia, always ultra-disciplined, would have skipped dessert all together.

Jasmine wondered how the three of them could share the same genes and have turned out so differently. Their features were remarkably similar: oversized teeth and big smiles, pointy noses and long, dark eyelashes framing big eyes. Their coloring was absolutely different, though. Sequoia had long, dark brown hair, which she almost always wore in a bun (at work) or a ponytail (at home). Her eyes were so light they almost looked like they belonged in someone else's face. And her skin tanned beautifully, which irritated both Jasmine and Holly to no end. Jasmine, who their mom always called, "blonder than blonde," had pale skin and bright green eyes and a sprinkling of freckles across her nose. And Holly kept her naturally-copper-red hair cropped close, constantly dyeing it raven-black or cotton-candy-pink or sky-blue. The short style brought out her dazzling blue eyes.

The differences went beyond just looks, Jasmine thought as the server returned with the dessert, a candle and three spoons. Sequoia was so Type A she was difficult to live with. And Holly was so free spirited they wondered if she'd ever settle down. Jasmine, of course, was the middle child, and her personality type fell somewhere in between.

Sequoia interrupted her thoughts. "So. Jasmine. Are you going to sleep with Parker, or with Hudson?"

Interesting question, Jasmine thought. She said, "Well, seeing as sleeping with Hudson isn't really on the table, I guess it'll be Parker."

Holly nodded. "You have been going through kind of a dry spell, lately."

Try a decade and a half, Jasmine thought. She smiled as she raised her glass again.

"To your most adventurous year yet," Holly said, and Sequoia said, "To success."

CHAPTER FIVE

The next morning, Jasmine woke wrapped in a blanket of heavy dread threaded with anticipation. Her dog, Ruby, apparently operated solely on excitement. She ran circles around the kitchen island, stopping every lap to take a bite of food and sniff Jasmine's foot. Jasmine put her tea kettle on the stove and took out a pan to scramble some eggs.

Throughout her eight-year career at the *Daily Trumpet*, Jasmine had never covered any hard news. When the hot tones came out over the police scanner, everyone else's ears perked up and a silence fell. Jasmine put in her earbuds and turned up her Relaxation playlist. When everyone else stayed late for election results, feasting on pizza and racing deadlines, Jasmine stayed home and watched straight-to-cable romance movies, curled up on the couch with Ruby.

She wrote stories about cookies and heroes, or surfing lessons. She covered performing arts festivals and new playgrounds, not deadly car crashes and criminals, which were completely out of her element. Those things—crumpled cars and tattooed hoodlums—scared the crap out of her.

Today, she was supposed to cover a press conference at the police station. She had no idea what it was about, although Liza had given her a stack of "notes" about six inches thick. It was more like a novel and she didn't have the time or brainpower to read it. Jasmine (and Liza, actually) had tried to insist Liza cover the press conference, but Mikey had overridden them, saying this would be a good way to begin the transfer.

"Liza can advise you on this first story before she hits the road, Carr. Now get on outta here, the both of you."

Jasmine slid her eggs from the pan to a plate. When she sat down at the counter to eat, Ruby flopped down next to Jasmine's feet and fell asleep.

The idea of heading toward danger freaked Jasmine out. She wasn't sure she could hang, even temporarily while Liza was gone. And, actually, it wasn't true that she'd *never* covered any hard news, she reminded herself. It was just that she tried to forget about the one and only time Mikey had sent her to cover a structure fire. She'd asked all the wrong questions. She'd interviewed the firefighters about how they felt when they got the call and when they arrived on the scene. She interviewed a little boy about what it was like to evacuate. She hadn't asked how the fire started, how many firefighters responded, or the monetary value of the damage it caused.

So when Mikey read the first draft of her story—which she'd written on deadline, leaving barely any time for edits—he pitched a fit about how she'd turned it into a fluff piece. Poor Liza had had to rewrite the story on such a tight turnaround that she didn't speak to Jasmine for a week.

(Jasmine could still picture Liza's face, red with rage, jabbing a fingertip yellow from gripping a cigarette into Jasmine's face as she chastised her, syllable by syllable: "Who, what, when, where, and HOW, Jasmine! It's simple. Real news.")

Mikey's face bright red and his teeth glowing yellow in his mouth, he made it perfectly clear what he thought of her news reporting.

"So help me, God, I'll never put you on another serious news story again," he said then.

And now, here he was, expecting her to go to today's press

conference and then write serious news stories for a few weeks until Liza came back from visiting her daughter.

That's where the dread was coming from.

How could this possibly turn out well? She wasn't a serious journalist. She was a fluff correspondent. In fact, maybe she should make her byline "Jasmine Carr, Fluff Correspondent." In fact, the only reason Mikey was putting her on Liza's beat was because her own beat was expendable.

She sighed, and Ruby adjusted her sleeping position.

Yesterday, Jasmine had chosen not to remind Mikey about how that structure fire situation had transpired, even though the memory was clear as a summer's day for her. Maybe he'd forgotten. *Probably not*, said a reasonable voice in the back of her mind.

Just as there were two sides to every news story (a concept even Jasmine understood by now), there were two sides to this new beat coin, too. If there was anything positive about it, she thought, hanging out with Hudson Stover seemed promising. He was definitely eye candy, although he might be too refined to find Jasmine appealing. Nevertheless, she could continue enjoying those vivid visuals of straddling his long muscular thighs. That's where the anticipation was coming from.

And Parker would be arriving in six days. That was something to look forward to. Maybe she *should* go buy some lingerie, like Holly suggested.

Maybe she was a terrible news reporter several years ago, but she could make it right. Hopefully. If not, her screw-ups would happen under the watchful green eyes of Hudson Stover, photojournalist, and everybody else.

Maybe Parker serving as a distraction was a bad idea, after all. *Or*, said a tiny voice coming from some deep corner of Jasmine's mind, *maybe it's a good idea.*

She cleaned up her dishes and got ready for work.

When Jasmine walked into the newsroom, she realized immediately that someone was sitting in her chair. She dropped her purse on the corner of her desk as Hudson Stover spun around to face her.

Her first reaction was that he was absurdly good-looking. How could someone even *be* so good-looking? It was unfair. For a split second she wondered if he'd ever had plastic surgery.

Then came her second reaction. Seeing him sitting there, looking so smug in her chair, Jasmine's teeth on edge.

"What are you doing?" she snapped.

"What are *you* doing?"

Jasmine's mouth dropped open. "Excuse me, please."

"Okay, pardner." Hudson stood up, but he remained in front of Jasmine's chair.

"Why are you talking like that?"

"Isn't that how you country folk talk?" Hudson drawled. Still, he didn't move.

"Excuse me, please," Jasmine said.

Now he bowed, an exaggerated movement, and walked away. Jasmine thought she heard him whistling but she couldn't be sure. Shaking her head, she sat down and turned on her computer. Before even a moment had passed, Liza strolled up, an unlit cigarette between her pointer and middle fingers, and her thumb flicking the filter. She propped a hip up on Jasmine's desk.

"Have you studied up on those notes I gave you?" she said.

"Good morning," Jasmine said.

Liza waved her cigarette, dismissing any further pleasantries. "So?"

"No," Jasmine said. "I haven't had time."

Liza crossed her arms. "Do you have any idea what you're walking into?"

Jasmine rubbed her eyes, then tapped the button on her mouse to open her email program. "No, Liza. I thought I was walking into a press conference."

"If you'd tear your eyes away from your computer screen for just a moment," Liza said, "I'd love to give you just a hint. So you don't go in there looking like an idiot."

Jasmine huffed out a sigh.

"It's nothing personal," Liza said. "Look. I was going over some financial records for the police department, and I found some discrepancies. I asked the public information officer for some information. You'd think he'd give it to me, right? Public information officer. Public information." She lifted both hands now, like they were two pans on a balance scale and she was the Lady Justice. "But no. He refused to comment. So I published the story without his input. I'm sure you saw it, right? Page One this past Sunday?"

Jasmine didn't answer. She rarely looked at the newspaper. That same voice from a dark and cobwebby place in her mind piped up: *Maybe that's a problem. Why* don't *you look at the newspaper?*

"You didn't read it," Liza said. "You didn't even see it. You really have no idea what's going on."

"It's not that I—"

"It's fine," Liza said. "I understand. It's not your beat, not your area of interest or whatever. Here's the thing. It's your tax money. And it's our readers' tax money. So you really should know this. Money is missing, okay? Somebody is siphoning money. Laundering it. Whatever. It's just gone. Lots of it."

"Who?"

"That's the million-dollar question, Jasmine. And I have a feeling you're going to spend some of your time *trying* to answer it during the next couple of weeks. With that lip-smacking Hudson at your side. I saw the way you looked at him."

"Like I wanted to claw his eyes out for sitting in my chair?"

"No," Liza said, putting her cigarette between her lips. "Not like that at all."

"Like what, then?" Jasmine said.

"I can't say. It'll offend my sensibilities. It's obscene, really."

Jasmine rolled her eyes and Liza walked to the door, lighting her cigarette exactly at the moment she opened it. Jasmine broke out of her Liza-watching trance with the realization that it was probably almost time to head to the press conference.

In the parking lot, Hudson straddled a sleek motorcycle. He was putting on his helmet, and he gave Jasmine a cocky grin as she walked to her own car.

"Want to ride together?" he asked.

She shook her head. "No. Thanks, though."

As she approached her car, he cleared this throat. "That your car?"

Jasmine felt her shoulders tense. "I'm getting into it, aren't I?"

"Sure you don't want to ride together?"

"Do you ever speak in full sentences?"

"Will that thing even make it to the police department?"

"For your information, this thing has made it to more places than I can count, for more years than your precious motorcycle has even revved its obnoxious engine. It's dependable."

Jasmine opened the driver's door of her bright orange Volkswagen Golf and inhaled its old-car scent. She loved this car, and she wouldn't tolerate some sexy, city-slicker newcomer making fun of it. Wait. Had she just called him sexy in her own mind?

With jerky movements, she put on her seatbelt.

Then, before she had time to set up her purse and cell phone and check behind her car three times, Hudson peeled out of the driveway so fast her head spun.

THE SEABREEZE POLICE DEPARTMENT'S public information officer, Earl Little, stood at the podium, his giant hook nose pointing at each attendee in turn as he scanned the room. Earl Little had a mustache like a broom head and a countenance like a guard dog. He could sit quietly for hours, but one misstep and someone was going down. The incident would probably involve blood.

Hudson leaned over to whisper in Jasmine's ear: "Glad you made it."

While one part of Jasmine's consciousness cringed at this stranger's proximity to her own body, another part of her relished the feeling of his breath against her ear. She hissed back, "Of course I did."

"I can't believe you drive that rattletrap."

Jasmine put a finger to her lips to silence him. Hudson nodded at

Earl Little and kept whispering. "He's kind of an ugly dude, isn't he? I think he knows who siphoned the money."

"How do you know someone siphoned it?"

"I've been doing this a long time," Hudson said.

"Shouldn't you be taking pictures, or something?" Jasmine said. The comment was out of character for her—it was more like something Sequoia would say—but sitting this close to Hudson made her uncomfortable and twitchy.

He laughed, a sharp, short sound, as if he knew what she was thinking. "I've got to come up with a creative angle."

Jasmine nodded. She wanted to whisper, "You're not going to find it, sitting on your ass like you are now," but couldn't get up the courage. Instead, she said, "You'd probably do better standing up."

Hudson didn't answer because Earl Little began to speak. "It has come to our attention that some investigative reporters have discovered a case of missing money in our department budget. Obviously, reporters are not trained financial professionals, and I can assure you that every step is being taken to discover whether money is, in fact, unaccounted for, and where it is, if so. As we all know, money does not simply … disappear."

On this last word he held up his hands, palms out, as if he were a magician.

A couple of reporters began asking questions, and Earl Little focused his beady, close-together eyes on Jasmine. She looked behind her, but there was no one there. Everyone else seemed oblivious to Earl's glare.

"Well, our good friend Liza done pissed Earl off," Hudson said to Jasmine, the, "Howdy, pardner," drawl returning.

This time, Jasmine giggled. She couldn't help it. Earl raised a bushy eyebrow at her. She glued her gaze to the notebook in her lap, the sheet on top still blank.

Also, though, she felt her reporter's intuition kicking in. (She hadn't thought she possessed any, but maybe it was just dormant.) Why was Earl glaring at her? The answer, she knew, was that he was angry at Liza, and, because Jasmine was Liza's counterpart, he was angry at Jasmine, too. Earl would be angry at Liza only if she was onto something. Liza was a great reporter. She'd won lots of awards and uncovered lots of stories that got dozens of reader comments on the *Daily Trumpet's* website. So she knew what she was doing. She was definitely on the right track with her story about missing money. And Earl Little was probably involved. How much money was missing? And where was it going?

Wait, Jasmine thought. *Am I actually interested in this?*

Earl began speaking again. "The fact is, financial reporting is a complicated business, especially at a department as big as ours. There can be a delay between when money comes out and when its use is properly accounted for. For example, we provide our officers with new bulletproof vests every five years. So every month, we hand out thousands of dollars to pay for the vests. The officers are then responsible for turning in their receipts."

Jasmine nodded. That made sense. But the Seabreeze Police Department wasn't that big.

"That doesn't make sense," Hudson said, his breath on Jasmine's ear again making her skin tingle. "That would still be a line item on the reports. He's totally lying."

Jasmine wondered how it would feel if Hudson was whispering against her ear while they were horizontal, and what he'd be whispering. Then she kicked herself for wondering that. Just then, Jasmine felt her phone vibrate against the side of her body. She'd put it in her purse to avoid having to look at it, and now someone was texting.

"Terrible timing," she muttered as she looked at the screen.

It was from the same Denver area code from which Parker had called.

Looking forward to seeing you.

Something, some emotion, some feeling, began fluttering around Jasmine's body, with particular concentration in her lady parts. She texted back: *I'm looking forward to seeing you, too.* Then, because she thought that seemed kind of cliché, she typed, *And I can't wait to hear what you've been up to.*

Although, who really knows? she thought. Maybe hearing what he'd been up to would be a turnoff. Maybe he'd been selling fish at a pet store or something. Or maybe he drove an ice cream truck. That would be pretty creepy.

He wrote back: *What are you wearing? ;)*

This was the thing about texting, especially with someone you didn't know anymore. At one time, Parker had been a part of her. She knew every nuance of every word he spoke. But that was before texting, and, she reminded herself, they were practically strangers now. For a brief moment, she considered replying with something like, *I'm going commando* or *Just whipped cream*, but she settled for *Wouldn't you like to know?*

A radio reporter in the front row was saying something about how the financial records were suddenly unavailable, and Earl Little was tapping his fingers on the podium. The microphone picked up the sound. He said, "I realize they're public information, but as you know, seeing as we're a police department, our staff members have duties other than making copies for the news media. Duties like preventing crime. Stopping aggressive drivers in school zones."

Hudson leaned close to Jasmine again and caught a glimpse of her phone screen before she could darken it.

"What are you doing?" he hissed. "We're in the middle of a press conference. You're sexting in the middle of a press conference."

Jasmine realized was inhaling Hudson's clean, pine tree scent and liking it, and she bit down on her bottom lip to stop those visions from materializing again. She shrugged as if sexting during press conferences was a totally normal activity. Hudson rolled his eyes, shook his head and sat up straight again. Then he lifted his camera with sharp, jerky movements, and pointed it at Earl Little. Properly chastised, Jasmine uncapped the pen she'd stuck through the wire spiral of her notebook and began taking notes.

Her phone vibrated again. She ignored it.

"Unbelievable," Hudson said.

Earl Little was saying, "I'm not taking any more questions."

John Herald, a newspaper reporter Jasmine knew from The Breeze, said, "I heard from a source that you and your cronies recently attended a conference in Long Beach."

Earl Little cleared his throat. "They are my colleagues, and yes, we did attend a conference in Long Beach," he said. He nodded, which made Jasmine think he was lying.

"I looked up law enforcement related conferences in Long Beach, and there haven't been any in the past several months," John Herald said.

Earl nodded again, as if he'd been expecting this turn of events. "That's because we didn't go to a law enforcement conference."

Jasmine's phone buzzed.

"Would you mind sharing what kind of conference it was?" John Herald said.

"Of course not," Earl said. "It was a marketing conference."

Jasmine wondered why a police department would send its people to a *marketing* conference. Was that a thing? It couldn't be. Although it would make sense to send a public information officer to a marketing conference, she thought. Wouldn't it? Or would it? Liza was a veteran reporter, and she had a good sense for whether something was on the up and up. On her notepad, Jasmine wrote: *Ask Liza about police marketing.*

Her phone vibrated yet again. She looked at it. Parker: *Aren't you coy? Send me a picture of yourself.*

Hudson elbowed her, and her fingers flew over her phone's keyboard: *I don't do selfies.*

Parker's reply came in immediately: *Ask someone to take a picture of you.*

She almost handed her phone to Hudson, but came to her senses before creating that catastrophe and stuck it in her bra. Then she realized that a bright blue phone case sticking out of her bra would undoubtedly attract attention. She wasn't sure whether she liked or hated the idea of Hudson's attention on her cleavage, so she pulled the phone out and put it back in her purse.

Earl Little was walking out of the room to a cacophony of shouted questions and clicking cameras. The press conference was over, and all Jasmine had written on her notepad was: *Ask Liza about police marketing.*

She'd doodled a unicorn, too, but somehow she didn't think that would be much help when she sat down at her computer. She stood up and walked quickly out of the conference room, planning to high-tail it to her car before Hudson caught up with her.

Unfortunately, that didn't work out quite as she'd hoped.

Outside, Hudson cornered Jasmine in the parking lot. She'd already opened the door to her car, and he stepped in close, trapping her there. She couldn't move enough to extricate herself or sit down, so she took a deep breath and waited, without exhaling. She didn't know what she was waiting for, but her errant imagination dished up an image of his lips on hers. She knew that was completely inappropriate, but she felt a little thrill anyway.

The thrill dissipated like cotton candy in water when she saw that Hudson's eyes were flashing with anger. She flinched.

"What the hell was that?" he said.

"What do you mean?" she said, even though she had a pretty good idea of what he meant.

"I mean, what the hell were you doing in there? Because you certainly weren't reporting."

Jasmine shrugged before she realized the movement may come off as insolent. "I was just a little distracted," she said.

"Yeah, no shit," Hudson said. "I can't believe they're letting you cover this."

Immediately, Jasmine felt defensive. "What do you mean? I'm an experienced reporter."

She didn't tell him about that other experience, the one where she'd failed miserably in covering the structure fire.

"You may be experienced at writing fluff," Hudson said. "But you're crap at real news. In fact, I think I saw your byline some-where. Jasmine Carr, Fluff Correspondent."

That stung, partly because he'd only just met her and partly because Jasmine knew it was true. Before she could come up with a proper retort, something about how she'd already thought of that one, Hudson walked away. She sank down into her driver's seat and shut the door. But she didn't start her car.

She spent a moment watching Hudson put his camera in its bag and then stow the bag in his motorcycle's saddlebag before he strad-dled the bike and drove off without looking back.

I'm not crap at covering real news, she told herself as he disappeared from sight. A vision of Mikey's angry red face came to the forefront of her mind, and she blinked it away.

She drove back to the office, a new mantra on repeat in her mind: *I am a serious journalist.*

CHAPTER SIX

"So, how'd it go?" Liza, all long legs and swirling hair, stood on the patio as Jasmine approached the back door of the newsroom.

"Fine," Jasmine said. She tried to breeze past, going for casual, but Liza put up a hand to stop her.

"Well, what did he say?"

"Who?" Jasmine's train of thought had covered quite a bit of ground since the press conference, through the prickly lands of Hudson and the scorching heat of Mikey's disappointment.

Surprise made a quick trip across Liza's face, but she covered it up quickly. "Earl Little."

Ah. Of course.

"He said there can be a delay in the reporting sometimes. Like, if the department gives the officers money to go buy a bulletproof vest, it can be a few days or a few weeks until the receipts come in and it's accounted for."

"That's bull," Liza said.

"Yeah," Jasmine said. "I thought it sounded a little fishy."

"So did you ask any questions?" Liza said.

Jasmine looked down at her feet, pretending to take an interest in the tiny ants that wove their way into and out of the crack in the concrete.

"Unbelievable," Liza said. "You didn't ask anything, did you?"

Jasmine didn't bother answering. What would she say? *I wasn't sure what to ask. I should have looked at the reports you gave me. Something seemed off, but I was afraid to ask a stupid question for which he'd have a callous, humiliating comeback.*

Liza snorted and walked away, muttering about how she should have covered the press conference, herself, and how she'd wring Mikey's neck for making her let Jasmine start fresh with this piece of shit story.

Just when Jasmine was thinking things couldn't get worse, Hudson pulled up on his motorcycle. Jasmine turned to walk inside, but he called out, "Hey, wait up. I have something to show you."

His tone was neutral, maybe even bordering on friendly. Jasmine sat down on the bench next to the door.

Hudson had already pulled his camera out of the bag when he approached her and sat down. He turned the screen toward her so she could see the photos, and he began scrolling through them. The first few were impressive action shots of surfers, which he'd obviously taken on his way back from the press conference. If the situation were any different, Jasmine would have complimented his photography skills. But after the way he chastised her, she didn't want to make nice with him.

He scrolled right through the photos of Earl Little and the mustached men who flanked him earlier that day. When he stopped scrolling, Jasmine sucked in a breath.

Hudson had taken a photo of *her* at the press conference. She was sitting in the tiny conference room seat, her notebook forgotten on her lap, her eyes glued to her phone, and a strange smile on her face, like she wasn't sure whether to cry or take off her panties right there. Not that Hudson could tell that's what the smile meant, but still. As if it weren't mortifying enough, Hudson pointed at the time stamp on the first photo (ten a.m. exactly) and then clicked the scroll button to display the next one. He pointed at the time stamp. Three minutes earlier, and she was still staring at the phone, a hand over her mouth, which, again, was smiling strangely. He kept scrolling, through twelve minutes' worth of photos, until the scene finally changed to the empty conference room. He'd taken that final picture one minute before the press conference began.

"Just getting the lighting, before things started," he said, confirming her thought.

Jasmine knew she had a choice, here. She could apologize, because really, her behavior was ridiculous—and they were supposed to be partners. If she just explained, Hudson would understand, even though it was unlikely that he'd ever been kind enough to experience love lost and then reclaimed. But she had a feeling he wouldn't be receptive. So she went with another tactic.

"So, is that all?" Jasmine said, straightening her posture to convey that she was finished here.

"No, not hardly," Hudson said. Jasmine closed her eyes, and he said, "Look, Jasmine. I know this whole hard news thing isn't really your cup of coffee. I don't know why people say, 'your cup of tea.' I hate tea."

"Well, I hate coffee," Jasmine said. "And prefer tea."

"Whatever. I know this scandal isn't your deal. Okay? But it's mine. I'm going to be completely honest. This whole small-town thing isn't my cup of coffee. I have almost no interest in being here except to use it as a stepping stone for something bigger. I figure if I can capture some great news, make some great images, win some awards, I can get a job anywhere. I'm moving up. But here's the thing. Because Mikey Stockman has us paired up for some stupid reason, I'm stuck with you. We're a chain right now, and we're only as strong as the weakest link. And the way you were acting today," he said, gesturing at his camera's screen, "that's you."

Jasmine opened her mouth to respond, but he kept talking. "None of the images I capture are meaningful if you're doing a mediocre job of telling the story. Okay? That's all I'm saying. If you don't give a shit about covering this story for yourself, do it for the people who read the newspaper, the people who pay Earl Little's salary. Because they're the ones paying for his trip to Long Beach. Or do it for Liza, who has worked her ass off building this beat into something respectable. You may not be letting yourself down right now, but you're letting down a whole bunch of other people. And I'm one of them."

With that, he walked inside. Jasmine remained outside, her mouth open and her face on fire. Well, she wouldn't be sleeping with Hudson Stover, that was for sure. He was an arrogant jerk with something to prove.

Instead of heading into the newsroom to write a terrible story, Jasmine remained on the patio bench and did what any woman facing career crisis would do: she called in reinforcements.

She texted Sequoia: *I need help with a story.*

Sequoia texted back: *See? It's already starting. I can't be a source for you. You should know that.*

Jasmine responded: *I would, if I was a serious reporter.*

Sequoia: *What's that supposed to mean?*

Jasmine: *Never mind. Is Earl Little as much of an ass as he seems like?*

Sequoia: *Yes. But you can't use me as a source, Jas.*

Jasmine: *I know. So where'd all that money go?*

Sequoia: *We all have our theories.*

Jasmine: *Care to share?*

Sequoia: *I can't, Jas.*

"Ugh." Jasmine squeezed her hand into a fist and pounded it on the bench. Which hurt more than she expected. Her eyes began to tear up. Her throat constricted. She couldn't do this. The resolve she'd felt just that morning was evaporating quickly. The parking lot blurred. She stood up.

Her phone dinged with another text. Hopeful that it was her sister, having changed her mind and become willing to give her the scoop, Jasmine wiped a tear from under her left eye, took a deep breath and unlocked her phone. No, it wasn't Sequoia. It was Parker again.

Even though she knew texting with him had cost her whatever story would have resulted from the press conference, even though she knew she should go inside and try to cobble something together, even though she knew Mikey and Hudson and Liza were waiting to see what would appear on tomorrow's front page, she sat back down on the bench to read his text: *So, where's the selfie you were going to send me?*

Jasmine smiled.

She was wearing a nice dress today. It was a deep blue with a collar and little pink flowers and tiny buttons up the front. A selfie would be fine. But the cement block walls of the *Daily Trumpet's* building certainly would not serve as an acceptable background. Jasmine got up and walked across the parking lot to the huge honeysuckle vine that climbed up one of the lampposts. She snapped a selfie, reviewed it before she sent it to Parker.

"I'm squinting," she said aloud, and then she took another one. "That's better."

It would do, anyway. She had a tendency to take dozens of pictures until she got one that was "just right" (and Sequoia had started to call her Goldilocks whenever Holly tried to take selfies of the three of them). The phone had captured the moment the breeze lifted a strand of her hair and sent it swirling around her face. Her smile looked a little on the big side, but then it always had. For thirty, she didn't look too old. Tiny lines had formed outside the corners of her mouth, and at the corners of her eyes. Smile lines. All in all, she still had it. Parker would think she was at least decent-looking. At least. Nodding with approval, Jasmine attached the photo to the text message and hit "Send."

She decided at that moment that she wasn't going to look at her phone again until she had a rough draft of her story done.

Only, she had no idea what to write for a rough draft.

"Shit."

It was time to finally read through Liza's reports. But first, she checked her phone. The photo was still sending.

"Nothing to see here, folks," she said, and she walked into the newsroom.

CHAPTER SEVEN

WHEN JASMINE'S PHONE SIGNALED A TEXT MESSAGE MOMENTS LATER, before she'd even typed in her byline, Jasmine Carr, Fluff Correspondent, couldn't resist looking at it. When she saw the text was from Parker, her stomach began to flutter.

Wow, Jasmine. You're as gorgeous as ever.

In Jasmine's research for an online dating site, she'd read that men were three times less likely than women to take selfies. Of course, the online dating thing never came to fruition. Jasmine was too shy to list any personal attributes in an online environment and instead dated men she met in person at the gym or the grocery store. Petey from the free weights section had turned out to be a pretty decent guy, but the romance fizzled out after they'd gone on a few dates and she discovered a huge jar of marijuana in his kitchen cupboard. That would never do.

Jasmine shook her head. What did Parker look like now, and would it be weird to ask him to send her a photo of himself?

For now, she just responded, *Thanks.*

That done, she faced her computer again. She didn't want to think about how badly writing the Earl Little story was going to go. She swore she could feel Hudson staring at her back. Liza, too. She typed in her byline and the dateline, and tried to come up with a headline.

Earl Little Says Missing Money Is Not Actually Missing

With a groan, Jasmine deleted the headline and tried again.

Seabreeze Police Department's Missing Money Will Be Accounted For

Again, she held down the backspace button. Passive voice.

The Money's in the Mail, Promises Seabreeze Police Department

She deleted that headline, too, and decided to skip ahead to the story. It would come to her. Or it wouldn't, and Mikey could write the headline.

SEABREEZE, CALIFORNIA — Officials from the Seabreeze Police Department said Wednesday that the "missing money" is not actually missing.

"Wow, Jasmine," she said. "That's pretty damned good. You're finally a serious journalist."

She put her forehead down on her desk and stayed there, completely aware that she was having a pity party, but not ashamed of it. That is, until Mikey Stockman emerged from his office lair and came to stand next to her.

"How'd the press conference go?"

He must have read what she'd typed into her document, because he said, "Jesus, Jasmine. Is that your idea of a good lead paragraph?"

"It's just a first draft," she said, not bothering to sit up. "I've still got to polish it."

"Well," Mikey said, "polish it early so I can give it heavy repairs before deadline."

He walked away, and out of reflex, she turned her head just slightly so she could watch him. As he passed Liza's desk, he jerked a thumb towards Jasmine's.

Jasmine closed her eyes, and when she opened them again, Liza was standing there, one fist on her hip and her eyes on the computer screen.

"Today's my last day here, Jasmine," Liza said. "And that doesn't give me much time to fix this. What did Earl Little actually *say* at the press conference?"

Finally, Jasmine sat up. She covered her face with her hands. "I don't know."

"Uncover your face. You're mumbling. I thought I heard you say, 'I don't know.'"

Jasmine let her hands fall into her lap. "I did," she said. "I don't know."

Liza broke out of her usual calm demeanor and stomped one foot. Before she could come up with anything horrible to say, though, the police scanner came alive, blasting hot tones through the newsroom. Out of habit, Jasmine opened her desk drawer and reached for her headphones, but Liza used a knee to shut the drawer. Jasmine yelped and withdrew her hand and Liza pointed at her own ear.

"Listen," she said in a growly voice.

"You're treating me like a preschooler," Jasmine said.

Liza's eyes widened and she shrugged a shoulder. Jasmine, properly censured, broke eye contact and looked at her fingernails.

"All units in the southern command area, we have a nine sixty-three at Highway One and Artichoke Road. That's a nine sixty-three at Highway One and Artichoke Road. All units in the southern command area, please respond."

In the brief span of silence that followed as all the reporters paused to listen, Jasmine avoided the urge to ask what a nine sixty-three was, because really, she should know. She should have learned by osmosis or something. But for the past several years, she'd sat in this newsroom almost oblivious to the action going on around her. She'd have to figure it out when she got to Highway One and Artichoke. Hudson was already packing his gear, moving with a sense of urgency that gave Jasmine anxiety. She took a deep breath and picked up her notepad. "I'll just head out, too," she said.

Liza nodded. "Why don't you do that. Want me to work on this missing money story while you go to the accident? I could just make a few calls."

So it's an accident. I wonder why Hudson's in such a hurry.

"Sure," Jasmine said as Hudson dashed out the door. "That would be great. Since I'm going to have to work on this story about the nine sixty-three. Who knows how long I'll be out there?"

Liza rolled her eyes.

Jasmine later wished she'd put her pride aside and asked Liza what, exactly, a nine sixty-three was. The knowledge would have mentally prepared her. But she was so determined to come across as a serious journalist that she decided to find out on her own.

During the fifteen-minute drive from the *Daily Trumpet's* office to the intersection of Highway One and Artichoke Road, Jasmine planned out the questions she'd ask. Fortunately, because Liza's desk was just a couple of feet away from her own, she'd learned *something* from osmosis. She'd heard Liza fire away a standard set of questions whenever she called a public information officer about an accident: What caused the accident? Was anyone injured? Were any of the drivers drunk?

Jasmine pulled up next to Hudson at a stoplight, and he revved the engine of his motorcycle. As soon as the light turned green, he looked both ways and sped off. For the briefest of moments, Jasmine considered speeding, too. She decided against it. It wouldn't do to get a speeding ticket on the way to the scene of a car accident. Still, she found herself exceeding the speed limit by eleven miles per hour—two miles per hour over her typical allowance. Her hands sweated on the steering wheel and her eyes checked the rearview mirror for cops.

Jasmine's phone chirped. She picked it up and unlocked her screen, then had to slam on the brakes to avoid rear-ending a truck at the next stoplight. It was from Parker again: *So what have you been up to?*

"Isn't this the purpose of meeting up next week?" Jasmine said aloud. "I can't answer this right now. Don't you know I'm a serious reporter?"

She tapped the voice-to-text button on her phone and responded, "I'm working. I'll text later."

He wrote back within a fraction of a second: *All work and no play…*

"Haha," Jasmine said into her phone.

He wrote back again: *When do you get off?*

"Seriously," Jasmine said. "Is he that person who has to have the last word on every text? This conversation is over."

When she looked down at her phone, she realized it had recorded that last couple of sentences, and hurried to delete them. Someone behind her honked. She tossed the phone onto the passenger seat, realized she must be really out of sorts not to position it carefully in her cupholder, and pressed down hard on the accelerator.

Hudson Stover, photojournalist, was already on scene, crouching low to the ground, capturing images of twisted steel and broken glass. She hoped he wasn't preserving the image of all that blood. Jasmine Carr, serious journalist, gathered her wits while simultaneously wishing she hadn't been embarrassed to ask Liza what a nine sixty-three was.

The setting was eerily quiet. The click of Hudson's camera and the low murmur of evidence technicians setting up some kind of fancy equipment were the only sounds Jasmine heard as she stood behind the tidy boundary of cones. Like bright orange sentries, they held a comforting line between her and the carnage.

Suddenly, a cop's face appeared in her line of vision. "This is a police scene, ma'am. I'll need to ask you to leave."

Her automatic reaction was to take a step back, but then Hudson was there, grabbing her upper arm. "She's with me," he said.

The cop nodded, a brief movement, and walked away. Hudson yanked Jasmine across that boundary and into the chaos.

She didn't have time to ponder the little thrill she felt at Hudson's declaration, except to tell herself it was purely professional. Hudson was hissing, "Where's your media badge? Of course they're not going to let you in. What were you thinking?" Rather than waiting for her to answer, he began rattling off details faster than she could get her mind working. She shook her head quickly, and pulled the cap off her pen to start writing.

"So it's two fatalities, an old man and a kid, a ten-year-old girl. They're not releasing names, yet. The mom of the kid crossed the center line and hit the old man's car head-on."

"Fatalities?" Jasmine's pen froze on the pad.

"Yeah," Hudson said. "Didn't you hear it on the scanner?"

Jasmine shook her head again. "No. I mean, yes. I heard it, but I didn't realize that's what it was. A ten-year-old girl? How sad."

"Yeah, it sucks," Hudson said. "They airlifted the mom to a San Francisco hospital. Not sure she'll make it."

"Do they know why she crossed the center line?" Jasmine asked.

"Ask a cop, Jasmine. That's your job. Mine's to take pictures, but I've already learned more than you have in the five minutes you've been here."

Jasmine didn't want to ask any questions. She didn't want to know. It was too horrible. How was she supposed to do this job? She picked her way carefully around the edges of the scene, unsure of how to describe it in a story. The mom and her daughter had been riding in a dark-colored SUV, northbound on the Highway. The old man's gold sedan was southbound. The two cars now rested in the southbound lane, their front ends completely crushed. Broken glass sparkled in the afternoon sun, the shards throwing out rainbows like prisms. The little girl's head had hit the passenger side windshield, leaving a spiderweb pattern, laced with blood. Firefighters had cut off the driver's side door to get the mom out. A dark pool of blood, still fresh, spread below the driver's side of the old man's car where Hudson said the paramedics had worked on him before he died.

"This your first accident scene?" A grizzled patrol cop had come up next to Jasmine, and he hooked his thumbs in his pants pockets as he spoke.

"Yeah," she said, struggling to make her voice audible.

"You get used to it," he said. "I'm Tony Walker, by the way."

They shook hands. "And you are?"

"Oh. Sorry, I'm Jasmine. Jasmine Carr. The *Daily Trumpet*."

"Where's Liza? I guess her daughter finally had that baby, huh?"

"Not quite," Jasmine said, "but Liza's leaving tomorrow so you get me today."

"Want me to show you around?" Tony said.

"Not really," she said. "But I guess you should."

Tony Walker took Jasmine's elbow and, as if he'd given tours a million times before, led her through the scene. "So the RP—"

She cut him off. "The RP?"

He cleared his throat. "Sorry, that's reporting person. Anyway, she called in the accident at eleven twenty-six. Said she'd seen the SUV cross the center line and hit the sedan. We believe the first victim, a ten-year-old girl, died instantly, and the old man suffered severe lacerations and went into cardiac arrest. Paramedics got his heart started again, but he died before they got him to the hospital."

"Can you give me their names?" Jasmine said.

"Not yet. We have to notify next of kin."

As Tony steered her around the other side of the cars, she wondered who the old man's next of kin was. Who would answer the door when the police knocked? Would it be his wife? Or one of his children? Did he have grandkids? And what about the little girl? How would her mother feel? What about the kids in her class at school? Jasmine felt the beginning of tears, and took a deep breath.

"Hey. Are you still with me?" Tony stopped and turned Jasmine to face him.

Hudson, who had followed them on the little tour, taking notes between shots, froze. Jasmine could tell he was listening but pretending not to.

"I'm listening," Jasmine said. "I was just thinking, that's all."

"You know, it might help you understand if you were able to see how our accident reconstruction equipment works. Would you like to come back to the office when they're all done here, check it out?"

"It's not that I don't understand," Jasmine said, forcing herself not to stammer. She was uncomfortably aware of Hudson's presence. She could feel him breathing next to her. She went on, "It's just—I just wonder about the victims, you know? Who they were. The old guy, what did he do for a job when he was younger? Does he have a dog or a cat at home? And the little girl. What kind of cereal did she eat? What TV shows did she watch? What was her favorite color? Do their relatives, their friends, want to see this story in the paper? Do they want to see the pictures? It seems so, I don't know, so—callous."

Tony squeezed Jasmine's arm and took a deep breath. "I hate to say this, kid, but it gets easier. People die. Yes, it's sad. It sucks. But it happens. And then it happens again. And it doesn't seem fair. You're going to hear about—and maybe even write about—that little girl's favorite foods, her quirks, the stuffed animal she slept with. And it's going to be hard."

Jasmine's throat closed and her eyes burned. Tony kept talking: "But that's exactly why you do what you do, Jasmine. To honor her life. It's my job to figure out what happened, to make sure her death doesn't go unnoticed, to hope any information we can provide will prevent another little girl from dying. That's all we can do."

"You're right," Jasmine said, but his words didn't make her feel any better. She blinked a few times to stop the tears from forming. "I just don't want to have a front row seat, I guess."

Tony dropped his arm to his side. "I hear you, sweetheart. But you've got one."

As soon as she was encased in the safety of her own car, Jasmine let herself cry. The whole way back to the *Daily Trumpet*, she wailed like she had as a kid. Why did a little girl have to die? She'd probably had so much potential. If only she'd grown up, she might have become a loving teacher or developed the cure for cancer or saved someone else's life. And her mother. If the mother lived, she'd never escape the guilt. The accident had been her fault, by all accounts. And her daughter was dead. It seemed so unfair. Jasmine growled when her phone dinged with yet another text.

Parker. Again.

He'd sent a photo, and her phone was still downloading it. The irritation that took root—didn't Parker have something worthwhile do do?—dissolved immediately when the photo finished loading.

"Oh, my," Jasmine said. From what she could tell in that one peek, he looked like a manly, totally edible version of his teenage self. Light stubble covered his jawbone and his eyes twinkled with mischief. "Oh, my," she said again.

Murphy's Law kicked in, and she didn't hit a single red light between the scene of the fatal car accident and her office, which meant she didn't have a chance to drink in the photo like she would have liked to. So when she finally pulled into the *Daily Trumpet's* parking lot, she stared at her phone's screen for way longer than necessary.

A tiny voice originating somewhere behind her left ear piped up, saying that just because Parker was still mouthwatering didn't mean he was the same great guy he'd always been. Still. His hair curled around his ears just as it had thirteen years ago. His lips quirked to the right, in the same way she'd memorized when they were still in high school. He was wearing a gray hoodie. Jasmine wondered if he wore that hoodie all the time. It really made his eyes stand out. They were the color of honey.

Maybe I should call him. Get the talking over with now so we can get straight to the action when I see him in person.

Jasmine jumped when someone knocked on her window. Hudson.

She dropped her phone and shut off the ignition, and then opened her door and stepped out of the car as if she'd just arrived in the parking lot. "What's up?" she said.

"What's up with you?"

"What do you mean?"

"I mean," Hudson said, "why are you just sitting here? You have two major stories to write on deadline."

"You're right," Jasmine said. "Just going over my notes from earlier."

"You were looking at your best friend. I mean, your phone. Again. Your notepad is still on the passenger side floorboard."

"I dropped it," Jasmine lied.

"Whatever. Just remember what I said, okay?"

"About what?"

"About taking this seriously," Hudson said. "I heard you talking to Tony Walker at the scene of that accident. I admit, I didn't realize you felt that way. I thought you were just self-centered."

Jasmine opened her mouth to respond, to defend herself, to explain that she was socially awkward and completely out of her comfort zone, but he just flashed her a smile that bordered on acrimonious, and continued. "I totally get what you were saying about the victims' relatives seeing the story and photos in the paper. But at the same time, it's our job to let people know what happened. Maybe your story or my photo will stop one person from texting and driving. Maybe a guy reads it and realizes how quickly life can end, and he finally takes that trip he's dreamed about for a lifetime. Or maybe a woman reads it and decides to stop waiting for her boyfriend to propose, so she proposes to him. I guess what I mean is that, through the story and photos, the deaths of the little girl and the old man can play a role in making the world better. So instead of feeling sorry for yourself, suck it up and write the story."

He stalked off.

Jasmine watched him go. She shook her head. Where had *that* come from? Of course she planned to write the story. In fact, after the dose of perspective she'd received from Tony (and, she hated to admit it, Hudson), she planned to write a damn good story.

First though, she planned to think more about meeting Parker Abbott again. She dug her phone out from under her seat and examined his photo. Parker Abbott, all grown up. She looked at the date on her watch. Six more days… which suddenly felt like an eternity. She got out of the car, still looking at Parker's face, and walked across the parking lot.

It was only when she got to the door that she realized Hudson was waiting for her. She jumped when she saw him there, camera out, ready to upload his photos. Of course, she fumbled her phone and dropped it, and Hudson sighed as he entered his employee code, but still, he held the door for her. As she walked past him, she smelled his aftershave—pine trees. He nodded curtly. She nodded back and wondered if her back end looked okay. Then she wondered why she wondered that.

Then she realized she'd left her notebook on her passenger seat. She did an about face, and Hudson said, "Notebook?"

When she didn't answer, he grunted.

Back at her desk, Jasmine struggled with a good lead paragraph, for the second time that day. Everything sounded stupid. Finally, she settled for boilerplate: *Two people died and one person suffered serious injuries in a head-on collision at Highway One and Artichoke Road Wednesday morning.*

It would do. She squared her shoulders and went on: *Police are withholding identification of the victims pending notification of next of kin.*

So far, so good. Then her phone vibrated and her mind

wandered. Was it Parker? She'd never responded to his photo text. She should really do that, or else he might think she thought he was ugly now. Which certainly was not the case. What words would she use to describe how he looked now?

She picked up her phone. Mouthwatering. Yummy. Super duper sexy? His lips looked exactly the same. Full and skilled. And his eyes. She could just stare into them for hours. *How sappy.*

Jasmine's computer signaled that she had an email, and the sound—a cricket chirp—jerked her back into reality. She turned off her phone and stuffed it into her purse, which she stowed under her desk.

The new email was from Hudson, and it included a photo attachment. *Great. Like I want to see the car accident again.*

Still, she opened it. It wasn't a photo of the car accident scene. Not even close. Anger hit her with the force of a wave against a cliff, and she pushed away from her desk and stormed across the empty newsroom to Hudson's.

"Who do you think you are, the paparazzi?" Jasmine said.

Hudson turned slowly towards her, his demeanor so calm she wanted to reach for his throat. Which, she reminded herself, was quite unlike her.

"It's my job to use powerful images to illustrate what's happening. What's happening here is that you're obsessing over some girly-man with mascara and shaggy hair, instead of doing your actual job, which is to at least pretend like you give a shit about the news." His voice was still calm, and her own anger bubbled to the surface, especially when he said, "You work for a newspaper. Remember?"

Jasmine glanced over her shoulder at her computer screen and the image she'd just found in her email: a collage of images of Jasmine, looking at her phone. At the press conference. In her car. At her desk. On the patio outside the newsroom. In some of them she wore a flirtatious smile. In others, her cheeks burned pink with the heat of imagined passion. In all of them, her eyes were absolutely glued to the screen of her phone. Like it was cool, clear water in the desert. Or a mug of hot chocolate in the snow. Or something. She looked obsessed. Desperate.

"I remember," she said. "But aren't you being hypocritical? You say I should focus on my work, but you're taking photos of me when you should be taking photos of the news!"

"Oh, I have photos of the news," Hudson said. "Would you like to see?"

"No. I absolutely would not," Jasmine said. "I'd imagine I'll see them when they come out in the newspaper. Alongside the stories I've been writing."

Not that she ever looked at the newspaper, she reminded herself.

"You mean, the stories you've been failing miserably at writing? How many inches do you have on the car accident story? Not even one, right? Because it stirs up your feelings?"

"Why don't you just focus on your job, and I'll focus on mine?" Jasmine said. "You're the photographer, and I'm the reporter. So let's just stick to our roles."

"Actually, let's not. Because the quality of your work is related to people's perception of mine. With your story alongside my photos, it's highly unlikely that I'll ever move on out of this banal little town. If you want me out of your hair, then you're going to have to step up your game."

"Fine," Jasmine said, giving a curt nod of her head.

Hudson smiled, then, and Jasmine's heart beat faster. She told herself it was a result of the adrenaline their argument had caused.

"Great," he said. "Thanks so much."

He spun his chair around, then, and she was left staring at the back of his head. He'd made fun of Parker's hair, and this was the first time she'd taken notice of his. It was cut short in the back, and curly on top. She quickly quashed the image of running her fingers through it and instead spun herself around and went back to her desk, where she deleted the email from Hudson and finished up the car accident story.

SAFE FROM SPYING eyes on her living room couch that evening, Jasmine said to Ruby, "I hate to admit it, but Hudson's right. I've been so caught up in the Parker scenario that I haven't been focusing on my work. I'm still kind of pissed that he made that little photo collage, but he does have a point."

Ruby cocked her head to one side, and then put her paws on Jasmine's chest and licked her chin.

"I know. My excitement is totally understandable. But I need to focus. Hudson might be right, but he's still an ass."

The next morning, Jasmine chose her outfit carefully.

"Professionalism begins with your wardrobe," Sequoia would say. Holly would say, "It's all in how you feel on the inside. You've got to *be* professional."

While chanting, "I *am* a professional," she pulled on black slacks and a white collared shirt. She added pearl earrings and a pearl necklace, and a pair of black high heels she rarely wore because one of her sisters, Sequoia, probably, told her they looked like "fuck-me" shoes.

Checking her work in the mirror, Jasmine felt satisfied. The heels were definitely "have-sex-with-me" shoes (Jasmine renamed them because she'd always hated the f-word), but she looked pretty good. Maybe she didn't quite believe she *was* professional, but she looked it. This was a good first step.

During her short commute, she thought about how a professional reporter would act. How did Liza carry herself? Shoulders thrown back, chin slightly lifted, she exuded confidence. And what about the men? Perry Marks always seemed so relaxed, even when he rushed into the newsroom after a City Council meeting to write a big story on deadline. When he talked to sources, on the phone or in person, he was constantly smiling, laughing as if he were at a cocktail party eating canapés and drinking champagne rather than covering an important news event.

Jasmine wished she could be as comfortable in her skin as Liza and Perry were in theirs. She wished she didn't shrivel like a dead flower in the winter whenever anyone turned the spotlight of their gaze on her. The problem: she didn't know how to change.

The outfit was a good first step.

She thought of something she'd seen on a reality show once. On the show, a panel of judges critiqued singing performances, and one of the performers had been shy, despite the fact that he had a very good voice. The judge told him, "When you're out there on stage, just pretend to be a confident person. The more you pretend, the more you'll feel like you really are confident."

That made sense. So maybe pretending to be confident could be a good second step, here. When Jasmine and her sisters were younger, they'd often strut around the house with books on their heads, perfecting their trips down an imaginary runway. Could muscle memory aid her in feigning confidence? Probably.

Jasmine took a deep breath as she parked and shut off her car. She got out and pulled herself to her tallest possible height. She lifted her chin just slightly, like Liza. She pushed her shoulders back and pretended she had a book on her head. What was the one they always used as kids? The kids' version of "Encyclopedia Britannica." It was maroon. *Relax. Just relax.* She approached the back door and took one more deep breath before reaching for the door handle. Then she realized she'd left her purse in the car.

"Dammit," she said. She stalked back to the car, her special posture forgotten for the moment.

She started over.

And of course, as she reached for the door handle the second time, Hudson emerged.

"Dammit," she said again.

"I'm happy to see you, too," he said. "What's going on?"

"What do you mean? I'm just getting to work."

"You look nice," he said.

"Different from how I normally look?" she said. "Why did it make you ask what's going on?"

He looked baffled, and for once, unsure of what to say.

Suddenly mortified, Jasmine said, "Take a picture. It lasts longer. And that's what you do, anyway." Then, just as she cringed at her own middle school retort (maybe practicing model struts from her middle school years wasn't a good idea, after all), Hudson smiled.

"Actually, I wanted to talk to you about that. Do you have a minute?"

Jasmine huffed out an exaggerated sigh, as if she were too busy to give him even a minute of her time. "I suppose so."

He followed her over to the bench on the patio and sat down next to her. His thigh touched hers, and she scooted away, not because she didn't like her body's reaction to the contact, but because she did. *Even though he's a jerk.*

Of course, he noticed, and made a point of looking down at the gap between them.

"So?" she said.

"So," he said. "I wanted to apologize."

Shocked, Jasmine froze, waiting for him to speak again.

"I wanted to say that I'm sorry for taking all those photos of you. And making a collage. And pointing out your less-than-professional behavior. It's not really my business, even though it kind of is."

"In other words, you want to issue an apology that is not really an apology, even though it kind of is."

Hudson laughed. "Precisely. No, really. I am sorry. That was totally rude of me. I still think you were acting unprofessional, but I'm sorry about all the photos. Okay?"

"Okay," Jasmine said.

Hudson put out a hand to shake Jasmine's, and she took it.

CHAPTER EIGHT

"So, Parker's coming tomorrow, right?" Sequoia stood in Jasmine's kitchen, cutting vegetables into precise cubes for a salad.

"Yeah," Jasmine said. Her stomach went all fluttery at the mention of his arrival. To quell it, she made herself busy getting out plates, silverware and wine glasses, and began setting the table. "He said he's not sure when he'll get into town. So basically, I'll be looking out the office window all day, waiting for him to show up."

"Are you nervous?" Sequoia said. "Excited? Horny?"

"All of the above," Jasmine said. "I'm just not sure if it'll be the same as it was back then."

"Do you want it to be?"

Jasmine pursed her lips as she opened the silverware drawer, looking for forks. "I'm not sure. I mean, we were so young. I want the feelings to be the same, I think. You know, those breathless, can't-live-without-you feelings?"

Sequoia used the knife to scrape the vegetables into the salad bowl. "I know what you mean, but I guess I wonder if those feelings were intensified back then, especially at the end, because you knew he was leaving."

"True." Jasmine realized she'd already put forks on the table.

She'd be so relieved when the initial Parker meeting was over. The anticipation was making her crazy.

The doorbell rang, and Ruby, startled from her spot under the dining table, went berserk, barking and running laps. Holly came through the door at a million miles per hour, and Sequoia sighed in such a dramatic fashion Jasmine had to laugh.

"I hate that dog," Sequoia said.

"I know," Jasmine said. "You've said so innumerable times."

"Can't you shut it up?" Sequoia said.

"It's a her, and no," Jasmine said, and although she normally would have said something about how it was Ruby's job to guard the house, she stopped short when she saw Holly's hair.

"Your hair!" she said.

"Oh, my God," Sequoia said. "It's white. It's like snow or something."

"Do you like it?" Holly said.

"What is this, the fourth hair color in as many months?" Sequoia said. Jasmine elbowed her.

Instead of answering, Holly crouched down just inside the door, and Ruby put her paws on Holly's shoulders as she licked her face in greeting. When Holly straightened up, Ruby ran back to her spot and flopped down, eyes alert.

"So, Jasmine," Holly said, drawing out her sister's name, "tomorrow's the big day, right? The famous and mysterious Parker Abbott hits Seabreeze for the first time in more than a decade. What are you wearing? Did you buy new lingerie?"

Sequoia shook her head and Jasmine giggled. "I have no idea what I'm wearing, and—"

A sharp inhale from Holly stopped Jasmine short. "Surely you've thought about what you'll be wearing when you see the love of your life after more than a decade."

"Okay. I'll admit that I have run through a few outfits in my mind, but I remain undecided."

"Salad's ready," Sequoia said. "Come and get it before your stupid she-dog eats it."

"My little vegetarian niece," Holly said.

Jasmine pulled the chicken out of the oven, and Holly opened the wine she'd brought. They sat down at the table, and Ruby inched her way over to Holly's side.

"Here to beg for carrots?" Holly said.

"Don't feed her from the table," Sequoia said. "She'll turn out like that dog we had as kids. That one you always used to sneak spaghetti to. Remember him? He died of obesity and I'm pretty sure it was your fault."

"Hulk," Jasmine said. She slid a chicken breast onto each of her sisters' plates and then onto her own before sitting down. "He died of cancer, which was not related to obesity, and was not Holly's fault."

Holly reached down to scratch Ruby behind the ears. "True," she said. "And I give Ruby vegetables only, so I think we're safe."

"Great. Long live Ruby," Sequoia said. She scooped salad onto her plate and passed the bowl to Jasmine. "You get it last, Holly, since you're touching that mangy beast under the table."

"How's it going with your new boss?" Jasmine asked.

Sequoia groaned. "It's horrible. Totally hate the woman. In fact, just the thought of her makes me want to puke, so let's change the subject."

"I still want to know what you're wearing tomorrow," Holly said to Jasmine.

"You can help me decide after dinner," Jasmine said. "Did you get the info on the personal trainer stuff? Are you going to start your certification?"

"This makes me nauseous," Holly said. "It feels like settling down. But yes. I'm going to do it. I got all the information, and I need to take some classes. It'll take a little time, but that's okay. It should be fun. So, that's it."

"What's up with that guy you were seeing?" Sequoia said through a mouthful of salad. "Are you guys still hitting it? Or did you break up? Wait. I know. You got a different boyfriend. Thus, the different hair color. Good. I didn't really like the leopard print."

"Really? I couldn't tell," Jasmine muttered.

"Oh my gosh, I can't believe you said hitting it," Holly said.

"We're in our thirties now. And yes. We're still seeing each other. Kind of."

"What's his name again?" Jasmine said. "Jimmy?"

Holly waved a hand. "It's Jimmy. But it's not serious."

"Never is," Sequoia said. "Jimmy's a little kid's name anyway."

Jasmine looked at Holly, whose face turned a shade of red as brilliant as her hair as she stared down at her plate. Just when Jasmine would have stepped in to mitigate the situation, Holly looked up at Sequoia and said, "Well, what's worse, Sequoia? Having a handful of less-than-serious boyfriends, or living alone, perpetually, because you're afraid of commitment?"

"Touché," Sequoia said, stabbing a piece of baby kale with her fork. One eyebrow raised and her lips quirked into a half-smile, she said, "I apologize."

"Well," that was unexpected," Holly said to Jasmine. "She never apologizes."

"I'm right here," Sequoia said.

"Oh, I'm sorry," Holly said. "Due to your unprecedented apology, I thought it was someone else sitting at your spot. And how come you never pick on Jasmine about her dating life?"

"Because she never tells us anything about it," Sequoia said.

"That's because there's nothing to tell," Jasmine said.

Which was kind of an understatement. She'd dated guys, here and there, but they were mostly subpar; that is, if Parker was the standard against which they were measured. Now, as an adult, she was embarrassed to admit that none of them did quite stack up. To her high school boyfriend. So she deftly avoided the topic whenever it arose. Like right now. Eager to change the subject, even as an image of Hudson flashed through her mind, she said, "Now hurry up and finish eating. We have an outfit to plan."

AT HOLLY'S INSISTENCE, Jasmine went with dark skinny jeans and a green sweater with a darker green scarf, and little black boots with tiny heels. Sequoia had pushed for khaki pants and a button-up blouse with cowboy boots, but Holly insisted that getup might look kind of manly. ("And cowboy boots with khaki pants? No wonder you can't get a date.") Anyway, she said, the tiny-heeled boots paired with the skinny jeans would show off Jasmine's calf muscles and make her look slimmer. "And slightly sluttier," Sequoia said, to which Holly responded with a sly wink. "Plus, that scarf really brings out your eyes," Holly said.

"Let's just hope I don't get stuck having to walk in the grass," Jasmine said.

Sequoia, put out by the fact that Jasmine had taken Holly's suggestion and not hers, said, "Put the cowboy boots in your trunk. They go with your sweater, and at least you won't ruin your kitty boots if you do get stuck in the mud. Or wherever."

Jasmine left the house Monday morning with her cowboy boots in one hand and a spring in her step. The spring in her step might have come from the lacy lingerie Holly had dug out of the back of Jasmine's drawer (it pinched a little), but she wasn't telling.

Yes, she also spent a little extra time on her hair, curling the ends and pinning her bangs back. And she put on extra makeup. This amount of effort when it came to her dating life was unusual. After Parker's family left for Spain, Jasmine swore off serious relationships. "I'm just looking for fun," she said to guys she met, and then after some time she realized she had to add the caveat, "Not that kind of fun."

She liked men, she thought, but she never let things get too serious … never let her expectations get too high. Because when your expectations are high, they have farther to fall.

When she walked into the newsroom, Hudson glanced at her, and then did a double take, raking her from face to sexy boots in a once-over so obvious Jasmine felt herself tingling. Then she felt herself heating up from the visions her mind created—visions of his hands giving her a once-over. When Hudson realized she'd caught him ogling her, his face turned bright red. Surprised and more than a little charmed, she smiled, but felt her face fall when he said, "A little heavy on the mascara, Jas."

She wasn't sure what to make of him calling her Jas. Her inner voice, though, was quick to remark, *How awkward.*

"Jasmine Carr," Mikey boomed from his office, saving her from having to come up with a retort. "A moment of your time, please."

She changed course and was just a little taken aback when Mikey said, "You look nice, Carr."

So what if he was her boss and ten years her senior? She did look nice and didn't mind hearing someone say so.

"Nice job on that story," he said. "The one about the fatal car accident."

"That was a week ago," she said. "And Liza spoon-fed me all the information after she made some calls. But thanks."

"Well, your second installment, the one that ran yesterday, where you wrote about the identification of the old man and the little girl, just hit the wire," he said, handing her a printout of the story he'd gotten off the national news wire. "Your first time, right?"

Jasmine smiled. It was her first time having a story picked up by the national news service. This meant newspapers all over the country would have access to it. They might even print it. None of her features had ever been quite big enough for the wire. Maybe she should go and request a couple of copies of yesterday's paper.

"Apparently," Mikey said, "the old man was some big muckety muck of this big corporation out of Pennsylvania or somewhere. He was here on business. They wanted to put a warehouse in, down south, off Artichoke Road. Anyway, it's a pretty big deal. Good thing you did a decent job on the story. Your name's all over the country."

Jasmine felt a tiny stirring of pride as she looked at her name on the printout.

"Don't get a big head or anything," Mikey said. "Keep that." He nodded at the paper she held. "Frame it, maybe. Now get outta here. I got work to do."

Jasmine walked out of Mikey's office, struggling to keep the goofy smile off her face, not wanting anyone to see how pleased she was about her first-ever wire story. She sat down to check her voice messages and her email. Parker still hadn't confirmed his arrival time, and Jasmine felt an absurd need to check and recheck her appearance in the bathroom mirror.

Finally, on her umpteenth trip back from the bathroom before noon, Hudson stopped her. He was standing in hallway between the men's and the ladies,' and when she exited the ladies' he stepped forward so their bodies were almost touching. She backed up, and he moved forward again. When her back touched the wall, she emitted a tiny yelp. He placed one hand on each side of her head and smiled. His face was inches from hers and his expression was a combination of menacing and hungry, and most of all, challenging. It was almost as if he was daring her to stop him. Only, she didn't want to. Maybe he was daring her to *not* stop him.

She swallowed. Her heart started doing that thing again, like it wanted to beat right out of her chest and touch him. If only she could climb right out of her skin to get away from the feeling that she needed him to touch her.

"You look really good today," Hudson said. "You should stop worrying about it. In fact, if I hadn't just apologized for taking photos of you, I'd be taking more, right now."

He leaned even closer to her and she realized that if either of them moved, they'd be touching, from ankle to chest. This man was maddening. One moment, he thought she was ridiculous. The next, he was almost on top of her in the hallway. Next to the restrooms, for goodness sake.

Jasmine found herself maddening, too. She was preparing for the arrival of the man she'd always believed was her soul mate, her one true love, and she was getting all ... to use Mikey's word ... *twitter-pated* over a guy who didn't even like her.

But if he didn't like her, why was he acting this way?

"You're incorrigible," she said to Hudson.

He smiled, a humorless smile that lasted a split second, and then he leaned forward to whisper in her ear. "If you rearrange that scarf one more time today, so help me, I'll use it to tie you to the bed the first time I make love to you."

And that was the exact moment Parker Abbott made his re-entry into Jasmine Carr's life.

CHAPTER NINE

JASMINE HEARD THE NEWSROOM DOOR OPEN AND CLOSE, BUT AT THE moment, she was incapable of removing herself from Hudson's trap. Her entire body was magnetized, and it was pulling away from the wall, towards Hudson. She wanted to feel the pressure of his chest against hers, his hips against hers, his arms around her waist. She could feel her pulse in her lower belly and between her legs and she wondered why she'd avoided sex for so long.

Hudson pushed away from her, never breaking eye contact, when whoever had just entered cleared his throat. Jasmine peeked around one side of Hudson's body and saw Parker standing there. His face registered surprise, and then uncertainty. Jasmine adjusted her scarf. Hudson narrowed his eyes at her, and she realized what she'd done. Apparently, she had a not-very-deeply-buried subconscious desire for him to tie her up.

Shit, it's a conscious desire, isn't it?

Then Hudson turned around slowly, and before walking away, he said under his breath, "Great. It's the guy with the hair."

Jasmine had always pictured her reunion with Parker as a joyous affair. Most likely in the rain. She would run to him, and he'd open his arms and catch her. They'd kiss passionately, unaware of any bystanders. It was possible that someone would shed tears. Maybe her, maybe Parker. Maybe bystanders. Then she and Parker would both laugh, because they were so happy to see each other after so long. They'd each start to say something, and then stop, and then giggle because they were interrupting each other. Just like in high school.

But that imagined scene never followed Parker walking in on her pinned up against the wall by another man (and liking it).

Parker stood there now, just inside the newsroom door, his hands in his jeans pockets. He had over-texted all week—why hadn't he texted her to let her know he was on his way? Surely, that would have prevented this awkward version of the scene that was their reunion.

"Hi, Parker," she said. For some reason, she didn't feel quite like running up to him.

Hudson had gathered his camera and gear, and, from behind Parker, he winked at her before walking out the door.

Finally, now that Hudson was out of the room, Jasmine was able to shake herself out of her stupor and direct all of her attention at the man who'd occupied most of her romance-related thoughts over the past decade and a half.

"Hi, Jasmine," he said.

Yes, he was still heartbreakingly handsome. He'd aged perfectly. He'd been a boy when they'd last spoken, and now he was a man. He was stocky and built, and stood with his feet set wide, like he was bracing himself. A light stubble covered the planes of his face. The joy Jasmine had always anticipated wasn't evident on his face. Jasmine sighed, unsure of how to proceed.

She opened her arms and walked toward him. He wrapped his arms around her shoulders, and she could hear him inhaling the scent of her shampoo. As he did, his body relaxed. The tension ebbed away.

"It's been way too long," he said after what seemed like several minutes.

Jasmine nodded. "It has."

Now, Parker put his hands on her shoulders and took a step back so he could examine her. His eyes rested on her face, lingered on her mouth and then traveled slowly down her torso and all the way down to her boots.

"Lookin' good," he said.

She laughed. "Same to you. Come on, let's get out of here. Want to hit The Grind?"

"Don't tell me you drink coffee now, Jasmine Carr. If you do, then my whole world has turned upside down."

Jasmine hated herself for scanning for Hudson as soon as she and Parker got out to the parking lot. She breathed a sigh of relief when she didn't see him or his motorcycle.

"So that was awkward," Parker said.

Rather than walking out to his car, he started pacing the patio. Jasmine leaned against the wall, her mind going a million miles an hour trying to figure out what to say. She finally decided on honesty.

"I know," she said. "It was. I'm so sorry. That guy, Hudson? He's new. Our editor has paired us up while the regular crime reporter is out of town. We just had a little—tension this morning."

"Tension of the sexual variety," Parker said.

Jasmine shook her head, too quickly, even as her body reacted to the word, "sexual."

"No, it wasn't that. We haven't been getting along well. Hudson thinks—"

"Hudson thinks you're hot and he wants to sleep with you, Jasmine."

Was it weird that her insides went all quivery at hearing Parker's voice say her name in the same way he had when they were younger? Or were her insides already quivery, thanks to Hudson and the scarf comment?

"It's not that," Jasmine said again.

"Trust me," Parker said. "It is. And if you think it's not, you're crazy."

"Well, it's not like that for me," Jasmine said. "It's purely profes-sional." Parker shrugged, his expression saying he didn't believe her. She went on, "Now, can we forget about it and go get something to drink or something? And to answer your question, no, I don't drink coffee. Still a tea drinker through and through."

He exhaled, as if he'd been waiting to hear her say that exact thing. "Yeah. Let's get drinks. I'll drive."

She'd been on the crime beat for one short week, but half a dozen scenarios jumped into Jasmine's head. What if Parker was a serial killer and he drove her out to the forest and killed her and buried her body? Or what if he was a serial killer and he tied a huge weight to her feet and dropped her over the side of the wharf? Or what if he was a serial killer and he took her to some remote cabin and forced her to eat rats?

Or what if he's the same Parker he's always been? said a tiny, more reasonable voice.

For a moment, she wondered where Hudson was going and what he was doing. She wondered if he was thinking of her.

Parker led her to a Volkswagen bus, and she laughed out loud. "This is your ride? I thought you'd have a rental car or something."

"I had it shipped here last week from Colorado. Didn't think it'd make the drive so I had it waiting at a parking lot when I got to the airport. It's my rebellion against my dad and my regimented military upbringing. Fits right in here in Seabreeze, doesn't it? Check it out, it even has a mural on the passenger side."

Jasmine's stomach lurched when she saw the mural: against the light blue body of the van, a jasmine vine flowed from the passenger side door all the way to the tail lights.

"Oh, my gosh," she said. "Did you buy it like this?"

"Nah," he said. "I had it done. You like it?"

"That's really sweet," she said.

And although she meant it—it *was* a sweet gesture—she also felt a little strange about it. He'd painted the entire side of his car with her namesake vine, when they hadn't seen each other in more than a decade? Sequoia would say it screamed stalker. And Holly would be charmed. Hudson would probably be freaked out. Jasmine, always relying on the opinions of others in order to form her own, wasn't sure how she felt about it.

Riding through town in Parker's van, Jasmine replayed the moment of the reunion she'd anticipated for so long. Why hadn't there been any fireworks? Why hadn't they kissed with the deep passion they'd felt as kids? Why hadn't they both laughed with pure joy like she'd always imagined they would?

Maybe because I was this *close to kissing someone else when he first saw me.*

Jasmine pushed thoughts of Hudson out of her mind, but her body couldn't quite keep up. Her entire nervous system fluttered with anticipation as her mind flashed on an image of Hudson standing over her, running her scarf through his hands.

"So, Jasmine Carr, serious journalist?" Parker said. Jasmine was grateful his voice transferred her train of thought to a different track. She could see smoke rising from the Hudson Express.

"Hardly," she said. "More like, Jasmine Carr, features reporter, thrust into serious reporting against her will. What have you been up to?"

"For the past decade? A lot," Parker said. "Just living in the fast lane, I guess. You've probably heard through the grapevine that after we moved to Spain, we lived in Germany for a few years."

"I haven't heard anything through the grapevine," Jasmine said. After his letters and phone calls dropped off, she heard the silence as if it were the soundtrack to her new life. The movie would be something like, "Life Without Parker," or, "Silent and Lonely," or, "Lonely Girl Cries … a story of life after teenage love."

"I guess I went kind of radio silent," Parker said. "Anyway, after we lived in Germany, I went to college on the East Coast, got my degree in electrical engineering. I probably could have gotten a job in the field, but for now I've been traveling. When I was a kid, especially when my dad moved us away from here, and away from you, I always thought I'd want to settle down right away. But I figure, we spent so much time following someone else's plans, and this is the time in my life to make my own, to be footloose and fancy free, you know?"

Jasmine wondered—briefly—why it had taken Parker so long to seek her out if he was footloose and fancy free, but he answered the question before she got the chance to ask it.

"I've always thought a lot about you," he said. "And the truth is, the idea of calling you freaked me out. I mean, I figured you'd be tied up with a husband and two-point-three kids by now. And a dog."

Why did he have to use the words, "tied up"? Again, images of Hudson flashed into her mind, vivid and totally inappropriate.

"I have a dog," she said. "Ruby."

"I felt like our pact gave me an excuse to call you," Parker said. "Not that I needed an excuse. But you know what I mean. I thought you'd be less likely to shut me down. I figured it was now or never."

"I wouldn't have shut you down, now or any other time," Jasmine said.

She had to resist the urge to clap a hand over her mouth. That made it sound like she'd been pining away after him for years. Which she had been. But she didn't want him to know that.

Parker, apparently oblivious to Jasmine's embarrassment, said, "So before calling you, I cyberstalked you a little bit, and found out you weren't married. I took a chance."

They smiled at each other, and that connection they'd shared so long ago finally sparked to life. Jasmine wanted to ask him so many questions: Did he still want to stick to the terms of the pact, or had he just used it as an excuse to call her? Did he want to be exclusive? Did he still find her attractive? Had he experienced the same phenomenon she had, where no one quite measured up to their teenage love? But all of these questions seemed so childish. She'd just have to wait it out.

Meanwhile, it seemed as though none of these questions plagued Parker. He seemed comfortable in his skin, relaxed, content. He parked in a spot outside The Grind, flashed her a grin that she couldn't help but return, and got out of the van.

The Grind sat on the top floor of a little red brick historical building downtown. Jasmine ordered her tea and Parker's coffee to go so they could sit outside on the benches overlooking the ocean.

"So you can just leave work like that?" Parker said when they sat down. "Without letting anyone know?"

Jasmine put her feet up on the low concrete wall in front of the bench. "Trust me, they won't miss me."

"Oh, I know of one guy who will."

Jasmine should have known the Hudson situation would come back to haunt her. "Now, now," she said, keeping the tone of her voice light. "Hudson is practically a stranger to me."

"He didn't look anything like a stranger to you when I walked into your office."

Jasmine shrugged and watched a fat seagull walk along the concrete wall. "I can see how that's true. But that was a one-time deal. He actually doesn't like me at all."

Parker didn't answer, but Jasmine could see his jaw set as if he was stopping himself from saying more on the topic. The seagull fluffed its feathers and then settled down in front of them, probably hoping they'd drop crumbs. Jasmine sipped her tea.

After a moment, Parker spoke again. "When I first left Seabreeze, I was devastated. I felt like I'd lost my soul mate."

Jasmine's own memories of that time in her life caused her throat to constrict. "I know. Me, too. I cried myself to sleep every night for two weeks." She laughed, but only to ease the tightening in her chest. "Actually, I spent two entire days in bed before my mom dragged me to the spa to get me out of my funk."

"Yeah, I slept the entire flight to Spain, and then I hid in my new bedroom for a week, listening to angry music," Parker said. "Ryder finally convinced me to go sightseeing. He promised we could get beer in Spanish bars. I spent the next few weekends completely sloshed. So did Ryder. He called it empathetic drunkenness."

At that confession, the seagull squawked and flew off.

"Let's walk," Jasmine said.

"Did you forget you're at the beach?" Parker said, pointing at her feet. "Those boots were not made for walking."

They both took their shoes off and set them on the bench before heading towards the ocean. The tide was going out, and seashells covered the beach. Jasmine stooped to pick up a sand dollar, and handed it to Parker. They began walking north, their feet leaving vanishing side-by-side prints on the wet sand.

Jasmine wanted to slip her hand into Parker's, just as she would have done years ago, but something stopped her. She wasn't sure how he'd react, especially after the Hudson fiasco. So they walked, next to each other, and talked about the paths they'd traveled since they'd last seen one another.

Parker had lived in too many places to count, and Jasmine was fascinated by his stories of making new friends, playing guitar on street corners in every town where he lived, and earning a living by taking freelance jobs whenever he needed to. Jasmine told him how she'd come to be a reporter, almost by accident.

"So you just walked in and asked for a job?" Parker said.

"Yeah, basically. I mean, I never intended to do it long-term, but I had to get a job. I had the experience in college, and during one of our Garden Club meetings, Sequoia kind of dared me to become a reporter. I think she was tired of me freeloading off her. You know, we lived together and even though I made a little money, she always had to buy the extras. Like wine."

"Wait—so you guys still call yourselves The Garden Club?" Parker said.

They turned around and headed back. The tide was coming in, and as Jasmine ran away from the water to keep her jeans dry, Parker walked right through it.

"Totally," Jasmine said when the latest wave receded and they joined up again. "Probably always will."

"So now that you've done it for a while, do you think you'll keep reporting?"

Jasmine shrugged. She took her time answering, watching the foamy waves roll in and swish out. "I just don't know. I mean, I feel like I've always wanted to find my calling, you know? My passion. I'm just not sure if this is it. I enjoy it. I like talking with people, hearing their stories, putting those stories into words to share with other people. But do I want to do it forever, day after day? I'm not sure."

"What if you didn't have to have a calling?" Parker said. "Have you ever thought about that?"

"You mean, if I just went where the tide took me?"

"Yeah," he said.

"I shudder at the thought," Jasmine said. "I mean, how would I ever know what to do next?"

"You might like it," Parker said. When she didn't answer, he added, "Just think about it."

Jasmine's phone rang, and she fished it out of her purse. "It's the paper," she said.

She heard Parker say, "The old ball and chain," as she answered.

"You need to meet Hudson at the bowling alley." Mikey's voice cut through the soothing sound of the ocean like scissors cutting through a pristine sheet of white paper.

"What's up?" Jasmine said.

"Apparently, some jerk committed suicide on lane twelve."

"Geez, Mikey, have some compassion," Jasmine said.

"Why? He's dead. Anyway, as you know—I'm sure you know this, Jas—we don't cover suicides."

"So why—"

"Because the asshole did it in a public place. Everybody and their mother is going to wonder why all of Seabreeze's cops are over at the bowling alley today. Check in with me when you get back to the office. I've gotta run."

Jasmine shoved her phone back into her purse and turned to Parker. "See? This is exactly what I dislike about journalism. My editor has no compassion. No empathy. This guy committed suicide, and it's just another dumb jerk who killed himself. And now, I have to go write about it."

They'd arrived back at their starting point, and Jasmine turned toward Parker. He put his hands on her upper arms and kissed her on the forehead. It was so chaste Jasmine had to keep herself from gasping. This first encounter with Parker wasn't what she'd expected at all. Not from the moment they'd seen each other.

DOZENS OF EMERGENCY VEHICLES—POLICE cars, fire trucks, and ambulances—parked at odd angles, clogged the bowling alley's parking lot. Their lights twirled and flickered in different patterns and rhythms, and Jasmine felt dizzy as she approached the building.

Parker had driven her back to the newspaper office, and by the time they got there, Jasmine felt rushed and anxious. She thanked him and slammed the van door without even making eye contact. The fifteen-minute drive to the bowling alley gave her some much-needed time on two fronts.

First, she had time to think about Parker and that chaste forehead kiss. Where was the passion? Where were the fireworks? She felt foolish for thinking they'd be unable to keep their hands off each other when they finally met up again, more than a decade's worth of memories and sexual angst just boiling over. Maybe the teenage Parker had shown wisdom beyond his years when he suggested they date for a month as part of the pact. They'd need time to get to know each other again. Or maybe they had both been stupid. Was it even possible to reignite a thirteen-year-old passion?

Second, she needed to mentally prepare for what the scene of a suicide might look like. She imagined herself walking into the bowling alley and seeing it—a place where she'd hosted and attended innumerable birthday parties as a child and downed innumerable beers as an adult—from the perspective of a reporter. Or a suicidal person. This thought sent her stomach to churning. No wonder Liza popped antacids all day long.

Pulling into the parking lot, Jasmine noticed the coroner's car pulling out. That meant she didn't have to see the victim's body. She exhaled the breath she'd been holding and felt her shoulders relax, just slightly.

She pulled open the building's glass door and was hit with the usual bowling alley scent: dirty socks, grease and popcorn. For the first time ever, she didn't hear the sound of pins falling down or people cheering. Instead, the near-silence that follows death muffled everything else.

The wide-open room absolutely teemed with people, and Jasmine made it as far as the arcade before she froze with overwhelming uncertainty. She didn't know who to talk to or where to go.

Firefighters and paramedics stood in small groups in the corridor between the entryway and the bowling lanes. They talked quietly, their expressions somber and their movements small. Suddenly, someone was standing next to her. She jumped when Hudson started to speak. "Glad you could make it."

Jasmine swallowed, hoping to increase air flow to her brain. "Sorry, I—"

"You were on a date, right?"

She looked up at him, hoping to gauge his feelings. She was startled to see that he looked sad—deeply sad. Still, his eyes twinkled, just the tiniest bit. So he was teasing her. How could he tease at a time and place like this? She shook her head.

"It wasn't a date, Hudson. It was a ..." Her voice trailed off and she found she didn't want to explain.

"Whatever," he said, still subdued, his voice relaxed. "Look, I don't think you should walk any farther. Seriously. I can just tell the PIO you're over here and he can come talk to you. Or whatever."

"You don't think I can handle it?" She tried to keep her tone light, but she felt defensiveness creeping in.

"It's pretty gruesome," Hudson said, his expression turning serious as he maneuvered his body to block hers.

Jasmine straightened her spine, and Hudson grabbed her arm. "I can tell what you're thinking," he said. "Don't march over there just to prove to me that you can handle a scene, okay?"

Something like real concern colored his voice, and this, along with Hudson's apparent ability to read her mind, caused Jasmine to pause. Then she pulled her arm out of his grasp. She had no idea why something about this man made her want to prove herself. "I'm fine."

Because the bowling alley was so crowded, Jasmine had to weave her way through a maze of people. This prevented her from seeing the scene until she was right there. When she did, her hand automatically came up to cover her mouth, and she heard herself gasp.

Police and evidence technicians gathered at the front of lane twelve, taking measurements and placing evidence tags. For a brief moment, Jasmine thought, *this isn't so bad. I can totally handle this.* And then she saw the blood. At first she had the insane thought that the blood had crossed over the foul line, and she wondered if it had set off the buzzer. Then she noticed—really noticed—the sheer volume of the liquid on the floor, and the chunks in it. Brain matter.

Without warning, black swirls overtook her vision. Her last thought as she felt her body crumple was, *I'm passing out.* And then there was something like a thought, something that didn't quite form before she hit the floor: *Hudson was right.*

Jasmine came to a little bit at a time, her consciousness grasping at threads of information. When she finally strung together the details, all in bits and pieces (bits and pieces of brain matter), she had no idea how much time had passed. Hudson crouched over her, his hand pressed hard against her head. She winced.

"Ouch," she said. "Why are you pushing on my head?"

He looked strangely relieved for someone who disliked her and simultaneously wanted to tie her up with her own scarf and make love to her. That was confusing.

"Ice pack," he said. "You bumped your head pretty good."

Fortunately, with all the activity in the building, no one aside from Hudson was paying her any attention.

"Can you sit up?" he asked.

She nodded, and winced again. "Ouch," she said.

"Uh oh," Hudson said. "I think the fall has your brain stuck on repeat."

She laughed at that, and he helped her to a sitting position.

"Holly would be so relieved she chose pants for me to wear today," Jasmine said.

"Who's Holly? Your personal assistant?" Hudson said.

"No, my sister."

"Your sister picks your clothes? What are you, like, twelve?"

Jasmine shrugged one shoulder. "Where's my notepad?"

"It's in my bag. Let's get you up and into a chair or something."

She shouldn't have been surprised at how easily Hudson hoisted her to her feet. He was strapping. Still, she was. She was also surprised at how gently he led her to a nearby chair, handed her the ice pack, and then brought her hand up to hold the ice pack on her head. And all without a single, "I told you so."

"Thank you," she said, offering him what she hoped was a

grateful smile. It felt like a grimace, but she couldn't be sure. "I think I'm going to throw up now."

"Hold that thought," he said. "Let me grab a garbage can."

He returned a moment later and set a small waste basket at her feet.

"At your service." He bowed, and Jasmine giggled.

"I think I'm okay now," she said.

"Okay," he said. "I think I got some good shots of you, passed out next to the pool of blood on lane twelve. I can see the headline now: Ace reporter passes out in a pool of someone else's blood and brain matter."

"Ugh," Jasmine said, and she thought, *How about fluff correspondent?* but didn't say it.

"I know," Hudson said. "That's why I'm a photographer. I can't write for crap. Sit tight. I'm going to go get you some coffee."

She didn't have time to tell him she didn't drink coffee. He dashed off and left her alone. It was only then that she realized he had positioned her so she was facing away from the grisly scene that had caused this mess in the first place. *How very thoughtful. Surprises aplenty today.*

"I can't help but brace myself for the next one," she said aloud.

A cop passing by looked at her as if she were crazy, and she smiled. "I'm fine," she said. "Just talking to myself."

Hudson returned and handed her a paper coffee cup. He sat down next to her.

"Sorry for the delay. The bartender made me brew it myself. Said she never has to make it until closing time."

"You brewed me coffee?"

He held up his own cup. "I'm having some, too."

Feeling oddly touched, Jasmine put a hand on Hudson's arm. "Thank you," she said. "Really."

"You're welcome," he said. After a pause, he said, "You know, when I got my first photojournalism job, I had one of the reporters write all my cutlines for me. I was so terrible at writing."

"I'm sure she didn't mind," Jasmine said.

Hudson scoffed. "Nice. It was a he. And you're right. He didn't mind, because I paid him in beer. We used to go to this little bar in Long Beach and have beers after work. I bought him one beer per cutline. On busy days, we went home drunk off our asses. When I was going to move, I finally had to break down and ask him to teach me how to write them myself. Paid him with a twenty-four pack. Anyway. Are you going to have any of that coffee?"

"I don't really drink coffee," Jasmine said. "But you were moving so fast I didn't have time to say so."

"Try it," he said. "Recipe for a hard news reporter who won't pass out cold when she sees blood: add one cup of coffee."

"It wasn't the blood," Jasmine said. "It was the brain matter."

She took a tentative sip of the coffee and grimaced. Hudson laughed. "Take another sip. It's like wine. You can't judge it on the first sip."

Jasmine obeyed, and nodded after swallowing. "It's not so bad."

"It's about half milk and a quarter sugar," he said.

"And something else, too, right?"

Hudson smiled. "Caught me. I figured since the bartender made me brew it myself, I'd take brewer's license. I added a couple shots of whiskey." When Jasmine's mouth dropped open, he said, "What? You needed something to relax you."

"You drink wine?" she said.

"Now and then."

"My sister's a whiskey drinker," Jasmine said. "Sequoia. She loves the hard stuff. I have no idea why. Well, I should amend that. Before today, I had no idea why. Now I feel this warm, comfortable sensation. No wonder she always settles down with a glass at night."

"I've never had much of a taste for it, myself," Hudson said. "But a veteran cops reporter gave me the same treatment when I lost my lunch at a scene very similar to this one."

"Did you end up friends?" Jasmine said. She could tell she was wrinkling her nose, but the whiskey made it difficult to control her expressions.

"Lifelong," he said. Then he stood up, tossed his empty coffee cup in the trash, and raised a hand to signal a plainclothes cop who was walking by.

The cop changed course and came to sit across from Hudson and Jasmine. Hudson said, "You're the spokesperson on this case, right? Whittaker?"

"That's me," said the cop. He didn't look friendly.

"I'm Hudson and this is Jasmine. We're from the *Daily Trumpet*. Can we ask you a few questions?"

Whittaker looked at Jasmine. His expression was serious, but his eyes held just more than a hint of humor. He jerked a thumb at lane twelve. "You the one who hit the floor a few minutes ago?"

Normally, this kind of treatment would embarrass Jasmine and make her prickly, but again, Hudson came to her rescue before she could provide Whittaker with a retort that resulted in instant dislike.

"Take it easy on her, man," he said. "First suicide."

Whittaker grimaced. "I've been there, myself, actually. I would have passed out at my first scene, too, if my training officer hadn't given me a pep talk and promised me a shot of whiskey after we cleared and processed the scene."

Hudson elbowed Jasmine. "See?" Then he looked at Whittaker and pointed at Jasmine's coffee cup. "I spiked her coffee."

Whittaker smiled, and without any more prompting, he began rattling off details about the incident.

CHAPTER TEN

In a rare display of unity, Sequoia and Holly insisted that Jasmine talk to Parker about whether he wanted to adhere to the terms of their pact—and date, exclusively, for thirty days.

"You have to know," Sequoia said, and Holly nodded to emphasize the point.

Jasmine, flabbergasted at her sisters' unusual concurrence, didn't argue. She did have to know.

She didn't want to push Parker into sticking with her for a month, if he didn't want to. She wasn't sure if she really wanted to stick with him, but she couldn't say why. Was it because of the subdued kiss he'd planted on her forehead at the beach that day? Was it because she'd changed? Because she thought he had? Or— and this was a strange thought—was it because of Hudson?

It didn't matter now. Jasmine was set to meet Parker for dinner in five minutes. She stood outside Waves, a cozy, casual diner Parker had suggested. It had been one of their haunts when they were teenagers, because it was inexpensive and delicious. Jasmine hadn't set foot inside in years. At some point, her interest in the place had fizzled out. Maybe it was when, during college, she'd had a sudden epiphany that the place was coated in grease and the dishes were never quite clean.

Standing as close to the window as she could without looking like a stalker of some kind, Jasmine looked inside. Okay, so it wasn't Pâtisserie, with its linen napkins and twenty-dollar cocktails. But with its cozy booths—covered in cracking glitter vinyl—it did have a certain charm.

Jasmine remembered Parker always being on time, and she felt jittery waiting for him. The soft summer fog felt cool on her cheeks, and she could smell the ocean. She closed her eyes and inhaled, and she heard Parker's voice.

"Does this remind you of anything?"

Jasmine smiled. "Yeah. That smell reminds me of that time we we went to Treasure Cove and played Skee Ball for hours, and then got corn dogs and walked down the beach. It smelled exactly like this."

She opened her eyes and saw her own nostalgia reflected in his. "It did smell exactly like this," he said. "I remember it distinctly because I beat you so badly at Skee Ball."

When she began to protest, he took her face in his hands, and brought his lips to hers. No fireworks. No sparks. But there was a low, slow burn, and it felt so familiar, so good, so comfortable. Jasmine wrapped her hands around his wrists and kissed him back. The bell on the restaurant's door jingled as someone came out of the restaurant and Parker pulled away.

"Shall we?" he said.

He opened the door for Jasmine, and she went in, her body on high alert. The hostess seated them next to the window, at a booth with a view of the never-ending ocean and a crystalline sky.

"Are you going to get your regular?" Parker said.

Jasmine laughed. She hadn't gotten her teenage self's regular— chili cheese fries and a Dr. Pepper—in years. The last time she'd come—when she was in college—she opted for the house salad and water with no ice and no lemon. Still, she nodded. Why not get her regular, for old times' sake? "Yeah. I'll get my regular. You?"

"When I was away," he said, "I dreamed of the bacon guacamole burger."

"With curly fries," they said at the same time.

It was so easy to fall into old routines. Parker ordered for both of them, and when the server walked away, Jasmine put both palms flat on the table.

"We need to talk."

"So serious," Parker said.

Jasmine's laugh came out nervous, high and breathy. "Well, here's the thing. I mean, you called me last week because of the pact we made, right?"

All of a sudden, Jasmine felt stupid. What if he'd just mentioned the pact because it was their birthday? What if he'd just used it as an excuse to call her? What if he was coming into town anyway? What if he hadn't taken the pact seriously at all? She froze.

"Definitely," he said.

"We don't have to stick to it," they said at the same time.

"I mean—" he said, and she said, "If you don't want to."

They both laughed.

"Sorry," Jasmine said. "Kind of awkward."

"No, it's fine," he said. "I'm the one who mentioned it when I called you."

The server returned with their food and drinks and they ate without talking. When they finished, Jasmine felt like the moment had passed, and instead of talking about the pact, she talked about the weather.

"SO?" Holly buttered French bread at Jasmine's kitchen counter while Sequoia chopped bell peppers. Jasmine flitted around the kitchen like a moth in the dark, bumbling from one cabinet to the other in search of dishes and silverware.

"You know where everything is, right?" Sequoia said. "I mean, this is your kitchen."

Jasmine huffed out a sigh. "I'm just distracted, okay? And the salad bowl is so big it never seems to fit anywhere. I keep moving it and I can never remember where I put it."

Ruby sat at Sequoia's feet, motionless except for when she periodically pushed on Sequoia's shin with one paw. "What's wrong with your creature?"

"She wants those bell peppers. They're her favorite," Jasmine said.

"That's weird," Sequoia said. "Call her off. I'm not feeding her bell peppers." She looked down at the dog. "Go eat some meat, dog. This is our dinner."

Jasmine finally retrieved the salad bowl—it was on the top shelf of the pantry—and set it next to Sequoia's pile of bell peppers.

"So?" Holly said again.

"Oh. Right," Jasmine said. She'd known what Holly was getting at a few moments ago, but for some reason, she didn't want to talk about it. "To answer the unspoken question, no. I didn't talk to Parker about the pact."

"What?" Holly said. "Why not? I mean, you guys were so in love back then."

"We were," Jasmine said, drawing out the second word as she set glasses next to the fridge and began filling them with water. "But I don't know, it almost feels like that same spark just isn't there. I mean, there's *something* there."

"You don't sound excited," Sequoia said. She'd finished with the peppers and scooped them into the bowl. She dropped one on the floor and Ruby pounced on it. "You should teach this dog to capture mice or something."

"It's not that I'm not excited," Jasmine said. "It's just that there's a lot going on right now. Anyway. We can talk more about that later. What I really want to know, Sequoia, is why you're cutting those vegetables with such force. What's up?"

Now Sequoia sighed. "I don't know. So our new boss lady is cutting our overtime budget. You know how much I count on that overtime."

"Maybe this will be good for you," Holly said. "I mean, you can finally go on some dates or something. You know, with men. Do you remember what those are? Men? They're a subsection of the human species. Sort of a mystery, but necessary in the proliferation of human life."

"I date," Sequoia said.

"Yeah, five years ago," Jasmine and Holly said.

"Okay. Do you guys have to pick on me?" Sequoia said.

"I want to hear more about your conversation with Parker," Holly said to Jasmine.

"Let's sit," Jasmine said.

They gathered the various dishes and went to sit at the table. Ruby followed them, and hopped up onto the chair next to Jasmine's.

"Gross," Sequoia said.

"So we get to dinner," Jasmine began, and Holly immediately interrupted, speaking with her mouth full of French bread: "Where'd you go?"

"Manners, Holly," Sequoia said.

Holly dismissed her comment with a wave of her hand, and Jasmine said, "We went to Waves."

Even Holly winced, and Sequoia said, "How very grown-up of you."

"I know," Jasmine said. "Parker wanted to go there, you know, for old times' sake. I mean, it wasn't as good as I remember, but it was cozy for sure. And nostalgic."

"Anyway, do go on," Sequoia said.

Jasmine nodded. "At first the conversation was kind of stilted. We kept talking over each other. I brought up the fact that he called me about the pact, but then I suddenly felt stupid. Like, what if he'd just used that as a cover? What if he didn't remember the terms?"

"Yeah, I'd feel stupid too," Sequoia said. She stuffed a huge bite of salad into her mouth and Holly said, "Don't say that. Of course he remembers the terms. He was totally smitten with you. He has every moment of your past together memorized."

Sequoia rolled her eyes and made a "get on with it" motion with her fork.

"Right," Jasmine said. "So anyway. I was about to ask if he wanted to, you know, stick to the original terms, or whatever, and then the food came and I lost my nerve."

"You *lost* your *nerve*?" Sequoia said. "It's not like you were bungee jumping, or skydiving. You were having a conversation."

Jasmine looked down at her plate. She cut a piece off her chicken breast and ate it.

"Don't get your feelings hurt, Jas," Sequoia said. "Geez, everybody's so sensitive tonight. I just expected a little more excitement, I guess. After all this time."

Jasmine nodded, still looking at her plate. "Well, me too. But I mean, that was so long ago."

"Just give it time," Holly said. She put a hand over Jasmine's.

"Let's change the subject," Jasmine said. "Holly, have you started your certification for personal training?"

THAT NIGHT as Jasmine lay in bed, she found that her train of thought was carrying a stowaway.

She started out thinking about Parker and the pact they'd made and the time they'd spent together so far. She thought about that kiss outside of Waves. She wondered whether he was thinking about her right now.

Could this even work? They had each grown in the past decade, and not together. But just because they hadn't grown together didn't have to mean they'd grown apart, did it? Ruby, in her usual spot beside Jasmine's left hip, adjusted her position and began snoring.

For so long, none of the men she dated were as caring, as considerate or as handsome as Parker. None of them had that "Parker quality." If a new guy held her hand too tightly or kissed her too softly or walked with too large of a stride, she crossed him off her list.

So, none of the other men she met stirred her interest.

Until Hudson (and here was the stowaway, emerging from the secret compartment where he'd been hiding).

Most notably, he was showing up in her thoughts right now, when she was supposed to be thinking about Parker. She was picturing his face, reliving the way her body reacted when he cornered her outside the bathroom at work, realizing how thoughtful he might actually be.

She couldn't identify the reason she found him so attractive. He didn't even seem to like her most of the time. But there was something, wasn't there?

She just had to decide whether that something was worth noticing, or whether it was a tiny blip on her radar, one worth discarding, writing off.

Jasmine stayed awake most of the night, her mind bouncing between Parker and Hudson like a ping-pong ball.

CHAPTER ELEVEN

"So what's up with the longhaired guy?" Hudson wanted to know.

Jasmine had just arrived at the newsroom and barely had time to put her purse down before he sauntered over and sat in her chair.

"What do you mean?" Jasmine said.

"I mean, are you guys an item, or what?"

Jasmine leaned against her desk, crossed her arms. "Here's what I don't get about you, Hudson. You go from being this superior jerk one minute, to being this sweet guy who brings me coffee laced with whiskey the next minute, to being this weird needy high schooler, sitting in my chair and bugging me about guys I'm seeing."

Hudson shrugged. "Sounds like you get it just perfectly. So you're seeing him?"

Jasmine flung a hand in the air and leaned over to turn on her computer. This put her in such close proximity with Hudson that her body started to hum. She almost wished she'd worn a scarf. "Why are you sitting in my chair?"

"Just so I could talk to you."

"So talk," she said, using one of Sequoia's most frequently spoken lines from childhood.

"Mikey and I were talking about doing a series, about—"

"Can't this wait until Liza gets back?" Jasmine said.

She straightened up and stood facing Hudson, who looked even more relaxed now, with his elbows on the arms of her chair and his hands folded across his stomach. That same vision she'd had the day they met, the one of her straddling him, came unbidden to her mind and she shook her head to send it packing.

"It's relevant right now, Jasmine," he said.

He did have such a nice voice, deep and gravelly. And she liked the way it made her name sound. "What is it?" she said.

"It's about unicorns. And fairies."

"Have you been talking to my sister?" At his blank expression, she closed her eyes, briefly. "Never mind. Anyway, what's it about? And can I sit down, please?"

He stood up, and she remained where she was. They stood there facing each other, centimeters apart, and it took every last drop of Jasmine's will power to resist the urge to lean forward. Hudson's body issued a kind of challenge, she thought, and then she thought that was silly. Finally, she moved aside so they could switch places. When she sat down in her chair he propped a hip on her desk.

"It's about suicide," he said. "Kind of like a suicide prevention series."

Jasmine's throat emitted a growly noise.

"Wait," Hudson said. "Before you say anything, let me tell you my idea."

"Wait," Jasmine said. "I thought this was yours and Mikey's idea."

Hudson shrugged. "So I'm thinking three to five stories. We can share statistics, talk to experts, maybe a feature story about someone who tried and failed to commit suicide. I know some of this is hard news, but some of it is right up your alley. Like the feature stories."

"So," Jasmine said, "I hate to be dense, but what's the point? To be morbid?"

"This is called journalism, sweetheart," Hudson said. He softened his tone when he went on: "The point is to increase awareness. We just had a suicide in our own town. It affects us all. If we can increase awareness, let people know they're not alone and that there are resources, and that they can come back from that dark, dark place, we can save lives."

"Wait a second," Jasmine said. "This isn't even your town. You plan to skip out as soon as possible. Onto bigger and better things, or whatever."

"It's my town right now, and I'm a journalist," Hudson said. "I take what I do very seriously, no matter where I am. Maybe you should do the same."

It took a conscious effort not to flinch, but Jasmine managed.

"Do me a favor and just think about it, okay?" Hudson said.

With that, he stood up and walked right out the newsroom door. She heard his motorcycle start up and chastised herself for wondering where he was going.

The police scanner squealed, the hot tones breaking through the otherwise quiet newsroom. This time, she remembered she was supposed to listen to the scanner before her hand even reached for her headphones. She stood up and went to stand next to the spot where it sat on the bookshelf.

"All available northern units, please report to Seabreeze Shopping Center. We have a report of a missing child. All available northern units, please report to Seabreeze Shopping Center."

Jasmine wondered how dispatchers could remain so calm all the time, or at least make their voices sound calm. Her own body was already filling with adrenaline as she gathered her purse, keys, notepad, and pen. Should she call Hudson? His own portable scanner wasn't on its charger on his desk, so he probably already knew about the missing child. What would Liza do?

As she backed out of her parking spot, Jasmine called Hudson's phone. Then she felt stupid. First of all, he'd gotten along just fine without her until now. Second, he couldn't even answer his phone, could he? He was undoubtedly driving and she had no idea how he'd pick up his phone on the motorcycle. After letting it ring a few times, she pressed End and set her phone carefully in the cup holder.

The Seabreeze Shopping Center's parking lot swarmed with cops. Jasmine felt smugly professional when she immediately spotted the satellite- and antenna-laden Seabreeze Police Department mobile command post. She had her notepad and pen out by the time she approached the on-duty lieutenant, who was briefing some uniformed officers who'd assembled.

"His name's Kevin Shoemaker. He's eight, and his mom said they were having lunch at the food court."

Determined to do this story justice, Jasmine took careful notes, holding her pen tighter than usual, writing more neatly. The lieutenant continued: "Kevin's mom went to the bathroom, and when she came back, he was gone. I don't have photos printed out yet, but you guys can pass this around."

He handed his phone to the nearest officer, who looked at the screen, nodded, and passed it on. Someone handed it to Jasmine, probably out of reflex, and she felt her throat tighten when she saw the image of Kevin Shoemaker's face. He had white-blond curly hair and chocolate brown eyes that smiled at the camera. In the photo, he was holding up a fish he'd apparently caught, his excited grin showing adult-sized teeth that were too big for his face.

Someone elbowed Jasmine. "Pass it on."

"Sorry," she said, handing the phone to the police officer next to her.

"So search and rescue should be here in a couple of minutes," the lieutenant was saying. "We're going to break the mall up into sectors."

He went on, laying out the plan, and Jasmine found herself looking for Hudson. Finally, she spotted his motorcycle next to her car, but she couldn't find him. She mentally kicked herself. Why was she looking for him? Was it because she was out of her element and needed support? Was it because she wanted him there in case she had questions about how something worked? Was it because she wanted to make sure his photos matched her story? The answer to all of these questions, she knew, was no. It was because of the strange attraction that sizzled between them. She wanted to explore it. She wanted to see how it changed depending on setting. And she hated herself for that.

She decided to go inside the mall. A change of scenery would do her good, and she could watch the scene unfolding. Readers would be interested in a description of the search, wouldn't they? Just as she turned around to go inside, someone stopped her with a hand on her shoulder. "You're with the paper, right?"

"Jasmine Carr," she said, and he said, "I'm Erik Whittaker, from the bowling alley."

Jasmine groaned. "How embarrassing."

"Oh, you're fine. I'd already wiped your fainting spell from my memory. Anyway, I saw you were listening to the briefing, so you have a pretty good idea of what's going on. But just hang tight and let me know if you have any questions. I know it's not up to me to decide what you emphasize in your story, but if you wouldn't mind mentioning the importance of calling the police right away when a child is missing. Some parents wait hours. They don't want to bother us, or they feel silly, but the longer they wait, the smaller our chances of actually finding the kid."

Erik Whittaker waited until he'd watched her add his advice to her notes before walking away.

Inside, she spent an hour in a chair on the fringe of the food court, watching the police as they worked. Some of them went from store to store, searching behind jewelry displays and in storerooms she imagined were full of shoe boxes. Others went through bathrooms and storage closets. The search and rescue teams came next. Jasmine knew some of them had remained outside, while others walked through the mall.

Still, no sign of Kevin Shoemaker. Or Hudson.

Kevin's mother sat at the same food court table where they'd eaten lunch, sobbing. She wanted to help search, but police detectives insisted she stay where Kevin had last seen her. Jasmine found herself staring, even more anxious now about this poor woman's reaction if police didn't find her son.

Despite her best intentions to remain separate from the situation, Jasmine felt her nerves coming to life. The anxiety built like a snowball rolling downhill, and before she knew it, she was up and walking through the mall, her boots clicking on the tiled floor. She didn't even know this Kevin kid, but her stomach twisted at the thought of what could have happened to him. There were so many exits and hiding places. The kid could be anywhere, with anyone, inside or outside of the mall.

Someone's phone rang, and Jasmine jumped. She had no idea how long she'd walked laps from one end of the mall to the other, and back again. Then, because she realized she hadn't looked at her own phone in a while, she checked it and saw that she had a missed call from Parker.

"Your timing is impeccable," she said when he answered.

"Are you busy?" he said.

After she explained where she was and what she was doing, Parker said, "Want to take a quick break?"

"I really shouldn't," she said. "What if they find this kid?"

"Then you can come back. I'm sure that photographer guy would be happy to call you."

Jasmine rolled her eyes. "He's not even here."

"Perfect. I'll pick you up outside the food court."

He disconnected and Jasmine shrugged. She told herself it wouldn't hurt to take a break, to clear her mind, to gain a fresh perspective. It's not like she was part of the search team, or anything. At the same time, she realized her compulsive internal justification of this "break" meant it wasn't really the right thing to do.

She walked through the food court, past Kevin Shoemaker's crying mother, and out into the afternoon sun.

———

AS THEY DROVE FURTHER and further away from the mall, Jasmine asked countless times where Parker was taking her. Every time, he responded with, "It's a surprise."

Part of her was heading into panic mode. This probably wasn't the best time for surprises. She really should be at the mall, or at least within sprinting distance. She wanted to ask him how long this surprise would take. This part of her knew she was making a bad choice, that she should have told Parker they could meet up after deadline this evening. But—probably out of her middle-child tendency to keep everyone happy—she hadn't. And here they were.

Quieting that part of herself required quite a bit of effort, but Jasmine managed by trying to solve the mystery of where they were going.

Maybe Parker was taking her to a romantic spot. Somewhere like The Point, where people went to make out. If so, she could postpone the make-out session long enough to talk about the pact, to get a handle on Parker's expectations—and her own. Yes, she decided. She'd talk to him about it. Today. That would be a good, practical use of her time while the search for Kevin Shoemaker unfolded at the mall without her.

When they pulled into the bowling alley parking lot, though, Jasmine almost passed out in the passenger seat. Her fingers felt tingly, right down to their freshly painted nails, and her head spun with images of evidence technicians in latex gloves and chunky blood spilling down lane twelve. In reflex, her hands gripped her armrests.

"Parker," she said, "this was a great idea, but I can't do it. I can't go in there."

"Why not?"

"Haven't you been reading the paper?" Her voice sounded harsher than she meant it to, but she didn't apologize.

"No," he said. "Why, what's up?"

"I had to cover a suicide here last week. It was horrible. I just don't think I can go in there right now."

"You used to love to bowl."

She remembered. As soon as Parker had his driver's license, they went to the bowling alley at least once every weekend, and sometimes on school nights.

"I do remember," she said. "But I don't love it, today. Let's go for a drive."

He shrugged, the disappointment etched in lines around his mouth. "Okay."

She put a hand on his arm. "Maybe another time," she said. "Okay?"

"Where do you want to go?" he said.

"Let's go to East Cliff. Like old times."

"Remember that time we got drunk, bowling?" Parker said.

He shifted the van into reverse and it chugged a little as he pulled back onto Riverside.

"Oh, I remember," Jasmine said. "My first time getting drunk, and you had to pour me into your car when we finally headed home."

"And then you puked three times between the bowling alley and your house."

"That was awful," Jasmine said.

"But you got your best score ever that night," Parker said.

Jasmine nodded. "Did you ever tell me how you scored that beer?" she asked.

"I always kept it a secret from you," he said, "because I was afraid you would balk at my lack of moral principles."

"I would never," she said, laughing. "I was as much of a participant as you were."

Parker laughed. "That's true."

Still, he didn't say anything about the source of the beer.

Jasmine elbowed him. "So how'd you get it?" she said again.

"My parents were going to have some people over, and Mom went to the grocery store to get food. Dad made this big deal of her getting a bunch of beer. So she got a few of those variety packs, you know? They come in those big cardboard boxes? Anyway, Mom was notorious for leaving stuff on the bottom of the shopping cart when she loaded her car. Toilet paper, paper towels, dog food, you name it. She came home from the store missing items more times than I can count. So, with that in mind, I just took a whole variety pack out of the fridge in our garage, and both Mom and Dad assumed she'd left it on the bottom of the basket. Some lucky person scored in the parking lot."

After stowing the beer in the trunk of his dad's car, Parker picked Jasmine up, and they parked in a service alley behind the bowling building, sipping beer. At first, Jasmine thought the beer tasted bitter, and she wrinkled her face every time she put a bottle to her lips.

"Just chug it," Parker kept saying, and finally, she did, slamming three additional beers in the span of a few minutes.

They'd gone in and she'd bowled nearly a perfect game before she started feeling queasy.

"I was in so much trouble that night," Jasmine said.

When Parker laughed, she said, "It's not funny. And that's not the only time you got me in trouble. Always with your little catch-phrase. 'Live a little,' you'd say."

He shrugged. "Teenage wisdom."

"And look at you now," she said. "Getting me to play hooky from work. Parker Abbott, you're a terrible influence."

Grinning, Parker pulled the van into a spot at a little lot at one end of East Cliff. "Want to walk?" he said.

At first, they walked side by side, like acquaintances or maybe even strangers. After a few minutes, though, Parker took Jasmine's hand. They'd held hands for hours as teenagers, so much that it became an inside joke. They did everything—eat, ride bikes, roller skate—while connected like Siamese twins.

She wondered if he remembered that. Right now, his hand in hers felt foreign, which she never would have expected thirteen years ago. Thirteen years ago, she thought they'd fit together perfectly forever.

They stopped at the viewing platform overlooking one of Seabreeze's most popular surfing spots. Parker put his arm around Jasmine's waist, and she leaned into him, resting her head on his shoulder. Despite her earlier resolution to talk to him about the pact, and despite the brightness of the sunny day, the excitement of surfers catching waves below, Jasmine's mind wandered to Kevin Shoe-maker and even more so, to his mother. As a mother, how would you go on with life if your son disappeared? Would you still go into the kitchen each morning to pack his lunch for school?

Parker's voice, steeped in nostalgia, interrupted her thoughts. "Remember that time we were sitting on those pilings and that huge wave came in?"

Jasmine smiled. "I was just thinking about that the other day, actually. That was so funny."

"Why do you sound so sad?" he said.

"Do I?"

He didn't answer.

"I was just thinking about that missing kid and his mom," Jasmine said. "I mean, can you imagine your kid going missing?"

"Just one of the many reasons I don't want kids," he said.

"You don't?"

"Nah," Parker said. "Don't get me wrong, I like kids just fine. I just don't want any of my own."

Had they ever talked about kids when they were kids? Probably not. She would have remembered this one. The portraits her imagination had created—the ones of their future children, handsome boys with Parker's chin and delicate girls with his eyelashes—went up in smoke.

"Nevertheless." Jasmine cleared her throat. "It's just weighing on my mind, is all. That mom was so upset."

"I guess she should have been more responsible," Parker said.

"She went to the bathroom, Parker. He's eight. She probably figured he'd be embarrassed to go into the women's restroom, and that he was old enough to sit at the table for three minutes while she went."

"Sorry, geez. You're probably right."

"Anyway. This was a really nice idea."

"I thought so," Parker said. "Just like old times."

"So, what's your plan?" Jasmine said. "Do you have one?"

"I guess you could call it the anti-plan. Just going where the road takes me. I mean, my dad always had his life so planned out, and I was always at his mercy. Well, the Army's mercy, actually. I don't want my life to be like that. I want to be able to choose my own path."

What he said made sense. After being dragged from state to state, country to country throughout childhood, a person would probably wish for the autonomy and freedom to do what he wanted. Jasmine's first reaction was to wonder whether he was really choosing, or whether he was just living by default. Then she realized her inner voice sounded like Sequoia's when she was talking to Holly. She didn't want to sound like Sequoia, so she said, "That sounds like a good idea."

The truth was, she didn't think it sounded like a good idea at all.

"You know, I should check my phone," she said after a moment.

"Why? Got somewhere to be?"

"Well, I kind of left the scene of a major story. Mikey would probably kill me if I missed out on the conclusion."

When Jasmine pulled out her phone and pushed the button to illuminate the screen, she gasped. She had six texts and four missed calls. Two of the texts and one of the calls were from Mikey. The rest were from Hudson.

"Shit."

She knew Hudson would be awaiting her call. So she dialed Mikey.

"Carr. Where the hell are you?"

"I—uh, I needed some fresh air, I guess."

Jasmine could practically see Mikey's face: bright red cheeks, lips pressed together, steam coming out of his ears. He said, "But where are you? Stover said you went MIA. I thought you were covering that missing kid case."

Jasmine nodded, then rushed to answer him. "Yes. I am covering it."

Beside her, Parker sighed and shifted his weight from one foot to the other.

"So, I'll ask you again," he said. "Where the hell are you?"

"East Cliff."

"East Cliff? East Cliff! What the—never mind, Carr. I don't even want to know. They found the frickin' kid. Get the hell back to the mall. Perry Marks said I should give *him* Liza's beat. Maybe he was right. I don't know what the hell I was thinking."

Tears leapt to Jasmine's eyes. She was so relieved, so happy, that the police had found Kevin Shoemaker. And she was humiliated. She wasn't surprised Perry and Mikey questioned giving her Liza's beat. And this was why. She wasn't cut out for journalism. Maybe she should quit reporting and join Parker on the road. They could be gypsies together. Visions of their future children rematerialized.

Parker looked at her, his brow wrinkled. She covered her mouth, and Mikey's harsh voice came through the phone again. "Stover's waiting on your skinny little ass," he said.

I'll just bet he is. Jasmine's memory flashed to that moment when Hudson had pinned her against the wall in the office.

"Let him know I'll meet him at the food court," Jasmine said.

Mikey disconnected, and Jasmine said to Parker, "I've got to go. Can you take me back to the mall, please?"

"WHERE THE HELL WERE YOU?" Hudson greeted Jasmine in the parking lot, before she even reached the entrance to the food court.

He yanked the door open before she could do it herself, and made an exaggerated gesture for her to go in ahead of him. She rushed in, saying, "What are you guys, my keepers? Babysitters? I'm here now."

"Don't get snippy with me, woman," he said as she walked past him. "You're the one who disappeared."

Jasmine gasped and turned around to face him. "Where was *I*? Where were *you*? I was here all morning, and I didn't see hide nor hair of you, mister!"

In a move Jasmine didn't expect, Hudson laughed. "Did you just call me mister?"

She felt her defenses slipping away, along with her anger. Because her defenses and her anger kept her safe from her strange, complicated feelings where Hudson was concerned, she fought to keep them close. "Let's walk," she said. "I need to find the PIO."

"You're too late, Jasmine," Hudson said, falling into step with her. "He already left, along with most of the cops."

"So what happened?"

"One of the cops said it was like a comedy of errors. Kevin's mom went to the bathroom. Kevin decided he had to go, too. So even though his mom told him to stay put, he got up and went to the bathroom. The men's, of course."

"Of course," Jasmine said. She felt almost giddy now.

Hudson continued, "When his mom came out, he was still in the bathroom, as far as anyone can figure. She went to look in the arcade, right over there." Hudson pointed, and Jasmine saw how easily such a situation could unfold. "So, Mom's in the arcade, and Kevin comes out of the bathroom. He doesn't see his mom, so he decides to go look for her in the bookstore, over there. They just kept missing each other. By the time the cops found Kevin, he was at the fountain, tossing in pennies, wishing for his mom to come back."

Again, Jasmine felt tears threaten. "That's so precious."

Hudson looked like he wanted to laugh, but he didn't. Something else caught his attention. "Oh, look. Even better than the PIO. You can talk to Kevin, himself. He's right there with his mom."

CHAPTER TWELVE

"Cute kid," Hudson said twenty minutes later as they walked out to the parking lot. In yet another surprising move, he'd sat through Jasmine's interview with Kevin Shoemaker and his mom, Katie. Now, he opened the mall door and held it as Jasmine stepped into the cool evening fog.

"He is," Jasmine said. "It's a good thing, too. It'll help soften his poor mom up a bit. I felt so bad for her. He really put her through the ringer this afternoon."

"I admit, I did the same to my mom a few times," Hudson said.

By now, they'd reached her car. She paused at the trunk, about to apologize, yet again. Before she could, he said, "Want to grab some dinner before we go back to the office?"

Jasmine felt a jolt of surprise. *Dinner? As in, a date?*

She hesitated, thought about Parker, and wondered what he'd think of her going out with Hudson.

It was just a casual dinner, though, wasn't it? Co-workers sharing a quick bite to eat before going back to the office? They had a deadline to meet. They had to have fuel.

But what would they talk about, alone together? She was almost certain they didn't have anything in common. Other than work, which he'd made perfectly clear wasn't common ground for them at all. She imagined stilted conversation, awkward beginnings.

Of course, because she'd been too chicken to talk to Parker about the pact and its terms, she wasn't sure whether they were supposed to be exclusive. It's not like a quick dinner with Hudson was really a date, with candles, but still.

"Wow," Hudson said, drawing out the word. "I can see your thoughts spinning around like one of those metal tops. You know, the ones where you push down on the stick and then let go? Jasmine. It's dinnertime. It's also deadline time. I'm proposing a solution. Food."

Inspiration struck. Jasmine could come up with a solution, too. She made an exaggerated show of checking her watch. "Look. I know you're used to working on deadline, but as you know, I'm not. I'm just afraid we won't have time to eat and still make deadline."

"I'll tell you what," Hudson said. "You start driving. I'll call in a pizza order and you pick it up, since, obviously, I can't carry pizza on the bike. Can you fit pizza in that tin can of yours?" She rolled her eyes, and he winked at her, then pulled a couple of bills out of his wallet. "My treat."

"I couldn't, really," Jasmine said. "We'll split it."

"Don't be weird," Hudson said. "Just go pick it up. What do you like?"

When she quirked an eyebrow at him, he added, "I mean, on your pizza."

Hudson waited for Jasmine in the parking lot. The fog glowed orange in the light from the lamps, illuminating Hudson's magazine-ad-worthy silhouette—leather jacket and everything—as he leaned against a lamppost.

What would it be like to lean up against him, right here in this otherworldly mist?

What would it be like to have sex with him?

"Jasmine Carr, you've officially lost your mind. Salivating over a man who doesn't even like you."

At the knock on her window, she jumped. Hudson opened her door and insisted on carrying the pizza. Inside the dark building, she paused—just long enough to picture Hudson taking her in the break room, on the table maybe, or against the vending machine and then to chastise herself—before flicking on the lights. She retrieved paper plates from the cupboard, and he bought a couple of sodas from the vending machine.

"Eat fast," she said. "I've got to get on this story."

He nodded. "Thanks for picking up dinner, by the way. Now tell me, did I see a tear of happiness leaking out of the corner of your eye when you finished interviewing that kid?"

Jasmine hung her head. "You totally did. I don't usually get so emotional about stories. Okay, that's a lie. I'm an emotional person. I was just so relieved, you know? I saw his mom earlier, bawling her eyes out and I really felt for her. So the happy ending made my day."

Her throat tightened again. She took a bite of pizza and shrugged.

"You're going to cry again right now, aren't you?"

"Shut up."

They finished eating, and then cleaned up together before moving into the newsroom. When Jasmine thought about how well they worked as a team, even if it was just setting up and breaking down an impromptu dinner, she pushed the idea out of her mind. This was a one-time deal.

"So where did you go today, anyway?" Hudson asked as they waited for their computers to boot up.

Jasmine, rifling through a stack of mail someone had left on her desk, noticed Hudson's voice didn't contain any animosity. She wasn't sure whether it was a trap, though, so she said, "Where were you?"

"I was there the whole time. If you'd have been paying attention, or, I should say, if you didn't have your nose in your phone the entire time, you would have seen me at the mobile command post when you first showed up. And then you would have seen me following one of the search and rescue teams for an hour. And then you would have seen me scouring the arcade. And then—"

"Fine! I get it, okay? I didn't have my nose in my phone the entire time, by the way."

"Every time I saw you, you did."

"How many times did you see me?" Jasmine spun her chair toward her computer—away from Hudson.

"Several," Hudson said. "Probably more than several."

Jasmine shook her head. "I have a story to write, okay? And then, apparently, I have some financial records to look through. Want to text Mikey and tell him we'll have our stuff done soon? I'm sure he just ran out to get food or something."

"What financial records?" Hudson said.

"Do you ever just answer a question?"

"Yeah, sometimes. See? I just did."

Jasmine groaned and opened her word processor, but Hudson's presence beside her desk distracted her. He had opened the envelope from the Seabreeze Police Department and was leaning on her desk, looking at the spreadsheets.

"These the records you requested?" he said.

"I didn't request them. Liza did, before she left."

Hudson shrugged. "Do you know what you're looking for?"

"Nope," Jasmine said. "But I'm sure I'll figure it out. It's a chart. Columns, rows, all that stuff. I'll look at it after I finish this story."

"Okay," he said. He dropped the papers and walked back to his own desk.

Hudson broke the silence a few minutes later. "I know it's that Earl Little guy," he said. "At least, he's involved. But he can't be working alone. There is no way that guy signs checks."

"Stop talking," Jasmine said. "I'm working."

An hour later, Mikey had come and gone, and even congratulated Jasmine on a job well done. On an actual news story. As much as Jasmine could consider his, "Thanks, Carr," a congratulations. Nevertheless, it was better than a "What the hell were you thinking?" so she basked in it as he walked out the door.

"Ready to look at those reports?" Hudson said when they were alone again.

"Wait. You were packing up your stuff. I thought you were leaving," Jasmine said.

"I'll stick around. I thought you'd want my help going through the records."

"I don't need your help."

"I thought you'd want my company," he said.

"Ha," she said.

He rolled his chair over to her desk, and after she cleared away the stack of mail, they worked together to lay out the spreadsheets from the Seabreeze Police Department. As they both leaned over the desktop, Jasmine couldn't help but inhale the scent of his cologne. She wondered what the description on the cologne bottle would say. Probably something like, "Smell like a manly man who just stepped out of the forest, axe in hand, and who is ready to ravish a woman on a bed of pine needles." Only, that left out the citrus. Good thing she hadn't attempted a career writing product descriptions.

"Earth to Jasmine," Hudson said. "Where did you go?"

She laughed. "The forest."

"Focus," he said, and she became hyperaware of his arm touching hers.

She blinked, hard, and began examining the spreadsheet. Finally, amidst the jumble of numbers, something stood out. "Check out these lawyer fees and miscellaneous expenses," she said. "Don't you think these are exorbitant?"

"So you do know how to read a spreadsheet." After a few moments, Hudson said, "You're right."

"Don't sound so surprised," Jasmine said, and Hudson went on, "Fifteen grand is way too much for miscellaneous expenses. That much should be categorized. Lawyers are expensive, though. Maybe we should request records from some similar-sized departments and see how much they spend on attorneys."

"Oh, good thinking," Jasmine said, and Hudson said, "Don't sound so surprised."

"Well, I think we've found a starting point, anyway," Jasmine said. "All this hard news stuff has me wiped out. I'm going to call it a night."

She stacked the papers into a neat pile and slid them back into the envelope. Then she shut down her computer. She was surprised when she turned around and noticed Hudson still sitting in his chair next to her desk.

"You staying here?" she said.

"I have an idea."

"THAT IS A BEAST OF A MOTORCYCLE. I'm not getting on that thing."

Jasmine's stomach fluttered at the thought of flying through the night, the wind caressing her body, *this* close to danger … and even closer to Hudson's body. She shivered.

"Oh, come on," he said. "Just let me take you for a ride."

Jasmine thought he might be talking about more than just motorcycles. He confirmed her suspicions when he added, one eyebrow raised, "I'm fairly confident you'll enjoy it."

"I'm very safety conscious," she said.

He glanced at her car, which, she had to admit, didn't look very safe or very fun. Then his eyes met hers again.

"So am I," he said. "But I still like to have my fun."

He held up a helmet, and she took it and put it on. Goosebumps raised on her skin when his fingers brushed her chin as he adjusted the strap. He put on his own helmet and climbed onto the bike. She climbed on behind him, and put her hands on his hips.

"You're going to have to hold on tighter than that," he said.

She could have sworn she heard laughter just at the edge of his voice. He started the bike and pulled out of the parking lot. Jasmine blamed her reaction on physics. The acceleration threw her body backwards, and she had no choice but to lean into Hudson and wrap her arms around him. She practically felt him smile as he shifted gears and headed west, toward the ocean.

He turned northward when they hit the coast. The lights from boats moored in the bay twinkled off the water, and the lighthouse illuminated each section of the scene as its light spun in slow circles. Jasmine forced herself to pay attention to the salty smell of the ocean air and the feel of the wind rushing over her face. She tried not to notice the way Hudson's body felt between her legs, or the sensation of her breasts pressed against his back. Because it was late, traffic was minimal, and Hudson drove on without stopping.

Why did she feel such a draw to this man, this incorrigible hotshot who wanted nothing more than to win his shiny awards and move several rungs up the proverbial ladder? Especially when she finally had Parker here, with her, in the same town? It was craziness. Her feelings were absurd. He'd never be interested in her anyway. She was a small-town girl, a country mouse.

They came to Treasure Cove, and the colored lights from the games and rides and little shops cast wavy patterns on the sea. Jasmine wanted to talk to Hudson, to tell him how beautiful everything was, but she knew he wouldn't be able to hear her. So instead of talking, she tightened her grip on him, even as the fleeting image of Parker in front of the Skee-Ball game made its way across her consciousness.

For a moment so brief she thought she imagined it, Hudson seemed to lean back against her when her body melted against his.

They kept driving, winding their way along the coast in the dark, passing only a few cars as the moon arced higher in the sky. Hudson turned around at some point, after a length of time that seemed at once seemed like short seconds and hours long. He drove east, into the redwood forest, and took the small, winding roads back to town. As they approached the office, Jasmine felt a little disappointed. She would have liked to keep riding around, pressed against Hudson, all night long. Which was totally impractical.

When he pulled up next to her car and cut the engine, she scooted back. The front of her body suddenly felt cold, and she shivered.

"I know you're not cold," Hudson said. "Here, hand me your helmet."

He hung the helmets on the handlebars, and then swung a leg over the motorcycle's seat and offered a hand to help Jasmine off.

Jasmine smiled and took his hand. Even when she was standing on solid ground, he didn't let go. He took her other hand, and leaned forward so their foreheads touched.

"See?" he said. "Wasn't that fun?"

She was afraid to make eye contact with him, because she was afraid they'd kiss. And if they kissed, she'd probably explode.

"It was all right," she said.

He chuckled, and the sound put her entire body on alert. Especially her lady parts.

"You liked it," he said. "A lot."

He let go of one of her hands and lifted her chin so their eyes met. He brought his lips to within millimeters of hers and whispered, "We'll have to go farther next time."

CHAPTER THIRTEEN

"So, I've been thinking," Parker said, and Jasmine's ears perked up.

The two of them sat on a picnic bench at the park, eating ice cream cones.

Was he thinking about the pact? Was he about to bring up the thirty-day timeframe they'd originally discussed? Maybe she'd change the subject before he even said it.

"You've been thinking you're finally ready to switch flavors?" She offered him her cone.

Then she almost kicked herself for making a statement she knew was true ... about herself. She was maybe, *possibly* ready to give Hudson Stover a try.

"No," Parker said. He wrapped a hand around hers, though, and tasted the chocolate and peanut butter ice cream. "I've been thinking we should go somewhere overnight. To get away. You're kind of distracted with your new work assignment, and it might do you some good to get out of town for a night."

"Out of town?"

"Yeah," he said. "We could go to Monterey or San Francisco for the night."

Jasmine nodded, but didn't answer. Why was she reluctant? It was a good idea. Or, it should be, anyway. It would give them time to focus solely on one another.

"Well?" Parker said.

"It's a good idea," Jasmine said, "but I don't know if I can leave town right now. With Liza—that's the senior crime reporter—visiting her daughter, I feel like I have to be here in case any big stories break. It's just for a few more weeks."

"What if we do a staycation, stay overnight at a hotel here in Seabreeze?"

"That might work, but still, there's my dog to worry about."

"Can't Sequoia or Holly dog-sit?" Parker said.

Inside, Jasmine cringed. She was making excuse after excuse, and she wasn't sure why. "I suppose," she finally said. "Holly'd probably do it. Forget Sequoia, she hates Ruby."

"Okay, you ask Holly and I'll do some research," Parker said. "Maybe I can find a pet friendly hotel. We can have a romantic evening with Ruby and your cell phone. If a big story comes up, you won't miss it. And we'll still enjoy the feeling that we're on vacation."

"Don't you have that feeling all the time?" Jasmine said.

Parker grabbed her ice cream cone. "Yes," he said. "I sure do."

The next day, Jasmine bribed her sisters into meeting her for a quick lunch at Beach Park. She arrived a few minutes early and laid out the picnic: egg salad sandwiches, watermelon and potato chips.

"You even brought lemonade," Holly said, coming up from behind Jasmine. "You're so on top of it."

Sequoia arrived next, and Holly said, "Why are you wearing jeans and a t-shirt instead of your uniform?"

"Why are you wearing a wig?" Sequoia said. "Just kidding. I changed at the station. I didn't want anyone to see us together while I was in uniform."

Holly sat down on the picnic blanket and picked up a slice of watermelon. Sequoia started with her sandwich. "Geez, it's not like we're criminals," she said.

"Your hair color is criminal," Sequoia said. "Just kidding. You know how it is. I'll bet you twenty bucks we'll see someone I've arrested before we leave here. I don't want them to see me with you and then follow you home and kidnap you."

"Wait," Holly said. "So you're protecting us?"

"Awww," Jasmine said, before Sequoia could answer. "Anyway, I lured you here so I could talk to you. Let's sit."

They did, and Jasmine dived in: "I'm torn. I don't know what to do. As you know, Parker came all the way here to reconnect. Meanwhile, this new photojournalist is smokin' hot and took me for a ride on his motorcycle and almost kissed me but didn't and I don't know what to do."

"So…" Sequoia said. "What are you torn about?"

"I want to date Parker and see what happens, but my body is telling me it wants to sleep with Hudson."

"I repeat," Sequoia said, "what are you torn about?"

"Yeah," Holly said. "Just date Parker and sleep with Hudson."

"I'm scandalized!" Jasmine put a hand to her heart. "I can't sleep with two men at the same time!"

"I didn't say you had to sleep with Parker," Holly said. "Just date him. And sleep with Hudson."

Sequoia finished her sandwich and took a slice of watermelon. Jasmine picked up her sandwich and stared out over the ocean.

"Yeah," Sequoia said. "It's not like you're committing to marrying either one of them."

Jasmine nodded. "Here's the thing, though. Parker wants to do an overnight date. He wants to go to a hotel or something. He says I've been distracted."

"Well, have you?" both of her sisters said.

"Probably. Serious news reporting is all-consuming, especially for a novice like me."

"So go on the overnight date," Sequoia said. Holly said, "Yeah, just give it a try. You haven't committed to the thirty-day thing, yet, right? It's not like you have to stick to the terms of this pact if it doesn't work out. I mean, I understand your reluctance to date Parker again anyway. Remember how angry you were at him?"

Hindsight was supposed to be twenty-twenty, Jasmine thought, but until now, she'd forgotten the boiling, all-consuming anger she'd felt when she found out Parker and his family were moving to Spain. She'd woken up the morning after the revelation and thrown magazines, broken a plate, and possibly kicked a hole in the bathroom wall.

The anger had ebbed and flowed after that, rearing its ugly head at random places and times.

"Remember the outbursts?" Sequoia said, as if she were reading Jasmine's mind. "That one time at the beach when you took that piece of driftwood and beat it against the sand like a cavewoman?"

"You were scary," Holly said.

Jasmine shook her head. "Anyway. Can you babysit Ruby overnight while I'm with Parker?"

"Absolutely not," Sequoia said.

"She didn't mean you," Holly said. "Sure, I'll watch her."

"That's settled," Sequoia said. "Go on the overnight date with Parker. Turn off your phone. And then come back and scratch the itch you've got over this Hudson guy."

Holly nodded. "I second that. Sounds reasonable."

Jasmine opened her mouth to speak, but Holly interrupted her. "Jas, you're overcomplicating this. You've got two great guys on the roster. I mean, just pick one. If it doesn't work out with one, and the other one's gone, well, by golly, there are other fish in this great, wide sea."

"It *is* a vast sea," Sequoia said.

Jasmine wished it were that simple. She felt like she wanted to give Parker a chance. But she didn't want to miss her chance with Hudson. He could, and likely would, move on from her without a qualm, just as he planned to move on from small-town life. Since she'd never slept with anyone other than Parker—which she wouldn't admit to Sequoia and Holly—she didn't have a frame of reference. Sex with Parker was sex with Parker. But what was sex with Hudson?

Sex with Hudson involves being tied up with that scarf.

"Okay," Sequoia said, saving Jasmine from the movie reel playing in her mind. "I have another idea. Sleep with Parker this weekend. If the chemistry's still there, great. Date him. If not, end it. No use wasting your time. Then, you're wide open for Hudson."

"Decisions, decisions," Holly said, her voice singsongy.

CHAPTER FOURTEEN

Parker and his Volkswagen bus picked Jasmine up Saturday morning. Parker carried Jasmine's bag down the walkway, and opened her passenger door for her. Holly, who stood on the front porch holding Ruby, waved at them and hollered to Parker, "Brownie points for romance and chivalry."

Jasmine rolled her eyes and Holly yelled, "Have a great time!"

Parker climbed into the driver's seat and smiled at Jasmine. "You girls haven't changed."

Jasmine knew she'd feel that comment all weekend, like an invisible sticker in her sock.

He pulled the van away from the curb. "You know, we could have stayed overnight in the van. The back seat folds into a bed. We could camp out by the beach, open the windows, and listen to the waves roll in all night long."

"It would have been very romantic," Jasmine said. "We can still do that, you know. We can cancel our hotel reservations."

"No way. I've heard this hotel is incredible. We're doin' it."

Jasmine wondered if he meant, *Doin'* it, doin' it, but she didn't ask. It was a double entendre Holly would jump on and Sequoia would roll her eyes at so Jasmine just let it slip by. Still, the thought of a hotel room, a bed in a hotel room, and making use of that bed, made her inexplicably nervous.

The Bayside Hotel stood along the cliffs, overlooking the ocean. Its bright white exterior contrasted the blue of the sky, and deep green vines with brilliant red flowers framed the windows. Inside, tile floors and a huge fountain featuring a mermaid playing the flute made Jasmine feel like she was in the Mediterranean rather than her hometown.

"I love it," she said when they'd pulled up in front of registration. Parker kissed her on the temple, and then went to the desk check in.

She stood by the fountain and noticed countless shiny pennies in the water. She decided it must be a successful wishing fountain since its entire floor was covered in copper. Parker came up behind her just as she was about to toss in her own penny.

"What are you wishing for?"

"I can't tell you, and you know it."

Jasmine wasn't sure she knew, herself. She could wish for a fun overnight date with Parker. She could wish for some sign that she should choose Parker over Hudson, or vice versa. She could wish for a dark and handsome stranger to ride in at this very moment, sweep her off her feet and take her to the real Mediterranean, snuffing out the Parker-Hudson Debate for good. She closed her eyes. Parker put his arm around her waist.

She made her wish, and immediately began hoping it would come true, and hoping it wouldn't.

Some genius had designed the hotel room for romance. The windows faced the water, of course, and Parker opened them immediately to let in the salty ocean air. The giant, deep bathtub sat directly beneath them so someone taking a bath could see both the sky and the sea at the same time.

Against the opposite wall, the four poster bed sat under a domed skylight. A tiny table and a pair of chairs stood in the corner, and on the table, someone had placed a tray that held champagne and chocolate covered strawberries.

"I told them it was our anniversary," Parker said. "I mean, it kind of is, right?"

Jasmine laughed, but didn't answer. She walked over to the windows and stood, looking at all the anchored boats bobbing close to shore. She could hear seagulls calling, and the air from the open windows felt balmy on her face.

"I could stand here all day," she said.

Parker came up behind her and put his arms around her waist. "It's a beautiful view. Even more so because you're here to look at it with me."

He turned her around and brought his lips close to hers. Before kissing her, he said, "What do you say we christen that enormous bed?"

"I like the sound of that," she said, although, at the suggestion, she felt a whole school of slippery fish flapping their tails in her stomach.

Now their lips came together, and Parker framed Jasmine's face with his hands. Where she'd expected an explosion, there was that sweet, gentle heat. Where she'd expected desire to knock her off her feet and onto her back, there was a quiet longing.

Still kissing her, Parker began unbuttoning the back of Jasmine's blouse, and she felt ultra-aware of every inch of skin his fingers skimmed. He pulled the shirt over her head and tossed it onto the foot of the bed, and then ran his fingertips up and down her arms once. He held her hands in his and backed up towards the bed. Jasmine pulled his shirt off and set it on top of her own.

Parker led Jasmine around the side of the bed and sat down on its edge, pulling her toward him so she stood between his legs. Jasmine deepened the kiss and Parker unhooked her bra and tossed it aside. His mouth moved to her neck and then her collarbone, and then his lips locked onto her breast. It brought her body, which until then had been thrumming with that low simmer, to a full boil.

She groaned, and she felt Parker's mouth smile against her skin. "Yeah, I still got it," he said.

Now she giggled, and he clamped down gently with his teeth. She brought her head down to inhale the scent of his hair, and so many memories came rushing into her mind. Parker that first day they'd met, standing there looking angry in the rain, but then taking so much care with his brother's science fair project as he loaded it into the car. The two of them purposely confusing the cashier at the drive-through ice cream shop, changing their orders repeatedly, laughing like maniacs as the poor girl tried to get them straight. ("No, not peanuts! I wanted sprinkles. No, not strawberry sauce. Chocolate, please.") Parker, head down at his family's dining room table, when his dad broke the news about them moving to Spain. Jasmine, lying in bed for days after they left, her pillow soaked and her face swollen.

"Hey," Parker said then, interrupting the flood of memories. "Where'd you go?"

He was looking up at her, his expression serious.

"Whoa. Just having some serious flashbacks," she said.

"It doesn't look like they were all that heartwarming," he said.

Jasmine sighed. "Most of them were."

Parker turned his head to one side and rested it on Jasmine's chest. She rested her cheek on the top of his head, and they stayed that way for a few moments before he pulled himself up to sitting again and then patted the bed next to him. She sat down and, suddenly feeling exposed, grabbed a pillow to cover herself. Parker put an arm around her shoulders.

"You know, we've been apart for a long time," he said. "And several times throughout the years, I've thought that I never really apologized for the way things ended. I know I said I was sorry then, but that was in the heat of the moment. I'm really sorry I kept the move from you for so long. I should have told you as soon as I knew."

Jasmine nodded, unable to form a coherent response. A jumble of thoughts raced in: it was so selfish of him not to tell me, my heart was broken. Not just broken, but shattered, smashed, pulverized. My life was ruined. I've never been able to have a real relationship since then.

The anger that had overcome her when he'd left came back with a vengeance and she hugged the pillow tighter.

"I fell apart when you left," she said. He nodded, and she added, "Actually, 'fell apart' is the understatement of the year. I was only a kid, but I felt like it ruined my life. Nothing was the same. We didn't ride to school together, we didn't do our homework together, we didn't go for tea and coffee on Friday mornings. I was alone. And lonely. Every part of my life was missing something."

Jasmine mentally kicked herself for being near tears now, more than ten years after the fact. "This is stupid. I'm sorry. I can't believe I'm letting it get to me like this."

Parker went to put an arm around her, but seemed to think better of it and settled for a hand on her knee.

"I understand," he said. "I do. It was like that for me, too, but I coped by living on the edge. Walking the wild side. You know? But I was hurting."

She nodded and he went on, "Look. Maybe we're rushing things. Why don't we go for a nice lunch on the wharf?" He stood up, kissed her on the top of the head, and grabbed his shirt. "I'll give you some privacy."

He went into the bathroom and shut the door behind him.

Jasmine set the pillow on the bed, retrieved her bra and shirt and put them on, then walked over to the mirror.

"I look like a wreck," she said to her reflection. She wiped the smudged mascara from under her eyes and smoothed her hair. "And I feel like one, too."

They snagged an outdoor table at Mario's on the Wharf. The ocean rolled underneath the pier, washing over the sand and sending up sprays of water. Seals barked from the aptly named Seal Rock, and kids tossed little fish over the railing at them. Couples strolled along, hand in hand, and people came out of the nearby ice cream shop licking cones and scooping sundaes.

A magician stood outside the magic shop, performing card tricks while people clapped.

Everything seemed so festive, and Jasmine felt dismal. After a nearly silent walk from the hotel to the restaurant, Parker got their table and ordered fish and chips. The server brought them the fried pickles they'd chosen as an appetizer.

"I'm sorry," Jasmine said when the server walked away. "I

shouldn't have agreed to this just yet. I didn't realize how strong my feelings still are."

"I understand," Parker said. He dipped a pickle in the creamy garlic dipping sauce and chewed as he spoke. "I wish it wasn't this way, but I get it. Let's not rush this, okay? Let's enjoy our weekend date. You're getting away from work, I'm enjoying your company, and we can both be content with that, right?"

Jasmine went through the motions during lunch. She ate her fish and chips, drank her iced tea, ordered a chocolate-dipped, frozen banana from the ice cream shop and ate it slowly, like the decadent treat it was.

She stood at the railing and watched the seals flap their flippers and slide off the rock into the waves. She smiled. When a little boy exited the magic shop and produced a rainbow-colored scarf from a top hat, Jasmine clapped. It was all mechanical, robotic, forced.

He had hurt her so badly, and he had just moved on. He left her in Seabreeze and partied his little heart out while she binged on brownies and took Cosmo quizzes with her sisters: *Will You Be A Spinster?* (The answer: most likely) or *How Old Will You Be When You Get Married?* (At least sixty).

They'd both been so young. It was only fair to forgive him, to move forward from here.

Back in the hotel room, Parker flopped down on the huge, cushy bed and patted the empty spot next to him.

"Let's talk," he said.

"Can't we nap?" she said, and he laughed, even though she was only half-joking.

"So, I know you remember talking about reconnecting when you turned thirty."

Jasmine was at the foot of the bed, taking off her shoes. She froze, her right foot bare and her left foot halfway out of the ballet flat she'd put so much thought into.

"Yes," she said. "I do remember that."

Parker nodded and pressed his lips together. He's nervous, she thought.

He cleared his throat. "Do you remember all the other terms of our little pact?"

Jasmine slid her left foot the rest of the way out of its shoe and climbed onto the bed. She sat on her knees facing him. "I remember some of them, I think," she said, even though it was a lie. She had the entire conversation memorized, as she'd played it and replayed it in her mind millions of times the first year after he'd left Seabreeze.

"So you remember how we said we'd give it thirty days." A statement, not a question.

She nodded. "I do remember that."

"Do you think we should try it?"

Breathing required conscious effort. Should they?

Before she could answer, Parker spoke again. "I mean, it would give us the chance to get to know each other again, without rushing, you know?"

Jasmine nodded. "Yeah, it would…"

"But?"

"Let me think about it."

CHAPTER FIFTEEN

Sunday morning, Jasmine walked through her front door and dropped her bag on the floor. Ruby ran up to greet her, squirming and licking and wagging her short little tail.

"So? How was it? Dish, sister!" Holly came out of the kitchen, a coffee mug in one hand and a muffin (no doubt a zucchini bran or something, Jasmine thought) in the other.

Jasmine felt her body slump. The past twenty-four hours had left her emotionally exhausted, especially since she hadn't slept at all. "It was okay."

"'Okay'? You look terrible. I know you want some coffee. Come on in."

"You know I don't drink coffee. Well, there was the one time. But it had whiskey in it."

"I think I can take care of that."

When they were settled on the couch, steaming whiskey-laced coffee in hand and Ruby on Jasmine's lap, Holly said, "All right. Spill it."

"Do you remember how I felt when Parker left?"

Holly cringed. "I remember how I felt. I'm not sure if it was empathetic or what, but remember the day we sat on your bed and ate ice cream with honey and cinnamon, all day long?"

"Oh, do I. I also remember the stomach ache I got afterward."

"Remember how we slept together for the first five or six nights, and we both cried ourselves to sleep?"

Jasmine gasped. "I knew *I* cried myself to sleep! But I had no idea you'd cried yourself to sleep, too!"

"I tried to suffer in silence. I didn't want to make things worse for you."

"Well, things were as bad as they could get, in my opinion," Jasmine said. "You couldn't possibly have made it any worse."

"Anyway," Holly said. She made a "go on" motion with one hand. "The details, please."

"Anyway," Jasmine said. "We were getting, you know, hot and heavy in the hotel room."

"Ooh," Holly said. Jasmine waved her off. "It was nice, at first. But then all of a sudden, I got a whiff of his shampoo—I swear it's the same stuff he used back then—and all these memories just hit me, you know? I was right back there with Parker, so in love with him, and so hurt by him. I was all alone again. I was broken. And then, out of nowhere, I was angry. I was so pissed, Holly. I mean, how could he leave me like that? And without even giving me a warning? You know this already, but his dad spilled the beans. He wasn't even going to tell me."

Holly reached across the couch cushion between them and took Jasmine's hand. "That definitely ruined that hot and steamy romance, didn't it?"

Jasmine giggled. Then, she couldn't help it, and the giggle turned into a laugh. She couldn't stop. She laughed until the laughter turned into wailing. Ruby looked from Jasmine to Holly, and back to Jasmine. She licked Jasmine's face. "It did." Her voice came out high and squealy and Holly broke into laughter, too. "Totally ruined the romance."

When they finally stopped howling, Holly said, "But you still spent the night with him. Did you guys consummate the renewed relationship?"

Jasmine shook her head. "No. We barely touched again after the shampoo-induced flashbacks. We had lunch, and then we went for a walk. It was a beautiful day. We slept in the bed together, but we didn't even touch. My weird emotional state cast a shadow over everything."

"Have you ever heard of forgiveness?"

"I forgive him."

When Holly raised her eyebrows at Jasmine, she said, "No, really. I do. But I just don't think I ever resolved those feelings, way back then. You know?"

"I get it," Holly said. After a beat, she asked, "So what do you do now? Where do you go from here?"

"I guess we just move more slowly," Jasmine said, "and we do so under the terms of our teenage pact."

Holly left an hour later, with a promise to call and check in on Jasmine that evening.

That afternoon, as images of Parker and images from her favorite home-makeover reality TV show warred for space in Jasmine's mind, her phone cut in, alerting her to a text message. She heard it ding from the kitchen counter but decided to ignore it.

"I can't get up now," she said to Ruby. "I want to see which carpet the homeowners use in this house. Whoever it is can wait."

Ruby obviously agreed; she adjusted her position on her special cushion and closed her eyes. Within moments, Jasmine had forgotten about the text and the homeowners on the show were choosing cabinets and fixtures.

When she finally got up to refill her water glass and her bowl of popcorn, the blinking light on her phone nagged her. She picked it up. The text was from Hudson: *Did you even bother looking at the paper this morning?*

She huffed out a loud, exasperated sigh.

I was on staycation, she typed back. She left out the part about stepping over the newspaper as she arrived at home after spending the night with Parker.

He responded immediately: *Don't they deliver the newspaper to Seabreeze? Oh, yeah. It's PRINTED in Seabreeze.*

She wrote back: *Unlike some people, I can step away from work for 48 hours. Also, did you hatch that phone? You sure responded quick.*

He didn't answer this time, and she went into the driveway to look for the paper. Ruby followed her and sniffed at the several days' worth of rolled-up newspapers like they were an alien life forms. Jasmine identified that day's paper—it looked the least weather-worn. She picked it up and began pulling the rubber band off. Then she stopped.

"Wait a second," she said out loud. "I'm not a puppet. I'm not going to jump just because Hudson says to jump."

She let the rubber band snap onto her wrist, then walked inside and flung the newspaper onto the kitchen counter, where it lay open.

Then she saw the photo on the front page. She'd recognize that beaky mug anywhere. It was Earl Little, the public information officer for Seabreeze Police Department. Curiosity got the best of her. She didn't have to tell Hudson she was looking. She unfolded the newspaper, smoothing it onto the counter.

She'd never seen a headline so big: *Seabreeze Police Department PIO Found Dead.*

Earl Little was dead? *Dead?*

The photo was one Hudson had taken at the last press conference. Earl Little looked directly at the camera, no doubt because Hudson was sitting right next to Jasmine and Earl had been glaring at her the entire time. There was no story to accompany the photo, just a simple cutline. She figured Hudson had written it, and wondered if he felt like the twenty-four pack of beer he'd bought his cutline-writing friend was worth it.

Following an anonymous tip, police from the Seabreeze Police Department found Earl Little dead in his apartment Saturday evening. They're asking for the public's help in solving this case.

Why hadn't anyone called her? She was supposed to be covering this sort of thing. She could have written a real story. Jasmine walked back to the couch and snatched up her phone to text Hudson back. *Earl Little is DEAD? Why didn't you call me?*

Her phone beeped right away, and she smiled at Hudson's

response: *I hate myself for responding right away after your snarky comment, but I see you've played into my hands, my little puppet, and read the newspaper as I intended. Yes, he's dead. I saw his body, myself.*

She wrote: *Do you think someone killed him?*

Most definitely, Hudson wrote. *No doubt it's the same people who are stealing money from the PD. Did you ever get those reports back? The ones on attorney fees?*

She wrote, *I got them Friday afternoon but didn't have a chance to look at them.*

Want to go in now?

"I can't believe I let you drag me here on a Sunday afternoon."

Jasmine and Hudson sat in the *Daily Trumpet's* conference room, reports from four nearby police departments spread across the massive table. Each of them used a highlighter to highlight line items related to legal fees.

"How was your weekend?" Hudson said as he skimmed a page, running his finger down a column. "Romantic?"

"How did you even know it was supposed to be romantic?" Jasmine stood up and glared at him. Then she realized she'd confirmed his suspicions. She kicked herself, mentally. When he kept skimming without making eye contact, she went back to work on her report.

"Just this weird sixth sense I have," Hudson said, tapping his temple.

"It was okay," she said.

"Was it that long-haired guy?"

"Why are you asking me this?"

"Just curious," he said. "Because we're partners and all that."

"Huh." Jasmine took extra care highlighting another item.

"Must have been really great," he said. "You're so chatty. Borderline effusive."

Jasmine straightened up. "Look, Hudson. I—"

"I like it when you say my name like that. So angry."

"Oh, my God. Parker and I—"

"That's his name? The longhaired guy? Parker?"

Jasmine rolled her eyes. "Yes. His name is Parker."

Hudson scoffed. Jasmine continued, "Parker and I used to date. In high school. We just reconnected."

She debated telling him about the pact, but decided against it. It was juvenile anyway.

"And?"

"And nothing. We just reconnected. End of story."

"*Is* it the end of the story?" Hudson said. Elbows on the table, he looked up to make eye contact with her. "Because you don't look all, what did Mikey say? All twitterpated. You don't look all twitterpated today. You look like a woman who most definitely did not get her itch scratched last night. If you know what I mean. I can practically see the tension. I mean, I can taste it."

Her first thought was that Hudson was exceptionally perceptive. Her second thought was that she wouldn't mind letting him scratch her itch, right now, right here on this huge table. Her third thought was that he was staring at her like he could read her first two thoughts. So she went back to highlighting.

"This is a big table," Hudson said.

Forty-five minutes passed, during which Hudson and Jasmine highlighted, read and highlighted some more, all in silence.

"So the results are in," Hudson said after punching a long list of numbers into his calculator. "The Seabreeze PD spends significantly more on legal fees than any of these other police departments. But the question is, why?"

"Are Seabreeze's demographics different?" Jasmine said. She gathered up the spreadsheets and carried them to her desk, still talking. "You know, does something about our population make people more likely to sue or less likely to settle in court? Is our tax rate similar to the tax rate in these other areas? Are these so-called 'legal fees' actually going somewhere else? Like on vacation?"

"Wow," Hudson said. He'd followed her into the newsroom. "Now you're thinking like a real reporter."

She swatted his arm, and simultaneously enjoyed the feelings of pride his comments had created.

"Seriously, though. Those are good questions," he said, sitting down at his own desk. "Now you have a starting point for tomorrow. You know you're going to have to do a follow-up on that Earl Little story, too. Since you were out getting romanced—or, *not* getting romanced—when he was getting offed."

"Nice cutline, by the way," she said. She shivered at the idea of poor Earl Little getting offed while she was semi-enjoying a weekend at a fancy hotel. Not that she'd liked the guy, but still. Did it happen quickly? Did he put his hands up to protect himself?

"Thanks," he said.

She began to tidy her desk, and Hudson stood up, sauntered over, and put an elbow on her chair. "So? Was it romantic?"

"What?" Jasmine said.

"Was your overnight date thingy romantic?" He straightened up and crossed his arms, and he was staring right at her now, his deep green eyes piercing.

"How do you even know I was on an overnight date thingy?"

For a second, Hudson looked guilty. His gaze flicked to one side, and then back to meet hers again. He shifted his weight from one leg to the other. "I just knew."

"My reporter senses, as mediocre as they are, are perking up right now. How did you know?"

"I, uh—I kind of ran into one of your sisters."

"You're stalking me. Which sister? No, wait. Don't tell me. Sequoia. You ran into her at the police station. Actually, no, she's too smart, and borderline paranoid. She wouldn't tell you where I was."

As the thoughts started to form, the story fell into place. "Holly. That scoundrel. She probably told you the whole thing, didn't she?"

"What whole thing?" Hudson said.

Uh oh. Maybe she hadn't told him the whole thing.

"You called the house, and she answered, and you thought she was me, and she, assuming you and I are actually friends, told you way more than she should have."

"You're close," Hudson said. "I called your house, she answered. I—"

"Wait. You did call my house on Saturday? Were you calling about Earl Little?"

"When Holly answered, I knew right away it wasn't you, and she told me in an offhand way that you were on a date. Wouldn't be back 'til the next day. I put one and three together and got four."

"Great."

"Was that the whole thing?" Hudson said. Now he looked like a predator, his body completely still and his eyes watching her every move.

"What whole thing?" Jasmine said, infusing her voice with innocence.

"You said Holly probably told me the whole thing. What were you talking about?"

"Why were you calling me, anyway?" Jasmine said. "You didn't need me for the Earl Little thing. I'm sure you didn't want to work on these spreadsheets. It was a weekend, and even Hudson Stover, Photojournalist Extraordinaire, has to take a day or two off every now and then. So why were you calling?" Jasmine had heard Liza on the phone—she knew how to get a source to crack.

"It was the spreadsheets." He said it like he was grasping at the end of a thread and finally managed to capture it between his fingers. And if Jasmine wasn't mistaken, his cheeks were looking a little rosy. "Friday evening, when I saw the envelope on your desk, I was so busy I didn't think about it," he said.

"Really?" Jasmine said.

"Yeah."

"Huh."

"What is that supposed to mean?" Hudson said.

"I don't believe you, that's all. You've been really into this case ever since it started. I think if you saw the envelope on Friday you would have called me from right here in the newsroom. While opening it, yourself. Or texted me. Goodness knows you're a bit heavy-handed with the texting."

Hudson shrugged. "Maybe. Or maybe I forgot."

"Doubt that's the case," Jasmine said.

He didn't answer, but he didn't turn to walk away.

"So why'd you call my house?" Jasmine said. "On Saturday."

"Oh, that."

"Yeah. That."

Hudson looked down. Jasmine found his embarrassment endearing, but didn't want to let him off the hook.

"I called to see if you wanted to go to dinner."

"Wait. You called to ask me out? Like, not professionally?"

CHAPTER SIXTEEN

"I KNEW IT!" HOLLY'S VOICE SOUNDED TRIUMPHANT, AND JASMINE pictured her sister, one hand in the air, her finger pointing at the ceiling.

It was Monday morning and Jasmine had called an emergency meeting of The Garden Club via conference call. Jasmine was in the newsroom, wearing headphones plugged into the phone. Sequoia was sitting on the side of the road somewhere, patrolling for speeding drivers. And Holly was home, sitting in front of her computer, taking a study break from the online portion of her personal trainer certification course.

"I knew he was calling to ask you out!" Holly said. "He tried to act all smooth, like he didn't really care that you were out on the town with someone else. But I could tell he was peeved."

"You're having way too much fun with this," Sequoia said. "I mean, this Hudson guy is clearly smitten with our sister. How could you take his feelings so lightly?"

"Funny," Jasmine said. "And he's not smitten. In fact, although I think he stopped despising me, he still considers me a fluff reporter who doesn't take the news seriously, and it drives him crazy. He's planning to move on to bigger things, anyway. He'll never stay in

Seabreeze. If anything, we have chemistry. That's it. It's nothing personal."

"Oh, I think it's something personal," Holly and Sequoia said at the same time.

"Anyway," Sequoia said. "Look, why did you want to talk to us, Jas? What was so important that you actually called an emergency meeting?"

Jasmine let out a big breath and tried to find some way to expel her nervous energy. She tapped her fingers on the surface of her desk, and when that didn't work, she bounced her leg. "I don't even know. I just wanted to tell you that Hudson was planning to ask me out. He didn't want to admit it. But I got him to crack. I don't know how I feel about that."

"Oh, I do," Holly said.

Of course, Hudson chose that moment to walk through the door of the newsroom. He didn't even spare Jasmine a glance, but she could tell he took note of her presence.

"He's here," she hissed into the mouthpiece of her headset.

"Go jump him," Holly said. "He obviously wants to."

"He didn't even look this way," Jasmine said. "He's going to avoid me all day. I know it."

"Wait. So what happened after he admitted he wanted to ask you out?"

"Sequoia," Jasmine said, her voice a harsh whisper. "I can't tell you that right now."

Holly giggled, and Jasmine found herself smiling widely. She covered her mouth with one hand so Hudson wouldn't see her grin.

"Look," Sequoia said. "I've got to get back to work, but I expect you'll fill me in soon."

"Ditto," Holly said. "You owe us this info, sis."

They hung up, and Jasmine turned on her computer.

She thought back to the night before, when she'd asked Hudson if he called her house to ask her out, not professionally. Hudson stared right into Jasmine's eyes and she thought, *That's what they mean when they say, "smoldering gaze."* Then, reason piped up: *That's totally lame of me to think.*

"Totally not professionally," he said.

Her eyebrows had shot up. She guessed he felt stupid, or on the spot, or some combination of the two, because he looked at the floor after that.

"Well, that's unexpected," Jasmine said. "I don't know what to say."

"If you don't know what to say, then it's obvious you already have an answer."

"But you never actually asked me out."

His eyes met her again, and he grinned. "Touché."

Then he walked away.

Now what? Jasmine wondered whether Hudson would get around to actually asking her out. Or had that ship sailed?

She sneaked a peek at him out of the corner of her eye. He was definitely handsome. Mouthwatering. What would it be like to step into his arms, to feel his lips against hers, to feel his bare skin warming under her hands?

As if he sensed her thoughts, Hudson looked over at her. When they made eye contact, he smiled.

That smile said so many things. It said he could tell what she was thinking. It said he wanted her to step into his arms. He wanted to feel her lips against his and her skin warming under his hands. It said her panties were about to incinerate.

Or did it just say he thought her whispering was juvenile?

"Shit," Jasmine whispered.

She stood up quickly, causing her chair to roll back into the center of the newsroom. "I'm taking a smoke break."

As she pushed open the door to the patio, she heard Hudson laugh. "You don't even smoke," he called.

It was true. She didn't even smoke. Instead, she sat down on the patio bench and wished she did.

"I can't believe this is happening," she said to herself.

Of course, the door opened a few seconds later, and Hudson Stover emerged.

He sat down next to Jasmine, and she got up to pace.

"Have you made any calls yet this morning?" he asked.

She had her back to him when she answered: "You just saw me on the phone."

"Sounded like a personal call to me."

"Are you eavesdropping?" she said.

"For sure," he said.

She spun around to face him, and put her fists on her hips. She was going for menacing, but he just laughed.

"Anger really brings out the color of your eyes," he said. "Reminds me of liquid kryptonite."

He took a pack of cigarettes out of his shirt pocket and offered her one.

"I'm going to make those calls," she said.

She went to stalk past him to the door into the newsroom, but before she could get her fingers on the keypad, he grabbed her wrist. Her entire body went on alert.

"Jasmine. Just settle down. I want to ask you something."

She arched an eyebrow. Was he going to ask her out? What would she wear? The accessory-obsessed Holly would insist on a scarf, but what would Hudson think of that over spring rolls? Her stomach fluttered at the thought.

Then she remembered he was still holding her wrist, and she shivered.

"Are you going to sit down?" he said.

She thought, *Get control of your mind, woman. It's a runaway train.*

She said, "Sure."

Once she settled next to him on the bench—so close she could smell his skin—she said, "What's up?"

Before he spoke, she noticed how thick his eyelashes were. She also noticed that he didn't light his cigarette.

"Are you going to follow through on the terms of your little pact with that long-haired Parker clod?"

Quickly, she averted her eyes. She looked at his hands, instead. Her runaway mind took off on its own track again: How did he know about the pact? Holly. She must have told him when he called the house. He acted like he didn't know what Jasmine meant when she asked if Holly told him, "the whole thing," but obviously he did know. Why didn't he say so, then? Why was he asking her about it now?

She couldn't really focus, though, because she was admiring Hudson's clean, square fingernails.

"Wow, I didn't think it was that hard of a question," Hudson said. "Your mouth is opening and closing like you're a goldfish."

Jasmine snapped her mouth shut and looked him in the eyes again.

"So?" he said. "Are you?"

"Is it really any of your business?"

"Why are you answering my question with a question?"

"Well, that's easy," she said. "It's because I don't want to answer it with an answer."

This time it was Jasmine who walked away, leaving Hudson staring after her.

THREE DAYS HAD PASSED since the surfacing of The Parker Problem (which is what Jasmine was now calling the overnight date gone wrong), and while Jasmine was tempted to obsess over The Parker-Hudson Debate (which is what she was now calling the strange tug-of-war she experienced whenever she thought about the two of them), the workweek served as a potent distraction.

On Monday, Jasmine put together what Mikey Stockman referred to as her "first-ever kick-ass news story," comparing Seabreeze Police Department's legal fee expenditures with those of other, similarly-sized police departments, and, of course, highlighting the discrepancy.

She couldn't get a comment from Seabreeze Police Department's people on Monday, since their primary public information officer was dead and everybody seemed preoccupied with that, but she received a call on Tuesday from a very prickly man saying he was taking over as public information officer and would like to meet with her.

Elijah Sawyer arrived at the office wearing the non-uniform

uniform of plainclothes policemen: khaki pants, a polo shirt and a badge and gun. Jasmine noticed right away that he was almost startlingly handsome. He belonged in a catalog for men's clothes. Or men's lingerie. He probably had a six-pack.

But his eyes glittered with distaste as she walked through the lobby to shake his hand.

"Jasmine Carr," she said. "You must be Elijah Sawyer."

He gripped her hand, a little harder than necessary, she thought, and scowled. "I would say I'm pleased to meet you, but that's not the case."

Even though Jasmine felt intimidated—beyond intimidated, actually—she also felt a strong urge to laugh. Probably nerves.

She used the defense mechanism she'd developed throughout childhood and feigned confidence. "Wow. Quite a greeting. I can tell we're going to get along famously. Let's talk in the conference room."

She made a conscious effort to tune into the sound of her heels clicking on the tile floor. It made her feel more grown-up, more serious, more important. When she and Holly were little, they'd wear their mother's high heels all over the house, pretending to be "professional ladies." If she wasn't home, they'd sneak her jewelry until their dad caught them (or until Sequoia tattled on them) and made them put it away.

Once they were all decked out in heels, pearl necklaces, and jangling bracelets, they'd walk straight to the dining room, where they'd start their procession and parade through the kitchen, clicking and clacking and saying things like, "Oh, dahling, could you get me some tea?" and "Oh, I couldn't possibly drink tea, could you get me some coffee?"

Being the oldest, Sequoia had no desire to be more grown up than she already was. Instead, she'd sit at the kitchen counter, looking down her perfect nose at them, correcting their posture or telling them how to adjust their jewelry.

Suddenly, a realization struck Jasmine, and she stopped several feet short of the conference room and whirled around. Elijah Sawyer managed not to bump right into her, but it was a close call.

"You know," Jasmine said, "you remind me of my big sister. Sequoia. I think you two would really hit it off. In fact, you've probably met her. Sequoia Carr? She works for Seabreeze PD, too."

He tried to hide it, but Jasmine didn't miss the flash of a grin that appeared before he pulled on his poker face.

"Sequoia Carr?" he said. "I've met her." There was something final in his tone, and Jasmine didn't miss it.

"I'll just bet you have," Jasmine said. "And I have a feeling she'd give you a run for your money. Anyway. Just in here."

She nodded at the conference room's open door and followed him in. As she turned around to shut the door, she made a mental note to ask Sequoia about Elijah Sawyer, and to do so in person so she could gauge her sister's reaction. First, though, she had business to take care of.

"So," Jasmine said.

She remembered from something she'd read (probably in some teenager magazine years ago) that you should never start a conversation with anything like, "so," or, "okay." She shrugged it off. Elijah stared at her, waiting.

"Earl Little," she said.

Elijah nodded as if he'd known she was going to ask about Earl Little. Of course he'd known, Jasmine thought. Earl Little's death was the obvious story, wasn't it? He didn't know what she had in her little bag of tricks, though. Elijah opened the briefcase he'd set on the table and pulled out a thin stack of papers.

"I've prepared a statement," he said. He set the papers on the desk in front of him, but didn't move. He just sat there, staring at the first page.

"So … are you going to read it to me?" Jasmine said.

"Can't you read it, yourself?"

"You're still guarding the papers."

He slid them across the desk to her. She skimmed the text. "Just what I expected," she said. Someone had typed up all the usual blither about Earl Little: how long he'd been on the force, which positions he'd held and how he'd be, "greatly missed."

"Look, Elijah. This is great. But you can't really believe you could show up here and get away without talking about the real news." He looked surprised, and Jasmine went on. "As you've probably heard by now, your department is missing some money. My colleague and I pulled up some financial reports from the PD, and it seems that someone has allocated a bunch of that money into categories related to legal fees. Does this seem at all fishy to you?"

"Fishy? You want me to base my answer on whether something seems 'fishy'?" He made finger quotes on the word, "fishy," and Jasmine shrugged. He was like her sister, and she knew how to play this game.

"Don't mince words, Elijah," she said. "You know what I'm getting at as well as I do."

"Well, obviously, someone has allocated that money to legal fees. So we must have had legal fees," he said. "I'm not really qualified to talk about that. I don't allocate funds."

For the briefest of moments, he stumped her. Jasmine wasn't sure how to proceed. An unexpected vision of Hudson made an unwelcome appearance. He'd know what to do, what to ask, what to say to get Elijah to open up. But he wasn't here. Jasmine was on her own.

What Elijah said was probably true. Poor guy was coming in cold. He'd likely never had anything to do with funds, much less allocating them. Jasmine wondered what he'd done to earn the dubious distinction of public information officer.

"Well, I recommend you get qualified," she said.

Elijah Sawyer did the last thing Jasmine would have expected him to do: he laughed. And then he said, "I guess I'd better."

"So be straight with me," Jasmine said. "Doesn't everybody at the PD know somebody's stealing money?"

Elijah sighed. "I can't tell you that."

"Your answer just confirmed it."

"What?" he said.

"Wow, you really aren't good at this, are you? You're getting whomped by a total newbie reporter."

"Whomped? Really?" he said.

"Well, when you put it that way. Not whomped. But you know. You would have said, 'No, nobody thinks somebody's stealing money.' But you said, 'I can't tell you that.' Which confirms that you think someone is stealing money."

She felt a tiny bit victorious and tried to tone it down by avoiding eye contact. She looked out the window. Hudson was climbing onto his motorcycle. She could have sworn he looked right at her before he put on his helmet and the motorcycle roared to life. Hudson drove away, and Jasmine turned back to Elijah. His hands were on the desk in front of him, palms down, and he tapped his thumbs on the wood surface.

"Look," he said, and Jasmine smiled. Sequoia always said, "Look."

Elijah cocked his head to one side, and she said, "Never mind. Carry on."

"I don't know why you are so convinced someone is stealing money. But I'm on Seabreeze PD's payroll, and I'd like to stay there. So I'm not going to comment on your little conspiracy theory."

Put in her place, Jasmine felt her ears turning red. Then Elijah continued: "But if you find some kind of proof, I'll be happy to look into it. Okay?"

Jasmine nodded.

"Now," Elijah said. "Do you want to look over the notes I typed up about Earl Little, or do you think you have what you need?"

Ten minutes later, Jasmine was at her desk, trying to come up with a lead paragraph.

Earl Little had lots of enemies, but one enemy finally took the lead and took action.

"God, that's horrible. Why do I even try?"

Jasmine flopped back in her chair, letting her arms and legs dangle. She was tempted to procrastinate. She could easily justify getting herself a soda and a snack from the vending machine. Or taking a smoke break even though she didn't smoke.

The one thought that stopped her from doing either of those things was that if Hudson saw her, he'd know exactly what she was doing. She had no idea why she fostered this strange need to prove to him that she wasn't an air-headed loser. Then she had an epiphany: she didn't have anything to prove to Hudson. She had something to prove to herself. Which was that she didn't have anything to prove to Hudson Stover.

With that thought bolstering her, she selected a chocolate bar and a diet cola from the vending machine and walked outside to enjoy them.

The chocolate tasted so good, and the soda felt so sweet and bubbly on Jasmine's tongue. She sat on the patio, the sunlight slicing through the slatted roof in bright blades. And so what if her stomach jumped a little when she heard Hudson's motorcycle come rumbling into the parking lot?

He cut the engine and Jasmine watched him swing a long leg over the seat before he opened one of the saddle bags and took out a white paper bag with the Seaside Deli logo printed on it.

What did a sandwich order say about a man? That was probably a quiz in one of those magazines. Chicken said he was cautious. Turkey and avocado said he liked variety. And roast beef? *Well, we all know what that says.* Jasmine chuckled to herself as Hudson walked toward the patio. Either he didn't notice her, or he was pretending he didn't notice her, but he avoided eye contact as he approached.

He confirmed that he was pretending not to notice her when he sat down on the bench next to hers, just a few feet from where she sat, and didn't acknowledge her presence.

"Hi there," Jasmine said.

Hudson grunted a greeting as he unwrapped his sandwich.

Roast beef. Of course.

"Are you ignoring me?" she said.

He took a huge bite. "Nope," he said, through a mouthful of beef and bread. "Just eating my lunch."

"Oh. Right," Jasmine said. "I'm so sorry."

After what seemed like a very long time, Hudson spoke to her. "Hello," he finally said. "Procrastinating, huh?"

For half of a split second, she debated whether to argue. She decided not to. "I knew you'd know what I was doing out here," she muttered.

"You're kind of obvious," Hudson said. "If you were really just taking a fake smoke break you'd be drinking water. You barely ever drink soda and I've never seen you eat a candy bar."

The last time they'd spoken about anything other than work was the day before, when Hudson asked if she was planning to stick to the terms of her pact with Parker. Of course, she'd evaded and then left the office without ever answering. How much longer could they avoid that topic? Probably not long, considering Hudson was a real journalist. Well, a photojournalist, Jasmine reminded herself. But still. He had a nose for getting to the root of an issue. Maybe she should just break down and tell him. Maybe. But if she did, he would never ask her out again.

She sighed when she remembered how he'd said he planned to ask her out, "Totally not professionally."

"What's going on with you?" Hudson said. "First, the soda and chocolate. Then ignoring me when I sit down." Jasmine gasped at this, and Hudson smiled at her before continuing, "Then that big sigh, like you've got a ball of tangled yarn in your brain and you're trying to untangle it right now."

"You could say that," Jasmine said.

She didn't mention to Hudson that he and his long legs made up a good deal of the yarn. Her mind balanced on the edge of the decision, and then he made it for her. "Well, I've got to get to work. I was heading back to the office and got some great shots of these kids practicing for a circus performance this weekend. Totally cute. I thought Mikey might want to use them as standalones since we don't have anything else page-one worthy for tomorrow."

"I'd love to see them," Jasmine said.

He pulled his camera out of the bag and turned on the photo viewer. As he scrolled back to the beginning of the circus performance photos, she moved over to his bench and scooted close enough to see the screen. And to smell his cologne. The first photo featured a little kid on stilts, juggling batons, while a group of younger kids danced in a semi-circle around him. In the next photo, Hudson had captured a girl midair as she performed a flip. The kids in the background watched her, some of them with grave expressions on their faces and others showing pure delight.

"I love that one," she said.

"Me too," he said. "Talented kids."

"My sisters and I once fancied ourselves circus performers," she said as he continued to scroll through photos. "We'd set up my parents' huge video camera on the tripod and tape ourselves in the backyard, doing cartwheels and trying to juggle. We were never very good."

"You could still learn," Hudson said. "I could teach you a thing or two."

"Wait." Jasmine sat up straight. "You know about circus performing?"

Hudson set the camera on his lap. "I know how to juggle. And I know how to do a handful of magic tricks."

"Will you teach me how to juggle?"

Just asking the question gave Jasmine an idea. She knew what she had to do.

"I need to tell you something," she said before Hudson could answer.

"Wait. Let me guess. Your dream circus specialty is that silk scarf dancing where you wear a skimpy leotard?"

"Absolutely not," she said, nudging his shoulder with hers.

"Remember how you asked me if I'm going to stick to the terms of my pact with Parker?" Hudson nodded and looked down at the camera on his lap.

"I remember. I also remember that you didn't answer."

"Well, I'm not."

He raised one eyebrow at her. "You're not?"

"No. Why do you sound so surprised?"

"Well, when I talked to your sister—"

"Ugh! Holly has no idea when to keep her mouth shut," Jasmine said.

"She has a romantic heart, I guess," Hudson said. "She said you and Parker were high school sweethearts and she was really hoping it worked out with the two of you. So naturally, I assumed you'd be giving it longer than a few days."

He was a good judge of character. But she'd prove him wrong.

She shrugged one shoulder. "No, I decided not to. It's just too much."

"Too much what?" Hudson said.

"With all the stuff we've been doing at work lately and everything," Jasmine lied.

"That's it?" Hudson said. "That's not very much."

It was true. She didn't really have anything else going on, besides a desire for Hudson to get around to asking her out.

She shrugged again. "So. I just thought I'd let you know."

"Well, thanks, Jasmine," Hudson said. He stood up and slipped his camera strap over his shoulder, stretched, then crumpled up his deli bag and threw it in the trash. "For letting me know. I take your social life very seriously. Now, I've got to get to work."

When the newsroom door closed behind him, Jasmine thought, *Well, that was unexpected.*

When she walked back to her desk after polishing off her soda and chocolate bar, Jasmine had a text from Parker: *Want to grab dinner tonight?*

She glanced at Hudson, who was apparently immersed in photo editing. He didn't even look up. Jasmine wrote back, *Sure. I can meet you somewhere after deadline. 8 p.m. at The Burger Shack?*

Parker responded, *Sounds great.*

Jasmine tucked her phone into her purse and sat down to work on a feature story about Earl Little and what a great guy all his co-workers claimed he was.

She didn't need Hudson to teach her to juggle, she thought. She was going to figure that out on her own. It was sink-or-swim time.

CHAPTER SEVENTEEN

"You won't believe what I did."

Jasmine sat with her sisters around Jasmine's dining room table Friday night, an empty Merlot bottle serving as a centerpiece while a fresh one made the rounds.

Ruby sat near Sequoia's feet, looking at her with sad eyes.

"Gross," Sequoia said. "I can feel your dog's drool dripping onto my shoes."

Jasmine called Ruby over, and Sequoia sighed. "Sorry," she said. "It's been a long week. After the stuff I saw today, I'll believe anything you tell me, Jas. Seriously, can you believe a woman would leave her kids in the car on the highway to walk three miles to get gas? How does a grown woman even run out of gas?"

Holly, of course, gave the woman the benefit of the doubt: "Probably she ran out of money, you know, between paychecks. She thought she could make it through to today."

"Well, she was wrong," Sequoia said. "It would be one thing if she was alone. But she had her kids with her, little kids, and she just left them in the car. On the highway. Where, might I remind you, drivers are driving at highway speeds. A guy called it in because one of the kids was standing outside the car. On the highway. He was hot and she'd taken the keys so he couldn't roll the windows down."

"Yikes," Jasmine said.

"Sorry," Sequoia said. "I didn't mean to steamroll the conversation."

She rubbed her forehead with one hand, took a sip of wine and refilled her glass. "Tell us what you did, Jas."

"Oh! First of all, I've been meaning to tell you something else," Jasmine said.

"And now *you've* steamrolled the conversation," Sequoia said, "preventing yourself from telling us what you set out to tell us in the first place."

Holly laughed.

"I know, I know," Jasmine said. Then she went on, carefully watching her sister so she wouldn't miss her reaction. "But anyway. There's a new PIO for Seabreeze PD. Elijah Sawyer."

And there it was. Sequoia looked down at her hand on the table, just for a fraction of a second, before returning her gaze to Jasmine's.

"Aha!" Jasmine said. "I knew it! You think he's hot! You think he's sexy, don't you?"

"What?" Sequoia said. She took another, bigger drink of her wine.

"You do," Holly said. "You did the thing. You've always done it. Your left eyebrow went up, just a tiny bit, and your lips pressed together in that weird crooked way they do when you're trying to keep a secret. And you looked down. Just for a second, but you did it. Spill it, sister. Tell us about this Elijah character."

"I will not spill it," Sequoia said. "We work together, and that's it."

"I noticed you didn't deny there was something to spill, or that you think he's hot," Jasmine said, "and he totally is."

"Wait," Holly said. "You met him, Jas?"

Still watching Sequoia, Jasmine said, "Yeah. He came into the office."

She relayed the entire story, including every detail she could remember about his stony countenance and the way he'd laughed when she'd recommended he "get qualified" to talk to her about his department's financial matters.

"Ohmigosh," Holly said. "He sounds exactly like Sequoia."

"That's what I was thinking!" Jasmine felt triumphant.

Throughout the conversation, Sequoia had carefully examined the wine marker Jasmine had put on her glass. It was a tiny pewter ballerina. Graceful, lithe. And probably a tiny bit snooty, like Sequoia.

"Anyway," Sequoia said. "What was the other thing you were going to tell us, Jas?"

"Well, we're letting you off the hook only because I have been waiting to tell you guys this," Jasmine said. "I can't believe I did this."

Holly scooped some salad onto each of their plates. "What did you do? This sounds very juicy."

Jasmine's words came out in a rush. "I told Hudson I wasn't going to stick to the terms of my pact with Parker. But I told Parker I was."

Both of her sisters stared at her.

"You did that?" Holly said.

"Jasmine!" Sequoia said. "You didn't!"

Sheepish now, she said, "I know. It was weird. I don't know why I did it."

"You want your cake, and you want to eat it, too," Sequoia said.

"This is kind of like cheating on Parker." Holly said. "I mean, I'm sure he assumes you're exclusive."

"He probably does," Jasmine said. Now she twirled her own wine marker, a little dog. Wanting to please her owner while still sneaking sausage off the table. Make that roast beef. "But, I mean, who knows if he's even going to stick around? What if we get through the thirty days and then leaves, anyway? Am I supposed to drop everything and go with him?"

"You are right in the middle of building up a reputation as a kick-ass reporter," Sequoia said. "I'd hate to think of you starting over."

Jasmine rolled her eyes. "I just didn't know what to do," she said.

"I don't blame you," Holly said. "But how are you going to handle this? I mean, Seabreeze is a small town. What if you're with

Parker and you run into Hudson? Or what if someone sees you with Hudson and mentions it to Parker?"

"I know," Jasmine said. "What was I thinking?"

Ruby jumped up at the excited tone in Jasmine's voice, and trotted over to lean against Jasmine's leg. "What if I tell Parker I'm also seeing other people? The pact doesn't say anything about exclusivity."

"No," Holly and Sequoia said at the same time, and Holly added, "He's too sensitive. He'd be offended."

"Okay," Jasmine said. "What if I tell Hudson I'm seeing Parker, but that I'd love to see him, too?"

"He won't go for that," Sequoia said. "He retracted his date invitation after he found out about the pact from Miss Big Mouth over there."

"Ooh, that's true," Jasmine said. "But on second thought, now he thinks I've given up on the pact."

"But what if he finds out you lied?" Holly said.

"You're in deep mud," Sequoia said.

"Yeah," Jasmine said. "I know."

"Good luck with that," Holly said.

Jasmine said, "Thanks. Thanks a lot."

Maybe she wasn't cut out to be a juggling circus performer, after all.

After Holly and Sequoia left her house, Jasmine put on her favorite love songs CD, filled her bath tub with almost-unbearably hot water and sank down into it.

While her body heated and sweat rolled down her temples, she thought about her most recent dinner date with Parker. He'd taken her to a cozy, upscale steakhouse on Beachside Drive downtown. The host walked them to a private table in the back corner. Parker pulled out Jasmine's chair and draped her napkin over her lap with a flourish. They grinned at each other. Between them, Jasmine felt a stirring of energy. He sat down across from her, then slid the candle to one edge of the table. He offered his hand, palm up, for her to hold.

As they sat there, looking at each other, Jasmine felt a pang of guilt. Why had she told Hudson she wasn't going to fulfill the terms of the pact? It might have been one of the stupider things she'd done. No, it definitely was one of the stupider things she'd done, and she couldn't take it back.

"So, let's start over," Parker said, the flickering candlelight making him look like a ghoul one moment and a sex god the next. "I'm sorry for rushing things, before. Tell me again how you decided to become a reporter."

"Okay," Jasmine said. "I like this story. You know, I always wanted to be an English teacher."

Parker smiled. "Yeah. I remember how much you loved Mrs. Erickson. You wanted to give the same kinds of quizzes she did, right? Those Latin root quizzes?"

"Yes! You do remember," Jasmine said.

"I definitely remember," Parker said. "In fact, I also remember having a fantasy about you being my teacher, between the sheets."

"You did not!" Jasmine said.

And just like that, they slipped back into their roles, as comfortably as if they were sliding their feet into old pairs of slippers. Now, in the bath, Jasmine opened her eyes and stared at the ceiling. Old slippers sometimes wore out, didn't they?

"I was just going into college," she told him, "and I went to campus to take a tour. I went into the English department, and it was all these people reading fat books and discussing archaic stories. I don't know what 'Beowulf' has to do with today's world, but they sure seemed immersed in it. And then I went into the journalism department. It was so lively, so vibrant. The students were talking, debating, discussing, even yelling. I mean, some of them were just there, typing away, smoking cigarettes and sipping coffee. But the differences between the English department and the journalism department were so stark. And I knew where I wanted to be."

"So it wasn't that you wanted to cover hard news," Parker said. "It was because you wanted that atmosphere."

"And more than just the atmosphere," Jasmine said, hating that she had to explain herself. Of course she hadn't chosen a career based on atmosphere. "It's the purpose, you know? The feeling that every single day, you're doing something worthwhile."

"So … you're saying teaching English isn't worthwhile?"

She could tell his tone was playful, but uncomfortable, she rushed to explain. "No, I'm not saying that at all. I'm just saying that in that moment, at that time in my life, I just felt this deep sense of purpose. You know?"

"But you write, like, feature stories. I mean, is there a purpose to that?"

In the bath, Jasmine closed her eyes again. She groaned.

At the restaurant, the server set their plates on the table, which gave Jasmine a moment to collect herself so she wouldn't reach across the table and grab Parker's throat. When the server walked away, she said to Parker, "You're seriously asking me that?"

"Whoa, don't get all prickly on me. It's just a question."

"Of course there's a purpose," she said. "Feature stories are inspiring. They tell important stories. Stories about ordinary people in extraordinary circumstances. Anyway. Enough about me. What's the purpose of you wanderlust? Tell me, how does *that* make the world a better place?"

"Ouch," Parker said.

Jasmine fake-toasted him with an asparagus spear, and he said, "Okay. I get your point. Right now, the point of my wanderlust is to bring the joy of my own personality everywhere I go."

"Are you kidding?"

"A little," he said. "But in reality, I feel like I'm content right now, you know? I travel to different places and meet different people, and it's working for me."

"Any idea how long you'll stay in Seabreeze?"

Parker took a big bite of his burger and chewed for a long time before answering.

"No, no idea," he said, finally. "I just don't know."

Jasmine didn't answer. Why did the two men in her life both want to bolt at the earliest opportunity? Hudson wanted to move on to bigger and better things, and Parker wanted to spread his joy all over the damned globe.

"Well, shit," she said.

Parker laughed. "I know. I figure one day, this urge to travel will leave me, but for now I want to fulfill it while I still can."

"Yeah, I guess you've got to scratch that itch," Jasmine said.

Parker said, "I guess I've got to."

They got shakes to go and headed out to Beachside Drive, downtown's main drag. While they walked, sipping their shakes, Jasmine thought about the possibilities for her romantic future, assuming both Parker and Hudson left Seabreeze for adventure.

She could choose spinsterhood. Living alone or with Ruby for perpetuity wouldn't be half-bad. They had an understanding, they slept comfortably in the same bed and they liked the same TV shows. Ruby would die, eventually, but Jasmine could get a different canine companion. She wouldn't have any children to whom she could pass her final pet dog, and they couldn't count on Sequoia to procreate, but surely Holly would. Jasmine would be a doting aunt to Holly's kids, and her old, stiff dog would be her final gift to them.

Or she could become a serial dater, never settling down. She'd be an eighty-year-old, pink Spandex-clad, magenta-lipsticked, white-haired lady perusing dating websites and using too much breath spray.

Maybe that's what this world had come to. She could get accounts on some online dating sites and seek out men with varied interests to match her own. Maybe she'd find a sensitive poet who read Rumi aloud to her on the banks of a creek. And she'd definitely need a man skilled in sexual healing. Of course, she wanted at least one guy who could cook her fancy dinners. A workout partner would be nice. Runs along the beach could be very romantic. She'd never be lonely, she'd never get bored and she'd never have to worry about men leaving her, because even if they did, she'd have a bunch of others to fall back on.

She found herself nodding as she walked with Parker down the wide sidewalk.

Maybe she should just become a lesbian. Women were so much more sensitive, anyway. She could get herself to a nunnery like Juliet and become a nun. Forget romance completely. Or—and maybe this was the best solution yet—maybe she could become a hermit. She could build herself a little hut in the hollowed-out trunk of a huge redwood tree in the mountains. With computers and internet and phones, she could read and watch movies and live simply in her hut.

Maybe she'd even commission her sisters to help her with a "No Boys Allowed" sign like they'd made for The Garden Club twenty-five years ago. Thinking about the fact that anything in her life had occurred twenty-five years ago made her feel exhausted with old age.

For no reason at all, while she walked next to Parker down Beachside Drive, her mind wandered to Hudson Stover. She wondered whether he'd ever tried to breach a "No Boys Allowed" sign, and how he'd react if he knew she was, at this very moment, planning to erect an invisible one around her own consciousness. Maybe she wanted him to bust right through it.

"What's going on in that head of yours, Jasmine Carr?" Parker said then. "You're awfully quiet."

She'd almost forgotten she was walking side by side with the man who had caused her mind to run full speed down the Alone Forever Route. She looked up at him.

"Nothing," she said. "Just thinking, I guess."

"What are you thinking about?"

When they were teenagers, they'd always ask each other what they were thinking about, and the answers always took them into deep conversations about life on other planets, God and creation, people's spiritual nature. But tonight, Jasmine didn't want to have a deep conversation. So she said, "Oh, just how nice it is to be here with you again."

She slipped her hand into his and focused on the quaint storefronts and colorful clientele on Beachside Drive.

Now, she submersed her entire body in the bathwater, blocking out all light and sound.

In hindsight, she thought, she should have asked Parker, over steaks and asparagus, or walking down Beachside, whether he was seeing anyone else. They hadn't talked about being exclusive, but she knew they both assumed they were. It would be unfair for her to pretend otherwise.

When Beachside Drive ended at the beach, Jasmine told Parker she was getting tired and was ready to call it a night. Instead of answering, he turned toward her, cupped her chin with his hands and kissed her, his hands moving up and down her back in time to the ocean's swaying song. At first, it was a gentle kiss, reminiscent of their early time together. But the intensity deepened until she noticed his body pressed against hers and her body reacting.

There's definitely something here, still.

Some kid, whizzing by on his skateboard, yelled for them to get a room, and they broke apart, laughing. They walked back to their cars, which they'd parked near the restaurant, talking about their old teachers and classmates, getting each other caught up on news and gossip about friends and enemies. Could it be this easy to fall back into their old relationship? And did she want to?

Parker gave her one more lingering kiss before she climbed into her car.

Now, twenty-four hours later, she stood alone and lonely, freshly bathed, in her clean kitchen, her dog making laps from the living room to the front door, her toenails clacking on the floor in a rhythm that made Jasmine want to tear her hair out. Maybe lifelong companionship with a dog wasn't a great idea, after all.

"You know, Ruby? I think I'm going to make a phone call."

Hudson answered on the fourth ring.

CHAPTER EIGHTEEN

Jasmine felt slightly offended that Hudson had given her such a work-based greeting, and for a moment she was so flustered she couldn't even come up with a witty response. She later thought she should have said something like, "No, I'm offering you a lead," or "No, but I'd like one."

Instead, she fumbled through some lame opening line like, "Uh, no, I just—I just called to, you know, say hi."

She flopped down on the coach, stifling a groan with one hand, and Ruby stopped pacing to look at her, head cocked to the side.

"Oh," Hudson said. "Uh, that's unexpected. Hello, I guess."

I shouldn't have called. He has a woman over. Someone from the city. Someone sexy who wears expensive jeans. The ones with the rhinestones on the pockets. Or he's hanging out with his guy friends and I've embarrassed him. I should just hang up. No, that would be lame. I'd never live it down.

"Is this an okay time?" she said.

Hudson laughed and the sound was deep and rumbly. "Sure. Why not?"

"Uh, I don't know," Jasmine said.

"So..." he said. "What's up?"

She wished her sisters were here to coach her through this like they'd coached her through her first phone call to a boy in seventh grade. Noah Thomas. He was her dream guy, an athletic honors student with dark curly hair, skin the color of hot chocolate and eyes the color of honey. He had a smile a mile wide, and he always helped her with her daily crossword puzzles in their homeroom class.

One day, he gave her his number, and she froze when she finally got up the courage to dial it. But before she could hang up, his mother answered and her voice sounded so nice Jasmine couldn't put the handset back on the receiver. So she waited for Noah to come to the phone, meanwhile gesturing madly at her sisters to get her some paper and a pen. When they returned with the supplies, she scribbled, *What do I SAY?*

In silence, with lots of suppressed giggling, they wrote instructions: *I love you Noah Thomas. Let's do a crossword puzzle. Item one across starts with a P and ends with an S. Any ideas what it could be? What is your kissing style?*

Come to think of it, her sisters had been no help. She'd had to get herself through that call without giggling right along with them. She'd have to do the same thing now.

"What are you doing?" she asked Hudson.

"Just sitting here."

Wow. He wasn't making this easy. Then inspiration struck. "So I was just calling about those juggling lessons."

"That is so not what you're calling about," he said.

How does he know? "How do you know?"

And why does being around Hudson make me blurt out stupid stuff?

"I just know. You missed me, that's what it is."

Jasmine wondered if she could disappear into the couch. Ruby hopped up and climbed onto her lap.

"So ... what are you really doing?" she said.

"Playing solitaire," he said.

"You're alone?" She was still picturing him in a leather-and-steel bachelor pad, most likely with a naked woman in the kitchen mixing him cocktails.

"That's basically what solitaire means," he said. "You pictured me here with a bunch of naked women, didn't you?"

She barked out a laugh. "Not at all."

"Want to come over?"

"What?" she said.

"I know you heard me. But you're probably the type of person who'd like to hear it again. Want to come over?"

"Uh, actually, I was—"

"You were sitting around alone, or with your dog, and thinking about me. And you decided to call me. And now you want to come over."

She hadn't even told him she was willing to come over, but before she realized what was happening, he'd given her his address and she was slipping into shoes and starting her car, Ruby in her lap.

"What am I doing?" she said to the dog as she drove through town. Ruby put her paws on the window sill and licked the window until Jasmine rolled it down. "I know, it's crazy. He doesn't even like me. What if he thinks this is a booty call, Ruby? That's not really my thing, you know?"

Ruby looked at her, her expression meaningful.

"It's not!"

The dog turned away.

Not that Jasmine could participate in booty calls tonight. She hadn't shaved her legs in weeks, and because work had kept her away from home so much recently, she hadn't done much laundry. So she was wearing a gross pair of granny panties under her work pants, and she definitely didn't want Hudson to see those bad boys.

Still, she found herself making the quickest possible stops at every stop sign along the route, and tapping her toes on the brake pedal when traffic signals turned red. Maybe she should call Holly or Sequoia. But they wouldn't understand. Holly would tell Jasmine that seeing Hudson was like cheating on Parker. And Sequoia would say something about Jasmine being incapable of making a decision. She drove through town, her phone safely in the cupholder. She cranked up the volume on the radio.

The streetlights glowed in the evening fog's mist, blurring into shimmering circles hanging in the sky. Hudson lived on the west side of town, close to the water. Jasmine found a parking spot on the street, and Ruby led the way to his little bungalow, trotting up the sidewalk as if she'd been there before.

It wasn't at all what Jasmine expected. Neat shrubs framed the doorway, and a textured Welcome mat squished under her feet when she approached the front door. She didn't even have time to knock; Hudson pulled the door open just as Jasmine held up her fist.

"Hi," he said. His deep voice made Jasmine's entire body vibrate, and that simple, "Hi," was colored with so many different images, her head spun.

Although, maybe her head was spinning because he looked fresh-out-of-the-shower sexy, his hair wet and his skin smooth where it was visible on his chest.

"Hi," she managed. At her feet, Ruby barked.

"Hi, Ruby," Hudson said. "Come on in, ladies."

His apartment wasn't what she'd pictured on the inside, either. Framed black and white photos hung equally spaced on the living room walls. From the furniture to the floor rugs to the dishes in the sink, everything was black and white, with the exception of a few red throw pillows. Acoustic guitar music played on the stereo.

"Nice place," she said to him. "Modern, but cozy."

"That's me," Hudson said, and Jasmine wondered how that translated to his dating life. "I was playing Solitaire, but you can join my game, if you want."

He gestured to the coffee table and she wondered if there was any hidden meaning in his words. "Sure," she said.

"Can I get you a drink?" Hudson said.

Jasmine sat down on the couch. "What are my options?"

"Beer and water. Sorry, I wasn't expecting lady company tonight."

"I'll take a beer," Jasmine said. He went into the kitchen, and she stood up to follow him. "So tell me, Casanova, what kinds of drinks do you stock for your lady company?"

"Oh, you know. Wine, daiquiris, flavored vodka, the regular girly stuff." He switched into a Spanish accent. "Anything to make my lady friends more comfortable."

"How many lady friends do you host?" The question came tumbling out of her mouth, and the heat of embarrassment followed it. She was positive her cheeks were bright red. What was it about him that made her so outspoken? Grinning, he handed her the beer, then clinked the neck of his own bottle against hers. They sat down on the couch, and Hudson scooped up the half-finished Solitaire game and shuffled the cards.

"So, my lady friend," he said, tapping the deck on the table to straighten it. "May I inquire as to what brings you here tonight?"

Charmed, Jasmine said, "I was just looking for some company."

"You were looking for a good time?" Hudson said, still in a Spanish accent.

"No! I mean, yes. But not in that way. You know what I mean."

"Surely the long-haired clod—what was his name? Oh, yes, that was it. Parker. Surely Parker is available. I can't imagine he'd be wrapped up in a riveting game of Solitaire on a weekend night."

Jasmine shrugged. "I didn't even call him."

"So tell me how the famous Jasmine Carr comes to be alone on a weekend night."

He began dealing out the game, laying the cards in a tidy row on the table.

"First, you tell me how the infamous Hudson Stover comes to be the same." Jasmine leaned back into the couch cushions.

"That's not a long story," he said. "I typically have quite a healthy roster of eager single women, waiting to spend weekend evenings with me. But, alas. As you know, I just moved to Seabreeze. I immediately found that a certain single woman, whose name shall not be mentioned in present company, captivated my interest." Here, he stopped dealing Solitaire for a moment and looked at her. "So I have been a bit, shall we say, delayed in setting up my roster here in town."

Wow. I've captivated his interest.

"Hmm," she said. "Very interesting."

"It is," he said. "This phenomenon occurs only in very rare circumstances. Very rare, indeed."

He handed Jasmine the stack of cards and she made a play, moving a black six onto a red seven and laying a red five on the black six. She handed the stack back to Hudson. Jasmine wanted to ask why he hadn't asked her out yet, if she so captivated him, but she was afraid the question would come off as desperate.

Instead, she said, "Well, I'm sure you hold yourself to very high standards."

"That I do."

They played Solitaire for a few more moments, and Hudson said, "So, why are you alone on a weekend night?"

"To tell you the truth, that is not an uncommon phenomenon. I had my sisters over for dinner tonight, but they went home. And then I called you."

"Let me guess: you're the middle sister."

Jasmine laughed. "I'm not sure whether I should be offended that you say that like it's a jab, or impressed that you got it right."

Hudson shrugged. "I'm pretty good, aren't I?"

"You know, they've actually done studies about how well-adjusted middle children are. They get along well with almost everybody and they're quite self-sufficient."

"Kind of defensive," Hudson muttered.

"Let me guess. You're the oldest. That's why you're such an over-achiever. You plan your life around achievements rather than experiences."

"Achievements *are* experiences. And I'm an only child."

"Ha! Even more of a reason to be accomplishment driven! You have to be everything for your parents."

"Now you're going too far," Hudson said. "My parents are supportive of whatever I do."

"All right, fine. Why don't you have any houseplants?"

"I'd hate to uproot them whenever I move. My lifestyle isn't really conducive to nurturing living things."

"Hm. How'd you know I was the middle sister?"

"Just a good guess. I'm a great judge of character. And your character screams, 'middle child.'"

"What? How?"

"You need lots of direction. You're a peacekeeper. You don't want to offend anybody and you dislike conflict. That's why you like features reporting. You like the excitement of the newsroom, but you don't want your stories to be about conflict, especially if it means asking those tough questions."

"Wow. You know me as well as I know myself, Hudson. Cheers to that."

She held up her almost-empty beer bottle and when he smiled, her lady parts went wild. "Cheers," he said. "To being alone on a weekend night. Until now. Want another?"

"Sure. Just one more. I don't want a conflict with any cops on my way home."

"I'm going to force you into conflict right now."

When she raised her eyebrows, he laughed. "Want to play pool?"

Hudson's garage aligned more closely with Jasmine's expectations. Metal road signs hung on the walls, and a stained glass chandelier lit up the pool table, which stood in the center of the room. A row of bar stools stood against one wall, and a mini fridge sat in the corner.

"Is this your man cave, or what?"

"I guess you could say that. I like having something fun to do at home, you know? Have a few beers, hang out with the guys. Or gals."

He was busy racking the pool balls, and Jasmine wandered over to the wall opposite the road signs. There were photos of him as a kid, his eyes just as bright as they were now, twinkling at the camera as he held a fish on a line or stood next to a birthday cake. There were some of him as an adult, too, with friends at the Statue of Liberty and the Grand Canyon.

How did he maintain friendships if he was always chasing awards around the country, too bohemian to buy a houseplant?

"Want to break?" he said. She turned around and he handed her a cue.

"You'd better do it," she said. "I'm pretty rusty."

Hudson nodded and moved to the end of the table. "So, any ideas on who offed Earl Little? I'll take stripes."

Jasmine took a sip of her beer and set it down before taking her shot. "I mean, not really, but I have to assume it's someone related to all that missing money. Right? Maybe they thought he was going to talk. Who else would have a reason to kill him?"

She'd missed her shot, and Hudson walked around the pool table to stand next to her. He leaned down, and his body brushed against hers before she realized it would be polite to give him a little space. Of course, his shot was good. He grinned at her and put a hand on her waist as he went around her to take another.

"That's the question, isn't it? Who else would have a reason to kill him? I like your thinking."

"See? I can ask the tough questions."

"But that Elijah Sawyer guy intimidates the hell out of you." He missed his shot and Jasmine lined up hers.

"At first he did," she admitted, "but then I realized he's exactly like my older sister, Sequoia. I can handle him. And how do you even know he intimidated me? Are you spying on me, or what?"

In one smooth movement, she hit the cue ball, sending a solid into the corner pocket.

"Nice shot," he said. "And no. I just saw you greeting him in the lobby at the office. I thought he looked like a real jerk."

He looks like a model, Jasmine thought. She said, "He was, at first, but he came around. I think we reached an understanding. I get the feeling he's kind of a new guy. He's not really aware of the department's politics, you know? Or if he is, he's ignored them until now. So I think he's going to do some digging. He may turn out to be an ally."

"See?" Hudson said. "You're the middle sister. Your people skills are excellent."

"Did I imagine it, Mr. Stover, or did you just give me a compliment?"

She bent over to make her next shot, and he said, "You want another one? Your ass looks fantastic in those jeans."

Jasmine felt the heat rise to her face and the warmth drop to her belly. She straightened up before her cue even hit the ball.

"What I want to know," Hudson said, acting as if he hadn't just set her simmering, "is how much money is worth killing someone over? I mean, it had to be a lot. More than what we've seen is missing. It just makes me wonder if there's more to this than we know."

"Why don't you write news?" Jasmine asked. She hoped her tone didn't come off sarcastic. "I mean, you have such an interest in it, I'm surprised you stuck with photojournalism rather than getting into investigative journalism or something."

He nodded. "You're not far off," he said. "For me, it's just that photos have this raw power. You can tell the same story, but without the need for words. You can convey the essence of what's happening and how it affects people with a single image."

"So you're power hungry."

"Totally. And not to be cocky or anything, but I'm really good at it. I'm okay with writing, but not as good as I am with photos. I love the investigative stuff, for sure. But my gift is photography. I got the eight ball. Want to go again?"

This time, Jasmine racked the balls while Hudson watched her. "So did you take the photos in the living room?" she asked.

"Some of them. Some of them my best friend took. Dougie. Well, I call him Dougie still, but I'm pretty sure he goes by Doug. Anyway, we grew up next-door to each other, and we started our own little investigative agency. We always argued over who would take the photos of the evidence we found. So we made up this system where we took turns. Once we were old enough to travel on our own, we started taking annual trips. We still argue over who gets the best shots. So we share most of our photos—the ones we aren't entering in contests or submitting for publication."

So he was capable of long-term friendship.

"So you guys still talk?"

"Yeah. We talk almost every day."

When she raised her eyebrows in surprise, he laughed. "I know, we're like girls, right? If we don't talk on the phone, we're texting, or chatting on social media, commenting on each other's posts, whatever. He's like a brother to me. Anyway. He's coming to visit in a week or two, whenever he can get time off work. He's never been to the central coast, so I thought I could show him the sights. I'm sure he'll want to see the newsroom, so if you're around, you'll get a chance to meet him."

"I'd like that," Jasmine said, her mind running through all the possible meanings of this potential introduction. Did this mean Hudson liked her? How many women had Hudson introduced to Dougie?

"You know what I'd like?" Hudson said, saving Jasmine from the over-analysis that always plagued her.

She hadn't even realized he was standing behind her, but there he was. He put his hands on her hips and turned her around to face him. Without warning, he lifted her onto the edge of the pool table. Her arms encircled his neck. He leaned forward to put his forehead on hers.

"What would you like?" she said. Her heart beat fast. She could hear it pounding.

"I'd like to do this."

He brought his lips to hers in a kiss that was at once sweet and urgent, giving and demanding. Jasmine wanted to press her body against his, to feel his arms holding her close. But just at the moment when she would have pulled him even closer, he ended the kiss. He remained there, his forehead on hers, his hands on her waist.

"You can do that, anytime," she said. She hoped he wasn't being too forward. If it weren't for Parker, Holly would cheer for Jasmine's boldness. But Sequoia would say she was being pushy. She might even go so far as to call Jasmine a hussy, but maybe not, considering Jasmine wasn't wearing a low-cut top and purposely breathing hard to make her cleavage rise and fall.

She shook her head to clear it, and saw the twinkle of humor in Hudson's eyes. "I can practically see you debating with yourself," he said. "You want it, but you don't want to want it, right?"

"Something like that," she said. "So I guess I'd better get going."

HUDSON'S KISS had definitely increased Jasmine's temperature. But more than that, spending time with him had illustrated just how alone she was. He had an uncanny ability to decipher her thoughts, to understand her. Now, for the first time in as long as she could remember, her house felt quiet and empty, and she felt lonely.

Of course she had her sisters, and Ruby, but she didn't really have a go-to person with whom to share the details of her day. Strangely, she thought, Hudson had almost become that person, lately. She knew what he ordered for lunch (roast beef!) and he knew she only drank soda and ate chocolate when she was procrastinating.

Now here she was, slipping between the cold sheets, preparing to sleep alone. It was the norm for her, but her feelings about it had changed.

"What is the meaning of this?" she asked Ruby, who had wiggled her way under the covers.

Ruby grunted and curled into a tight ball, but she didn't close her eyes.

"It's not that you're not enough for me, Ruby," Jasmine said. "It's just that spending time with Hudson tonight made me realize how nice it could be to be with someone who just knows me. You know?"

For a half-second, she wondered if talking to a dog indicated mental instability. Even if it did, she didn't care. She was disappointed when Ruby closed her eyes and, a moment later, started to snore.

Nevertheless, she continued to speak. "Parker knows me, but he knows the old me. I'm not sure if he knows the person I've evolved into over the course of the past decade. Can we ever get that intimacy back? Isn't it worth finding out? With Hudson, it's like he knows me, on this weird, deep level. You know? And I like it. I wish you'd answer me, Ruby. I have no idea what to think."

As long as she could keep these two tracks of her life completely parallel—traveling side by side but never touching—maybe she'd have a chance to figure it out.

CHAPTER NINETEEN

"CARR. I NEED YOU IN HERE."

Mikey Stockman's brown tweed pants were visible through his office doorway. He was probably sitting in his go-to position—his butt in his chair, his feet on the desk and an electronic cigarette in his hand.

"Conversations that begin that way never seem to go well," Jasmine said.

She smiled at Hudson as she passed him, then dropped her purse on her chair. And so what if she sashayed, just a little, as she walked to Mikey's office, hoping Hudson would turn around and watch her? When Jasmine saw another young woman sitting across from Mikey, she forced her mind to switch tracks. The girl was about her age, and had bright orange hair and wide blue eyes. Her wardrobe was completely black, right down to her fingernails and the hundreds of bracelets she wore on each wrist.

Jasmine hoped her face didn't show her surprise, but she could tell from Mikey's amused expression that it probably betrayed her.

"This is Priscilla," he said. "Priscilla May."

Jasmine stepped forward and extended a hand. Priscilla May stood up and voiced exactly what Jasmine's mind had just been whispering. "I know, it sounds like a porn star name. That's why I go by my middle name. My second middle name, actually. You can call me Cara."

Jasmine laughed out loud. "Jasmine Carr," she said. "But I guess you already knew that."

"Jasmine," Mikey said. "Cara is the new reporter I was telling you about, that week Liza left. She was a little delayed in getting here, but she's here now. So anyway. I thought she could shadow you for a few days. I thought you could give her the lay of the land. Show her the ropes."

"Okay," Jasmine said. "I'd be glad to. Although, I can assure you there's someone more qualified than me for this position. Come on, I'll give you a tour, and then you can come with me to my first meeting. I have a feeling you'll find it very entertaining."

Mikey stood up. "I'll leave you ladies to it."

"I guess you know this is the newsroom," Jasmine said as they exited Mikey's office. "And the lobby's through those doors. This is Hudson. He's a fixture on the tour." Hudson nodded at Cara in greeting, and then winked at Jasmine. Her stomach responded with a little flutter.

"Where do you hail from, Priscilla May?" Hudson said. "Hollywood?"

"He has a habit of eavesdropping," Jasmine said, hoping Cara could read the apology in her tone. "He'll call you Cara from now on."

"It's totally fine," Cara said. "I'm used to it. I'm not from Hollywood. Although that would be infinitely more interesting than my actual home town, which is a tiny speck just outside of Omaha. Bellevue. Well, it's actually not that tiny any more. I wanted to see what the beach is like."

"It's fantastic," Hudson said. "This is a great little town. I'm sure Jasmine can include some highlights in your tour."

Something about the way Hudson called Seabreeze, "a great little town" raised Jasmine's hackles.

"I'll show you the printing press," she said to Cara. Hudson shrugged at Cara as if he didn't understand Jasmine's abrupt transition. Jasmine rolled her eyes and led Cara outside.

"So, you and Hudson are an item, then, right?" Cara said as they walked down the alley behind the *Daily Trumpet's* main building.

Jasmine stopped walking. "Why do you say that?"

Cara laughed. "Your expression is priceless. I just felt the, um, shall we say, *tension* between you. That's all." Now she shrugged. "Your secret's safe with me."

"It's not a secret," Jasmine said. She huffed out a breath and attempted a calmer affect. "It's complicated."

Jasmine started walking so quickly Cara had to jog to catch up with her. "Wow. Looks like I hit a sore spot. You can tell me about it over lunch."

Jasmine shook her head. "There is nothing to tell."

"Did you forget you're talking to a fellow reporter?" Cara said. "I can read people. And I ask lots of inappropriate questions."

They both laughed at this. Instead of answering, though, Jasmine opened the door to the cavernous room that held the printing press, and gestured for Cara to go in ahead of her.

A half-hour later, Cara gave Jasmine a sideways glance as they pulled up at the Seabreeze Dog Park.

"This is your meeting?" She put finger quotes on "meeting" and Jasmine grimaced as she turned off the car.

"I know I was a little misleading," she said. "But Mikey wants me writing feature stories even while I'm covering cops and courts. 'We've got to maintain balance, Carr,' he says. So here we are. At the dog park."

They got out of the car, and walked over to the picnic table, where a motley group of humans waited for Jasmine. Their dogs played nearby, jumping through brightly colored tires and climbing up obstacles, barking and waging their tails.

"Wow," Cara said. "I can't wait to see how you make a story out of this."

As Jasmine interviewed the humans about the park's recent renovations, Cara immersed herself in a game of fetch with the dogs, sending the entire pack of them tearing this way and that across the park.

Jasmine felt a little miffed that Cara didn't bother listening to the interviews, but she reminded herself Cara already had journalism experience. Jasmine was just supposed to be giving her the lay of the land, and nothing more. *Plus,* Jasmine reminded herself, *if Mikey had wanted an expert reporter to give Cara a tour, he would have assigned the job to someone else.*

In an effort to give Cara a feel for the real Seabreeze, Jasmine took her to the wharf for lunch. She pushed away memories of her last trip here—the failed overnight date with Parker—and ordered them fried calamari and lobster to share.

While they waited for their food, sipping on iced teas and watching the waves roll in under the wharf, Cara went into full investigative reporter mode.

"So tell me about your complicated situation with that yummy Hudson character."

"Wait. Are you asking because you're interested in him?"

"Woman, I could actually feel the electricity between the two of you. I'd be an idiot to step into the middle of that."

"Really?" Jasmine said.

"Really. I'd die of electric shock."

Jasmine barely knew this Cara person. She wasn't sure if she could or should tell her all the details about Hudson and Parker and the pact and the lie. The Lie. The three of them—Jasmine, Cara, and Hudson—would be working in close quarters, and what if Cara slipped and said something about Parker?

"Wow," Cara said. "I can practically hear your wheels turning."

"Why does everyone always say that to me?"

"You have a very readable face," Cara said. "Look, you don't have to tell me. I'm just trying to make conversation, that's all. You want to keep it to yourself, that's fine by me. And if you want to hear complicated, you should hear the real reason I was late to arrive here in Seabreeze."

"Do tell," Jasmine said.

Cara inhaled deeply, but the server appeared with their baskets of food before she could begin. When he walked away, she inhaled deeply again, and she and Jasmine both laughed.

"So. I was living with my boyfriend. Ollie."

"Wait," Jasmine said. "His real name is Ollie? I didn't know people actually named their kids that. I thought it was like, a joke or something."

"His existence is a cosmic joke, believe me," Cara said, and Jasmine found herself rather delighted. "We were living together in Bellevue. We had this little apartment, and we shared one car. My car. My baby. It was an old Trans-Am. It was a classic, a convertible. The color—they call I cosmic purple. I loved that car."

"I think I actually see a tear forming in your eye," Jasmine said. "Things don't sound promising for you and that car."

Cara dabbed at the corner of her eye with her linen napkin, and they both laughed again. "Your instincts are dead on. Things don't end well. So originally, we were going to move to California together. We weren't really a 'til-death-do-we-part kind of couple, but we planned to stay together, you know? Anyway, we had a huge fight just before we planned to move. I'm sure you can guess what it was about."

"The car," Jasmine said. She took a bite of calamari.

"The car. Ding, ding, ding. You got it," Cara said. She picked up two lobster claws, and as she spoke, she used one to illustrate her own thoughts, and one to illustrate Ollie's. "I wanted to bring the Trans-Am out here. I thought we could rent a moving van and tow it. Ollie didn't like that idea. He wanted to sell the car and buy a pickup truck. Can't you just imagine how awesome it would be to have a convertible out here?"

Jasmine nodded. "It would be. Although, wait 'til you see how foggy it gets sometimes. I mean, it's chilly! You might not want a convertible."

"Not year round, but still. It's a beach town."

"That it is," Jasmine said.

"Not that it matters, now, anyway," Cara said. "Ollie crashed the car. Totaled it."

Now, as Cara took a big bite out of the lobster claw that represented Ollie, she really did look like she was going to cry. Jasmine reached across the table and placed a hand over Cara's. "I'm so sorry," she said.

Cara took a sip of her iced tea. "We should have ordered Bloody Marys."

"Mikey Stockman would never know."

Within a few minutes, the server had delivered their first round of Bloody Marys, and Cara finished the story of her breakup with Ollie.

"That was the first mean thing he ever did," she said, twirling her celery stick in her drink. "He was so sweet. So calm."

"That's a classic statement from an abused spouse," Jasmine said. "You got out just in time."

Cara didn't respond to that, but went on, "So he crashed the car. Obviously I didn't have a plan for buying a new one. As you know, he did, but obviously, we were no longer going to move out here together."

"Obviously," Jasmine said.

"So I had to cash out some of my retirement fund, and it took some time for the check to come in. Then I bought a new car—"

"A classic Trans-Am?"

"No. Unfortunately. Do you know how hard those things are to find?"

"I admit that I have never looked for one," Jasmine said.

"Well, they are. Needle in a haystack and all that. So I settled for a boring little sedan. It gets good gas mileage and has a big trunk. It was the fastest way to get the heck out of Bellevue. And here I am."

Jasmine was now halfway through her first Bloody Mary, and the combination of alcohol and Cara's willingness to air her dirty laundry loosened her up enough to dish on the Hudson and Parker Debacle.

After a moment of silence for Cara and Ollie's relationship—and Cara's car—Jasmine signaled for a second round before launching in: "Okay. I'm ready to tell you why the Hudson situation is complicated."

"I knew you'd come around," Cara said.

"Parker is my high school sweetheart."

"Not Hudson?" Cara said.

"Not Hudson," Jasmine said.

"Go on," Cara said. She leaned forward, her elbows on the table.

Jasmine filled Cara in, from the pact to Parker's call a couple of weeks ago to Hudson's panty-incinerating scarf-related threat. She included every detail, even her present-day anger at the teenage Parker and her lie to Hudson about ditching the pact.

"Woman, you've got yourself in a real pickle," Cara said when she was done.

By now each of them was through her second drink, and Cara's comment had Jasmine laughing so hard tears leaked out of her eyes.

"I do. I seriously do," she managed to squeak out. "And of course, my dear sisters, to whom I always turn for guidance on matters such as this, give me conflicting advice. I have no idea what to do."

"I say you ride it out," Cara said. "I mean, you want to give things with Parker a chance. But you don't want to miss out on your chance with Hudson."

"Exactly!" Jasmine said, vindication making her heart swell. "But I feel kind of like I'm cheating on both of them."

"Well, you should," Cara said. "Which is why you have to be very careful."

An hour later, Jasmine and Cara counted up the empty Bloody Mary glasses they'd lined up at the edge of their table.

"That's eight," Jasmine said. "Three for each of us."

"Wow," Cara said. "You're a serious drinker. And terrible at math."

"As are you, my friend," Jasmine said.

"I just wanted to bust through that secretive exterior," Cara said.

They fell into fits of giggles at that point, and Jasmine realized she shouldn't be driving them back to the newsroom. "I'm going to call Hudson to come get us," she said.

"I'm sure you are," Cara said. "Only, doesn't he drive a motorcycle?"

Again, the two of them were overcome by giggles, and Jasmine said, "I guess I'll call Parker."

"Here's where having two men at your beck and call comes in handy."

CHAPTER TWENTY

"Wow," Cara said, resting a hip against Jasmine's desk the next morning. "You actually did it." She pointed at the dog park photo on the front page of the newspaper. "You turned that dog park thing into a real story. It actually brought tears to my eyes."

Jasmine glanced at Hudson's back and could see him tensing. He was probably afraid Cara's comment would hurt Jasmine's feelings.

"Well, as I saw yesterday, you're prone to crying jags," Jasmine said.

"Ha. Seriously, though, it was a good story. That guy whose dog saved his life? I mean, how did you even get to that shit? How did you know what to ask?"

"Feature writing is the art of subtlety," Jasmine said. She was half-joking, but felt a tiny bit of pride.

Cara stood up. "Well, maybe you can share your secrets with me over lunch. Your treat. Except, let's stick to soda today."

Chuckling, Cara walked back to her own desk before Jasmine could say she had a lunch date. It turned out to be a good thing, though, because Jasmine's date was with Parker … and she couldn't have Hudson finding out about that.

Parker arrived a few minutes later. Jasmine had been watching for his van, and as soon as it pulled into the parking lot, she jetted outside.

"I want to try a new place," Jasmine said as she climbed into the passenger seat. "Somewhere we've never been."

The truth was that Hudson had a photo assignment downtown, so she'd found a restaurant uptown to ensure they didn't cross paths. But Parker didn't need to know that.

"How about that new bistro downtown?" he said. "I heard they have good salads."

"I was thinking something off the beaten path," she said. "Something out of the way."

Was that too suspicious?

He shrugged. "Okay. You call it."

"There's a little café on the west side. It just opened. I haven't really heard anything about it, but maybe we can try it out."

As they drove, Parker said, "Remember that time you wanted to go for a hike somewhere you'd never been before? You said to me, 'Somewhere off the beaten path, Parker. Something out of the way.'"

"I do remember," Jasmine said. "We ended up getting lost and hiking for three hours just to get back to the trailhead."

"Nice hike, though," Parker said. "I was miffed because I thought we were going to be hiking for an hour or so, and you were like, 'It's all about the journey. Enjoy it.'"

Yes, Jasmine remembered that day. They'd gone to the redwood forest. They started in the morning, and throughout the day the sun burned off the fog, coming down through the flat leaves in spikes. Birds chirped and butterflies flitted between the tree trunks. They came across a wooden viewing platform that faced a waterfall, and stood there, feeling the cool spray on their faces.

"You know, this would be a perfect place to have a picnic lunch," Parker said then, and Jasmine felt guilty for not having thought of packing food. She was getting hungry, too, but she was so enjoying the scenery, and being in it with Parker, that eating didn't seem strictly necessary.

"I didn't see this on the map," he said, and then he answered himself: "Oh, yes! That's because we didn't get a trail map. Jasmine insisted on flying by the seats of our pants."

"Well, I'm having a lovely time," she said, and Parker grunted and turned away.

Jasmine couldn't stand to see him unhappy, so she insisted on hiking back to the trailhead even though she could have spent all day in the forest. "You know, I could make us a little redwood salad," she said at one point as they trudged in what they thought was the direction of the parking lot. "Throw in some bark, some leaves, maybe even some pieces of that plant right there."

"That's poison oak."

"Oh. Right."

As they continued to walk, Parker became more irritated and Jasmine felt more guilty. They didn't speak again for a long time, and the scenery that had felt so welcoming just an hour before now felt like a vast maze, a complicated labyrinth through which Parker's anger followed Jasmine like a minotaur.

When they finally made their way back to the trailhead, Parker drove straight to a convenience store and bought several of the greasy hot dogs that spun continuously on the metal heater. He knew Jasmine hated those hot dogs, but handed her one anyway. She didn't eat it and instead sat in silence while he drove her home. She spent most of the evening in her bedroom, poring through magazines to find quizzes that would answer questions like, "Are you compatible with your boyfriend?" or "Are you and your boyfriend destined for the long-term?"

That night, she fell asleep with a feeling of foreboding heavy in her stomach.

He'd called the next morning as if nothing had happened, and they'd resumed things as normal. It was only a few days later that Parker's dad had announced their impending departure. Of course, that news colored the rest of their days with the rosy shade of tragedy and longing.

"Believe me," the present-day Jasmine said, "I have not forgotten that day. And now, they have GPS. Want me to enter the restaurant's address on my phone so you don't go hungry?"

Parker grinned at her. "I was starving. What can I say? I was a growing teenage boy."

The café was suitably out of the way, on the back side of a new shopping complex, facing a cement block wall and the freshly turned dirt of a just-completed construction project.

Not very romantic, but it'll get the job done.

"Didn't want to be seen with me, huh?" Parker said, elbowing her gently as they approached the hostess station.

She answered, a little too defensively, "No, that's not it at all, I just wanted to try this place, I swear." When she actually looked at him and saw that he was joking, she wished she had bit her tongue. She wondered if he'd noticed how intense her response was.

Inside, black and white pencil drawings lined black walls, and red chairs grouped around white tables. The floor was shiny concrete and the black linen napkins were folded into little teepees that stood on red-and-white checkered placemats.

The hostess—dressed in tight black slacks, a starched white shirt unbuttoned to the cleavage, and unreasonably high red heels—led them to a table in the corner. The menu was printed on one side of a long narrow piece of card stock with artfully torn edges. It featured three appetizers, three salads, and four entrées, an unusual meat like buffalo or quail playing a starring role in each. The average price point for the salads was well more than twice that of a good, fat burrito at the taco stand down the street from Jasmine's office.

"Well, you wanted something off the beaten path," Parker said under his breath, and they both giggled.

"No wonder we're the only ones here," Jasmine said. "Word must have spread fast."

"Would you like the duck breast with lamb wool or the lamb hooves with duck fat?" Parker said.

Again, they dissolved into giggles, both of them hunched over the table in hilarity until they realized someone was standing there, clearing his throat.

"Pardon me, Sir and Madam," the waiter said. He used one delicate finger to push his glasses up on his nose. "May I take your drink orders, please?"

Jasmine steadied herself with a deep breath. Parker said, "Two waters, please. Ice and lemon."

The server nodded, and with an air of superiority, glided away as if he were walking on air.

"Should we leave?" Parker said, before Jasmine could tell him she never ordered lemon any more because she read an article about how they harbor germs in restaurant settings.

"We just got here," Jasmine said. "What if we hurt their feelings?"

"Whose? The trendy waiter guy who can barely stand the sight of us? Or the hostess who moonlights as a porn star?"

Jasmine smiled, and it felt a bit wobbly. Panic-induced wobbliness, probably. If they left here, they may run into Hudson. She said, "I think we should stick it out. Give it a chance. Maybe duck breath soup is better than it sounds."

"All right," Parker said. He inserted quacking noises into the conversation every few moments throughout the meal. It was, in fact, better than Jasmine expected, although she wasn't sure if she would ever come back.

For a moment after they finished eating, she considered walking back to work so Hudson wouldn't see her arriving at the office with Parker. The unfortunate truth was that it was too far to walk. So she hatched a plan. Even though Hudson hadn't taught her to juggle just yet, she thought she was doing a fine job of it.

"I kind of feel like a coffee," she said as they walked out of the restaurant. "Want to drop me off at that Golden Bean place? It's just a couple of blocks from the office. I can just walk from there."

"Why don't I just wait for you to run in and then I'll drive you back? Wait. You don't even drink coffee."

Perhaps because of the self-induced pressure of hiding these two men from one another, she felt like snapping at him, "You don't know everything about me, Parker Abbott."

Then she had this strange urge to talk about how Hudson had converted her. And then she decided to play it safe.

"Well, I could use a tea. You know. Coffee, tea. It's a coffee shop, so…"

"I'll just drive you there and then take you back to the office."

"You know, actually, maybe I don't want one." She felt her smile spread wide across her face, bordering on crazed. "Never mind. Why don't you just drop me off at the paper?"

Parker took a step back from her, like he was afraid she might lose it. "Okay, Jas. I'll take you back straight away."

"Thanks, Park."

The drive back to the office was awkward, Jasmine thought, and it was her fault. Her strange attempts at ensuring Parker and Hudson didn't cross paths were definitely going to backfire. What would she say to Hudson when he saw Parker drop her off? What would he say to her?

She might say, "What pact?" No, that was too obvious. Maybe something like, "No big deal. We were just having lunch. What's the big deal?" And then Hudson might say, "What the hell are you doing with that longhaired clod?" or, "I thought you weren't sticking to that stupid pact."

Jasmine jiggled her leg, her heel banging repeatedly against the floorboards.

"Are you okay?" Parker asked at one point, turning down the music and peering at her.

"What? Yeah, totally."

She scanned the roadway, looking for signs of Hudson's motorcycle. She didn't see him. Did that mean he was at the office, already? As quickly as she could, she calculated the amount of time that had passed since they both left. He would have had plenty of time to drive to wherever he was going, shoot some photos and come back.

"I'm fine," she said.

"You're acting totally weird," Parker said.

Jasmine shrugged.

He turned the van into the alleyway behind the *Daily Trumpet*, and Jasmine felt herself sliding down lower in her seat. Involuntarily. Maybe she should buy a disguise. Dark glasses and a floppy sunhat.

"This is ridiculous," she muttered. Then she pressed her lips together and thought, *I have nothing to be ashamed of.*

"What?" Parker said.

She straightened up in her seat and lifted her chin.

"Thank you for a lovely time."

She opened her door before he even stopped the van. Then, with Parker staring after her, open-mouthed, Jasmine stepped down and waved good-bye. It was only then that she realized Hudson's bike wasn't in the parking lot. She simultaneously heaved a sigh of relief and mentally kicked herself for being an idiot.

"So what if I'm dating two guys at once," she said as she yanked open the newsroom door and stalked to her desk. "People do it all the time. It's not a crime."

"What's not a crime?" Cara, her smile impish, spun around in her desk chair to face Jasmine. "Couldn't help but overhear."

"Dating two guys at once."

"It's totally not a crime," Cara said. "But my question is, why are you working so hard to convince yourself of that?"

Jasmine didn't get a chance to answer Cara's question, because Hudson walked into the newsroom.

"Hello, ladies," he said, and Jasmine sagged into her chair with relief.

"Everything okay?" he said.

Cara shot Jasmine a look. Jasmine smiled at Hudson, and not for the first time that day, she had the feeling her smile was a little too wide. She made an effort to tone it down. "Everything's fine," she said.

He shot her an expression that said he didn't believe her. Jasmine jumped when her phone rang. Then, she dug around in her purse for it, fumbled it once she found it, and finally pressed it to her ear before she realized she hadn't pushed, "Answer."

Cara grinned at her. Hudson shook his head. Jasmine answered the phone.

"It's Elijah Sawyer," said a brisk, curt voice. "We need to talk."

His serious tone made her uncomfortable, like wearing a pair of shoes with one sole disconnected and flapping each time she took a step. This discomfort made her want to say something like, "Wow, that's the worst proposition I've heard all week," but she didn't. Instead she pressed her lips together before saying, "Okay."

Elijah said he'd be at the office in an hour. She wanted to ask whether he wanted to ask if she had any plans before he just showed up and commandeered her day. She hung up before she could do any such thing.

"You look like a little kid," Hudson said. "Like it's everything you can do to keep from laughing right now."

"That Elijah Sawyer is so serious. I don't know why, but it makes me feel like laughing."

"I'm sure he'd appreciate that sentiment," Hudson said. "What did he want?"

"He just said, 'We need to talk,' and said he'd be here in an hour."

"Want me to sit in with you?" Hudson said.

Jasmine went from hilarity to irritation in a split second. "Do you not think I can ask serious reporter questions?"

"It's not that at all, it's—"

"It's just that you think I can only report on fluff."

"You just said it yourself. The serious stuff makes you uncomfortable."

"No, I said Elijah Sawyer's serious tone makes me want to laugh."

Cara stood up and cleared her throat. "I'll just be in the break room. I think I saw some donuts in there. Or something."

Hudson watched her go. Jasmine flounced over to her desk chair and sat down in it. Before she realized what was happening, though, it rolled out from under her. She fell on the floor, her butt hitting hard and her feet in the air. For one second, the newsroom was totally silent. Hudson's mouth formed an *O*, and then he leapt out of his chair and offered his hand to help her up.

She declined his help, and wincing, managed to get onto all fours and then bring herself to a standing position. He stood there in front of her, blinking, his hand still out, palm up. Despite her bottom throbbing in a terrible way, she straightened her spine, adjusted her clothes and sat down (gingerly).

Hudson exhaled and walked back to his desk. Fortunately, Jasmine's desk phone rang. She snatched it up, grateful for the distraction.

"Hey." Sequoia's voice sounded even more tense than usual, if that was possible.

"You sound tense," they both said at the same time.

"I just fell out of my chair," Jasmine said, and Sequoia said, "I need to talk to you."

"What's up?" Jasmine said.

"Why'd you fall out of your chair? It's that good-looking guy, isn't it?"

Jasmine's face turned red and her eyes—completely of their own accord—flicked over to Hudson. *Why is he looking at me?* As she felt the heat spread across her cheeks, his expression went from curious to predatory. She looked at a paper on her desk and started doodling in the margins.

"What's up?" Jasmine said again.

"I think it's my boss stealing the money."

"But I can't quote you, right? This is off the record?"

"Stop talking in your weird spooky voice. You can't write the story, Jas. She's a horrible woman. She'll come down on me."

"What do you mean, 'come down on you'?" Jasmine said. "Don't you think you're being a bit dramatic, even for you?"

"I mean, before the story comes out, you're going to have to ask her questions, right? Isn't that what reporters do? They ask for comments?"

"Yes, but—"

"So you're going to ask her questions, which will give her a heads up."

"But I'm sure she'll know disciplinary action is coming from the department before I even publish anything."

"You've already published something, Jas. Remember? You published something about the missing money."

"Yeah, but—"

"She could demote me, before anybody even takes disciplinary action. Because of your stories."

"Because of my stories? Sequoia—"

"Yes, because of your stories. When is that old lady reporter going to be back?"

"I don't know, a few more weeks. Her daughter—"

"A few more weeks?"

"Stop interrupting me!"

"Aren't you just, like, the features reporter or something? I mean, when did you become an *actual* reporter? Why do you even care about this story?"

Jasmine's face heated up again, but this time it was with anger.

"You know what, Sequoia," she said, spluttering. Even as she struggled to come up with a solid retort, she felt Hudson's presence behind her. "I like features reporting. It's important to me. And you don't have to knock it. As for your boss, I'm sorry. But I'm just doing my job. Why don't you do yours, and then you won't have to worry about being demoted?"

She slammed the phone down onto the receiver and was surprised to notice her hands were shaking.

"You okay?" Hudson said.

Jasmine put her elbows on the desk and her head in her hands. "I'm fine. I feel like she's being overdramatic. Her boss wouldn't demote her over my stories. Anyway. I never have been able to come up with good comebacks for her."

"The older sister?"

"Of course."

"Want to talk about it?"

"Nope. Sequoia's just going to have to deal with me being a real reporter."

Hudson shrugged. "Want to go somewhere else, and not talk about it? Before your meeting with Elijah?"

Tempting, Jasmine thought. *Very tempting.*

"You're taking your time to answer," he said. "Which means you want to go with me. Come on, I'll take you for a quick ride. We still have a little time."

She caved. Of course she did. Cara returned from wherever she'd gone just in time to see Jasmine pick up her purse. She winked as she watched Jasmine following Hudson through the newsroom. When he opened the door for her, Cara gave her a questioning look. Jasmine shrugged as she ducked outside. She realized she always tried to make herself smaller, and though she suddenly wondered why, she didn't have the mental space to develop an answer. Hudson handed her the spare helmet and she pushed it onto her head.

If Parker saw her, he probably wouldn't recognize her with the helmet on. She tucked her hair into the back of her shirt to disguise herself even further.

"Wind. Tangles," she said to Hudson, even though he hadn't said anything.

"You could braid it," he said. He shrugged, then climbed onto the bike. She climbed on behind him, and was surprised at how natural it felt to slide forward along the seat until their bodies were touching. He leaned back against her, just for a moment, and she felt that deep yearning pulling at her lower belly. Then he put his hands on the handlebars and kicked the bike into gear. As he pulled out of the parking lot, Jasmine let her body soften against his.

After what Jasmine knew was miles, but what seemed like a few very short moments, Hudson parked the bike in a tiny lot Jasmine recognized as belonging to one of the state parks. She took just a moment longer than necessary to inhale the smell of Hudson's leather jacket and peel her body away from his. They stowed their helmets, and he offered her his hand. She took it.

The trail wound down through the redwood forest. The trees themselves shot into the sky and sun reached down through the leaves, sending shafts of light onto the creek so it twinkled like magic. Hudson pulled Jasmine further into the forest. She followed, willingly, and drank in the cool shade and musical birdsong.

"This is my favorite spot," he said when they'd come to a copse of deciduous trees whose leaves shimmered in the breeze and sunlight.

He pulled her off the trail to a place where the trees formed a circle, and the ground in its center was flat and smooth, almost as if it were manmade. Wildflowers in purple and yellow and fiery orange grew around the circle's edge.

"This is beautiful," Jasmine said. She stood at the center and turned around slowly as she looked up at the trees and the sky. "I've never been here before."

Hudson came up behind her and wrapped his arms around her waist. Jasmine imagined Sequoia's voice whispering in her ear that he might actually be a serial killer, having brought her to a remote location to perform his ritualistic killing. Then Hudson's actual voice whispered, "Like I said, it's my favorite. But it's even better when you're here, too."

She intertwined her fingers with his and leaned back against him. The longer they stood there, the more Jasmine felt like they were at the center of the world, motionless, the earth turning around them.

"We could just stay here for the rest of the day," Jasmine said. "Forget Elijah Sawyer and the money laundering and the newspaper."

"I like that idea," Hudson said. His breath in her ear made Jasmine shiver. Then he spun her around to face him. She thought he was going to kiss her, here in this magical spot, but he didn't. Instead, he began to dance with her. Jasmine turned her head so her cheek rested against Hudson's chest. They swayed to silent music.

At one point, Hudson inhaled as if he were going to say something, but apparently decided not to.

"What are you thinking?" Jasmine said.

"Just work stuff," Hudson said. "But we can talk about it later. I realized I was about to ruin the moment."

Jasmine smiled. "This is a pretty nice moment," she said.

"It is."

Jasmine and Hudson walked back through the forest in near-silence. She couldn't decide whether she felt disappointed that he hadn't stripped her down in that magical alcove and made love to her right on the ground, or relieved that she didn't have to return to the office with post-sex hair and redwood leaves inside the back of her pants.

Why didn't he want to ravish her? Was it something she'd done or hadn't done? Or maybe something she'd said or hadn't said. Maybe she smelled funny, but she couldn't really tell right now. She made a mental note to give herself the sniff test when she got a moment alone.

During the ride back to work, Jasmine couldn't discern between the rumble of the bike's engine and the vibration running through her body, making her entire being buzz.

When they entered the newsroom, Cara gave her yet another look. Jasmine was positive her expression showed some kind of guilt. She felt her ears turning red.

"Oh, Jas," Hudson said before they went their opposite directions. Her lower belly warmed at his casual use of her name. "I wanted to talk to you before you have your meeting with Elijah Sawyer."

Just like that, the buzz was gone. Jasmine nodded. Cara turned back around to face her computer. *Nothing to see here, folks,* Jasmine thought. *Unfortunately.*

"I guess we don't need privacy for this conversation," she said, under her breath. She didn't miss the quick, rueful smile he sent her before he became serious. She said, "Put on your game face."

Now, he laughed. "So I just wanted to say, don't let him off the hook. He's probably going to come in here and tell you he needs more time on the investigative end of things. But you've got to make him give you something. Our readers are expecting you to put something out there."

Jasmine nodded.

"Jesus. You're nodding at me like I'm a little kid, asking for a pet dragon."

Jasmine shrugged one shoulder. "Well, of course I know the readers are expecting something, but I can only take what he gives me. Right?"

"Wrong," Hudson said. Jasmine felt prickly. How could this man turn her into a puddle one minute and want to punch him in the face the next? "You've got to push him. You can get something out of him. Something new."

"Thanks for the advice, Hudson," Jasmine said. She spun around and started to walk to her desk, exaggerating her movements so he could read her irritation, but he stopped her by grabbing her wrist and spinning her back around to face him. He planted a firm kiss on her mouth, and said, "You're welcome."

Despite the kiss's brevity, Jasmine could feel something

simmering beneath it. He let her walk away, then, and when her cell phone indicated an incoming text message, she hurried to pick it up, just to give herself something to do with all the tension in her body.

The text was from Parker: *Dinner tonight?*

"I'M GOING to be up front with you," Elijah Sawyer said when Jasmine closed the conference room door behind them.

"Please do," she said.

"I think something fishy is going on with the department's budget. I'm investigating it myself. Right now, I don't have anything to give you. I can't tell you anything on the record."

"So…" Jasmine said.

"So, you're going to have to wait to print any comments from the department, I guess. For the time being, this is a non-story, in my opinion."

"Actually, it's not a non-story right now," Jasmine said. "In fact," she said, spreading her stack of papers on the table in front of him, "I've done some research and it looks like Seabreeze PD spends significantly more money on legal fees than other departments of a similar size. I can run the story with or without a comment from the Seabreeze PD. That's up to you."

Yes, she felt smug. Just a little bit. Hudson would approve. Elijah Sawyer almost had to say something now.

"You know, I'm surprised to hear you talking like this," he said.

That is not what I was expecting him to say.

"Like what?" Jasmine said.

"Well, your sister told me you're just the features reporter. Standing in for the regular cops reporter. She said to go easy on you."

These three sentences struck Jasmine on several different levels. First, she was peeved that, once again, Sequoia referred to her as "just" the features reporter. Second, she found it irritating that Sequoia had thought Elijah should "go easy" on her. Third, she realized Sequoia had spoken to Elijah Sawyer, and she wondered if this meant they might go on a date. Or if they already had. Or maybe they were just sleeping together.

"I don't even know where to begin," Jasmine said.

"Sequoia said you might say that," Elijah said.

"Yeah, I'm sure she did," Jasmine said. "But not for the reasons you're thinking. I can't believe she said that!"

"She's just trying to protect you," he said.

"I don't need protection."

"Maybe you two are more alike than you think you are."

"You don't even know us," Jasmine said, although she watched his face for any signs to the contrary. Nothing. He had a perfect poker face. "Anyway, that's beside the point. I'm writing a story. You can either have input, or not. It's up to you."

"I don't have any input to give you," Elijah said.

"Fine," Jasmine said. "Then why did you come here?"

"To tell you I can't tell you anything."

"You should have saved yourself a trip. You could have called or emailed."

Elijah shrugged, and Jasmine felt guilty. He seemed uncertain of himself, like he wanted to tell her more, but couldn't.

"I guess we're done here," he said. "I'll let you know when I have something to tell you. On the record."

"Is there anything you can tell me, off the record?" Jasmine said.

A small sound, something between a laugh and a grunt, escaped Elijah's mouth. "Nope."

"Fine. I'll see you out."

"I can see myself out."

"So?" Hudson caught Jasmine as she walked out of the conference room a few minutes behind Elijah. So what if she'd needed to get her composure after he stalked out? She had expected Hudson to be waiting for her, but not in the hallway. Now he knew she'd been sitting alone in the conference room for several minutes.

"Wait. Were you actually waiting for me outside the conference room? Did you have a paper cup against the door, so you could hear what we were saying?"

Hudson had the decency to look embarrassed, but he cleared his throat and said, "How'd it go?"

"It went fine."

"Did he give you anything?"

"He came to tell me he couldn't give me anything," Jasmine said.

"Wait. What? Did you just accept that?"

"Well, I told him I was writing the story, and that he could comment or not comment. It was up to him."

Hudson nodded. "And what did he say?"

"He said that's fine. And then he left."

"Wait. He left? You let him just leave? Without giving you anything?"

"Yeah. I can't make him."

Hudson shrugged. "Okay."

Jasmine pushed past him. "Oh, I'm so glad that meets with your approval."

She heard Hudson laugh as she walked back to her desk. Before he could see what she was doing, she grabbed her phone and responded to Parker: *Sure. Dinner tonight sounds great.*

CHAPTER TWENTY-ONE

Seabreeze was a small town. There were only so many places Jasmine could take Parker and feel reasonably assured they wouldn't run into Hudson. The Jupiter Café, with its bizarre alien-inspired decor and glittery red vinyl seats, was one such place, and although Jasmine's stomach lurched at the idea of gluten-free vegan crepes with flax seed blueberry sauce, she figured Hudson would never set foot in here.

"An entire gluten-free, vegetarian menu?" Parker said when they sat down. "And what is with this table?"

The table's surface was glass, and it revealed an otherworldly scene: tiny doll heads atop toy tractor bodies and plastic lizards eating rubber arms and legs.

"Ambiance," Jasmine said. "And you're welcome. I'm helping you expand your palate."

"Whatever you say," Parker said. "I'm just excited we're having new experiences together."

Jasmine smiled at him, and stretched her arm across the alienscape to reach for Parker's hand. They perused the menu, and Jasmine found herself laughing.

"This is so weird," she said. "I'm sorry. I mean, I'm all about trying new things, but none of this looks appetizing, does it?"

"I mean, the cranberry-walnut salad looks okay," Parker said. "But all it's got for protein is nutritional yeast. I'm kind of scared to try it."

"Maybe we should just order this 'nice cream,'" Jasmine said, pointing to the dessert section.

"Dessert for dinner? I like it," Parker said.

The server, a young man with a Mohawk, dark eyeliner and gauges in his earlobes, came to take their order. Parker ordered two, "Nice cream? Shakes?" and Jasmine giggled.

"Maybe we should go back to my place and cook dinner after this," Jasmine said when the server walked away. "I mean, it's going to get expensive if we keep eating out all the time."

"That's a great idea," Parker said. "After we drink these nice cream shakes, we can go to the store. I could go for a nice, juicy steak and some gluten-filled French bread."

Jasmine giggled.

Suddenly, Parker's expression became serious. His eyes bored into Jasmine's in a way that stopped her giggling immediately and replaced it with a nervous stomach and sweaty palms.

"There's something I need to say, Jas."

Jasmine nodded. She noticed that his thumb, which had been making slow circles on her palm, stilled. "Go ahead."

"Look. I know we talked about this before, but I just wanted to make sure we're still on the same page. You're not seeing anyone else, right? I mean, in order for this thing, this pact, to work, I really think we need to be exclusive. Give us a fair chance, you know?"

Panic set in. Jasmine's armpits tingled. If Parker hadn't been holding her hand, she was positive it would give her away, probably flitting from the table to her hair to her necklace. She wondered if he could feel her trembling. She nodded, concentrating hard on doing it slowly, as if it were a natural agreement.

He peered at her, obviously waiting for her to say something out loud. So she said, "Of course," and nodded some more.

"Glad we got that out of the way," he said. "I don't know why, I was just worried about it."

Jasmine smiled. "You've got nothing to worry about."

"Actually, I'll be honest, here."

Uh oh.

"I think I do know why I was worried. I think it's because of that Hudson guy. I mean, he's obviously into you. I saw the way he was looking at you. And I know you said it's not mutual. But the two of you spend so much time together. You know? I just want you to be honest with me, too. If this whole pact thing isn't working out."

"I understand," Jasmine said.

The nice cream shakes weren't bad, the two of them decided, but they agreed dinner was in order, so they went to the store. Grocery shopping with Parker offered a glimpse into what life could be like if Jasmine stayed with him. It was fun. Jasmine felt carefree. Parker convinced her to climb into the shopping cart and he pushed her around the store, running for a short distance to the French bread and then standing on the back of the basket to coast to the steaks. He tossed her the potatoes, one at a time, and cheered when she caught them.

He insisted on pushing her through the checkout line, and they both laughed hysterically when the cashier asked if Parker had gotten the four-digit code from produce so he could charge Parker for Jasmine.

Back at her house, Parker went through the cabinets like he lived there, too. Without asking where she kept the bowls or whisks or seasonings, he mixed up a marinade for the steaks and rubbed the potatoes with salt while Jasmine poured wine and rinsed vegetables for a salad.

At one point, while she was buttering the French bread, he came up behind her at the kitchen counter. He wrapped his arms around her waist and nuzzled her neck.

"This is so nice," he whispered. "I could do this all the time."

She set the knife down and turned around in his arms. "I know," she said. "It *is* so nice. We should do this more often."

Parker kissed her gently, and she let herself relax into it. He ran his hands down her sides. She sighed. He sighed. They leaned into each other. His body felt so good against hers.

"What dinner?" she said against his mouth.

He chuckled, a lazy sound that made her want to forget about everything else, for this night and every night, and just stand here with him in her kitchen.

Then her stomach growled.

"Okay, okay," Parker said. "I was really enjoying that, but hungry is hungry."

He kissed her one more time on the nose.

Over dinner, they talked about their high school friends and classmates.

"Remember that guy who we dressed up as a mermaid for our homecoming float junior year?" Jasmine said.

"The guy who was at the bow of the pirate ship?"

"Yes!" Jasmine said. "He's a dancer at Jungle now."

"Wait. So he's a drag queen?" Parker said.

"Yes!" Jasmine said. "I was so surprised. I mean, he was always pretty manly, with the big muscles and the six-pack. But the mermaid thing must have been the gateway into his going drag."

"That's crazy. I totally wanted to be that guy."

"We should go see him perform one night," Jasmine said. "That would be fun."

"We should," Parker said. "Although I admit I'm not sure how I feel about going to a drag queen show."

"It'll broaden your horizons," Jasmine said.

"Okay. I'll take your word for it. But if I don't like it, you owe me one. I'm going to have to take you to a UFC fight or something."

"Deal," Jasmine said, and Parker said, "Deal."

They shook hands.

Dinner was done, the dishes were clean and the kitchen was wiped down. Parker leaned against the counter, arms crossed. "So what now? That was delicious, by the way."

Jasmine folded a dish towel, for the third time, and smoothed it onto the counter next to the sink. She didn't know why she had so much nervous energy. "We could watch a movie."

"Want to sit on the couch and talk?" Parker winked at her.

As teenagers, they often sat on the couch together, but talking always turned into making out. When their parents or friends would ask what they'd done on a particular evening, they'd glance at each other and then say, "We sat on the couch and talked."

Now, that memory brought a smile to Jasmine's face. "I'd like that. Why don't you pour us each one more glass of wine, and I'll go pick a movie to put on?"

He nodded, but when she picked up her phone to carry it into the living room, he set the wine bottle down and pointed at the phone. "You should leave that here."

"What if someone calls? From work?"

"What if they do? You're allowed a night to yourself, Jas. I'm allowed a night to yourself." He raised his eyebrows and they both laughed. "Put it on silent. Just for tonight. And leave it in here. I promise, you won't even think about it. Not once."

That promise sent a surge of adrenaline through her body. She followed Parker's advice without another thought.

Jasmine chose one of her favorite movies, a romantic comedy about a woman so bad at dating that her friends take over her dating life. Parker came into the living room carrying the two glasses and the bottle of wine. He set everything on the coffee table. Again, nervous energy commandeered Jasmine's body. Although she'd already put the movie in the DVD player, she ejected it and put it in again. Then she spent more time than was strictly necessary finding the remote control and lining it up with the edge of the coffee table, centering it between the two wine glasses.

Why am I so nervous?

Parker sat on the couch. He picked up his wine and patted the couch cushion next to him. Jasmine smiled, but didn't feel quite ready to sit down.

"I'll just make some popcorn." She went into the kitchen and busied herself digging through the pantry.

Maybe she was afraid she'd freeze like she had the last time they started to get intimate. Poor Parker had planned that romantic weekend staycation and she'd shut him down before the romance even began. Maybe she was just unsure of how they would fit together after all this time. Would he still like the same things, like when she sucked on his fingertips? Or had his preferences changed?

Was this it? Were they about to have sex again? Was she ready for that? And if they did have sex, what did that mean for them? Would she feel like they had to be a couple, indefinitely? Did she want that?

"Jas? Everything okay?"

Jasmine spun around to face Parker. He stood in the doorway of the kitchen, one arm propped against the doorframe and the other still holding his wine. His smile was uncertain. Only then did Jasmine realize the microwave had stopped. She had no idea how long the popcorn had been done. Her body jerked into action.

"Everything's fine! Fine! I was just getting the popcorn. I had a hangnail. I was just trimming it real quick so it didn't bother me all night. Sorry about that."

Parker tilted his head, but didn't say anything. Jasmine retrieved the popcorn from the microwave, dumped it into a bowl and followed Parker back to the living room. She'd eaten so much at dinner, she didn't really have room for popcorn. She set the bowl on the table. Parker picked up the remote and started the movie. Jasmine leaned back and he draped his arm over the back of the couch.

The movie started.

"I'm too full for popcorn," Jasmine said.

"I was waiting for you to confess that," Parker said. "I am, too. That was a pretty big dinner. So, why are you so nervous right now? I can practically feel your nerves and you're sitting a foot and a half away from me."

Jasmine sighed. "I have no idea. I just feel like my body is full of this … tension."

"Maybe I should help relieve some of that tension."

Jasmine turned towards him, and he laughed. "Deer in the head-lights, woman. I didn't mean what you think I meant. Why don't you sit on the floor, right here, and I'll give you a massage?"

That didn't sound too intimidating. Once she was settled in front of him, Parker began kneading her shoulders. His thumbs moved in circles, starting at her shoulder blades and working up towards her neck and the base of her skull.

"This is heavenly," she said.

"And I haven't even started undressing you," he said. "Not yet, anyway."

She shivered. The movie's opening credits ended and the story began to play out. Parker kept massaging, and Jasmine found herself relaxing, finally.

"This is really nice," she said.

"It is," he said, "but my hands are getting tired. Why don't you come back up and sit next to me?"

When she did, she said, "Thank you for that. I feel so much better."

Then she leaned over and kissed him. He brought a hand up to her face, and the kiss deepened. There it was again: that slow burn, waking up from a long nap. No, it wasn't fireworks like she felt with Hudson. But it was like the warmth of the sun on her skin on an almost-cold spring day. Parker pulled away just long enough to say, "You're welcome," before kissing her again with an urgency that left her breathless.

Maybe this will be easier than I thought.

Parker laid down, and pulled Jasmine down next to him, so they were facing each other. He stopped kissing her just long enough to smile at her, and then covered her mouth with his again, running his fingertips up and down her arms until she practically melted against him. They didn't see much of the movie.

CHAPTER TWENTY-TWO

Jasmine's phone rang early the next morning. Actually, she realized when she saw the clock, it wasn't that early. It just felt early. Noticing the caller ID was secondary to noticing the time.

"Hudson," Jasmine said.

"Are you still sleeping?" he said.

She hadn't realized she'd answered. "Not anymore."

"Sorry. Want me to call you back?"

Jasmine shook her head. "No. It's fine. What's up?"

Now her heart pounded in her ears. He was probably calling to ask her out. It was the weekend, after all, which meant they could have a daytime date. What should she wear? The scarf? Or maybe not the scarf. She didn't want him to think she was baiting him into her bed. Although, maybe she did want him to think so.

"I wanted to talk to you about something," Hudson said.

He sounded so serious, Jasmine groaned. Maybe he wasn't calling to ask her out, after all. "I have a headache," she said.

"Out partying last night?"

The pain in Jasmine's head couldn't stop the visions of Parker underneath her on the couch, his hands on her skin and her legs intertwined with his. They hadn't actually had sex, she thought, but the intimacy was there.

"Not partying, no," she said. "Maybe a little too much wine. But I was home."

"Huh."

"So, what's up?" she said. She rolled onto her stomach and propped herself up on her elbows.

"I wanted to run a couple of ideas by you," Hudson said.

"Ideas about what?"

"That suicide prevention series."

Now, Jasmine dropped her face into her pillow.

"Hello?" Hudson said.

Even though she knew her voice was muffled, she said, "What about it?"

"Can we meet?"

"This is so not what I was expecting when I saw your name on the caller ID. Can we rewind and I just don't answer?"

Hudson barked out a laugh. "Uh, sure, Jas. I'll call you back."

When the line went dead, Jasmine flung her phone across the bed. She groaned into her pillow. "I was joking," she said to Ruby, who, apparently disgusted with her, jumped off the bed.

"Well, kind of," Jasmine said.

The phone rang again. Jasmine groaned again.

"Jasmine Carr, here," she said when she picked it up.

"Um, yes," Hudson said in a nasal voice that made Jasmine laugh despite herself. "I was calling to set up a meeting with the alert, enthusiastic Jasmine Carr. Is she available?"

"It depends," Jasmine said. "What's in it for her?"

"Tea and muffins?"

"Fine."

The English Garden Teahouse sat against a backdrop of redwoods and boasted a huge multi-tiered flower garden and an archway covered with wisteria.

"You look different this morning," Hudson said when Jasmine arrived at the appointed time.

Of course, this five-word sentence threw Jasmine into a panic. Could Hudson tell Parker had finally scratched her itch last night? Did she have post-almost-sex hair?

Was this like the Walk of Shame in college when she'd slept with Charlie Winston and left his dorm room early the next morning? They really had just slept, but naturally, all the college guys who were awake way earlier than seemed normal and saw her walking (tiptoeing, actually) down the hallway, believed they'd knocked boots. Jasmine arrived home and Sequoia, who had already finished a three-mile run and an egg white omelet, chastised her for being anywhere with post-sex hair.

Too mortified to correct her bossy big sister, Jasmine hadn't bothered answering and only confirmed Sequoia's suspicions when she headed straight to the shower.

So what did Hudson mean when he said she looked different this morning? She smoothed her hair.

"It's not your hair," he said.

She cringed.

"You just look so relaxed. Actually, I think this is the most relaxed I've seen you in a long time."

Jasmine brushed past him to walk into the English Garden. "You've rarely seen me on the weekends," she said over her shoulder.

While they waited in line to order, Jasmine obsessed over whether it was possible for Hudson to tell that she'd been with Parker last night. A make-out session with Parker felt a lot like cheating on Hudson. Especially when he insisted on paying for her tea and muffins, and then carried her tray to the table and pulled out her chair.

He'd worn a soft green sweater, and Jasmine had the strange urge to rub his back before she sat down. Instead, she put one hand on his shoulder and smiled. "Thank you."

He sat across from her and spent some time arranging her tea and muffins and his coffee and scone on the table.

"So?" Jasmine said. "What did you want to talk about?"

"All business this morning," Hudson said.

"Well, you woke me up on a Saturday to get together and talk about work stuff. Sounds like you're all business."

Hudson looked down at his plate and stirred his coffee with a little wooden stick. Suddenly, a realization dawned on Jasmine. Maybe he'd used work as an excuse to see her this morning. Otherwise, he wouldn't look so embarrassed, would he?

She softened her tone. "But we don't have to get right down to work stuff, if you'd rather chat first."

Still looking into his coffee, Hudson said, "It's fine. You're right. That was kind of weird of me to call you on a Saturday. I'm sorry. I thought I had a good reason, but I guess it could have waited until Monday."

Without warning, Hudson stood up. The legs of his chair scraped against the tile floor, and he stepped aside and shoved the chair back under the table. Jasmine felt her mouth drop open in surprise.

He looked down at her one more time, and she saw what looked like genuine sadness on his face. Then he walked out the door, leaving his coffee on the table. She wasn't sure if she should follow him or let him go.

But she knew heartbreak when she saw it. She wrapped her blueberry muffin in a napkin, grabbed their drinks, and followed him outside.

"You don't have to follow me," Hudson said.

He had walked past his motorcycle and was already halfway across the street. Jasmine found herself traveling at a near run to catch up with him. Her tea sloshed out of the hole in the lid of her to-go cup, and it burned her hand.

"Shit," she hissed.

Hudson didn't even slow his pace.

"Wait up," Jasmine said. The plea reminded her of her childhood, when she and Holly would beg Sequoia to "wait up" whenever they walked anywhere. Not only was Sequoia the oldest, but she'd also experienced an early growth spurt and her legs doubled in length before Holly or Jasmine even grew out of clothes in the Little Girls' department. When she discovered she could, she stalked everywhere at double-speed, Jasmine and Holly rushing along in her wake like little quail babies trying to keep up with their mama.

Of course, this memory made Jasmine feel like an idiot, and she yelled, "Stop!" in as strong of a voice as she could muster without making people nearby think she was being kidnapped.

Hudson turned around, then, and Jasmine was horrified to see tears in his eyes. Before she realized what she was doing, Jasmine ran to Hudson and wrapped her arms around his waist. Again, her tea spilled out of her cup. She managed not to flinch. But Hudson didn't.

"Holy crap!" he said. "Your tea is still really hot!"

Jasmine couldn't help it. After setting both of their drinks on the edge of the sidewalk, she laughed. At first, Hudson tensed. But after the briefest of seconds, she felt him relax, and then she felt him begin to laugh, too.

They stood there in the middle of the road, clinging to each other, laughing. When they finally broke apart, she saw him wipe beneath his eyes with his fingertips. She wanted to take his hand, but wasn't sure if he'd be receptive to that. Instead, she put a hand on his shoulder.

"Do you want to talk about it?" she said.

Hudson rubbed a hand over his face. "I don't know. I mean, you probably think I've lost my mind."

Jasmine nodded, and he elbowed her. She said, "I've just never seen you like this. Normally, you're so, I don't know. So composed. Happy go lucky, even." When he didn't answer right away, she said, "Yes. Happy go lucky, for sure."

Hudson laughed, but it was a dry, humorless laugh and even his small, tight smile looked wobbly. "Remember I told you a while ago about the friend who brought me whiskey-laced coffee when I passed out at a bloody news scene?"

"Yes. That story held special meaning for me," Jasmine said.

"His name was Will. Will Richardson. He was one of my best friends. Let's walk."

He picked up their drinks, handed Jasmine's to her, and started walking up the sidewalk, away from the English Garden. Jasmine followed him.

"Anyway," Hudson said, "Will. He was a cops reporter, like I said, at my first newspaper job. We were the same age at the time, early twenties. Will was that guy, you know? He was that guy every-body liked. Cops would practically throw information at him, even when other reporters had to beg for it. Other reporters were always hanging around his desk, just waiting to see what he'd do next, who he'd call, how he'd talk to them. He'd call a source who was pissed off at the editor for that day's editorial and by the end of the call, he'd have that source eating out of his hand, giving him everything he needed for a kick-ass story, and offering to buy him a beer. Anyway. We were inseparable. We rode to stories together. That was back when I had a real car. We ate together. We hung out together after work, shooting pool or having beers and watching movies. You know? The girls teased us that we were BFFs. So one day, Will doesn't show up for work."

A seed of fear took root in Jasmine's stomach. She had a feeling about where this story was going. Even though she still wasn't sure whether it was appropriate to do so, she took Will's hand. He didn't resist. Noon was approaching, and the street became increasingly busy. Hudson's voice barely rose above the sounds of the traffic.

"So at first, I thought it was something dumb," Hudson said. "Like he was hungover. Or he overslept. Or his car wouldn't start. He had this piece of shit little hatchback, and it was always giving him trouble. And you know how it is, working for a newspaper. You show up when you show up in the morning. You're never really late for work, right? But Will never came in past eleven or noon. And he *never* just didn't show up. Until that day. It was a Wednesday. I remember because the convenience store where we used to stop for coffee always had a special on Wednesdays where you could buy a coffee and get a free pastry. As usual, I'd bought two coffees and picked up two pastries. I love bear claws, and Will loves—loved—croissants. Don't ask me why. So I put them on his desk, as always, anticipating that he'd be in the office shortly. We almost always showed up within fifteen minutes of each other, because, like I said, we were inseparable. Our schedules were pretty much the same."

They came to an intersection threw their empty cups away when they stopped for traffic. Hudson led Jasmine across the street and she wondered how much farther they'd walk. He seemed to have lost his sense of time and place.

"By noon," Hudson went on, "everybody was talking about Will. 'Where's Will?' 'Probably hungover.' Or, 'Shouldn't Will be here by now? His coffee's getting cold.' 'Someone should do him a favor and eat that croissant before it dries out.' You know, all the normal stuff people say. Before worry sets in."

Jasmine didn't imagine Hudson was much of a worrier. He seemed so practical.

"I know you're thinking I'm not much of a worrier, and you're right. At first I was having all the same thoughts as everyone else. I was even considering practical jokes I could play on him. Fortunately, it was a busy morning and I didn't get time to put a Post-It note over his mouse tracker or foil all over his desk. Someone suggested moving his entire workstation to a different cubicle. Which would have been funny, right?"

Jasmine nodded. She swallowed, hoping that would loosen the tightening in her throat.

"So finally, it's one p.m. and somebody asks if anybody's called Will. I tell them I texted him at eleven that his coffee was getting cold, but that I didn't get a response back. Somebody else suggests that one of us should go to his house and see if he's there. Of course, everyone looks at me. I'm the natural choice. Our editor back then is this old lady, Midge Henechek. She chain smoked and wore silk blouses and never smiled. But she always brought us homemade soup if we were sick. So, everyone's nominating me to go to Will's. And Midge, she looks at me with her beady eyes, real carefully, and says, 'I think I'll go. Hudson, you hold down the fort.'"

"That must have made you really worried," Jasmine said.

Hudson nodded. He must have realized then that he was squeezing her hand pretty hard, and he massaged it as they continued walking. "Yeah. It suddenly dawned on me that maybe I should be nervous. So I sat at my desk and tried to write some cutlines, schedule some photo assignments, that kind of thing. But I was too distracted. I couldn't do anything. Every time someone's phone rang, I jumped. Time just ticked by, so slowly. It was the longest hour of my life. Finally, the call came. Of course, old Midge didn't call me. She called another reporter, a girl I kind of had a crush on."

He sneaked a smile at Jasmine, who smiled back.

"Anyway, it was like everyone in the newsroom knew. This other reporter, her phone rang, and we all watched her answer it. Her body stiffened, and she became closed off, you know? Like she was keeping a secret. The rest of us started looking at each other, then back at her. She was practically whispering. None of us could hear what she was saying, only that she was murmuring. After she hung up, she sat at her desk, completely still. None of us spoke. It was eerie. Finally, she turned around, and her face, it was just so pale. It was then that I knew he was gone. Even though we were in a roomful of reporters, nobody asked her what had just happened. We all just waited. She looked at each one of us in turn, her eyes resting on one face after another, and then she looked at me. She said, 'Will's dead.'"

The present-day Hudson broke into sobs. Jasmine stopped walking and pulled him into an embrace. They stood there on the sidewalk, in the dappled shade of a sycamore tree, and he cried and cried.

"I'm so sorry," Jasmine whispered. She wasn't sure if he could hear her over his crying, but she didn't say it again. She rubbed his back, and waited.

Finally, Hudson straightened up and took a tissue out of his pocket.

"That was a year ago, today," he said. His voice was still shaky. "I guess I felt like I needed company. Maybe work stuff was just an excuse to spend the day with you."

Jasmine smiled. She took both his hands in hers.

"Now I understand why you wanted to do that series, though," she said. "I mean, it's a good idea either way, but now I see the personal connection. I see why it's so important to you."

Hudson nodded. "If we could help just one person, give him hope or a place to find support, then maybe we could prevent people like Will's parents from losing their children. Or people like me from losing their best friends. At the time, I didn't even realize he was, you know, suicidal. I still have trouble saying that word. He was usually upbeat, you know? We had so much fun together. He was always smiling, laughing, joking around. I never would have guessed he'd feel so hopeless."

"I'm so sorry," Jasmine said again. "That must have been so hard for you."

Hudson gritted his teeth. "It was. Especially because in hindsight, I could think of so many warning signs, you know? I mean, even though he was usually in a great mood, there were little things he said or did that should have tipped me off. One day, a week before he died, he gave me this black and white photo print that used to hang in his living room. You probably saw it when you came over the other day. I was checking it out, and he asked if I liked it. I said I did, and he took it down and handed it to me. 'It's one of my favorites,' he said. 'I want you to have it.' Almost like he was planning his death, even then."

"I know this is morbid," Jasmine said. "But did he leave a note or anything? To let people know why he did it?"

Hudson shook his head. "No. Not a word. I guess he had some issues with depression as a teenager, but his family thought he'd overcome them. I've always wondered if he just tried to hide it so no one would worry about him. And then he just couldn't keep up the façade."

"That makes sense, actually," Jasmine said. "That's so sad."

"I just wish he'd known how great life can be," Hudson said. "I just wish he'd known he wasn't alone." His voice wavered again.

"We'll do the series," Jasmine said. "For Will. And for you."

Somehow, Jasmine and Hudson ended up at the beach. They stood on the wet sand and let the small waves lap at their feet while they tossed pebbles and pieces of broken shells into the ocean. In a flawless sky, the midday sun cast a ribbon of white across the bright blue sea. For more than an hour, they stayed there, following the tide. They barely spoke to one another, except when Jasmine pointed out a huge pelican swooping down into the water, and when Hudson found a sand dollar, which he gave to Jasmine.

"I guess I should get home," Hudson finally said, his voice scratchy from lack of use. Jasmine reached out to squeeze his hand and they walked back to the English Garden's parking lot without letting go. They hugged, and Jasmine held him for a long time before they went their separate ways.

Driving back home, Jasmine felt emotionally exhausted. Everything seemed brighter. The sun shone harsh on the red tile roofs of the buildings, and the sky was so blue it hurt her eyes. She couldn't imagine feeling so hopeless that ending her life was the best option. She also couldn't imagine finding out one day that someone she thought she knew was gone. Out of nowhere.

In her own house, everything seemed quiet and lonely. The sounds of ceramic dishes clinking as she put them away made Jasmine flinch. Ruby's toenails on the tile floor sounded like the pounding of a hammer.

Even so, she spent the evening brainstorming about the suicide prevention series. She could find statistics to work with. That would be a good starting point. And she could interview social workers, counselors, psychologists, and doctors. Where could she find someone who struggled with suicidal thoughts? She imagined herself walking along downtown, asking random people, "Have you ever been suicidal?"

Feeling out of her element, she thought she could probably ask another "real" reporter to take on this series. But she didn't want to. For the first time in her career, she felt like this project was something she should take on. Hopefully she could handle it.

What was it about Hudson that made her want to help him? What was it about him that motivated her to delve into a serious news topic—one that made her really uncomfortable—as a serious journalist?

She wasn't sure, but it didn't really matter. Hudson Stover was bringing out a new part of Jasmine. Even more importantly, she liked it.

CHAPTER TWENTY-THREE

"Okay, I'm ready to get to work." Jasmine spread her computer printouts across the conference table, and Hudson gave her a low whistle.

"I'm impressed," he said. "It's nine a.m. on a Monday and you already have a whole ream of papers to work off of."

"So I printed all this stuff out yesterday," Jasmine said.

"What? Researching off the clock?"

Jasmine gave him a fake scowl, and he smiled at her. She rested her head on his shoulder, and he sighed. "Thank you so much for doing this," he said. "It really means a lot to me."

"Well, you kind of guilt-tripped me at the English Garden."

"Ha," Hudson said. "I guess I did."

They worked seamlessly together, outlining story ideas and photo ideas, lists of known sources, and ideas for finding new ones. When they'd finally developed a prioritized project plan—which Hudson labeled "PPP"—Jasmine tossed her pen on the table and leaned back in her chair. "I think we have our starting point."

Five stories published over a five-day period, Jasmine thought. It would be her first-ever series. The thought put a flutter in her stomach. She couldn't tell whether it was nerves or excitement, or both, but Hudson must have sensed it because he reached over and tucked her hair behind her ear.

"I feel like I should buy you a beer," he said.

"I won't turn it down," Jasmine said. "But it's not even noon. So I'll have to take you up on it later."

"Tonight," Hudson said. "We can go to that new sports bar downtown. I'm pretty sure there's a game on tonight."

How likely was it that Parker would be downtown tonight? Jasmine ran through her recent conversations with him, trying to remember whether he'd mentioned any plans. When she came up with nothing, she nodded.

"Sounds great."

For the first time since she could remember, Jasmine worked straight through until lunchtime without looking at her email or her cell phone. In addition to the suicide prevention series, she worked on the Seabreeze Police Department story, making calls and scribbling notes. Since Hudson had told her about Will, Jasmine thought, her work as a journalist had taken on new meaning. She felt as if, maybe, just maybe, her stories, her writing, could make a real difference.

Just after noon, Hudson walked over and sat on the corner of her desk. "You've been very immersed in your work today, Carr."

She turned her chair toward him. "And now you're here distracting me."

"I could take you for that beer now."

"Only, it's lunchtime," Jasmine said. "If I drink a beer now, I'll be sleeping in my chair by three p.m."

"I'd settle for the taco stand over on Sand Dollar."

Jasmine shrugged. "You're driving."

She didn't know why she'd said it. Hudson managed to hide his surprised expression just a split second after it appeared on his face. Her own face burned with embarrassment. It was very likely that he could tell she was, at this very moment, imagining the feel of his hips between her thighs on the motorcycle, his back against her chest and her arms around his waist.

"Jasmine Carr wants to ride my motorcycle," Hudson said in a singsongy voice.

She stood up with jerky movements. "Stop gloating. Let's go."

Cara gave her a thumbs-up and a goofy, open-mouthed smile as she followed Hudson out of the newsroom, and Jasmine rolled her eyes.

At the moment, humiliation seemed like the worst possible scenario. Later, though, Jasmine would realize she wasn't thinking clearly. Things could always get worse.

"I LIKE your hair in a braid like this," Hudson said. They'd returned from lunch, and he had just taken off Jasmine's helmet. He ran her braid through his free hand, stopping when he got to the end. He pulled on it just hard enough to tip her head back, and he kissed her before releasing it.

"You taste like tacos."

"And you're making me all twitterpated," she said. "We have serious work to do."

Hudson laughed and stowed the helmets in the bike's saddle-bags. "I'll show you serious work."

They were both smiling when they reached the patio outside the newsroom door. Cara, who sat on the bench with a soda in one hand and a sheaf of papers in the other, leapt to her feet as soon as she saw them. Her eyes darted from Jasmine to Hudson and back to Jasmine, where they rested even as she said, too loudly, "Hudson, can I talk to you for a minute?"

Hudson looked at Jasmine, and Jasmine looked at Cara. Cara nodded slowly, like an evil witch luring children to her candy cottage in the woods. "It'll just be real quick. I know you two are working on that series. Can I just get you to take a look at these photos?"

Cara angled her stack of papers so Hudson had his back to Jasmine. When he seemed distracted, she jerked her head at Jasmine, hurrying her into the newsroom. Jasmine, hoping for more information, gave her a quizzical look, and Cara widened her eyes and jerked her head again.

As soon as she walked inside, she saw—and smelled—the explanation for Cara's odd behavior. A huge bouquet of flowers, in a palette of pinks and purples, sat on her desk. The scent of lilies hit her as she approached. Even though, in the back of her mind, she knew who'd sent the arrangement, she ran through a list of potential secret admirers. Maybe it was her parents or Mikey, congratulating her on her first national wire story. Or maybe it was one of her sisters. Holly would make a gesture like this. A late birthday bouquet, maybe?

Of course, the list was pointless. She didn't need to read the card to know who they were from.

The note read, *It was so nice being with you the other night.*

It was in Parker's own handwriting, which meant he'd actually gone into the shop and chosen the bouquet himself.

"Shit," Jasmine said. Fortunately, no one was in the office to hear her, or to ask her any questions. Nobody ever received flowers at the office. And Jasmine never received any flowers, anywhere. She thought they were a waste of money because they died within days, and she always made that clear on first dates to prevent suitors from sending them. "If you want to send me a gift I'll appreciate, make it wine," she'd say. "Or chocolate. Or even a Thai takeout gift card." (Now, she realized, maybe that's why she rarely went on second dates.)

What if Hudson walked in here, right now, and saw the flowers on her desk? They'd never agreed to be exclusive. But he'd know they were from Parker and she'd told him she wasn't planning to fulfill the terms of the pact. She couldn't really throw them in the garbage. First, it would be exponentially more wasteful to throw them away before they died. They were too big to fit in the can under her desk, anyway. She couldn't take them out to the Dumpster, because she'd have to walk right past Hudson and Cara.

That was it! Cara. Jasmine picked up the flowers and marched them over to Cara's desk, where she set them on an empty corner. "Special delivery," she murmured.

Just then, the newsroom door swung open and Cara entered, her eyes darting wildly between Jasmine's desk and her own. Jasmine saw the relief cross her face when she saw the flowers on her own desk. "Carr," she said. "What are you doing to my flowers?"

Jasmine buried her face in the bouquet and inhaled deeply. They did smell good, even if they were a little overpowering. "I'm just smelling them, that's all," she said. "I love the smell of lilies. These are beautiful."

Hudson had been holding the door for Cara, and he came up behind her. "Don't get any ideas," Jasmine said. "I don't like it when guys buy me flowers."

"Waste of money," she and Hudson said at the same time.

Cara, obviously delighted, laughed.

"I don't know where you got the idea that I'd buy you flowers, anyway," Hudson muttered as he walked to his desk. "But those are nice flowers, Cara. Who are they from?"

"Oh, my ex. Trying to win me back, I guess. Flowers aren't going to do it, though."

Hudson grunted. "I should think not."

Cara winked at Jasmine, Jasmine mouthed, "Thank you," and they all sat down to work.

Jasmine's desk phone rang fifteen minutes later. When she heard Parker's voice on the other end of the line, she flinched. "Did you get my special delivery?"

She clapped a hand over her mouth. How could she have forgotten to text him and thank him for the flowers? Now, because she was so focused on keeping him a secret, she risked exposing everything. If Hudson heard her thank Parker, he'd know the flowers were really for her. And if she didn't, Parker's feelings would be hurt.

What have I gotten myself into?

"I did," she said. "It was totally awesome."

Totally awesome? Come on, Carr, you can do better than that.

"Totally awesome?" Parker said. "I don't think I've heard you say that since we were teenagers."

Jasmine laughed. "Thank you so much for sending that over."

"Wait. Are you trying to pretend this is a work call?" Parker said.

"Yes," Jasmine said. "Absolutely."

Parker laughed. "Let me see if I can get you to say something unprofessional. I'm getting penis enhancement surgery. I know I told you I tried that Swedish pump thing, but it didn't work. So I'm going in tomorrow morning for the surgery. They say it'll increase the girth by one hundred percent."

"That's—that's wonderful," Jasmine said. She could barely contain the hysteria that threatened to destroy her professional façade.

"I think you can sample it within a week. If you like."

"Look, I really appreciate you sending over those materials," Jasmine said. "I'm going to get to work on that story right now. You have a great day."

She heard Parker laughing as she hung up the phone. Her email program dinged a minute later. Cara had written, *I can't save your ass every time you hit a snag, you know. You're going to have to get this out into the open. And thanks for the flowers.*

Jasmine rolled her eyes and responded, *You're welcome. And thank YOU for saving my ass. I owe you one.*

She thought the conversation was over, but Cara responded again: *You totally do. You're buying me a drink tonight.*

After work, the two of them went to Starboard, a bar adjacent to the beach.

"Cheers to an act of friendship," Cara said, holding up her wine glass. "Oh, and an act of deceit."

"Cheers," Jasmine said.

The two of them tossed back the shots of tequila Cara ordered, and Jasmine shuddered.

"I'm too old for this stuff," she said.

Cara smacked the tabletop and laughed, bringing to life images of Liza. Is this how serious reporters managed not to go crazy? By leaving work at the office and partying hard in their off hours?

"You're not too old," Cara said. "You're just out of practice. Shall I order another?"

Jasmine shook her head. "No, let's go easy. Let's get something we can sip."

The girls sat on the low wooden patio. Jasmine could smell the sand and hear the ocean rolling in and out. She sighed. "I really owe you, Cara. Thank you so much for today."

"Woman, you already know I don't think there's anything wrong with you dating two guys at once. But you've got to come clean. Not only are you going to get caught, but you're also not going to be able to maintain this whole thing, emotionally."

"People date two guys at once all the time," Jasmine said.

"Yeah," Cara said. She signaled the server. "But you've got two guys on the hook who both think you've only got eyes for them. You know? That's different than casually dating two guys who know there are others. You must be exhausted."

For the first time in weeks, Jasmine realized she *was* exhausted. She didn't know how much longer she could keep up this way. "You're right," she said to Cara. "I am. I guess I didn't even realize it, myself, until now. Whenever I go places with Parker, I feel like I'm constantly on alert, hoping we don't run into Hudson. With Hudson it's a little easier, because I can always pass it off like we're working."

Cara nodded. The server came over and Cara ordered a couple of margaritas. Jasmine realized she was already feeling a little bit dizzy. She ordered chips and salsa.

"So. You've got to tell them, or pick one," Cara said. "That's all there is to it."

"Ugh. I know you're right. It's just so hard. I feel like I can't tell them, you know? If I do, then they'll both know I was lying and I just can't go down like that."

"But if you don't tell them and they find out, then things will be even worse. I mean, right now, you can still spin it like you weren't really planning to get serious with either one of them. But if they find out independently, you're screwed."

"So, option B," Jasmine said. "I need to choose one."

Cara nodded. The server brought their margaritas and chips and salsa. Jasmine selected a chip, salted it and scooped up some salsa.

Cara licked some salt off the rim of her glass and then took a long drink of her margarita.

"So who's it going to be?" she said. Her eyes twinkled.

Jasmine took a long drink of her margarita, considering. When she didn't answer right away, Cara took a chip, too. With a flourish, she dipped it and ate it, and then licked her fingertips.

"I'm waiting," she said.

Jasmine groaned again. "I know you're right, but I have no idea how to choose. Can't you just make the decision for me?"

"That Hudson is really yummy," Cara said. She paused, pursing her lips and looking up. "So, you take Parker. And I'd be happy to take Hudson off your hands."

"I know what you're doing," Jasmine said. "Stop baiting me."

Cara laughed. "Yeah. Hudson is totally not my type. He is yummy, though. I know. Maybe you can have sex with both of them. And then decide."

"Scandalous," Jasmine said. "I don't know if I can do that."

"Oh, I think you can."

"I just don't know what to do," Jasmine said. "I mean, being with Parker has been, like, a lifelong dream. But being with Hudson is so … I don't even know. So new, I guess."

"Sometimes when you finally get around to living your lifelong dreams, you realize they've changed," Cara said. "And sometimes someone who makes you feel itchy and uncomfortable is necessary for your growth. I mean, sometimes they just have an STD, but you get the picture."

Jasmine crumpled up her napkin and threw it at Cara, who caught it and threw it back.

"So you're saying I should choose Hudson," Jasmine said.

"I'm not saying anything about who you should choose, sister," Cara said. "You choose whoever your heart wants you to choose."

"But how do I know?"

"That's the question, isn't it?"

Two hours later, the girls were ready to head home.

"Good thing we don't need a taxi tonight," Cara said. "After what we spent on food and drinks, I'm not sure we can afford it. You'd have to call Parker to come and get us in his van."

"I'd have Hudson come get us on his motorcycle," Jasmine said. "You should really try the motorcycle. Although, Parker said the back seat of his van folds into a bed. You almost can't beat that."

They settled the imaginary scenario by splitting cab fare so Jasmine wouldn't be forced to make a decision.

"I think deciding who to call to pick us up is too much like foreshadowing," Jasmine said. "It's unfair. Hudson is practically disqualified because he drives a motorcycle."

"Oh, no. Is Hudson disqualified?" Cara said. "Because I really like him."

"I can't take this," Jasmine said. "And after all this talk, I think we do need a cab. I'm calling one."

THE NEXT MORNING, Jasmine woke up with the impression that thousands of tiny little dwarves had taken up residence inside her skull. With hammers. She groaned, and Ruby leapt up and licked her face.

Jasmine's first thought was that she never should have mixed wine and margaritas. Her second thought was that she should make herself some tea. Her third thought was to wonder whether Cara was in bad shape, too. Probably not. She drank more alcohol, more frequently, than Jasmine did. She'd probably bounce right back.

"Can I order coffee delivery?" Jasmine said to Ruby.

From somewhere out in the living area, Jasmine's phone crowed. She didn't think it was possible to get up and check her text messages, so she flopped back down and pulled the covers over her head. It didn't last long. Her phone made another noise.

Jasmine rolled herself out of bed. The wood floor felt cold against her bare feet. When she was completely upright, her head pounded worse than ever. Her phone was on the counter, its notification light blinking dutifully.

Before she could check her messages, she had to heat up some water. Instead of brewing it in the pot like she usually did, she opted for the microwave. When it was done, she dropped an Earl Gray tea bag into her mug and inhaled the steam.

Even though the tea was still too hot to drink, she took a tiny sip. Finally, she felt ready to check her messages. She groaned when she saw she had half a dozen of them.

Cara: *Are you still alive? I feel like death.*

Hudson: *Are you coming in this morning?*

Parker: *I didn't hear from you last night. Everything ok?*

Cara (again): *I'm bringing you coffee.*

Parker (again): *Hello?*

Hudson (again): *Seriously. Are you coming in?*

Jasmine responded to Cara that she didn't drink coffee and she would be at the office in an hour. She responded to Hudson that she'd be at the office in an hour. And she responded to Parker that she was alive and just a little tired.

So what if her thumbs hovered over the keyboard for several seconds before she explained to Parker why she hadn't texted him last night? For some reason, probably because she still felt like a teenager around him, she felt guilty admitting to him that she was hungover. Not that she needed to explain herself to him, but she didn't want him to think she'd been out with anyone else. She could probably say she was out with Cara. But that would sound fishy. He didn't even know she had a friend named Cara. She settled for, *Worked late last night.*

Jasmine brought her tea into the shower with her. She balanced it on the shelf that held her shampoo so she could take sips at regular intervals. The hot water alleviated some of the pain in her head, which allowed her mind to function again.

Of course, it picked up where it had left off the night before: smack in the middle of The Great Hudson-Parker Debate.

Between sips of tea, Jasmine shampooed her hair, which still held the scent of ocean air and cigarette smoke. Last night, Cara had suggested Jasmine fill imaginary Parker and imaginary Hudson into different parts of her life.

"Like the shower," she said. "Or the kitchen. Imagining each man playing different roles in your life will help you decide which one is a better fit. Like, who do you want to shower with? Who do you want to eat dinner with? Who will watch your favorite shows with you? Normally, during this exercise," she said, pulling up her posture so she looked professional, "I ask my client to determine which man gives her better orgasms. But you're obviously still in the dark about Hudson."

Cara's idea seemed like a good one, Jasmine thought now. In the shower, Hudson came to mind first, and she closed her eyes and imagined it was him scrubbing her scalp. That was nice. What else would he do? Just as the imaginary Hudson began rubbing soap all over her torso, the imaginary Parker knocked on the shower door and stepped in, pushing the imaginary Hudson out.

This would never do.

The imaginary Parker did things a little differently. He kissed her mouth while he rinsed her hair. He rinsed her body while he kissed her neck. And then the imaginary Hudson, apparently angry at having been pushed out a minute before, returned.

He massaged Jasmine's shoulders, neck, and head, and ran his thumbs down her back to the tops of her hips. The imaginary Parker knocked on the bathroom door. In all her discussions with Cara, Jasmine had never considered both men in the shower at the same time. What would *that* be like? Somehow she didn't think either of them would like the idea. She wasn't sure she would, either, when it came right down to it.

The imaginary Hudson kept massaging Jasmine. He turned her around and rubbed the front of her body. The knocking continued. Hudson kissed Jasmine's mouth.

Then the bathroom door opened, and the sound of a real, actual voice made her jump, her illusions dissolving instantly.

"I know, I know, you don't drink coffee," Cara said. "But I'll just put it here on the counter for you. I brought you breakfast, too. I feel partially responsible for how I know you're feeling this morning. It's just a muffin."

"How did you get in?" Jasmine said.

"You left the front door unlocked."

"I feel like death, too," Jasmine said. "And you are partially responsible. But you didn't have to stop by. I've only myself to blame. No one forced me to throw both wine and margaritas down the hatch. That's something my dad would say."

"He'd be right," Cara said. "I know that from personal experience. But still. You wouldn't have gone out if I didn't come up with the idea."

"Well, thank you," Jasmine said. "And also, thanks a lot for ruining the shower fantasies I was just having. I was following your advice."

"So who's better in the shower?" Cara said.

"Undecided."

Cara snorted. "I'm leaving a couple of aspirin right here, next to your coffee. I'll see you at the office."

"Thank you," Jasmine called as Cara closed the door.

Try as she might, Jasmine couldn't get back to her shower fantasies, so she finished up and got out. She'd have to invite the imaginary Hudson and the imaginary Parker into her kitchen to see who provided a more enjoyable breakfast-making experience.

Jasmine knew a muffin wasn't going to cure her hangover. The shower and the coffee helped considerably, enough that she was able to stomach the idea of cooking up a bacon breakfast burrito.

As the bacon began to sizzle on the stovetop and its scent filled the kitchen, Jasmine thought about the real-life Parker and Hudson. Each of their fantasy versions was pretty darned good in the shower, but that wasn't necessarily indicative of what real life would look like.

If one of them was here now, how would it feel? Which one would she want handing her a teacup or a mug full of coffee? Which one would want his bacon crispy, the way she liked hers? Which one would feel right, standing there in pajama pants and bare feet?

Parker liked his bacon crispy. In fact, he had taught her how to cook it that way when they were juniors in high school and they decided to make her family breakfast for dinner one evening. She could still remember the way his body felt behind hers, the way his hand curved over hers on the tongs as they flipped the bacon.

For the past thirteen years, she'd cooked her bacon crispy, mostly because it was the only way she knew how.

How did Hudson like his bacon? Jasmine had no idea. Probably chewy. She could probably make chewy bacon. In fact, she'd make it that way today, just to prove she could. Did Hudson even eat bacon? Yes, he'd ordered it on the pizza the night of Kevin Shoemaker's disappearance at the mall. When she thought about how they'd spent that evening alone in the darkened newsroom, she smiled. That had just felt so simple, so easy.

Dating Hudson would mean installing a coffee maker in her kitchen. Where would she put it? And would he need a full-sized one or one of those single-serve ones? *He eats roast beef. He needs a full-sized coffee maker. And size does matter.* Jasmine chuckled at her own joke.

Parker didn't drink coffee regularly. But he almost always ate toast, which Jasmine almost never did. She would have to get a toaster, and those things took up lots of space.

She sighed. "This is so complicated," she said to Ruby, who licked one of her bare toes in response.

Maybe there was some kind of game show she could go on with Hudson and Parker to determine which one of them was a better match for her. "If there isn't one, there should be," Jasmine said.

She set the chewy bacon and scrambled eggs on a tortilla, and sprinkled cheese on top before rolling it into a burrito. She sat down at the counter, and Ruby, who'd lost interest because the burrito didn't contain vegetables, walked into the living room and jumped up onto the couch to sleep.

What kind of criteria would a game show take into consideration? Looks, obviously. Both Hudson and Parker scored high in that department. Hudson's long, lean frame made Jasmine want to stretch out beside it, and his bright green eyes focused so intently on hers that she could feel her panties smoldering. Parker's body was so solid, so steadfast. Whenever his arms encircled her body, she wanted to swoon against him so he could sweep her up and carry her away.

The chewy bacon was good. Really good.

Dating show producers also ranked contestants based on matching interests. Parker and Jasmine shared such a rich past. They'd made so many memories together. With Hudson, she shared an interest in riding motorcycles. So what if it was a new interest, to her?

The one thing dating shows couldn't measure was the way a woman felt when she was with a particular man. Was that even measurable?

One night, Jasmine had watched a reality show about dancers. Some exercise gear manufacturer had come to the show and hooked the dancers up to tons of sensors that measured heart rate, gravitational pull and energy expended. Maybe some dating company—online dating company, maybe?—had similar technology. She could use it to measure how her body reacted to Parker and to Hudson.

The burrito was gone. She hadn't even realized she'd eaten it all. The Great Hudson-Parker Debate was taking over her mind, and she was on a slippery slope to madness. She didn't know how much longer she could keep this up.

CHAPTER TWENTY-FOUR

Even during her short stint as the cops reporter, Jasmine knew driving distracted could be worse than driving drunk or high. She'd never read any statistics about driving distracted and hungover, but she should have known it was a bad combination.

For eight years, Jasmine had made the drive from her house to the *Daily Trumpet* at least once per day. She knew the route by heart. Back out of the driveway, head east on Duhame Street. Stop at the intersection. Continue east until Roper Avenue. The traffic signal was almost always green. *Almost* always. Almost every morning, she coasted through the intersection at Duhame and Roper.

But today, the morning after she and Cara decided she needed to choose between Hudson and Parker—and make that choice as soon as possible—Jasmine was distracted. She was running through scenarios in her mind, putting each man through the paces. She considered them in bed, and on her couch, and at the grocery store. And she didn't notice in time that the light at Duhame and Roper was red until it was too late.

Right in the middle of a scene where Parker was throwing potatoes across the produce department so she could bag them and put them in the cart, Jasmine drove through the intersection, against a red light. She had one more vision of Hudson in the grocery store, standing next to her in front of the cheese case, holding her hand, the electricity crackling between them.

Then the loud squealing of tires brought her back to reality—but only for a split second before she heard a loud crash, felt the impact, and everything went dark.

REALITY ENTERED Jasmine's consciousness in snippets, snapshots of moments. Silence and immense pressure against her chest. Shouting. The glaring sun, shining in her eyes and making her squint. Broken glass sparkling against black asphalt. Shouting. Sirens. More shouting. Someone touching her. Someone grabbing her under the arms and pulling her out of the car.

She could hear her own thoughts, broken and distorted. I ran the red light. I hit someone. Or someone hit me. Someone's pulling me out. My car is smashed. I'm smashed.

And then reality went dark, again.

WHEN SHE FINALLY WOKE UP ALL THE way, Jasmine knew immediately that she was in the hospital. She could smell that bleached-clean, alcohol-swabbed scent exclusive to hospitals and doctors' offices. She could hear the hospital noises: low voices, intermittent beeping, the paging system broadcasting information through the halls.

She tried to clear her throat, but couldn't. Suddenly she felt like she might gag. Did she have a tube in her throat? Full-blown panic set in, and she reached for her mouth. Her body twisted from side to side, but she couldn't move her hands. She couldn't call out. By some miracle, a nurse came in at that moment. When she saw that Jasmine was awake, she rushed to the side of her bed and placed her hands on Jasmine's shoulders.

"You're okay," she said. Jasmine figured the nurse's voice was supposed to be calming, but the tube in her throat felt so uncomfortable she couldn't calm down. "You weren't breathing well on your own when they brought you in, so we put you on a ventilator," the nurse said. "But now that you're conscious, I have a feeling you'll breathe just fine. Try to relax, okay? Let me see what I can do about getting it taken out."

Jasmine nodded, but she could picture herself lying there, eyes wide open and wild.

The nurse squeezed her shoulder one more time. "I'll be right back, okay? Remember, try to relax. I promise, it's not so bad once you get used to it."

Jasmine nodded as best she could, and the nurse left. Jasmine's eyes darted from one side to the other. Wasn't anyone here for her? Someone must have come. Sequoia must have heard about the accident on the scanner, but would she even realize Jasmine was involved? If Jasmine had had the courage to choose between Parker and Hudson, one of them would definitely be here. One of them would have been expecting her, and when she didn't show up, he would have figured out where she was.

Which was in the hospital. Alone.

Jasmine tried to moan, but the tube prevented any real sound from coming out. Instead, she emitted a kind of gurgling sound. Even as she was trying to figure out who would come to the hospital to be with her, Jasmine lost consciousness again.

SHE WOKE UP MOANING, and felt a vague sense of elation when she realized the sound was actually coming out of her mouth. The nurse must have returned to remove the tube. Jasmine coughed, then croaked out a, "Hello?"

No one responded. This was the first time she'd been alert enough to take inventory. A dull throbbing had taken up residence in her torso, and her arm ached like it was on fire. When she managed to look down at it, she saw that someone had wrapped a thick brace around it. She wondered if it was broken. The rest of her body felt tender.

And, she was still alone.

So. She'd alienated both of the guys she cared about, and her sisters, too. But where was Cara? Certainly their time together the night before meant something. Miserable, Jasmine closed her eyes again. She was now analyzing the meaning of the time she spent with another woman.

Someone knocked on the door to her room. Before she had the chance to welcome that someone, the door opened. Jasmine tried to hide the disappointment she felt when she saw her visitor. It was Holly, whose concern was etched across her forehead in long horizontal stripes. Above that, her hair was dyed a God-awful dark turquoise.

Jasmine tried to speak but her voice wouldn't work.

Holly, hands fluttering out in front of her like tiny hummingbirds —fun to watch but ultimately elusive—practically climbed into Jasmine's bed.

"I'm so glad you're awake! I was so *worried*!" she said, over and over again.

Jasmine managed a squeak.

"It's just that you're usually such a careful driver," Holly said. "You always check three times before you back out of a parking space. But the police said you ran a red light. That's just not like you. I assume you were either very tired or very distracted. Which one was it?"

Jasmine found that she didn't have the energy to answer any questions.

"You ran a red light?" Holly said.

Jasmine shrugged and nodded.

"Should I call Sequoia?"

This thought enabled Jasmine to find her voice. "Please don't."

"You don't want her to lecture you on running red lights? 'Driving distracted is worse than driving drunk, Jasmine. Put the phone down.'"

"Exactly. Only, I wasn't on the phone."

"Then what the hell happened?" Holly said.

"Geez, I feel like you're Sequoia in Holly's body right now. With turquoise hair."

Holly's right hand flew up to touch the hair at her temple. "Answer me, or I'll call her."

"Now you're interrogating me," Jasmine said, her voice a croak. "These are interrogation tactics."

Holly sat down on the side of Jasmine's bed and took her hand.

"Ahhh," Jasmine said. "This is more like the Holly I remember."

"How can you still be so sarcastic at a time like this?" Holly said.

"It's a gift."

Holly waited. Jasmine sighed. "Okay," she said. "I was distracted. I have this new friend, Cara, at work, and last night when we went out for drinks, she suggested I try a kind of ... *exercise* for deciding between Parker and Hudson. So I've been working on it all morning. The idea is that I imagine having each one of them with me at various points throughout the day. I imagined having each of them in the shower with me. Then I imagined each one in the kitchen with me while I made breakfast."

Holly nodded. "Okay," she said. "But then what?"

"You know," Jasmine said, "I never thought about this, but who knows if Parker would even be awake while I was making breakfast? He's got nowhere to be. He'd have to get a job eventually, wouldn't he?"

"You're getting off topic."

"Right," Jasmine said. "I am. But seriously."

"Seriously," Holly said. "So who was with you, imaginarily, when you were driving and ran a red light and crashed?"

"Ohmigosh," Jasmine said. "Is the other driver all right?"

"Yeah," Holly said. "He's fine. He tried to stop so the impact was pretty minimal. He walked away. Just minor injuries."

"Oh, thank goodness," Jasmine said. "I can't believe I did that."

"Why don't you tell me what happened?" Holly said.

"That light is almost always green," Jasmine said. "Today, it was red. I just didn't stop."

"That's it?"

"That's it."

"Wow, sister," Holly said.

"Tell me about it."

Cara came rushing in, then, a tornado of orange hair and black fishnet stockings. "I just saw you in the shower and now you're here?" she shrieked.

Holly raised one eyebrow at Jasmine, and Jasmine shrugged. The shrugging hurt, and she winced. "I don't even know what happened," Jasmine said to Cara.

"I'll say," Cara said. "Which guy was riding the car with you, imaginarily, when you ran the red light?"

"How did you know I ran a red light?"

"I quizzed one of the nurses on the way in. I pretended I was a reporter for the *Daily Trumpet*."

"You *are* a reporter for the *Daily Trumpet*. Anyway, do you think Hudson knows I got into an accident?"

"I'm sure he heard about the accident on the police scanner," Cara said.

Jasmine turned to Holly. "Do you think Parker knows about the accident?"

"I have no idea," Holly said. "Based on what you just said, though, I imagine he's still sleeping."

"He's not," Jasmine said. "Unless he texted me this morning to guilt trip me for not texting him last night and then went back to bed."

Cara laughed. "You've really got yourself in a pickle."

"No kidding," Jasmine said. She was starting to feel grumpy. Her arm hurt, her throat felt raw and her older sister, who *had* to know about the accident, wasn't even here to support her.

Sequoia rushed in at that very moment, for once looking out of sorts. A piece of hair had fallen from the bun at the base of her neck, and it covered her right eye. She tucked it behind her ear and when it fell back into her eye she brushed it away, impatient. Her plain-clothes uniform, khaki pants and a tucked-in collared shirt in Navy blue, was out of whack, too: a button on her shirt was undone, and in one spot on the back, it wasn't tucked in all the way. *She must not know about that*, Jasmine thought. Sequoia never went anywhere unless her shirt was evenly tucked in all the way around. She'd been obsessive about that kind of thing as a kid, throwing tantrums if her ponytail had a single bump in it or her shirt poofed out in one spot more than the others. She'd never outgrown it.

"Where's the doctor?" she demanded.

Jasmine and Holly exchanged a nervous glance, and Jasmine cleared her throat. "He should be by soon, Sequoia. It's fine. He's competent."

"I've seen the way they treat patients in this ER," she said. "Or the way they don't treat patients, I should say. How the hell did you get into a collision, Jasmine? Haven't I told you a million times that—"

Holly and Jasmine chimed in: "Driving distracted is worse than driving drunk."

"Yes," Jasmine said. "You have. And I wasn't on my phone, I swear. I was just distracted."

Cara snickered and Sequoia shot her such a dirty look that Cara immediately pressed her lips together and looked away.

"What are they doing for you?" Sequoia said. "Is anything broken? Do you need surgery?"

"I think my arm's broken," Jasmine said. "And I was hoping they were keeping visitors out, but obviously that's not the case."

When Sequoia inhaled and it was obvious she had a diatribe planned, Cara cut her off. "It's not you. It's Jasmine. She doesn't want Hudson and Parker crossing paths. Well, not here, anyway."

A hint of humor flashed in Sequoia's eyes, but she didn't address that particular news item. "I'll go find the doctor."

She spun on her heel and walked away.

The phone at Jasmine's bedside rang, and Holly, Cara, and Jasmine jumped. Cara answered it, and her eyes widened as the caller spoke to her. She thanked whoever was on the other end of the line and hung up.

"You have a male visitor," she said. "The nurse at the nursing station didn't want to let him in without checking, first. It's Hudson."

Jasmine had only a few seconds before Hudson arrived. She felt herself starting to sweat. Was she nervous? Why was she nervous? She saw him every single day.

"You're thinking about Hudson in the shower, aren't you?" Cara whispered.

Jasmine knew she was bordering on hysteria. She was thinking of Hudson in the shower, and it was so inappropriate. Hudson, in the flesh, appeared in the doorway, looking as tall and as gorgeous as ever. "Well, hello there," Jasmine said. Cara snickered again. Even Holly smiled.

Hudson said, "I feel like I've just walked in on a private conversation."

"You have," said the three girls, in unison.

"I heard the accident on the scanner," he said. "I was just coming to see if you're okay."

Jasmine began to answer, but Cara cut in. "Holly and I are just going to see if there's any fresh coffee in the cafeteria. We'll bring you a cup, Jasmine."

"I don't drink—"

Now Cara shot Jasmine a dirty look and Jasmine, slow to pick up on Cara's intentions, stopped herself short and said, "Thanks, guys."

Before Holly and Cara had even gotten into the hallway, Hudson was at Jasmine's side, sitting on the very edge of the bed.. He gripped her upper arm, hard, and said, "You really had me worried, Carr."

Then, he leaned forward and kissed her so hard she couldn't breathe. And then, as if things could get any less appropriate, her imagination placed this real-life Hudson in her bed. With her. And they were both naked.

Her entire body thrummed with anticipation following that single kiss.

When Hudson pulled away, Jasmine exhaled. "Wow," she said. "I'll have to worry you more often."

"Please don't," he said. "I can't take it."

The bedside phone rang again. Jasmine panicked. The only other person who'd call or visit was Parker. A call was fine, but what if he was at the nurses station?

She had no idea what to do. She couldn't let Parker see her here, like this, with Hudson. Even though they weren't kissing any more, he was sitting on her bed, holding her hand, stroking her hair. Definite signs of intimacy beyond what co-workers should share.

Maybe she shouldn't answer. If she let it ring, the nurses would assume she was in the bathroom or maybe getting x-rays or possibly dead. They wouldn't send a visitor in during any of those scenarios, would they?

"Are you going to answer that?" Hudson said.

"Oh. Um. Nah. Let it go to voicemail."

"I'm not sure if voicemail is included in your stay at this lovely, luxury destination," Hudson said. "Want me to get it?"

"No! No, thanks, I mean. It's fine. I'll get it."

The phone rang again.

"Are you going to get it?" Hudson said.

"Sorry," Jasmine said. "I'm just spaced out, I guess. Oh. It stopped ringing. Oh, well. They'll call back."

Hudson looked at her like he thought she might be losing her mind. "Did you hit your head in the accident?"

"I have no idea, but I'm sure I did," Jasmine said. "I don't remember any of it."

Besides the fact that I ran the red light because I was thinking about what it would be like to hold hands with you across the center console, and maybe to feel you rubbing my leg while I was driving.

"Jasmine, I—I don't know what to say. I was in the newsroom, and I heard the hot tones coming out for the accident. Of course, my ears perked up, like they always do, you know? But then I heard the description of the car. The dispatcher said the RP—that's reporting person—said the vehicles involved were a late model pickup, dark blue, and a bright orange Volkswagen Golf. A bright orange Golf is distinctive, you have to admit. And I knew right away. I knew it was you. And my heart stopped. Seriously. I felt it stop in my chest. It's kind of embarrassing, the reaction I had."

He leaned forward again and rested his forehead against hers. One part of her enjoyed this tremendously. He wrapped one of his hands around one of hers, and she stroked his hair. The other part of her, though, had her mind on overdrive. What if Parker was on his way here from the nurses station? If they'd let him through, he would be two doors down by now.

"Hudson," she said, pushing his body away from hers as gently as she could. When he was sitting up again, facing her, she said, "I am so sorry. I didn't mean to scare you. Look at me. I'm fine. Aside from the arm."

"I need to tell you something," he said.

Jasmine could feel her heart beating throughout her entire body. It pulsed in her ears, her fingertips, even her toes. This was absolutely the worst time for Hudson to tell her anything, much less *something*. What if Parker walked in?

"Is it important?" she said.

"Very," he said.

"I'm not sure if now is a good time," she said. "I mean, I'm in the hospital. You're in the hospital. We're both in the hospital."

"Exactly. Which makes now the perfect time to tell you. There really is no time like the present."

Jasmine nodded. "I just want to make sure I have full mental clarity when you tell me this very important bit of information."

"It's not actually information," Hudson said. "It's more like a feeling."

Alarm bells went off in Jasmine's mind.

Someone knocked on the door, two quick raps.

Jasmine's heart nearly beat out of her chest. Then she looked at the door and saw that her newest visitor was a nurse. Still, her entire body shook and her heart rate refused to return to normal.

"Oh, good," the nurse said. "You're awake. You had another visitor, honey. When we couldn't get an answer in your room, I figured you were sleeping, so I said you weren't taking visitors."

"Thank you," Jasmine said. She knew her voice sounded unnaturally high, and she rushed to change the subject. "I'm sure you saw my sister. Sequoia. She wants to know if I need surgery."

The nurse smiled as she checked Jasmine's IV and then wrapped a blood pressure cuff around her upper arm. "I talked to her, yes. She's just worried about you. You know, I have a sister just like her. You're blessed, really. Anyway, honey, I don't think you're going to need surgery. Your arm is broken, but it's clean break. Nothing a cast won't fix up."

"That's a relief," Jasmine said. Then, to prevent a silence into which the nurse could spill the identity of the visitor she'd turned away, Jasmine went on, "I mean, I wasn't as worried as Sequoia was. She's kind of a worry wart."

"She just cares about you, that's all. Your blood pressure's a little high."

"Is she okay?" Hudson said. "Is there something she should do for the blood pressure?"

The nurse clucked her tongue. "No, honey. It's probably just the pain from her arm. She'll be right as rain in no time. What a good boyfriend you are."

Jasmine felt herself blushing, and Hudson looked away but didn't contradict the nurse.

Holly and Cara walked in a few seconds after the nurse departed, and Sequoia followed shortly thereafter. With all the commotion, Hudson didn't have a chance to reveal the "feeling" he'd been so anxious to share, and Jasmine was relieved. *Relieved and curious*, her inner voice amended.

"I'll take you in tomorrow to get your cast," Sequoia said.

"I can take her," Holly said. "You don't need to take time off work."

"We can both take her, I guess," Sequoia said. "I don't want you to feel left out. But you know I can't trust the doctor to do the right thing. Someone responsible has to be there and I think you've both proven that you're not responsible. I mean" (and here, she finally smiled) "look at your hair, Holly."

Jasmine shrugged. After all, she'd crashed her car because she was living imaginary car-sex scenes. Holly looked offended. Cara looked like she wished she could be somewhere else. Jasmine smiled at her, and it came out feeling like a grimace.

Hudson chose that moment to interject: "I can take her, you know. We work together. It would be no problem."

"What are you going to do, drive our sister, who, may I remind you, has a broken arm, around on your motorcycle?"

Even Hudson blanched at Sequoia's words.

"I didn't think about that," he said. Then he added as an afterthought, "Wait. How did you know I drive a motorcycle?"

"I could ride on the back of his bike." Jasmine jumped in before Sequoia could blurt out that she'd done something creepy, like run a background check or stalked him.

"This is ridiculous," Sequoia said. "Holly and I will take care of it. It was lovely to meet both of you, and thank you so much for stopping by, but we'll take it from here."

As most people did in response to Sequoia's bossiness, Cara and Hudson obeyed. They both nodded and walked to the door of the hospital room without speaking.

Jasmine had no idea what to say. She wanted to call out to them, to tell them to stay, but she was afraid of Sequoia's reaction. So she squeaked out, "Thanks for coming, guys."

Being alone with Holly was one thing. Being alone with Holly *and* Sequoia was a whole different matter. After Cara and Hudson scuttled out of the hospital room, Sequoia turned toward Jasmine and crossed her arms.

"So. Do you want to tell me what's going on here?"

"Uh oh," Holly said. "She's doing the bad cop thing. She's about to interrogate you. Only, there's no good cop."

"I think you're supposed to be the good cop," Jasmine said to Holly.

"So?" Sequoia repeated. She widened her stance and looked hard at her sister.

Jasmine cringed. "So, I was driving and I ran a red light and someone hit me," she said. "I woke up here."

"But how did you run the red light?"

"Um, I didn't stop?"

"Ohmigod, Jasmine," Sequoia said. "Why are you doing this? This is like when Mom and Dad used to ask you something like, 'Why are the cookies all gone?' and you would say, 'Um, because I ate them all?' It's so irritating! Don't you understand the ripple effect of that one bad choice?"

"It wasn't a choice, really," Jasmine said, and Sequoia stomped her foot.

"Wait," Holly said. "Did you actually just stomp your foot?"

Now she rolled her eyes. Jasmine laughed, but cut her laughter short when Sequoia glared at her.

She held up one finger. "First of all, you and I are both missing work right now." She brought up a second finger. "Second, Holly's missing out on whatever she does while the rest of us work. And third," she said, adding another finger, "You're going to have a cast for, like, two months! Do you know how hard it's going to be to do your work with a cast?"

"I'm really sorry," Jasmine said.

"And all of this because you were distracted? What does that even mean? I mean, I get it if you're a mom with a bunch of noisy, crying kids bickering and fighting with each other in the backseat. Or if you were arguing with your passenger and just weren't paying attention. Or, and I've seen this in real life—if you were trying to sneak a drink of beer and then hide your beer can between your seat and the console. I could see you being distracted. But you were alone! And presumably, you weren't participating in any illegal activities. That is, except for running that red light."

Holly looked at Jasmine, her expression apologetic. Then she said to Sequoia, "Well, she wasn't alone, exactly."

"What? What is that supposed to mean? You're either alone or you're not alone. Which one was it?"

Mortified, Jasmine said, "Never mind. It's nothing. I was alone."

"Why did Holly say you weren't alone? Your stories aren't matching up. One of you is lying."

"And I'm going to do my best to find out who!" Holly said, in her best Sequoia impression. Jasmine broke down into giggles again, and Sequoia's dark look only made them worse this time.

Tears of hilarity streaming down her face, Jasmine explained through the laughter why she'd been so distracted. Holly's simultaneous laughter only made things worse. When she finished, hiccuping from laughing so hard, Sequoia sat down on the bed. It was as if someone had let all the air out of her, and she just deflated.

"This is worse than I thought," Sequoia said. "My own sister, distracted by imaginary men in her car, creating a real-life accident and scaring me half to death."

Holly, still breathless, said, "I mean, it's kind of funny when you think about it."

Jasmine could have sworn she saw a glimmer of humor in Sequoia's eyes and around her mouth before she shut it down. "You guys kill me."

Fortunately, the doctor chose that moment to come in.

"I could probably keep you overnight," he said to Jasmine. "But most people do better at home. They recover more quickly. Do you have help in getting around?"

He was a grandpa character, Jasmine thought, an old guy with bushy white eyebrows. He looked up at Sequoia and Holly. Holly nodded, her head bobbing up and down so quickly Jasmine was afraid she'd give herself a headache. And Sequoia sighed, heavily, as if the the doctor had asked her to cut off her own arm and give it to Jasmine as a replacement.

"I'm going to take her home now, and I'll chauffeur her to get her cast tomorrow. After that, she's on her own."

Holly jumped in. "I'll help her."

The doctor looked from Jasmine to Sequoia to Holly, and then back to Jasmine. He smiled at her. "You're so lucky to have your sisters here with you."

"She *is* lucky," Sequoia said. "She's also a pain."

The doctor chuckled.

"Let's go," Sequoia said.

With a characteristic lack of gentleness, Sequoia hoisted Jasmine to her feet and helped her change. Holly eased Jasmine into the wheelchair an orderly had brought in, and Sequoia, of course, insisted on pushing Jasmine down the corridor and out the sliding door.

Jasmine blinked in the bright sunlight. Her eyes and skin felt raw. Holly flitted around the wheelchair, looking for traffic and pedestrians even though the driveway and parking lot were silent.

"Just settle down," Sequoia said. "I'll get the car. Can I trust you to sit here with Jasmine for a few minutes? You won't become distracted, will you?"

Holly nudged Sequoia out of the way and took hold of the wheelchair's handles. Sequoia stalked into the parking lot without looking back. She returned a few minutes later, and after helping Jasmine into the passenger seat, Holly opened the back door to get in, herself.

"Wait," Sequoia said. "Why are you getting in, Holly?"

"I thought I'd help you get her home and settled," Holly said, "and then you can bring me back to my car."

"That's ridiculous," Sequoia said. "Just follow me."

If Holly had agreed, or if Jasmine had said Sequoia's idea was a good one, Sequoia may have checked the rearview mirror more than just habitually on the ride back to Jasmine's house. As it was, the three of them talked the whole way there.

"So why are you having such a tough time deciding between Parker and Hudson?" Sequoia said. Traffic was heavy, and Sequoia had to wait to turn out of the hospital parking lot. Her eyes bored into Jasmine's while she waited for an answer, with an intensity in direct contrast to the conversational tone of her voice. Jasmine thought she might catch on fire under the heat of that stare.

"Sequoia," Holly said, "give it a rest. She's recovering. From a car accident. Can't this wait?"

"No, it cannot wait." Sequoia turned right, pressing hard on the accelerator to squeeze between two cars. "She didn't run that red light because she was daydreaming. She ran the red light because she can't make up her mind. She can't decide between these two men and it's tearing her up. It's really affecting her."

"I'm right here. Can we talk about me like I'm in the car, too?"

"Of course," Holly and Sequoia said at the same time.

Jasmine wished she could crawl into some kind of shell. If only she were a hermit crab. Or a snail. No, not a snail. Too slimy. A hermit crab would be okay. Why was Sequoia so impassioned about this?

"Jasmine," she said, "you're a mess. This predicament is making you that way. It's messing with your mind. I just don't understand why it's such a tough decision."

Jasmine sighed. "It just is, Sequoia. You wouldn't understand because you never let yourself have feelings for anyone."

"Don't make this about me," Sequoia said. She slammed on the brakes to avoid hitting a car that had slowed to turn right onto a side street.

Holly said, "She's right, Sequoia. You have no idea what it's like to have real feelings for someone. Or two someones, for that matter."

"I'm not sure you're helping my case, Holly," Jasmine said.

"Anyway," Sequoia said, slamming on the accelerator. "Nice change of subject, girls. But why don't you explain, Jasmine, why it's so difficult for you to choose one of these men? Apparently they both have a lot to offer. So what's the deal?"

Jasmine sighed, again. Then she mentally kicked herself for being so dramatic.

"You're so dramatic," Sequoia said. "Just get on with it." They stopped at a traffic signal. "Look. This is me stopping at a red light," Sequoia said.

"Fine," Jasmine said, wishing for more green lights so they could get home. "I'll get on with it. Here's the thing. They're both great guys."

"Oh, my," Sequoia said. "I'm getting all worked up just thinking about these *great guys*. Dig in, Jasmine. There's more to it than that."

Holly said, "Wow. Is this a new interrogation technique? You use this on all the criminals?"

"Okay, you're right," Jasmine said. "'Great guys' is kind of lame. But they are. Parker is so sweet. He's such a gentleman. Did you know he still orders for me at restaurants, just like he did when we were teenagers? It's the sweetest thing."

"Wait," Holly said, and Sequoia chimed in with her: "He orders for you?"

Jasmine felt her face turning red. Again. "I mean, he asks me what I want, and then he orders it. I guess it's a throwback from when I was too shy to order my own food."

"How sweet," Holly said at the same time as Sequoia said, "How creepy." Under her breath she added, "and controlling."

"And Hudson?" Sequoia said.

"Hudson is … different," Jasmine said.

"Wow, for a writer, you're worse than terrible at describing people," Sequoia said.

"Yeah," Holly said. "That was a terrible description."

"Wait," Jasmine said. "I thought you were on my side."

"I was," Holly said. "I am."

"Okay," Jasmine said. "So Hudson just came into my life, like, a few weeks ago. You know? He doesn't know the old me. It's like he knows a new me. One I haven't even become yet. The thing is, I'm not sure if I'm that person. I'm not sure if I can be the person he sees me as. Or if I even want to be."

Sequoia nodded. "Now it all makes more sense."

Jasmine couldn't tell if she was being sincere or sarcastic, so she kept talking. "I'm really enjoying spending time with both of them. And I think it's because they represent different things to me. Parker is this ideal, you know? He's the standard by which I've measured all other men. For years."

Sequoia cursed as she slammed on the brakes again. Holly flinched. Jasmine braced herself for impact.

"And Hudson?" Sequoia said.

"He's the potential, I guess," Jasmine said. "He represents what things could be."

"That's actually pretty deep," Sequoia said.

Holly nodded. "You just have to decide which one is right for you, right now."

Then, the three of them spoke at once. "If only it were that easy."

CHAPTER TWENTY-FIVE

Finally, Sequoia pulled into Jasmine's driveway and put the car in park. Then she looked into the rearview mirror and said, "Wow. I don't know how I missed that the entire time I was driving you home."

Jasmine and Holly twisted around in their seats to see what she was talking about, and Jasmine yelped when she saw Parker's van pulling into her driveway behind Sequoia's car.

"Parker," Jasmine and Holly said at the same time.

"Wait," Sequoia said. "Is that jasmine painted on the side of his bus?"

"It is," Jasmine said, doing her best to keep her voice even and level.

"That's so sweet," Holly said, and Sequoia said, "It's creepy, is what it is."

By this time, Parker had already climbed down from the van and was walking to Jasmine's side of the car, his movements hurried and purposeful.

He lifted the door handle with a little pop, but then opened the door gingerly like Jasmine might fall out if he opened it too fast.

"Are you okay?" he said as soon as he got the door open wide enough to bring his face up close to Jasmine's. "I came to the hospital, but the nurse wouldn't let me in. Kind of a grumpy old lady."

Holly, who had gotten out of the backseat and was standing behind Parker, gave Jasmine a comically-serious look. Jasmine could practically feel her sister's relief at the Parker-Hudson Near Miss.

The whole situation suddenly seemed so absurd, and Jasmine had the urge to giggle. Again. Fortunately, Holly looked away, and Parker took Jasmine's unbroken arm to help her out of the car.

"One of the nurses took pity on me," Parker said. "Or maybe it's because I brought in a box of donuts. I don't know. Anyway, she told me they were just about to discharge you. So I decided to come here to see if you needed anything. It looks like I'm too late, though. Looks like your sisters have things under control."

Sequoia shut her car door. "I think we have it handled, Parker. Thanks for stopping by."

Parker withered. Any traces of self-confidence blew away in the wind like the tufts off a daffodil. "Um, okay," he said. "I'll just head home, then. Jas, you call me if you need anything, okay?"

Jasmine nodded, and Sequoia came around the front of the car to shepherd her into the house. Holly followed after Parker like a chick after a mother hen. She darted this way and that, but followed his general path. Sequoia took Jasmine's elbow and led her into the house.

"I've got to be more observant," Jasmine said when they were inside. "I should have seen him. If I'm not careful, Parker and Hudson are going to cross paths. And that's going to be messy."

"This is yet another side effect of your indecisive nature," Sequoia said. "Can I get you some water?"

"No, thank you," Jasmine said. "Can you get me something stronger? Wine?"

"I'm pretty sure you're not supposed to drink alcohol right now," Sequoia said. "They gave you pain killers."

"Where is Holly? Why isn't she back in here, yet?" Jasmine said.

"I'll assume that was rhetorical," Sequoia said. "Here's some water."

Jasmine took the water and sipped it. Then a realization struck. "Oh, no. If Parker came here to check on me, what if Hudson comes, too?"

When Sequoia didn't answer, Jasmine answered herself. "He's not really the nurturing type. If he does show up, it will be with coffee laced with whiskey. He won't hold my arm or help me stand up. But he and Parker don't know about each other. I mean, I think Parker suspects, or suspected at one point, but …"

Her voice trailed off. She had no idea what to do. Finally, she said, "What can I do to prevent Hudson from showing up?"

"Nothing," Sequoia said. "Anything you do will come across as awkward."

"What if I just text him that I'm home and settling in, and then I invite him to come over later?"

"Why don't you just tell him not to come over, at all."

"Wait," Jasmine said. "Why are we assuming he even wants to come over?"

"That's true," Sequoia said. "He may not."

"Well, I think we know he was worried. He came to the hospital."

"He's a reporter. He came to gawk at the scene."

Jasmine bristled. "He did not. He came to see how I was doing. If he'd wanted to gawk at the scene, he'd have gone to the actual scene. Where the accident happened."

"You mean, where you caused the accident," Sequoia said. "It didn't just happen."

For the first time since the accident, Jasmine thought about her beloved car. Was it totaled? She pictured bright orange paint and broken glass. Suddenly, she had to sit down. She sank into one of the barstools and put her head in her hands. "My car," she said.

"Yep," Sequoia said. "That piece of junk is totaled, my sister. Wiped out. I've been waiting for it to kick the bucket, but I admit, I didn't imagine it going down this way."

Before she realized what was happening, Jasmine saw tear drops landing on the kitchen counter, in tiny splashes. She began to sob in earnest, then. Sequoia, always practical and rarely nurturing, found a tissue and shoved it at Jasmine. She managed a quick pat on Jasmine's shoulder. "I can't believe my car is gone," Jasmine wailed.

"I know the right thing to say is, 'I'm sorry, Jasmine,'" Sequoia said, "but to be honest, it's about time. You're lucky you didn't get crunched to smithereens in this accident. Heaven forbid you'd been on the highway or something. You could have died in that little tin can. Now you can get a practical car. One they make for grown-ups."

Jasmine wailed again. Mid-wail, Holly and Parker walked back into the house. Holly rushed to Jasmine's side. She began rubbing Jasmine's back in big, swirling circles. Parker came to her other side and took one of her hands in his.

"I'm so sorry, Jasmine," Parker said. "Why don't you ladies go on home, and I'll stay with Jas for a while. I can make her some food, tea, whatever she needs. We can hang out on the couch and watch reruns of 'The Simpsons.'"

If Parker stayed, indefinitely, how would Jasmine set up a time for Hudson to come over? What if Hudson stopped by to check on her and he and Parker came face-to-face? How would she explain to either one of them what was going on?

What *was* going on, anyway?

Sequoia was right. The problem was that she was indecisive. And stupid.

"No one has to take care of me," Jasmine said. "I'll be fine on my own. I'm sure I have leftovers I can heat up for dinner. I can just hang out here with Ruby."

"Are you sure?" Parker said.

"Despite all appearances, Parker, my sister is an adult," Sequoia said. "She's perfectly capable of staying home alone. And ordering her own food. She can't drive anywhere, anyway. So I think she's safe."

Everyone, even Sequoia, hugged Jasmine. Parker kissed her on the temple. They left, and she was alone.

Typically, Jasmine enjoyed solitude, especially in the form of loud music and a good book. And probably a glass of wine. This evening, though, she felt antsy and irritable instead of soothed and relaxed.

Her favorite acoustic album played on her living room speakers. Guitar music flowed through the house. The book she'd been struggling to find time to read sat open to page one on her lap. A full cup of tea stood on the side table, steaming.

And she couldn't concentrate. Not on the book, not on a murder mystery she found on TV, not even on drinking the tea. Ruby, oblivious to Jasmine's struggles, snored loudly from her spot on the couch, where she lay on her back with her front paws folded neatly across her chest.

Every time Jasmine tried to focus, her mind drifted to Parker or Hudson. Maybe she should call it quits with both of them, and start fresh with someone new. Or maybe she should call it quits with both of them and spend some time—more time—alone. Dating was overrated, anyway.

Jasmine's phone rang, disrupting the flow of the quiet music. Her head throbbed as she leaned forward to pick it up off the coffee table. The Caller ID told her it was Hudson. Unable to deal with her feelings at the moment, she pressed "ignore" and set the phone back down.

She picked it up again and texted him: *Sorry, I'm in the bath. Can we talk later?*

Then she wondered why she'd said she was in the bath. At first, she'd thought being in the bath was a good excuse for not talking on the phone, but on second thought it sounded kind of sexual.

Hudson responded: *Why don't I come over now? ;) Just kidding. Sure, let's talk later. PS. Don't get your arm wet.*

"Oh, yeah," Jasmine said to Ruby. The phone dinged again. This time, it was Parker: *Just checking in. Are you doing okay? Can I get you anything?*

She responded: *I'm fine, thanks. I don't need anything now, but I appreciate the offer. :)*

Parker texted again: *What are you doing?*

Jasmine typed: *Just sitting on the couch with Ruby, reading a book.*
Want company?

Exasperated, Jasmine dropped her phone into her lap. Then she picked it up and answered: *No thanks. The peace and quiet is soothing my frazzled nerves.*

At least if she was texting both men at one time, it meant they were both somewhere other than at her house. This dance may be exhausting, but she could keep it up all night.

"I can do this," she said to Ruby.

Ruby rolled over onto her stomach and gave Jasmine a look that said she didn't believe it for a minute. Then she stood up, shook her tiny body, and sat down, alert, as if she was ready for the show.

Parker texted again: *Okay. Promise to let me know if you need anything?*

Jasmine responded: *Of course.*

When her phone dinged again, she said to Ruby, "He's being kind of a nuisance, isn't he?"

Again, Ruby gave her a dignified look, and waited. Jasmine read Parker's text out loud: "Remember our first date at Linda's? I'm stopping by there to get some chips and salsa."

Then she said, "I have no idea why he's telling me that."

She should have seen it as foreshadowing, she thought later. But she'd been so wrapped up in figuring out how to prevent the two men in her life from crossing paths that she didn't even pick up on the clues. Instead, she went back to staring at the first page of her new book.

One hour and fifty pages later, Jasmine's phone dinged again.

"Maybe I should just shut this thing off," she said out loud.

The text, another one from Parker, said, *Special delivery.*

Jasmine looked at Ruby, but the dog didn't offer any clues. So she got up and walked over to her front door. Her first glance through the side window didn't reveal anything, but then Parker came striding up the walkway, his arms wrapped around a pair of big brown paper bags. He looked so pleased with himself that she couldn't help but smile as she opened the door. All the irritation she'd felt at his over-texting melted away.

"I brought you chips and salsa," he said. "Fresh from Linda's."

"That's so sweet," Jasmine said. "Come on in."

Parker opened the Styrofoam box and set it in the middle of the coffee table.

"I got guacamole, too," he said. "I know how much you like that."

Jasmine actually didn't like guacamole any more. Five years ago, a fluke incident in which she'd overdone it on guacamole and beer had cured her of her insatiable hunger for guacamole. Sequoia was still holding a grudge over that one, Jasmine thought, and she couldn't blame her sister. Jasmine had thrown up all over Sequoia's pristine kitchen floor.

Still, Jasmine reminded herself, Parker was being so thoughtful, and it's the thought that counts.

She selected a less-oily chip and dipped it in the salsa.

"Do you remember our first date?" Parker said. When Jasmine nodded, he said, "I was so nervous. I can't believe you wanted to go on another date with me after that. Do you remember how I dripped a huge glop of salsa onto my pants?"

"No!" Jasmine said. "I don't even remember that. I don't think I even knew about it."

"How could you not have known? I was humiliated! It was like a great pink river on my pants."

He pushed the guacamole toward her, and she dipped another chip in the salsa.

"I probably didn't notice because I was so nervous, myself," Jasmine said.

"You were?"

"Of course. I'd been fantasizing about chips and salsa with Parker Abbott for months."

"You had not," Parker said.

"I had!" Jasmine said. "Ever since we picked you up in the rain that day."

"Then why didn't you talk to me?"

"I don't know. I was scared. You seemed so grumpy that day. I was afraid to approach you afterwards."

Jasmine's phone dinged, but she didn't bother checking it. She stuck it between the couch cushions.

"Aren't you going to check that?" Parker said.

Jasmine shrugged. "Anyway, I thought I really hit the jackpot when we ended up being biology partners."

"I did, too," Parker said.

When someone knocked on the door, Jasmine froze. Parker looked around as if whoever had knocked might materialize through one of the walls.

"It's probably Holly or Sequoia coming to check on me," Jasmine said. "Sequoia. She doesn't trust me to heal up on my own."

Parker laughed. "I know. I'm the oldest child, too. Remember, we met because Ryder messed up his science fair project. Couldn't get it right."

"True. You wait here. I'll be right back."

When Jasmine saw who was on the other side of the door, she was grateful the entryway was so far from the living room.

"Hudson," Jasmine said.

"Jasmine," Hudson responded. He looked as surprised by her reaction as she was by his appearance. "I texted you," he said.

It was only then that she realized he was holding a brown paper bag and a box of chocolates.

If she hadn't started panicking when she opened the door, she was panicking now. This was the very situation she'd been trying to avoid. By not answering Hudson's text, by sneaking around between the two men—by being so *indecisive*—she'd created this situation rather than preventing it. She wanted to cry, to throw her hands up, to disappear. But she couldn't.

What could she do, instead? How could she play it cool? How could she make this okay?

She could act as if Parker was just there as a friend. But would he notice? If only Hudson hadn't brought chocolates. She couldn't pretend he was there as a friend. A friend wouldn't bring chocolates.

"Is someone here?" Hudson said, at the same time as Jasmine said, "What's in the bag?"

"Come on in," Jasmine said, and Hudson said, "Whiskey and coffee. Decaf."

As he spoke, Hudson walked past her and into the house. She shut the door, wishing she could have run through it, first.

Jasmine hung back, and then brilliance struck. "Head to the left," she said. "Into the kitchen. Let's make some coffee right now."

"I wasn't sure if you had a coffeemaker so I bought the pre-made stuff. You know how they sell it in a box at The Grind now?"

"Good point. I don't have a coffeemaker."

Just tell me where the mugs are," Hudson said. "I don't want you doing anything extra."

How long would it take for Parker to hear another man's voice in the kitchen and come scope things out?

"They're next to the fridge," Jasmine said. "I can grab one."

"No, no," Hudson said. "I'll get it."

Maybe if Hudson poured the drink quickly enough, Jasmine could usher him out before Parker saw him. Jasmine could pretend someone else had brought them.

How could she hurry this process along?

"There's the sink," she said.

"Thanks, Jas," Hudson said. "I didn't see it there."

Jasmine flinched. This wasn't working out.

"Haha. Sorry, just delirious, I guess. I'm tired."

Jasmine heard Parker pause the TV. Any minute, he'd be walking in here. Where else would he go? Hudson kept searching the cabinet. He still hadn't chosen a mug. Jasmine tapped her toe. Where was Parker? Why wasn't he coming in? Maybe he'd gone to the bathroom.

Jasmine tapped her toe again. Hudson turned around. Empty-handed.

"Are you okay?" he said.

"What do you mean?"

"I mean, you're tapping your toe. I've never seen you do that. You seem really agitated."

"Huh? No, I'm fine. Everything's fine. This was really thoughtful."

"Yeah, I thought about flowers but—"

"Waste of money," they said at the same time.

Hudson removed the screw top from the box of coffee and poured it into a mug. Just as Jasmine handed him a spoon, Parker walked into the kitchen.

Jasmine would later look back and find this moment comical. Parker stopped in the kitchen's entryway. Hudson, just grasping the spoon, stopped, too. The moment was completely suspended.

The two men stood there, staring at each other for what seemed like an eternity. Jasmine could practically see the thoughts running through each of their minds. Parker was thinking something like, *What the hell? What is that newspaper guy doing here? Is that a box of* coffee? *Are those chocolates?* His eyes shot to the spoon, acting as a link between Jasmine and Hudson. He looked Jasmine in the eye. *What is really going on here?*

Hudson was thinking, *Oh, geez. It's the longhaired guy. He keeps showing up. What is he doing here, tonight? Why didn't Jasmine tell me he was here when I asked if someone was here? That makes his appearance very suspicious. What is she not telling me?*

And Jasmine, for her part, was thinking, *Oh, no. Ohhhh, no.*

Parker broke the silence. "Hey, man. Hudson, right? How's it going?" He extended a hand. "I'm Parker."

Hudson let go of the spoon. "Hudson," he said. He grasped Parker's hand. Jasmine wondered whether either of them was squeezing the other's hand in that strange show of strength and masculinity she'd heard about.

"Parker was just—"

"I was just bringing her some chips and salsa," Parker said. "And guacamole."

"You don't even like guacamole," Hudson said to Jasmine.

Jasmine's face immediately heated up. She cleared her throat.

"She loves guacamole," Parker said.

Hudson looked at Jasmine. "Does she?"

"Hudson was just stopping by to check on me," Jasmine said.

Both men stared at her without speaking. They were holding their positions. Neither of them offered to duck out, to make this moment less awkward.

"Parker and I were just about to watch some TV," Jasmine said. "Want to stay, Hudson?"

Hudson looked from Jasmine to Parker, and back to Jasmine again. "Uh, no. No, I don't think so. I'll leave you two to your TV show. Don't worry about walking me out."

In the silence that followed Hudson's departure, Parker continued to stand in the kitchen's entry, unmoving, staring at Jasmine. Jasmine found herself staring back at him, blinking in a way she'd probably find absurd if she could see herself from his perspective.

She cleared her throat again, but before she could speak (not that she knew what she wanted to say, anyway), Parker held up a hand. "Wait. When you said there was nothing going on between you and Hudson, I believed you. I trusted you. And you can say, right now, that he showed up as a friend. To cheer you up, offer you support, whatever. But first of all, a guy friend doesn't bring a girl boxed coffee and whiskey—and chocolate. Unless he has feelings for her. And second, I saw the way he looked at me, and at you. He has feelings for you, Jas, and he wouldn't have felt comfortable coming over with boxed coffee and whiskey and chocolate, and standing in your kitchen, unless he was reasonably certain you have feelings for him, too. Which means that even if you don't have feelings for him, your behavior has said otherwise. I thought we were giving this thing between us thirty days. That's not too much to ask after I came all this way to be with you, is it?"

Jasmine opened her mouth to answer, but Parker held up a hand again. "I don't think it is. Enjoy your chips and salsa. I'll take the guacamole. Since, apparently, you don't like it anymore, but you didn't bother to tell me."

Jasmine cringed. Parker walked into the living room, put the lid on the guacamole and walked out the front door without saying good-bye.

Now, Jasmine stood in the silent kitchen, having created the very scenario she'd spent the past several weeks building her life around avoiding. And now, instead of having to choose between Parker and Hudson, she was alone, the choice having been taken away from her.

"What do I do now?" she said aloud.

No one answered. Even Ruby, who had positioned herself near the counter in anticipation of dropped food, walked into the living room.

Jasmine found that her appetite had disappeared. She cleaned up the chips and salsa, and sat down on the couch. Rather than turning on the TV or putting on music, she sat in silence. Ruby hopped up onto the couch, but instead of laying against Jasmine's leg like she normally would, she walked to the farthest possible cushion and settled down with her hind end facing Jasmine.

"Great. Even you're mad at me," Jasmine said.

She closed her eyes. Why was this choice so hard to make?

For years, she'd considered Parker her soul mate, The One. She'd compared every relationship she had with that giddy, teenage-love relationship they shared. Could anyone ever stand up to that? The answer, she knew, was that no, no one could ever stand up that. No new man could ever compare to a girl's first love. Especially when said first love ended in tragedy and was reborn in hope.

Then Hudson came sauntering into her life. He was far from perfect, with his big-city swagger and his fast motorcycle and his almost-too-gorgeous grin. Even though they'd just met, it seemed like he knew her right away. Since that first day, he had pushed her beyond what was comfortable for her. The weird thing was, she liked it. She found it thrilling. From his threat to tie her up with her scarf to his suggestion that she work with him to put together a serious journalistic series, she liked the feeling of expanding. But was she expanding into the real Jasmine, or a Hudson-crafted Jasmine?

"Why am I even thinking about this, Ruby?" she said. "It's not like I have a choice anymore, anyway. Neither one of them will have me. In my efforts to choose the right one, I ended up choosing neither."

Sequoia would say something about how this was a good opportunity to learn a life lesson. What was life trying to teach her? That dating anyone was a bad idea? That she should be alone forever? That her ideal was shattered and she had to start over from scratch?

If Sequoia were sitting right here, she'd undoubtedly say, "Life is trying to teach you to make up your damn mind, Jasmine."

At this thought, Jasmine chuckled. Ruby seemed to think this was an appropriate time to forgive Jasmine, and she came back over to lay against Jasmine's leg.

Jasmine spent the rest of the evening there, petting Ruby and feeling sorry for herself.

CHAPTER TWENTY-SIX

The next morning, Sequoia arrived bright and early to take Jasmine to the orthopedic doctor. Jasmine had just finished telling Sequoia about the Hudson-Parker Face-Off when they came to the intersection where Jasmine had run the red light.

"What is life trying to tell me, Sequoia?" Jasmine said.

"You know, I think life is trying to tell you to make up your damn mind, Jasmine," Sequoia said. "I'm not sure whether to congratulate you or say something to the effect of 'I told you so.'"

"I knew you were going to say that," Jasmine said.

"I always speak the truth," Sequoia said.

"But how do I just choose? It's not as simple as that, you know?"

"I actually don't know," Sequoia said. "It seems relatively simple, to me."

"To you, who has no relationship experience to speak of." Sequoia rolled her eyes, but didn't answer. "Sorry. That was rude. Anyway, each of them just has different qualities, you know? They're so different."

"It's not really about them, Jas. It's about you. It's about how you feel when you're with them. When do you feel the most like your-self? When do you feel energized, happy, alive?"

"Not that it matters now, anyway," Jasmine said.

Sequoia shrugged. "You're right. It doesn't matter for this round. But other men will come into your life. We can count on that."

They'd reached the doctor's office, and Sequoia was out of the car before Jasmine could respond. Jasmine followed her big sister into the building, thinking that for once, Sequoia had provided some good relationship advice.

They were in and out of the doctor's office within a half-hour, which meant it was still before lunchtime when Sequoia dropped Jasmine off at work.

"Wait. Did you seriously get an orange cast?" Cara was up and out of her chair before the newsroom door closed behind Jasmine.

"It's in honor of my poor, wrecked car," Jasmine said.

Cara laughed. "Can I sign it?"

"You'll be the first."

"Wait. Your sister didn't sign it?"

"Nah, she got a work call on our way back here and I think we both forgot."

"What happened with Hudson?" Cara said.

"What do you mean?" Jasmine didn't really mean, "What do you mean?" She really meant, "How did you know something did happen?" and "How did Hudson's behavior tip you off?"

Cara said, "He's acting like a real ass, shoving papers around on his desk, snapping at everyone who asks him a question, speaking in caveman grunts. I recognize a broken heart when I see one."

"Huh," Jasmine said.

"Yeah," Cara said. "So what happened?"

When Jasmine finished telling Cara the story, Cara whistled, long and low. "I don't even know what to say. But that explains his behavior. Maybe we should work remotely today so you don't have to come into contact with him."

"That's your best idea yet."

Avoiding Hudson turned out to be relatively easy, Jasmine thought as the day went on. He left before Jasmine arrived ("with a squeal of his tires, in a cloud of smoke," Cara said), and didn't come back to the office at all. Even though Jasmine found herself distracted, she managed to make good headway on the suicide series, scheduling a few interviews and researching statistics to include.

She could only hope Hudson still wanted to work on it, and still planned to get the photos they'd discussed. Could the two of them complete an entire series without talking? It might be difficult, but it wouldn't be impossible. At least the newsroom was almost always busy, with reporters coming and going, the TV always on and dialed into CNN, people calling out to one another with crude jokes, the phones ringing. This made it unlikely that the two of them would ever have to be alone together. Unless a big story came up that required them to work late. Which had already happened more than once in the short time since Hudson had arrived in Seabreeze.

"Shit," Jasmine said.

Maybe she should apologize to Hudson, to air the situation out. But what would she say? "I'm sorry I lied to you." "I'm sorry I led you on." "I'm sorry I was an idiot."

"Ugh," she said.

"Stop talking to yourself," Cara said. "You're distracting me."

"Sorry," Jasmine said.

And what about Parker? Should she try to make amends with him? What would she say? "I'm sorry I lied to you." "I'm sorry I led you on." "I'm sorry I was an idiot."

Or should she just let both men go, free them from the mess that was Jasmine Carr?

JASMINE SHOULD HAVE KNOWN Hudson wouldn't let her off easy. As co-workers with whom women have (or ruin) romantic relationships must do, inevitably, he returned to the office. And of course, the timing couldn't be worse: she was sitting on the patio outside when he pulled into his parking spot.

She could have packed up her break materials—chocolate and soda—but it would have been so obvious that she was avoiding him. Instead, she played it cool, like it didn't give her deer-in-the-headlights syndrome to anticipate talking to him.

He didn't disappoint.

Hudson stalked right up to Jasmine and pointed a finger at her (a behavior she found highly annoying). "You," he said. "You don't take anything seriously. At all. You don't take your work seriously, you don't take your romantic involvements seriously, you don't take my feelings seriously, or the feelings of that longhaired clod. And you certainly don't take your injury seriously. An orange cast? An orange cast. I should have known. Jasmine Carr, purveyor of all things unserious."

His tone was light, but his eyes held such intensity Jasmine wished she could curl up into a ball and roll away.

She tried for indignation. "I do take things seriously."

He actually sneered in response. "Oh yeah? Like what? Name one thing."

"Like the suicide series."

"Yeah, because I made you."

Jasmine nodded. "Touché."

"Name something else."

Jasmine sighed. "I don't want to."

"You don't want to, or you can't?"

Why was he doing this? She took lots of things seriously. When she didn't answer, he practically spit, "Oh, I know. I know one thing you take seriously. One thing. Your high school, teenage romance. You let it rule the course of your adult life. Which makes perfect sense, Jasmine. Perfect sense."

With that, he walked into the building, shaking his head and muttering to himself.

Jasmine felt the overpowering urge to cry, and bit down hard on her lip and counted to thirty before throwing away the rest of her junk food and going for a drive along the coast.

CHAPTER TWENTY-SEVEN

Two weeks passed, during which Jasmine kept her head down at work. Hudson came and went, but never even looked at her, much less spoke to her. She didn't hear from Parker at all. Every day, she experienced at least one period of time during which she deliberated whether to reach out to each of them, to explain the irrational debate that raged in her mind when she was dating both of them. But every day, that deliberation ended with her reasonable inner voice telling her to let it go.

Over drinks at Starboard one night—beers because neither of them could stomach margaritas after the previous incident—Cara provided Jasmine with a list of options for her dating future.

"You could join one of those online dating sites," she said, "or one of those meet-up groups for singles in our area. Or what about taking Ruby to the dog park? I'm sure you could date a fellow dog-lover."

"Thanks, but no, thanks," Jasmine said. "I'll meet someone else one of these days, I'm sure."

"Or what about just going to restaurants alone? Ooh, or to bars? Someone is bound to pick you up."

"That's like wearing a sign around my neck that says, 'I'm

desperate,'" Jasmine said. "Forget it. I think what I really need is some alone time."

She looked around at the assortment of guys there, and wondered which one would pick her up if Cara weren't here. Probably the guy sitting at the bar with three empty martini glasses and his rolled-up necktie in front of him.

"Aren't you lonely?" Cara said.

"Aren't you?"

"Yeah." Cara took a deep breath and tore her straw wrapper into pieces. "I think I'm going to try out one of those online dating sites. I actually opened an account last night but haven't checked yet to see whether I got any bites."

"Sounds kinky."

"Shut up. You could also try choosing between the two men with whom you're obviously smitten."

"Oh, geez. Why does everyone keep saying that to me?"

"Oh, I don't know, Jasmine. Maybe because it's true."

Sequoia and Holly had said the same thing, countless times since The Face-Off. Jasmine couldn't even keep track of who had said what anymore, but each comment was some rendition of the one before it:

"*Just choose one, Jas. The right one will accept your apology before tossing you into the sack for a down and dirty romp.*"

"*I don't understand what's so hard about choosing one. It's all about how he looks at you.*"

"*It's all about how he makes you feel.*"

"*It's all about how he makes you feel ... between the sheets.*"

"*It's all about how he complements you.*"

"*No, no. It's all about how he compliments you.*"

Jasmine didn't know if any of what they said was true. All she *did* know was that she didn't know what to do. As she had done for the past couple of weeks, she compared and contrasted her suitors relentlessly.

Parker was short. Hudson was tall.

Parker was a drifter. Hudson was driven.

Parker treated Jasmine like she was fifteen and he wanted her to stay that way. Hudson treated her like she was fifteen and he wanted her to grow up.

Parker drove a van. Hudson drove a motorcycle.

Parker ignited a low, slow heat in Jasmine's belly. Hudson made her want to explode.

She viewed her time with Parker through one of those soft-focus lenses. And she viewed her time with Hudson through an extra-bright filter.

The two of them were so different. They complemented her differently. But which one complemented her better?

"I just don't know," she finally said aloud to Cara. "There is just so much to the question of which one to choose. Maybe it's better to scrap this whole thing and start from scratch."

Although Jasmine's communications with Hudson had been extremely limited during the two weeks following The Face-Off, she managed to finalize the suicide series. It was the first time she'd really sorted through heaps of statistics, tons of sources, and hours of interview notes to compile a comprehensive series on a complicated topic.

At first, she felt unsure of herself, questioning which numbers belonged in the stories, which would have the most impact in helping readers understand the widespread suicide problem. But the absence of anyone there to guide her—Cara, although supportive, insisted Jasmine figure it out based on all the research she'd done—forced her to follow her own intuition.

Even though her hands shook slightly as she uploaded the final versions of the stories to the *Daily Trumpet's* server for editing, she was pleased with the results. The stories were good. They were informative. They would remind people about the resources, support, and services available, and they would bring attention and real human connection to the topic.

Jasmine knew she should feel happy. Elated, even. If she said so herself, she nailed it. But something was missing.

Even when Mikey came bounding out of his office a half-hour after she uploaded the series to congratulate her on a job well done, even when Cara finished reading through the stories on her own computer and told Jasmine they were, "really, *really* good," Jasmine felt down, and couldn't put her finger on the reason why.

In retrospect, the answer seemed pretty obvious.

The following Sunday, when the first story came out on page one, Jasmine received several emails and voicemail messages from people whose lives suicide had affected in some way.

In one, a woman said, "Thank you so much for your article today. My brother committed suicide two years ago, and I always wondered if he even realized there were resources out there." In an email, someone wrote, *Wow. I had no idea all these resources were available. Great article. I've shared it on all my social media profiles. This is real journalism. Well done.*

And those represented a small percentage of the feedback she received.

Every time her email application alerted her to a new message, and every time she received a new voicemail, Jasmine experienced the strong urge to turn around and share the excitement with Hudson. She wanted to yell at him, "See? I can be serious! I am a serious journalist! I've even gotten phone calls!" She wanted to high-five him or hug him or beg him to tie her up with her scarf.

But his attention was elusive. Not once did he offer her any kind of kudos. Although she'd never admit it to anyone, not even (or especially not) to her sisters, Jasmine found herself hyperaware of Hudson's comings and goings despite the fact that he seemed completely blind to her.

"MAYBE THIS IS the new status quo," Jasmine said to Ruby one evening as they sat on the couch watching a cheesy romance movie. "You and me, ice cream, and the cheesy romance channel."

Ruby apparently didn't like the idea. She hopped off the couch and disappeared. Jasmine finished the ice cream. This wasn't so bad. After the resounding success of her series, she could sense that being a professional journalist could be fulfilling. Maybe this whole Parker-

Hudson Problem was a sign that she should focus on her work, and only on her work.

Isn't that what Hudson had done?

He'd focused on his work, devoting most of his spare time to work-related efforts. And he seemed happy. Happy enough, anyway. He had his bachelor pad and his photography and his friends. Jasmine could do that, too. Maybe it was time to make some renovations—life renovations. She'd start with the house, and come Monday, she'd throw herself into her work like never before. The suicide prevention series could serve as a launching point for a whole new phase of her career. Maybe, for the first time, she could even apply for some awards. With a hope of actually winning some.

She didn't need a man. She didn't need romance. At least, not right now. If she focused on building her own life into what she wanted it to be, maybe that would fall into place later. Or, maybe not. Being a lifelong bachelorette wouldn't be so bad. Ruby might not agree, but she'd get used to it.

What she did need was a car. Not just any car, but a serious, grown-up car. That would be the first order of business tomorrow.

Jasmine fell asleep that night feeling at peace for the first time in a long while.

The next morning, she ordered up a taxi to take her to the car dealership.

"You need a new car?"

The taxi driver, a grizzled smoker with chewed-down fingernails and rough white patches of skin on his elbow (which he kept propped up on the back of the middle seat), wanted to know what Jasmine was in the market for.

"Something serious," she told him. "Maybe a sedan or a little SUV, you know?"

"You want serious, you gotta go with a pickup truck," he said. "A big one. Those things are serious."

"Well, I don't really have any heavy lifting to do. I just need something to get me from point A to point B. I guess I should have used the word, 'sophisticated.' I need something sophisticated."

He shrugged. "Have it your way, sweetheart. They got a special on those old lady cars. You know, the gold ones? You always see 'em in gold. If you want sophisticated, that's sophisticated for ya."

Jasmine wasn't sure if she wanted something *that* grown-up. Maybe a pickup truck *would* be a good option. The taxi driver pulled up at the entrance to the dealership's sales office.

"Here ya go, sweetheart. Door to door service." As she handed him her payment, he said, "Remember, honey, you're a nice young lady. I know they got specials on those old lady cars, but now is the time in your life when you can drive something fun. Live a little. You know what I mean?" Jasmine smiled and thanked him, and shut the door. As she walked away, he rolled down the passenger side window and called, "Oh, and honey?"

She turned around. "You seem like a nice girl," he said. "Don't let 'em screw ya, okay?"

Jasmine nodded, and turned around again. She almost ran right into a salesman who'd come out to meet her. The taxi driver gave her a quick double honk before driving away.

"So I guess you need a new car," the salesman said. "I'm Dale."

Fortunately, once she decided against the pickup truck and the old lady car, her choices were slim, so the selection process went quickly.

"This one is sporty, yet practical," Dale said. He'd led her to a little two-door coupe. "You'll get great gas mileage and it also has plenty of power."

For the first time in a long time, Jasmine didn't run through her sisters' potential reactions to her decision before making it. The car was perfect. It looked like a young person's car, and it also had earned top safety ratings. Plus, it had a few bells and whistles, like seat warmers, a sun roof, and a touchscreen stereo system. These features probably came standard on most newer-model cars, but she was so used to her old Golf that they seemed like luxuries.

So, with minimal haggling or bargaining, she bought the car.

With that item checked off her list, she drove to the mall and went directly to Home Décor and More, the overpriced, trendy home furnishings store where Holly always shopped. After overcoming her initial sticker shock, Jasmine loaded a shopping cart with picture frames, candle holders and colorful throw rugs. Something about a multi-colored painting of a cow called to her, too, so she stuck it in her cart before she could change her mind. It would look perfect on her dining room wall.

"Perfectly ridiculous," she said to herself, mimicking Sequoia. Then she checked out, smiling.

CHAPTER TWENTY-EIGHT

Parker lived on the outskirts of town, in a low-slung one-story apartment building surrounded by asphalt. Jasmine tried to view it as anything other than depressing, with its oddly-placed potted plants and sand-filled ashtrays. He answered the door before Jasmine even finished knocking, his expression a mixture of happy and relieved. When he opened his arms, she stepped into them. She laid her head against his chest and as always, noticed how well they fit together.

"Let's go inside," she said.

He stood back, took her hand and led her into the apartment. Why hadn't she been to his apartment before this? Just like the outside of the building, the inside of his living quarters was indistinct. A few rock band posters hung on the wall and a gray sheet covered a futon in the corner. Parker led Jasmine to the futon and pulled her down beside him without letting go of her hand.

"I'm so glad you wanted to talk to me," he said. "I wanted to see you, but I wasn't sure what to do."

"I'm sorry," Jasmine said. "I just needed some time to think."

Although she knew she had to power through this conversation, her hands shook. What would he say? How would he react?

"Parker," she said.

He smiled. "You're nervous, aren't you? It's okay. I understand you've been going through a lot lately. Take your time."

He had no idea, she thought. She cleared her throat. "Okay. Thanks. As you know, you've always stood out as the archetypal perfect guy for me."

When she put finger quotes around "perfect guy," he grinned.

"I've compared every guy I've dated to you, to see how he measures up. 'Is he as tall as Parker, or shorter than Parker? As good looking? As generous? As good of a driver?'"

Now she was blushing. Yes, she was embarrassed, but she had to get it all out there. Parker was looking a bit smug, now, and she couldn't blame him. It was actually pretty cute. His expression reminded her of the time he'd picked her up to surprise her for a date, and he'd taken her to a circus performance she'd been wanting to see. The tickets sold out the first day, and Jasmine was so disappointed she'd cried. Parker teased her for crying over not getting tickets, but he ended up pounding the pavement until he found some from a third party seller. The night of the circus performance, he told her he'd take her out to dinner as a consolation, so she wouldn't be bored at home. When he arrived at the door, he presented the circus tickets to her with a flourish, looking so pleased with himself that she cried tears of laughter as well as tears of joy.

"Of course, the answer is always, unequivocally, no. No one can measure up to you, Parker. You're everything I've always wanted in a man."

"Jasmine, I—"

"Wait," she said. "Let me finish."

She withdrew her hand from his, then folded her own hands together and stuck them between her knees so she wouldn't fidget for this next part.

"You see, I was so stuck on you, I didn't even know what I was missing. I dated my share of guys, great guys, without ever really giving them—or myself—the chance to see if they were a good match for me. And with my career, I kind of did the same thing. I kind of put it on hold because I was always waiting for you to come back around. I always asked myself what you'd think of this. And I always remembered how you used to make fun of reporters on TV. Remember that?"

Parker nodded. Now he was looking a bit chagrined. "I didn't mean it," he said. "I mean, I meant it, but that was a teenage boy talking. I respect what you do, now, Jas. Of course I do."

"Of course you do. I know that. But I didn't, before. Because I was kind of stuck in that age group, you know? I was living as the teenage Jasmine, one-half of the teenage Jasmine-and-Parker duo. Until recently. You see, recently, I realized that I've changed. I'm still the same person, but I'm different, too. My teenage self was so in love with you, *beyond* in love with you, and almost died of sadness when you left."

Again, Parker tried to interrupt, but Jasmine held up a hand. "I'm so sorry to say this, Parker, but the adult me needs something different. I can't be with you."

JASMINE HAD JUST one more stop to make, and she felt more nervous than she had in weeks. Hudson's motorcycle was parked at the curb in front of his house, and she could hear music coming through his open windows. She steeled herself and knocked on the front door.

Of course, it was habit to compare the speed of his response with Parker's, but she nipped that thought in the bud and waited impatiently for him to answer. It was taking so long, she considered walking back to her car. He'd probably seen her through the window and decided not to answer. Or maybe he was preparing some speech to give her. A diatribe about how she hadn't been honest with him. She deserved it. Or maybe he couldn't hear her knocking over his music. She decided she'd knock one more time before going home.

Just as she raised her hand, the door swung open to reveal Hudson, naked except for an unreasonably small towel wrapped around his waist. His hair was wet and water droplets glistened on his chest.

If Jasmine's heart was beating hard before, it threatened to leap out of her chest now. He was so incredibly sexy. She wanted nothing more than to run her hands over his bare skin, but instead, she clasped them together at her waist.

Why was it that she felt so comfortable stepping into Parker's embrace, but not into Hudson's?

Uncertainty silenced her, and Hudson raised his eyebrows as if to ask why she was standing on his doorstep.

"Oh. Right. Hudson."

"Jasmine."

"You're not dressed."

"I was in the shower. You interrupted me."

Now that the door was open, the music, acoustic and soothing, made Jasmine think of dancing with Hudson, swaying in his arms. She'd forgotten how to speak.

"So," he said. "What's up."

"Sorry," she said. She gave herself a little shake. "Do you have a minute?"

He stepped back and gestured grandly for her to come in. He shut the door and crossed his arms, but didn't offer her a seat. She could smell his clean, soapy scent. She cleared her throat.

"So?" he said again.

"I just wanted to apologize for not being honest with you about Parker. For not being honest with myself about Parker. I mean, I should have told you I was seeing him, and I should have told him I was seeing you. And I should have told you, a long time ago, that I want to be with you. I have feelings for you, Hudson, even though you're completely wrong for me. You're arrogant, you're bossy, you're completely sweet and thoughtful. And you're the best thing that has happened to me in years. I feel like you've helped me redis-cover myself, or at least stumble upon the best version of myself. I don't know what it is about you, but I feel like I'm just on the edge of something new, something great, all the time. I'm more confident, more vibrant, more everything. I want to be with you, Hudson."

Silence.

Jasmine poured her heart out and Hudson responded with silence. What now? They stood there in his living room, staring at each other, guitar music and nerves in the air. Should she say something else? Normally, she'd just keep talking until he answered, but she had no idea what else to say. How many different words could she use to say the same thing?

So she waited.

Hudson looked thoughtful, pensive. He didn't seem angry or upset. It didn't look like he was going to kick her out of his house. But still, he didn't speak. Jasmine could see his heart beating. A bead of water that was caught in his chest hair escaped and dropped onto the towel. Jasmine took a deep breath.

"Jasmine," Hudson said, finally.

She nodded, careful not to make it seem too eager.

"Look, I—I need some time to think, okay? I appreciate your apology. But I need some time."

Jasmine nodded and swallowed the cluster of nerve cells that had clogged up her throat. Wordlessly, she turned around, opened the door, and walked out, turning to close the door behind her.

The last she saw of Hudson, he was standing there, holding the towel at his waist, staring at her. Walking down the path to her car, she experienced a barrage of half-thoughts: *So stupid, of course he doesn't want to, I missed my chance. I need to ask Cara about those dating sites. Maybe I'll be a spinster.*

Still, she thought, at least she'd said something. She wouldn't have to go through life wondering if things would have turned out differently if she reached out and apologized.

"No," she muttered to herself. "I'll just go through life wondering why I was such an idiot."

Just as she lifted the handle of her driver side door, she heard Hudson call her name. He was coming down the path, still in his towel. He looked determined. Or angry. Probably he was about to give her a piece of his mind. He would likely chastise her for dating two men at once, for not making a choice, for not taking herself seriously enough. She could take it. He was right. He'd been right all along. And because she knew that, she could hear him out. This was all about personal growth.

He came around the back of her car and stopped just inches from her, so she could feel his breath on her face.

"You're so right," he said. He gripped her upper arm, and turned her body so she was facing him. For a moment, he didn't speak. "We are so wrong for each other. You're shy and unsure of yourself and sometimes you drive me totally nuts."

Jasmine nodded. The motion bordered on manic, but he was right. And wasn't he agreeing with everything she'd said just a moment ago?

"You're so rigid, it kills me. You check three times before you back out of a parking spot. You're so beautiful, Jasmine. You're like the sunrise. I want to see you every single morning, every single night. You drive me nuts, did I mention that? You make me do crazy things, like play solitaire on a weekend night because I can't get my mind off you. The truth is, I'm totally crazy about you. I want you, so bad. I want to be with you, and only you. I've even been considering staying in Seabreeze. I bought a houseplant."

He leaned in then, pushing her back against the car, and kissed her. Relief flooded through her body, and a deep longing she'd only begun to recognize. She wrapped her arms around his waist and kissed him back.

***

"I KNEW IT!" Holly was triumphant, one finger raised in the air in victory. "I knew you'd choose Hudson."

Jasmine's sisters and Cara had come over to Jasmine's house to have a quick happy hour cocktail—and plan a romantic evening during which she'd seduce Hudson. He was due to arrive in an hour.

"I didn't," Sequoia said. "I was beginning to wonder whether you were even capable of making a choice. But I'm glad you chose Hudson. That whole jasmine-painted-on-the-side-of-the-van thing was borderline stalker behavior."

"I thought it was sweet," Holly said. "What did you think, Cara?"

Cara laughed. "I have no idea. I mean, it was sweet, but it was also kind of stalker-creepy. He seemed like a nice guy, but Jasmine was kind of his only purpose. He's just out there floundering around. Not good enough for our girl."

"He's not exactly floundering around," Jasmine said, feeling a little defensive. "He just wants to enjoy his freedom, for now."

"Whatever you want to call it," Holly said. "Should we choose your slutty outfit?"

"The one that's going to make Hudson drop his drawers the second he sees it?" Sequoia said.

"The one you're only going to be wearing for, like, five seconds before he rips it off you?" Cara said.

"We should," Jasmine said. "Let's do this."

When Jasmine's doorbell rang an hour later, she felt a jolt in her lower belly. Although she'd always found Hudson mouthwatering, they still hadn't consummated their relationship in the week since she told him she wanted to be with him.

One night, they came close. They sat on the couch, drinking wine and eating spaghetti. Hudson leaned over to lick a little bit of tomato sauce off the corner of Jasmine's mouth, and that, of course, turned into a kissing marathon. Just when Jasmine sensed it was getting hot and heavy, he stopped kissing her and, holding her at arm's length said, "I'm so proud of you for your work on that suicide series."

Hearing that from Hudson was *almost* as good as having an orgasm (okay, not really), but it stopped the steamy romance short— cold water on a fire.

Tonight was *it*, though. The tension had been building, and it had to come to a head or she might not live to see another day.

Holly had instructed her to open the door and drop the robe as soon as Hudson saw her. Sequoia had argued that it would be better to answer the door in the lingerie—no robe. And Cara had suggested a third option, in which Jasmine opened the door and then sashayed away, dropping her robe as she walked to the bedroom.

But Jasmine was tired of taking everyone else's advice. She was wearing the robe, but she had never even put the lingerie on. She planned to answer the door in her birthday suit … with one particular, special accessory.

For the briefest moment, she second-guessed the decision, but she took a deep breath and went with it. "Come in," she called.

When he opened the door, she dropped the robe. Its silky fabric pooled at her feet and its absence revealed the scarf around her neck. Hudson's mouth dropped open, and something in his eyes lit up. Still facing her, he shut the door. Then he walked toward her. He gripped her waist and pulled her close to him, bringing his mouth down to hers.

"You look delicious," he said.

"So do you," she said. "Would you care to join me in the bedroom?"

"You bet I would," he said, running the scarf through one hand. "Did you wear this for me?"

Jasmine smiled at him. "I wore it for both of us."

THE END

TURN **the page for a sneak peek of *Studying Sequoia*, the second book in the Garden Club series.**

PREVIEW: STUDYING SEQUOIA

BOOK 2 IN THE GARDEN CLUB SERIES

Chapter One

Sequoia Carr had a strange effect on men. She'd yet to nail down exactly why she had this effect, or whether she could change it.

Not that it mattered, she thought on this Monday morning as she came off her shift at the Seabreeze Police Department. Sequoia Carr was done with men.

In fact, she rarely thought about them. She hadn't been thinking about men while she stripped out of her uniform and examined the peeling paint on the walls of the department's locker room, thinking that it looked like moldy Swiss cheese. She hadn't been thinking of them as she pulled on her favorite fluorescent orange running shorts and inhaled the musty gym-sock smell that permeated every concrete inch of the place.

She'd been thinking about running.

Sequoia found it fitting that marathon running was one of the first Olympic sports. It was essential to human survival. Cavemen ran after their food. They ran away from predators who would turn them into food. And now, Sequoia Carr ran. Every single day, because it was essential for her survival.

She pulled on her tank top. After a quick examination in the full-length mirror, which revealed unusually toned thighs, nicely tanned shoulders, and a dark brown braid that reached her waist, Sequoia put on her shoes. In her hydration pack, she stowed the sandwich she'd bought earlier, along with some chips and a bottled water.

Even though she hadn't yet set foot outside, her body knew the routine. She could feel her heart rate picking up already, and she could taste adrenaline in her throat. The slam of her locker echoed in the empty room. She zipped her hydration pack and put it on, then exited the locker room and ran right into Elijah Sawyer.

He jumped back at the contact, and when he saw who he'd run into, he jumped back again. It was almost comical. It would have been comical, Sequoia thought, if she was the comic type.

She may not be the comic type, but she was observant. She'd spent twelve years being observant. She didn't miss the pine-and-citrus scent of Elijah's cologne or the interesting almost-brown, almost-green, almost-golden color of his eyes. She *definitely* didn't miss the once-over he gave her before stuttering out, "Good morning, Carr."

She expected him to say something like, "Nice outfit," because that's what her co-workers usually said when they saw her wearing anything other than a uniform, her hair braided and hanging down her back rather than tucked into a bun or twist.

But he didn't. Instead, the words, "Going for a run?" tumbled out of his mouth like he'd been trying to hold them in.

Before she could answer, he pressed his lips together, did an about face, and took off in the other direction.

"Morning, Sawyer," she called out after him. Even though he was no longer looking at her, she gestured to her outfit. "Yep, I'm going for a run."

Elijah's retreat did amuse Sequoia, but as soon as she noticed she was grinning, she forced her expression back to serious.

And now she swas thinking about men and the strange effect she had on them. Well, one specific man. She stepped outside to warm up, and blinked to let her eyes adjust. Fall was her favorite season in Seabreeze. The air was cool and the sun was bright.

There was something endearing about Elijah Sawyer, she thought as she walked, fast, away from the police station. She couldn't quite pin down whether it was his striking, model-worthy good looks or his standoffish demeanor, or maybe a combination of the two. Not that it mattered. Sequoia Carr was a lone wolf, unfit for romance of any kind. If she weren't, though, maybe she'd give Elijah a roll in the hay.

Now she barked out a laugh, and the sound had her slapping a hand over her mouth. She'd never roll in the hay. It was unsanitary. And Elijah probably wouldn't want to roll in the hay with her, anyway. They'd interacted a maximum of four times since they'd worked together, and he was usually terse and nearly silent … which was probably her own fault.

Actually, Sequoia thought, her lack of people skills extended beyond men. She was unfit for relationships of any kind.

She stopped at the concrete flower planter on the corner of Beachside and Grove to stretch her legs.

She had built-in friendships with her sisters, Jasmine and Holly, but she bungled those on a regular basis by the careless throwing out of words in thoughtless order at precisely the wrong time. She almost always managed to offend either Jasmine or Holly, or both, when they spent time together, and hated herself for how frequently she deployed her go-to phrase: "I'm not criticizing," she'd say. "Just making an observation."

Which was true. Usually. But all too often, her words came out sharp-edged. With the mindfulness she'd been practicing, Sequoia shook off the negativity and reminded herself that each encounter provided a new opportunity for making positive change. At least, that's what the books said.

She took a sip of her water and began to jog, then started her watch. Just as she did every morning, Sequoia headed down Grove Street first. She had a stop to make.

During the workweek, Sequoia spent a lot of time at the Seabreeze Public Transit station on Grove Street. It was a hot spot for the city's homeless population, and the Seabreeze PD received innumerable calls about vandalism or fighting there. One of the regulars spent his evenings carrying an open umbrella, rain or shine, and a sign declaring the end of the world was near. He often sang nursery rhymes as he paced the platform.

Julie Sandusky sat in her usual place, on the bench under the overhang. Because it was their routine, Julie stood up as soon as she saw Sequoia coming down the street.

As always, she looked so serious, and Sequoia was reminded of the first time she'd seen Julie here. It was five years ago, after Sequoia left Walt Walters—another man on whom she'd had a strange effect. Julie was easy to recognize, with her bright red hair, the coppery orange so many women pay hundreds of dollars to replicate, and her vivid blue eyes.

Sequoia had just taken up running, not because she wanted to, but because her sisters insisted that exercise would make her nicer (of course, they hadn't put it that way. Holly had explained that exercise created endorphins, which made people more cheerful).

When she rounded the corner near the transit station and saw Julie sitting there, their eyes had locked, for the briefest moment of recognition. But in each of their worlds, knowing one another was frowned upon.

Julie had been beautiful in her past life. Five years of homelessness had chapped her lips and hands, cracked her cuticles, and weathered her face. Her worn-out appearance and equally shabby jacket made Sequoia unbearably sad. So that first day, she'd run to the deli on the corner and bought a sandwich for Julie. But when she came back, Julie was gone.

Sequoia ate the sandwich, herself, and returned the next day with another. This time, Julie was there, and she smiled with so much gratitude Sequoia nearly cried. She made a mental note to get her emotions under control, then blamed her instability on Walt, and then returned every single day with a sandwich for Julie.

In all this time, they never spoke to each other. So on this cool, bright fall day, Sequoia stopped for just long enough to remove the food from her pack and hand it to Julie. Then she kept running.

Ninety minutes later, Sequoia inhaled the scent of bacon cooking as she took a long draw on a cold Stella Artois.

"Another six miles in the books," she said to herself as she laid out the tortilla for her breakfast burrito. "That's seventy miles this month. I think I can hit one-fifty before November."

Jasmine made fun of Sequoia for talking to herself, but Sequoia found it much more ridiculous that Jasmine talked to her dog, Rosie —or was it Roxie? Remy? It didn't matter. Jasmine talked to that little mutt as if it were a person.

"You may as well get used to talking to yourself, Carr," Sequoia said. "Call it Fate, call it Destiny, call it whatever you want, but there's pretty much no way you'll ever be standing in this kitchen, cooking breakfast with a man, cracking open a beer at eight a.m."

Although her sisters seemed way too interested in her romantic encounters, or lack thereof, Sequoia was okay with being alone.

"Keep telling yourself that, Carr," she murmured.

Not only was she decidedly not relationship material, but she was also too observant to make living with her pleasant.

"Some people call it critical," Sequoia said. "I call it astute."

Sequoia surprised herself by sighing as she sat down at the dining room table. It hadn't always been this way. As a child, a teenager, and even a young adult, Sequoia had imagined herself falling madly, passionately in love with a real-life version of Clark Kent. Then she met him and those dreams died, dissolving into steam.

Walter Walters. His parents had doomed him from the start by giving him that ridiculous name. However, genetics had been kind to Walt Walters. He was tall and broad and muscular, well-endowed in every department. At the start, she would have sworn he could transform into a superhero. But choices—starting with his parents' choice of names for their only son and ending with his choice to seek out the companionship of another female right under Sequoia's nose —made him undesirable.

Walter Walters was Sequoia's first love. She fell hard, headlong, head over heels for him exactly two months after she graduated from college. Ambitious and full of hope for the future, Sequoia had just been accepted into the police academy.

She was happy. Elated. So much so that, acceptance letter tucked into her purse so she could look at it whenever the urge struck, she went shopping for essentials like boots and sweatpants that would make Holly, the chic, trendy fashionista, cringe.

"Although Holly's ever-changing choice of hair color makes me cringe," Sequoia said as she stuffed packages of plain gray t-shirts into the trunk of her car.

Sequoia decided to treat herself to pizza and beer at Bob's Pizza and Wings downtown.

Walter Walters, stunning in his solitude as much as he was in his physical appearance, sat at the bar.

And who was Sequoia Carr to ignore a specimen like that?

As all people with strange names learn to be, Walter Walters was charming. He was witty. He lured her in with a joke about beer—a joke she couldn't even remember now.

Knowing Walt, it was something about the size of his penis. Despite being tall and broad, he always felt the need to hint at the magnitude of his natural bounty.

For some strange reason, probably because she was full of uncharacteristic hope and excitement, Walt's joke delighted her. Instead of walking away like she should have, leaving him at the bar, she poured herself into a taxi with him that very night.

Half a decade after the fact, Sequoia realized they had almost nothing in common, aside from a deep love for cushy socks and a hearty dislike for the St. Louis Rams. Still, they hit it off spectacularly. The sex was amazing—the best she'd ever had. They knocked it out of the park—three times. Would they call that a turkey in baseball? Or was that bowling?

It didn't matter. She gave all the credit to this mysterious stranger she met over pizza and beer.

An avalanche of personality clashes and discrepancies in values took things downhill from there, she thought now as she dug into her breakfast burrito with unusual ferocity.

Because Sequoia's parents had taught her the value of work, she'd always been career-oriented (a euphemism for obsessed with work). Straight back to her days as a barista when she boasted the record for number of cappuccinos made (and drank) in an hour.

So she didn't even notice when Walt began acting distant just a few months into their fresh love. He later pointed out that he skipped dinners and went to lots of weekend conferences out of town, but she was so wrapped up in the police academy—counting pushups and studying criminal justice textbooks every night—that she didn't pay attention.

It was true: she spent most of her free time studying or running or working out or interviewing seasoned cops on their roadside investigation techniques.

Of course, now that she could see it in hindsight, it all made sense: Walt's later-than-usual nights, the phone calls he didn't answer, the way he started shaving his chest hair.

(Which, she reminded herself now, was totally weird.)

The modern-day Sequoia took another sip of her beer as she contemplated the reason Walt had strayed.

He blamed her. Obviously.

"A guy needs sex more than once in a new moon," he'd said one evening, and she'd pointed out that he probably meant *blue* moon, and a blue moon occurs roughly every thirty-three years, and they'd definitely had sex more often than that.

The blue moon comparison was more of an exaggeration than anything, but, Sequoia admitted to herself now, it was a reasonable complaint.

Some people were cut out for love, and some were cut out for work.

Obviously, she was cut out for the latter, not only according to Walt, but also according to herself.

She didn't even want to spend time with Walt, and when he started making fewer and fewer appearances, returning fewer calls, and canceling more dates, she knew it wasn't about him.

It was all about her: Sequoia Carr was meant to be alone. Fly solo.

That evening—and not for the first time—Sequoia felt like her sisters had her in the interrogation room at the police department.

"What I want to know," Holly said, "is why you haven't talked about anyone you're dating in, like, forever."

The three of them sat at Jasmine's dining room table, snacking on vegetables Jasmine had set out. Eating together was a weekly tradition, a standing meeting of The Garden Club. Sequoia remembered with fondness how they'd given themselves that name the day they realized their parents had named each of them after flora.

Although she'd loved the meetings as a child, the adult Sequoia sometimes dreaded them. She couldn't put her finger on why, exactly, but it probably had something to do with the fact that the conversations always ended up veering toward her love life. This line of questioning made her heart race and her cheeks burn. Not having dated someone in, *like, forever*, was nothing to be ashamed of.

Only, Sequoia felt ashamed. She felt incapable. And she hated feeling incapable. Because she was the oldest of the three Carr sisters, her parents had constantly reminded her that she had to set a good example for Jasmine and Holly. She must work hard, try and try again, and then succeed, not only for herself, but as a role model.

This, right here, was a perfect illustration of why she sometimes lashed out. Tonight, though, in the spirit of mindfulness and new opportunities, she'd remain calm.

New start, she chanted silently. *New opportunity*.

"I want you to know that this is where I would normally say something like, 'I don't understand why you insist on changing your hair color as often as you change your underwear.' But I'm not going to."

"What?" Holly said. "Don't you like this shade? Jessica—that's my hairdresser—said it's called Auburn Sunset."

"It's better than the last one," Sequoia said. Jasmine kicked her under the table, but she steamrolled ahead: "What was that? Cotton Candy Throw-up?"

"Shut up, Sequoia," both of her sisters said.

"Hey, I thought we'd agreed not to use 'Shut up' during The Garden Club meetings."

"We founded The Garden Club when we were kids," Jasmine said. "And we only banned the term, 'shut up' because we didn't want Mom and Dad to hear us saying it."

Sequoia shook her head. "Fine. Let's get back on topic. First of all, asserting that I haven't talked about a date in 'forever' is unrealistic. Forever means forever. Not a month."

"It's been way more than a month since you said anything about romance," Holly said. Jasmine nodded for emphasis before putting a raw cherry tomato into her mouth.

"Well," Sequoia said, grasping at thoughts in the back of her mind before she finally got a firm grip on one. "I don't tell you lovely ladies everything, now, do I?"

That sounds good, Sequoia thought. It implied that her love life was more interesting and bountiful than parched, cracked desert soil.

Holly shrugged it off, and Sequoia had the shortest moment to experience relief and to come up with a subject change. But Jasmine, the newly-dogged newspaper reporter who wouldn't let go until she had an answer, pointed at Sequoia's face.

"I knew it!" she said to Holly. "She's hiding something."

Well, that backfired.

"Actually, I'm not," Sequoia said. "There's nothing to hide."

"Did you run today?" Jasmine asked.

Sequoia nodded. "Just six miles."

Every once in a while, she got the urge to tell Holly or Jasmine, or both of them, about Julie Sandusky. But she felt like that was a whole separate component of her life, and she didn't want to mix it with the sisters component.

As usual, Jasmine scoffed at Sequoia's use of "just" preceding six miles. But she didn't let the topic of romance slide.

"You know, you could find a running partner or running buddy," Holly said. "Then you might meet some new people. You know, people you could date."

Sequoia exhaled, loudly, hoping that signaled the conversation was over.

"You know, you could go on one of those dating websites," Jasmine said.

"Um, no thanks," Sequoia said. "Those sites are filled with felons and the very desperate."

"I don't know about that," Holly said. "But I do know that you're lonely."

"Don't project your feelings onto me," Sequoia said. "I rarely feel lonely, and even then, it's just because I use up the toilet paper and wish I had someone to bring me more, or because I can't decide what to make for dinner and wish someone else could make the decision. So don't worry about me. I'll either find that person or I won't."

"I just think it would be nice if you had someone," Jasmine said.

Sequoia rubbed her forehead with the tips of her fingers. "You guys are so weird," she said. "You're crazy weird. I'm not sure if this is the best idea."

"What?" Holly said. "We didn't even come up with an idea."

"The idea of me dating," Sequoia said. "Seriously, all this feeling lonely crap is your thing, not mine."

"Do you even have any friends?" Holly said.

"What is with you today?" Sequoia said. "I have you two. And my co-workers."

"Your co-workers don't count," Jasmine said. "You don't even talk to them."

"Yes, I do," Holly said, mimicking Sequoia. "We talk all the time. Like, 'Hey, did you see that box of donuts in the break room?'"

"Look," Sequoia said. "I'm an introvert."

"When is the last time you had a date?" Jasmine said.

Sequoia's mind flashed on a couple images of which her sisters wouldn't approve: her straddling Ryan Tucker in the bathroom at the Burger Stop during a casual sex encounter, and her bent over a stack of beer cases in the storeroom at Bob's Pizza and Wings, Dustin Myers standing behind her, during an even more casual sexual encounter.

A girl—even Sequoia—had needs.

Those were pretty recent, but she liked to keep them under wraps. And anyway, they didn't exactly qualify as "dates."

"I can't remember," Sequoia said. "Anyway, I think my relationship with Walt proved that I'm not capable of maintaining long-term romance."

Holly rolled her eyes. This time, Jasmine (ever the peace-maker) kicked Holly under the table, but she set her jaw, as if she, too, had a thought on the matter but was making a conscious effort not to reveal it.

"What?" Sequoia said. "You know it's true."

Actually, they didn't know. She'd never told them the demise of her relationship with Walt was her fault. Yes, she'd revealed Walt's affair with the long-legged, platinum blonde Barbie, and they'd defended her valiantly, promising to crush Walt's testicles with their bare hands if they ever saw him again.

But she'd never told them why he had an affair, which was because she was a cold, heartless woman who refused to think about anything other than her career.

"Whatever you say," Jasmine said. "But I don't think it would hurt to date once in a while. Keep your skills from getting rusty, you know?"

"Oh, I've got skills," Sequoia said.

Her sisters giggled, and Jasmine went into the kitchen to get the casserole out of the oven. This transition provided the perfect opportunity for a subject change, and Sequoia grasped it.

"Aside from the fact that there's nothing to talk about when it comes to my dating life," she said, "Jasmine's exploits with Hudson have trumped my stuff, anyway."

"True," Holly said. "How's it going, redecorating his place?"

Sequoia expected Jasmine to start glowing as she talked about wall sconces and curtains, and then morning coffee and late night pizza with Hudson Stover, her boyfriend and the photojournalist she worked with at the *Daily Trumpet*.

Instead, her sister sighed. "We can't even agree on a paint color for the living room. He thinks my choices are too ethereal and I think his are too industrial."

"Hm," Holly said. "Maybe you should start with a focus piece, like a throw pillow, and go from there."

"That's actually a good idea," Jasmine said.

She stood up and rummaged around in her purse until she found her notebook and a pen. When she returned to the table after having written down *focus piece - throw pillow?*, she sighed again. "And I really want to get rid of his gross couches. I mean, who buys black velvet couches?"

With the spotlight finally trained on someone else, Sequoia breathed a sigh of relief.

That night, walking out the door of Jasmine's house, Sequoia felt like she'd escaped from Alcatraz, swam across the San Francisco Bay and dragged herself onto the shore.

"Being on the receiving end of interrogations is exhausting," she said as she drove home to get ready for work. "I'll have to remember that the next time I'm questioning a criminal."

An hour later, she walked into the police station thinking about black velvet couches. Who, indeed, would buy such a thing? Sequoia had always liked Hudson but she had to go with Jasmine on this one.

Distracted, she came around the corner, narrowly missing another collision with Elijah Sawyer, who was finishing up his shift and on his way out.

Usually, she'd make some snarky comment about how he really should watch where he was going. But something happened. An unfamiliar feeling took root low in her belly and she knew she'd stutter if she tried to speak. Which, of course, was unacceptable. And weird.

They were almost exactly the same height. This typically turned her off, but at the moment, it gave her a chance to notice (again) that his eyes were the most interesting color. He smelled so good, like pine trees and citrus, that she wanted to nuzzle his neck and maybe even hug him. If she'd been alone, she would have said to herself, "Totally weird, Carr. Totally weird." But he was still standing there, frozen.

So she nodded curtly at him. "Excuse me, Sawyer."

He jumped into action, nodded back, and mumbled, "Morning," as he walked away.

For the second time in as many days, Sequoia had to force the smile off her face.

Elijah Sawyer had made his first appearance on Sequoia's radar a few months before, thanks in large part to Jasmine and a series of unfortunate events.

First, Liza, the cops reporter at the *Daily Trumpet*, noticed a bunch of expenditures unaccounted for in the Seabreeze PD's budget. This set off a string of press conferences, hosted by Seabreeze PD's public information officer, Earl Little, a rat-faced man with beady eyes.

It was simply bad timing that Liza's daughter had her first child (a little girl) at that same time. Liza flew across the country, leaving Jasmine, a features reporter, to cover the police beat. (It was supposed to be temporary, but Liza ended up staying on the East Coast, and Jasmine had surprised everyone, even herself, by asking to stay on the police beat.)

Almost immediately upon Liza's departure, Earl Little turned up dead. Actually, Sequoia thought with a snort, "turned up dead" was a bit of a euphemism. Someone shot the guy. Elijah Sawyer had the dubious honor of standing in for Earl Little. It was likely a wrong place, wrong time scenario, but Elijah took it like a champ.

It only made sense that Jasmine and Elijah crossed paths, and when they did, Jasmine noticed how "prickly" he was (and, of course, how good-looking). Thanks in part to his prickly factor and in part to the fact that she was already engaged in some kind of weird love triangle with Hudson and her high school sweetheart, Parker, Jasmine decided Elijah would be the perfect match for Sequoia.

Sequoia wondered if Jasmine would have snapped Elijah up, if circumstances hadn't been what they were. Probably not. He wasn't really her type. Not outgoing enough.

Anyway, Sequoia thought, it was only then—after Jasmine asked Sequoia if she knew or fantasized about Elijah—that Sequoia took any notice of him. She'd noticed him, to be sure. How could she not? He was good-looking in the tough, manly way that made her believe he could handle her. His face, chiseled perfection with a strong jaw and a cleft chin, belonged on the pages of a magazine, maybe in an ad for cologne. Or fast cars. But, there was the thing about her flying solo. And he was her co-worker. So she'd always observed him from a neutral perspective. But once Jasmine met him, Sequoia let her perspective shift, just a little. And she realized she found him border-line fascinating.

Next—and she blamed Jasmine for making her think this way—

she did begin to fantasize about him! She often imagined him naked. Sequoia had seen him at the end of his shift a few times, his t-shirt stretched tight across his chest. Elijah Sawyer had nice muscles.

Finally, he smelled so good.

Fortunately, she thought as she approached her desk today, the two of them rarely crossed paths. Except, of course, during the past two days. She felt that silly smile forming on her mouth again and shut it down as she sat at her desk to check her emails and read through the day's call log.

Recently, the shenanigans of her new boss, Beth Hardwick, had kept her distracted from thoughts (and fantasies) about Elijah. But their two near-collisions had brought him back into focus.

The computer finished booting up and Sequoia logged into her email, trashing junk mail and scanning the rest.

Beth Hardwick seemed to have something to do with the money the police department was missing, and for some inexplicable reason, she seemed pissed off at everyone else about it. She also seemed to have something to do with Earl Little's death. Not that the world was missing out on much now that he was gone, but he'd been in charge of sharing information with the newspaper and it seemed he was doing a good job of it. Too good.

And, of course, Jasmine had decided to morph from fluff reporter to serious journalist at the very moment things were spiraling out of control at Seabreeze PD. Her stories hinted that the missing money and the dead public information officer were inside jobs.

Sequoia tended to agree ... but she hadn't said as much to Jasmine. Jasmine was doing just fine on her own. Seabreeze was a small town. Everyone knew Jasmine was Sequoia's sister.

Which is why Beth Hardwick now hated Sequoia.

Email-checking complete, Sequoia moved on to the call log. She didn't see anything particularly interesting, but found herself scanning the list of responding officers for Elijah's name. She wondered whether he drank coffee.

Beth Hardwick's entrance cut Sequoia's musings short.

"Morning, Carr," she said, sidling up to Sequoia's desk. She leaned against the corner of the desk and crossed her arms.

Sequoia checked the time on her computer before clicking out of the call log. Five minutes until the official start of her shift. She stood up.

"Morning, Hardwick," she said. "I was just heading out."

"I need to talk to you."

"Can it wait? My shift starts right now."

"Your shift starts in five minutes."

Conscious of Beth Hardwick's ability to make her life miserable, Sequoia suppressed a sigh. Didn't the woman know that starting your shift five minutes early was actually starting your shift on time? Apparently not. Beth pushed herself away from the desk and stood with her feet set wide apart, her arms still crossed. She was blocking Sequoia's path, and she knew it.

Sequoia nodded. "What do you need?"

"I don't need anything. I want to tell you that I'm making some shift changes in the department. These changes may apply to you."

Feigning indifference, Sequoia shrugged. "Okay. Thanks for the heads up."

Beth inhaled as if she were about to say something, and Sequoia pushed past her. "Have a good day."

ABOUT THE AUTHOR

Hilary Dartt loves great adventures, whether she's writing, reading, or living them. The author of nine women's fiction novels, Hilary lives in Arizona's high desert with her husband, their three children, her Weimaraner and running partner, Leia, a failed barn cat, and a flock of chickens. She loves camping, exploring in the Jeep, and dance parties with her kids. Learn more at www.hilarydartt.com